SPEAK OF THE DEVIL

"Appearances can be deceiving."

"Indeed they can, Raphael, Angel of Light"—Flood laughed—"but appearance is the shadow at least of reality, don't you think?"

Raphael shrugged. "We're more casual out here on the coast."

Their conversation became general after that, and they both grew slightly drunk before they went to bed.

After Damon turned out the light, he continued a steady flow of random, drowsy commentary on the day's events. In time the pauses between his observations became longer. Finally he turned over in bed. "Good night, Gabriel," he murmured.

"Wrong archangel," Raphael corrected. "Gabriel's the other one—the trumpet player."

"Did I call you Gabriel? Stupid mistake. I must have had one martini too many."

By David Eddings
Published by Ballantine Books:

THE BELGARIAD
Book One: *Pawn of Prophecy*
Book Two: *Queen of Sorcery*
Book Three: *Magician's Gambit*
Book Four: *Castle of Wizardry*
Book Five: *Enchanters' End Game*

THE MALLOREON
Book One: *Guardians of the West*
Book Two: *King of the Murgos*
Book Three: *Demon Lord of Karanda*
Book Four: *Sorceress of Darshiva*
Book Five: *The Seeress of Kell*

THE ELENIUM
Book One: *The Diamond Throne*
Book Two: *The Ruby Knight*
Book Three: *The Sapphire Rose*

THE TAMULI
Book One: *Domes of Fire*
Book Two: *The Shining Ones*

HIGH HUNT

THE LOSERS

THE LOSERS

David Eddings

A Del Rey Book
BALLANTINE BOOKS • NEW YORK

A Del Rey Book
Published by Ballantine Books

Library of Congress Catalog Card Number: 91-58631

ISBN 0-345-38520-9

Manufactured in the United States of America

First Hardcover Edition: June 1992
First Mass Market Edition: September 1993

Fortuna Imperatrix Mundi

i

Mrs. Muriel Taylor was thirty-eight years old when she found that she was pregnant. Mrs. Taylor was a pale, almost transparent woman of Canadian background, who, until that startling discovery, had lived in a kind of dreamy reverie filled with semiclassical music and the endlessly reworked verses to which she devoted two hours every afternoon and never allowed anyone to read. The pregnancy ran its normal course, although Mrs. Taylor had miscarried twice before. She laid aside her poetry and devoted herself wholly to the life within her, seeming almost to wish at times that she might, like some exotic insect, be consumed from within by it and fall away like a dead husk at the moment of birth.

She labored with the selection of a suitable name for her unborn son (for he would surely be a boy) as she had never before struggled with the surly intransigencies of language, emerging finally with the one name that would lift her still-womb-drowsing infant above the commonplace, beyond that vast, ever-expanding mob of Joeys and Billies and Bobbies and Donnies. She would, she decided, call him Raphael, and having made that decision, she fell back into her drowse.

And in the usual course of time she was delivered of a son, and he was christened Raphael.

Mr. Edgar Taylor, Mrs. Taylor's husband, was a man best described as gray—his hair, the suits he wore to the office, even his face. Mr. Taylor was an accountant, much more at home with columns of figures than with people, and the sudden appearance of an heir, the product of his somewhat tepid passion, seemed to stun him. He gave up all outside activities so that he might hurry home each night to watch his son, not to touch him or speak to him, but simply to watch in a kind of bemused astonishment this prodigy that he and his wife had somehow wrought.

The Taylors lived in Port Angeles, a small, damp city on the extreme northwest coast. The peninsula below it is given over in large part to a national park, roadless and pristine; and the city thus has an insular character, cut off from the sprawling bustle of Seattle, Tacoma, and the other population centers of the state by a deep, island-dotted sound. All significant travel to and from Port Angeles is by ferry. The nearest major city is Victoria in British Columbia, a curiously European metropolis where Mr. Taylor had traveled on business some years earlier and had met and intermittently courted Mrs. Taylor. In due time they had married and he had brought her back across the twenty-six miles of intervening water to the dank clamminess of Port Angeles with its rain and fog and its reek of green hemlock logs lying low in the salt waters of the bay.

From the beginning Raphael was one of those rare children, touched, it seemed, by a singular grace that gave everything he did a kind of special significance. As an infant he seldom cried, and he passed through the normal stages of early childhood with a minimum of fuss. His mother, of course, devoted her entire existence to him. Long after he had matured to the point where her constant attentions were no longer necessary—or even desired—she was forever touching him, her hand moving almost of its own will to lingeringly caress his face or his hair.

Perhaps because of that special grace or perhaps because of some long-forgotten gene in his makeup, Raphael avoided the pitfalls that almost inevitably turn the pampered child into a howling monster. He grew instead into a sturdy, self-reliant little boy, gracious to his playmates and polite to his elders. Even as a child, however, he was adept at keeping his feelings to himself. He was outgoing and friendly on the surface, but seemed to reserve a certain part of himself as a private sanctuary from which he could watch and say nothing. He did well in school and, as he matured, developed into that kind of young man his infancy had promised—tall, slimly muscular, with glowing, almost luminous eyes and pale blond hair that stubbornly curled in spite of all efforts to control it.

Raphael's years at high school were a time of almost unbearable pride for Mr. Taylor as the young man developed into that boy athlete who comes along perhaps once in a generation. Opposing coaches wept on those golden autumn afternoons as Raphael, knees high, the ball carried almost negligently in one hand, ran at will through their best defenses. Important men in the lumber company where Mr. Taylor worked began stopping by his desk to talk about the games.

"Great game, Edgar," they'd say jovially. "Really great."

Mr. Taylor, his gray face actually taking on a certain color, would nod happily.

"Young Rafe really gave it to them," they'd say. "He's a cinch to make all-state this year."

"We think he's got a good chance," Mr. Taylor would say. Mr. Taylor always said "we" when talking about Raphael's accomplishments, as if, were he to say "I," it might seem boastful.

For Mrs. Taylor, however, the whole period was a time of anguish. There was always the danger of injury, and with morbid fascination she collected gruesome stories of fatalities and lifelong maimings that occurred with hideous regularity on high-school football fields across the nation. And then there was the fact that all the sportswriters and the disgusting man who broadcast the games over the local radio station had immediately shortened her son's name to Rafe— a name that smacked of hillbillies or subhuman degenerates slouching along in the shadows and slobbering over thoughts of unspeakable acts. Each time she heard the name, her soul withered a little within her. Most of all, however, she feared girls. As Raphael's local celebrity increased so did her dread. In her mind Mrs. Muriel Taylor saw hordes of vacant-minded little trollops lusting after her son, their piggish eyes aflame with adolescent desire and their bubble-gum-scented breath hot and panting as they conspired—each in her own grubby little soul—to capture this splendid young man. Mrs. Taylor had, in the dim reaches of her Canadian girlhood, secretly and tragically suffered such pangs for an oafish campus hero, so that she knew in her heart of hearts to what lengths the predatory adolescent female might go, given such a prize as this most perfect of young men, this—and she used the word only to herself in deepest privacy—this angel.

Young Raphael Taylor, however, avoided those girls his mother most feared as adroitly as he avoided opposing tacklers. This is not, of course, to say that he was celibate. It is merely to say that he devoted his attentions to certain local girls who, by reputation and practice, were in no position to make lasting demands on him. For the most part he avoided those girls who might, by the sacrifice of their virtue, have been able to make some kind of viable claim upon him. Once, though, in the summer of his sixteenth year, there was a girl whom he had deeply and desperately loved; but her family had moved away, and he had suffered, but had been safe.

During the fall of Raphael's senior year in high school, Mr. Taylor developed a serious shortness of breath. Despite his wife's urgings, however, he put off visiting the family doctor, maintaining that his condition was just a recurrence of an old bronchial complaint that had plagued him off and on for years.

On a splendid Friday afternoon in late September Port Angeles hosted their traditional rivals from across the sound. As had been the case since his sophomore year, Raphael dominated the game. Although it was obvious from the very beginning that he would carry the ball at least twice during every series of plays, the opposing players were unable to stop him. He scored three touchdowns during the first half, and when the visitors opened the second half with a booming kickoff, he scooped up the ball deep in his own end zone, reversed direction, and feinting, spinning, and dodging with the grace of a dancer, he started upfield. Every opponent on the field, even the kicker, tried to stop him, but he was unstoppable. For the last thirty yards before he crossed the goal line, he was absolutely alone, running in solitary splendor with all tacklers hopelessly far back.

The home fans, of course, were screaming wildly. And that was the last thing that Mr. Taylor ever heard. He had risen excitedly to his feet to watch his glorious son run the full length of the field, and the sound of the cheers surrounded him. The massive heart attack was like a great blow to his chest, and he toppled forward, dying with those cheers fading like distant thunder in his ears.

The funeral was very sad, as funerals usually are. Mrs. Taylor bore up bravely, leaning on her golden-haired son. After all the ceremonies and condolences, life once again returned to near normal. Mr. Taylor was so close to being a nonentity that he was scarcely missed at the place where he had worked, and even his widow's emotion at his passing might best be described as gentle melancholy rather than overwhelming grief.

Raphael, of course, missed his father, but he nonetheless played in every game that season. "He would have wanted it that way," he explained. He was touched, even moved almost to tears by the moment of silence dedicated to his father just prior to the game the Friday after the funeral. Then he went out onto the field and destroyed the visiting team.

Mr. Taylor's affairs, of course, were in absolute order. Certain wise investments and several insurance policies provided for the security of his family, and his elder brother, Harry, a Port Angeles realtor, had been named executor of his estate. Harry Taylor was a bluff, balding, florid-faced man with a good head for business and a great deal of sound, practical advice for his brother's widow. He took his responsibilities as executor quite seriously and visited often.

That winter, when the question of college arose, Mrs. Taylor faced the issue with dread. Money was not a problem, since her husband had carried a special insurance policy with some very liberal provisions to guarantee his son's education. There were also scholarship offers from as far away as southern California, since Raphael had twice been named to the all-state football team. In the end, however, the question was deferred by the young man's rather surprising decision to attend the local junior college. He had many reasons for the choice, not the least of which was his full realization of what anguish an abrupt separation would cause his mother, coming as it must so soon after her bereavement.

And so it was that Raphael continued to play local football, his uncle Harry basked in reflected celebrity, and his mother enjoyed the reprieve the decision had granted her.

At the end of two years, however, the decision could no longer be put off. Raphael privately considered his options and independently made his choice.

"Reed?" his uncle said, stunned.

"It's a good school, Uncle Harry," Raphael pointed out, "the best school in this part of the country. They say it's one of the top ten colleges in the United States."

"But they don't even have a football team, do they?"

"I don't know," Raphael replied. "I don't think so."

"You could go to Stanford. That's a good school, too."

Raphael nodded thoughtfully. "Yes," he agreed, "but it's too big."

"They've got a good team. You might even get a chance to play in the Rose Bowl."

"Maybe, but I think I'd rather go to Reed. I've had a lot of fun playing football, but I think it's time I moved on to something else, don't you?"

"Where is this college located?" Mrs. Taylor asked faintly.

"Portland," Raphael replied.

"In *Oregon*?" Mrs. Taylor asked even more faintly.

Raphael nodded.

Mrs. Taylor's heart sank.

Portland, the city of the roses, bestrides the banks of the Willamette River near where that stream joins the Columbia. It is a pleasant city, filled with trees and fine old Victorian houses. The campus of Reed College, where Raphael was enrolled, lies somewhat to the east of the river, and has about it a dreamy, timeless quality. The very buildings that rise from the broad lawns identify the place as a college, since such a random collection of Georgian manors, medieval cathedrals, and starkly modern structures of brick and glass could exist for no other reason.

In his car of recent vintage with its backseat filled with the new and expensive luggage his mother had bought and tearfully given him, Raphael Taylor pulled rather wearily into the student parking lot and stopped. The trip had been quite long, and he was unaccustomed to freeway driving. There was, however, an exhilaration about it all. He was on his own for the first time in his life, and that was something.

Thanks to his uncle's careful correspondence with the registrar and the bursar, all arrangements had been made well in advance, and Raphael knew precisely where his dormitory was located. With his jacket under his arm and two suitcases rather self-consciously swinging at his sides, he walked across to the manselike solidity of the dorm, feeling a certain superiority to the small crowd of bewildered-looking freshmen milling uncertainly around in front of the administration building.

His room was on the third floor, and Raphael was puffing slightly as he reached the top of the stairs. The door at the end of the hall was open, and billowing clouds of smoke were rolling out. Raphael's stomach turned cold. Everything had gone too well up until now. He went down the hall and into the smoke.

A young man with olive skin and sleek black hair brushed by him carrying a large vase filled with water. ''Don't just stand there, man," he said to Raphael in a rich baritone voice. "Help me put this son of a bitch out." He rushed into the room, bent slightly, and threw the water into a small fireplace that seemed to be the source of all the smoke. The fire hissed spitefully, and clouds of steam boiled out to mingle blindingly with the smoke.

"Damn!" the dark-haired man swore, and started back for more water.

Raphael saw the problem immediately. "Wait," he said. He set down his suitcases, stepped across to the evilly fuming fireplace, and pulled the brass handle sticking out of the bricks just below the mantelpiece. The damper opened with a clank, and the fireplace immediately stopped belching smoke into the room. "It's a good idea to open the chimney before you build the fire," he suggested.

The other man stared at the fireplace for a moment, and then he threw back his head and began to laugh. "There's a certain logic there, I guess," he admitted. He collapsed on the bed near the door, still laughing.

Raphael crossed the room and opened the window. The smoke rushed out past him.

"It's a good thing you came by when you did," the dark-haired man said. "I was well on my way to being smoked like a Virginia ham." He was somewhat shorter than Raphael, and more slender. His olive skin and black hair suggested a Mediterranean background, Italian perhaps or Spanish, but there was no Latin softness in his dark eyes. They were as hard as obsidian and watchful, even wary. His clothing was expensive—tailored, Raphael surmised, definitely tailored—and his wristwatch was not so much a timepiece as it was a statement.

Then the young man looked at Raphael as if seeing him for the first time, and something peculiar happened to his face. His eyes widened, and a strange pallor turned his olive complexion slightly green. His eyes narrowed, seeming almost to glitter. It was as if a shock of recognition had passed through him. "You must be Edwards, right?" His expression seemed tight somehow.

"Sorry," Raphael replied. "The name's Taylor."

"I thought you might be my roomie."

"No. I'm two doors up the hall."

"Oh, well"—the stranger shrugged, making a wry face—"there goes my chance to keep the knowledge of my little blunder a secret. Edwards is bound to smell the smoke when he gets here." He rose to his feet and extended his hand. "J. D. Flood," he said by way of introducing himself.

"Rafe Taylor," Raphael responded. They shook hands. "What were you burning, Flood?"

"Some pieces of a packing crate. I've never had a dormitory room with a fireplace before, so I had to try it. Hell, I was even going out to buy a pipe." He raised one eyebrow. "Rafe—is that short for Raphael?"

"Afraid so. It was a romantic notion of my mother's. You wouldn't believe how many school-yard brawls it started."

Flood's face darkened noticeably. "Unreal," he said. That strange, almost shocked expression that had appeared in his eyes when he had first looked at Raphael returned, and there was a distinct tightening in his face. Once again Raphael felt that momentary warning as if something were telling him to be very careful about this glib young man. In that private place within his mind from which he had always watched and made decisions, he began to erect some cautionary defenses. "And what does the J.D. stand for?" he asked, trying to make it sound casual.

"Jacob Damon Flood, Junior," Flood said with distaste.

"Jake?" Raphael suggested.

"Not hardly."

"J.D. then?"

"That's worse. That's what they call my father."

"How about Damon?"

Flood considered that. "Why not? How about a martini?"

"Is it legal? In the dorm, I mean?"

"Who gives a shit? I'm not going to start paying any attention to the rules at this late date."

Raphael shrugged. "Most of my drinking has been limited to beer, but I'll give it a try."

"That's the spirit," Flood said, opening one of his suitcases and taking out a couple of bottles. "I laid in some ice a bit earlier. I make a mean martini—it's one of the few things I've actually learned." He busied himself with a silver shaker. "Any cretin can swill liquor out of a bottle," he went on with a certain brittle extravagance, "but a gentleman boozes it up with class."

Flood's language seemed to shift back and forth between an easy colloquialism Raphael found comfortable and a kind of stilted eastern usage. There was a forced quality about Flood that made him uncomfortable.

They had a couple of drinks, and Raphael feigned enjoyment, although the sharp taste of nearly raw gin was not particularly to his liking. He was not really accustomed to drinking, and Flood's martinis were strong enough to make his ears hot and the tips of his fingers tingle. "Well," he said finally, setting down his glass, "I guess I'd better go get moved in."

"Taylor," Flood said, an odd note in his voice. "I've got a sort of an idea. Is your roommate up the hall an old friend?"

"Never met the man, actually."

"And I've never met Edwards either—obviously. Why don't you room in here?" There was a kind of intensity about the way Flood said it, as if it were far, far more important than the casual nature of the suggestion called for.

"They don't allow that, do they?" Raphael asked. "Switching rooms, I mean?"

"It's easy to see you've never been in a boarding school before." Flood laughed. "Switching rooms is standard practice. It goes on everywhere. Believe me, I know. I've been kicked out of some of the best schools in the east."

"What if Edwards shows up and wants his bed?"

"We'll give him yours. I'll lie to him—tell him I've got something incurable and that you're here to give me a shot in case I throw a fit."

"Come on." Raphael laughed.

"You can be the one with the fits if you'd rather," Flood offered. "Can you do a convincing grand mal seizure?"

"I don't know. I've never tried."

"The whole point is that we get along fairly well together, and I don't know diddly about Edwards. I *know* that you're white, but I haven't got any idea at all about *what* color he is."

"Is that important?" Raphael said it carefully.

Flood's face suddenly broke into a broad grin. "Gotcha!" he said gleefully. "God, I love to do that to people. Actually, it doesn't mean jack-shit to me one way or another, but it sure as hell does to old J.D. Sooner or later somebody from back home is going to come by, and if word gets back to the old pirate that his son has a nigger roommate—his word, not mine—thee shit will hit thee fan. Old J.D.'s prejudiced against races that have been extinct for thousands of years— like the Hittites—or the Wends."

"It won't work out then, Damon," Raphael told him with a perfectly straight face. "My mother's Canadian."

"That's all right, Raphael. I'm liberal. We'll let you come in through the back door. Have Canadians got rhythm? Do you have overpowering cravings for northern-fried moose?"

Raphael laughed. The young man from the east was outrageous. There was still something slightly out of tune though. Raphael was quite sure that he reminded Flood of someone else. Flood had seemed about to mention it a couple of times, but had apparently decided against it. "All right," he decided. "If you think we can get away with it, we'll try it."

"Good enough. We'll drop the Rafe and Jake bit so we don't sound like a hillbilly band, and we'll use Damon and Raphael—unless you'd like to change your name to Pythias?"

"No, I don't think so. It sounds a little urinary."

Flood laughed. "It does at that, doesn't it? Have you got any more bags? Or do you travel light?"

"I've got a whole backseat full."

"Let's go get them then. Get you settled in."

They clattered downstairs, brought up the rest of Raphael's luggage, and then went to the commons for dinner.

Damon Flood talked almost continuously through the meal, his rich voice compelling, almost hypnotic. He saw nearly everything, and his sardonic wit made it all wryly humorous.

"And this," he said, almost with a sneer as they walked back in the luminous twilight toward their dormitory, "is the 'most intelligent group of undergraduates in the country'?" He quoted from a recent magazine article about the college. "It looks more like a hippie convention—or a soirée in a hobo jungle."

"Appearances can be deceiving."

"Indeed they can, Raphael, Angel of Light"—Flood laughed—"but appearance is the shadow at least of reality, don't you think?"

Raphael shrugged. "We're more casual out here on the coast."

"Granted, but wouldn't you say that the fact that a young lady doesn't wear shoes to dinner says a great deal about her character?"

"Where's your home?" Raphael asked as they started up the stairs.

"Grosse Pointe," Flood said dryly, "the flower on the weed of Detroit."

"What are you doing way out here?" Raphael opened the door to their room.

"Seeking my fortune," Flood said, flinging himself down on his bed. Then he laughed. "Actually, I'm putting as much distance as possible between my father and me. The old bastard can't stand the sight of me. The rest of the family wanted me to go to Princeton, but I preferred to avoid the continuous surveillance of all those cousins. A very large family, the Floods, and I have the distinction of being its major preoccupation. All those dumpy female cousins literally slather at the idea of being able to report my indiscretions back to old J.D. himself."

Raphael began to unpack.

"J.D.'s the family patriarch," Flood went on. "The whole damned bunch genuflects in his direction five times a day—

except me, of course. I suppose I've never really forgiven him for tacking that 'Junior' on me, so I set out to be as unlike him as I could. He looks on that as a personal insult, so we don't really get along. He started shipping me off to boarding schools as soon as I lost my baby teeth, though, so we only irritate each other on holidays. I tried a couple years at Pitt, but all that rah-rah bullshit got on my nerves. So I thought I'd saddle up old Paint and strike out for the wide wide west— What do you say to another drink?'' He sprang up immediately and began mixing another batch of martinis.

Their conversation became general after that, and they both grew slightly drunk before they went to bed.

After Flood had turned out the light, he continued to talk, a steady flow of random, drowsy commentary on the day's events. In time the pauses between his observations became longer as he hovered on the verge of sleep. Finally he turned over in bed. ''Good night, Gabriel,'' he murmured.

''Wrong archangel,'' Raphael corrected. ''Gabriel's the other one—the trumpet player.''

''Did I call you Gabriel?'' Flood's voice had a strange, alert tension in it. ''Stupid mistake. I must have had one martini too many.''

''It's no big thing. Good night, Damon.'' Once again, however, something in the very back of his mind seemed to be trying to warn Raphael. Flood's inadvertent use of the name Gabriel seemed not to be just a slip of the tongue. There was a significance to it somehow—obscure, but important.

In the darkness, waiting for sleep and listening to Flood's regular breathing from the other bed, Raphael considered his roommate. He had never before met anyone with that mon-eyed, eastern prep-school background, and so he had no real basis for judgment. The young men he had met before had all come from backgrounds similar to his own, and the open, easy camaraderie of the playing field and the locker room had not prepared him for the complexity of someone like Flood. On the whole, though, he found his roommate in-triguing, and the surface sophistication of their first evening exhilarating. Perhaps in time Flood would relax, and they'd really get to know each other, but it was still much too early to know for sure.

iii

Raphael's next few weeks were a revelation to him. Always before he had been at best a casual scholar. His mind was quick and retentive, and neither high school nor the community college he had attended had challenged him significantly. He had come to believe that, even as on the football field, what others found difficult would be easy for him. His performance in the classroom, like his performance on the field, had been more a reflection of natural talent than of hard work; everything had been very easy for Raphael. At Reed, however, it was not so. He quickly discovered that a cursory glance at assigned reading did not prepare him adequately for the often brutally cerebral exchanges of the classroom. Unlike his previous classmates, these students were not content merely to paraphrase the text or the remarks of the instructor, but rather applied to the material at hand techniques of reason and analysis Raphael had never encountered before. Amazingly, more often than not, the results of these reasonings were a direct challenge to the authority of the text or of the instructor. And, even more amazingly, these challenges were not viewed as the disruptions of troublemakers, but were actually encouraged. Disturbed and even embarrassed by his newfound inadequacy, Raphael began to apply himself to his studies.

"You're turning into a grind," Flood said one evening.

Raphael pulled his eyes from the page he was reading. "Hmmm?"

"You study too much. I never see you without your face in some damned book."

"That's why we're here, isn't it?"

"Not hardly." Flood threw one leg over the arm of his chair. "A gentleman does *not* get straight A's. It's unseemly.

Haven't you ever heard the old formula? 'Three C's and a D and keep your name out of the newspapers'?''

"No. I hadn't heard that one." Raphael's mind was yearning back toward the book. "Besides, how would you know here? They won't let us see our grades." That was one of the peculiarities of what was called the "Reed experience."

"Barbarous," Flood snorted. "How the hell can we be expected to maintain a proper balance if they don't let us see our grades? Do you realize that a man could screw up? Stumble into so many high grades that his reputation's ruined for life?"

"I wouldn't worry too much about that, Damon. I don't think you're in any danger."

"Don't get shitty." Flood got up quickly. "Let's go out and get drunk—see if we can get arrested or something."

"I've got an early class tomorrow." Raphael turned back to his book.

"Talk to me, goddammit!" Flood said irritably, snatching the book from Raphael's hands. "What the hell are you reading, anyway?"

"Kierkegaard." Raphael reached for his book.

"The Sickness unto Death," Flood read. "Now there's a cheery little title. What class is this for?"

Raphael shrugged. "It came up in a discussion. I thought I ought to look into it."

"You mean it's not even *required*?" Flood demanded incredulously, tossing the book back. "That's disgusting, Raphael, disgusting."

"Different strokes," Raphael said, finding his place again and settling back to his reading. Flood sat watching him, his black eyes as hard as agates.

And then there was the problem of the girl. She sat across the room from him in one of his afternoon classes, and Raphael found his eyes frequently drawn to her face. It was not that she was exceptionally beautiful, for she was not. Her face was slightly angular with strong bones, and she was quite tall with a coltish legginess that made her seem somehow very young. Her voice, however, was a deep, rich contralto with a vibrance, a quality, that stirred Raphael immeasurably each time she spoke. But she spoke infrequently. Sometimes a week would pass without a word from her. While others in the class talked endlessly, arguing, discussing, pushing themselves forward, she would sit quietly, taking occasional notes and now and then stirring restlessly as Raphael's gaze became warmly obvious.

He began to try to challenge her—to force her to speak. He frequently said things he did not actually believe, hoping to lever her into discussion. He did not even care *what* she said, but merely yearned for the sound of that voice, that rich, vibrant sound that seemed somehow to plunge directly into the center of his being. She began, in time, to return his glances, but she still seldom spoke, and the infrequency of her speech left him frustrated—even angry with himself for his absurd fascination. Her name, he discovered, was Marilyn Hamilton, and she lived off campus. Beyond that, he was able to find out very little about her.

"You're Taylor, aren't you?" a large, bulky man with a huge black beard asked him one afternoon as he came out of the library.

"Right," Raphael replied.

"Name's Wallace Pierson." The big man held out his hand. "I understand you've played a little football."

"Some." Raphael shifted his books so that he could shake the man's hand.

"We're—uh—trying to put together a team," Pierson said, seeming almost apologetic. "Nothing very formal. Wondered if you might be interested."

"Intramural?"

"No, not exactly." Pierson laughed. "It's just for the hell of it, really. You see, there's a Quaker college across town— George Fox. They have a sort of a team—pretty low-key. They sent us an invitation. We thought it might be sort of interesting." He fell in beside Raphael and they walked across the broad lawn toward the dormitories.

"I haven't got the kind of time it takes for practice," Raphael told him.

"Who has? We're not really planning to make a big thing out of it—just a few afternoons so that we can get familiar with each other—not embarrass ourselves *too* badly."

"That's not the way to win football games."

"Win?" Pierson seemed startled. "Hell, Taylor, we weren't planning to win—just play. Good God, man, you could get *expelled* for winning—overemphasis and all that jazz. We just thought it might be kind of interesting to play, that's all."

Raphael laughed. "That's the Reed spirit."

"Sure." Pierson grinned. "If we can hold them to ten touchdowns, it'll be a moral victory, won't it?"

"I'll think it over."

"We'd appreciate it. We're a little thin in the backfield. We thought we'd get together about four or so this afternoon—see if there are enough of us to make a team. Drop on down if you'd like."

"When's the game?"

"Friday."

"Three days? You plan to put a team together in three days?"

Pierson shrugged. "We're not really very serious about it."

"I can see that. I'll think it over."

"Okay," the bearded man said. "Maybe we'll see you at four then."

"Maybe."

But of course he did play. The memory of so many afternoons was still strong, and he had, he finally admitted, missed the excitement, the challenge, the chance to hurl himself wholly into violent physical activity.

Pierson, despite his bulk, played quarterback, and the great black beard protruding from the face mask of his helmet made the whole affair seem ludicrous. On the day of the game their plays were at best rudimentary, and they lost ground quite steadily. The small cluster of students who had gathered to watch the game cheered ironically each time they were thrown for a loss.

"Hand it off to me," Raphael suggested to Pierson in the

huddle on their third series of plays when they were trailing
13–0. "If you try that keeper play one more time, that left
tackle of theirs is going to scramble your brains for you."

"Gladly," Pierson agreed, puffing.

"Which way are you going?" one of the linemen asked
Raphael.

"I haven't decided yet," Raphael said, and broke out of
the huddle.

After the snap Pierson handed him the ball, and Raphael
angled at the opposing line. He sidestepped a clumsy tackle,
found a hole, and broke through. The afternoon sun was very
bright, and his cleats dug satisfyingly into the turf. He reversed direction, outran two tacklers, and scored quite easily.

A thin cheer went up from the spectators.

In time his excellence even became embarrassing. He began to permit himself to be tackled simply to prevent the
score from getting completely one-sided. More and more of
the students drifted down to watch.

On the last play of the game, knowing that it was the last
play and knowing that he would probably never play again,
Raphael hurled himself up and intercepted an opponent's pass
deep in his own end zone. Then, simply for the joy of it, he
ran directly into the clot of players massed at the goal line.
Dodging, feinting, sidestepping with perfect coordination,
he ran through the other team. Once past the line, he deliberately ran at each member of the backfield, giving all in turn
a clear shot at him and evading them at the last instant.

The wind burned in his throat, and he felt the soaring
exhilaration that came from the perfect functioning of his
body. Then, after running the full length of the field and
having offered himself to every member of the opposing
team, he ran into the end zone, leaped high into the air, and
slammed the ball down on the turf so violently that it bounced
twenty feet straight up. When he came down, he fell onto
his back, laughing for sheer joy.

On the Saturday morning after the football game Raphael was stiff and sore. His body was out of condition, and his muscles reacted to the exertion and bruising contact of the game. He still felt good, though.

Flood was up early, which was unusual, since he normally slept late on weekends. "Come along, football hero," he said to Raphael, "rise and shine." His eyes glittered brightly.

Raphael groaned and rolled over in bed.

"Quickly, quickly," Flood commanded, snapping his fingers.

"What's got you all bright-eyed and bushy-tailed this morning?" Raphael demanded sourly.

"Today we go a-visiting," Flood said exuberantly. "Today I carry the conquering hero to visit the queen."

"Some other time." Raphael laid one arm across his eyes. "I'm in no condition for queens today."

"I wouldn't touch that line with a ten-foot pole—or a nine-foot Hungarian either. You might as well get up. I'm not going to let you sleep away your day of triumph."

"Shit!" Raphael threw off the covers.

"My God!" Flood recoiled from the sight of the huge bruises and welts on Raphael's body. "You mean to tell me you let yourself get in that condition for *fun*?"

Raphael sat up and glanced at the bruises. "They'll go away. What were you babbling about?"

"We go to visit the fair Isabel," Flood declaimed, "whose hair is like the night, whose skin is like milk, and whose gazongas come way out to here." He gestured exaggeratedly in front of his chest. "She's an old schoolmate of my aunt's, a fallen woman, cast out by her family, living in shame and obscurity by the shores of scenic Lake Oswego some miles to the south. She and I are kindred spirits, since both of us offend our families by our very existence. She's invited us to spend the weekend, so up, my archangel. Put on your wings and halo, and I will deliver you into the hands of the temptress."

"Isn't it a little early for all the bullshit?" Raphael asked, climbing stiffly to his feet and picking up his towel. "I'm going to hit the showers." He padded out of the room and down the hall to the bathroom.

After a hot shower his sore muscles felt better, and he was in a better humor as he dressed. There was no withstanding Flood when he set his mind to something, and finally Raphael gave in. Twenty minutes later they were packed and southbound on the freeway in Flood's small, fast, red Triumph.

"Just exactly who is this lady we're visiting?" Raphael asked.

"I told you," Flood replied.

"This time why don't you clear away all the underbrush and give me something coherent."

"The lady's name is Isabel Drake. She went to school with my aunt, which makes her practically a member of the family."

"I don't quite follow that, but let it pass."

"We have very extended families in Grosse Pointe."

"Okay."

"Helps us avoid contact with the riffraff."

"All right."

"Avoiding contact with the riffraff is a major concern in Grosse Pointe."

"All right, I said."

"Do I digress?"

"Of course you do, but I'm used to that. All right. Miss—Mrs.—Drake is a distant friend of your family's, a lady of middle years who happens to live in the area, and this is by way of a courtesy call, right?"

Flood laughed. "She'll love that," he hooted. "*Mrs.* Drake—definitely *Mrs.*—made, when she was quite young, an excellent marriage and an even better divorce. She's a lady of means now. The aunt I referred to is my father's youngest sister, so Isabel is maybe thirty at most—hardly what you'd call 'of middle years.' And as far as 'courtesy calls' go, you'll soon discover that the term is wildly inappropriate. Isabel Drake is probably who they had in mind when they invented the word 'fascinating.' ''

''Why did you call her a fallen woman?''

''That's a tale of dark passion and illicit lust, Raphael, hardly suitable for your tender ears.''

''Try me. If there are subjects I shouldn't talk about, I'd like to know in advance.''

''Besides which, you're panting to hear the details, right?'' Flood smirked.

''Pant, pant,'' Raphael said dryly. ''Get on with it, Damon. You're going to tell me about it anyway; nothing could stop you. I could have your mouth bricked up, and you'd still tell me.''

Flood laughed. ''All right, Raphael. Shortly after her divorce, Isabel conceived a passion for the husband of one of her cousins, a vapid, colorless girl of no lasting significance. There was a flaming affair which quite rapidly approached the status of a public scandal. The man in question was also of no lasting significance—some semipresentable shithead the cousin's family had bought for her. Anyhow, there were all the usual lurid developments—gossip, people falling over themselves to tell the poor cousin what Isabel was up to. She attempted suicide, of course.''

''You're kidding.''

''Not a bit of it. Sleeping pills, the tragic suicide note, all of it. Anyhow, there was a separation, and the poor klutz informed Isabel that he was ready to divorce the cousin and 'make an honest woman' of her. Isabel, who was getting bored with the whole thing at that point, laughed in his face. She was not about to give up that alimony for *anybody,* much less some cretin who couldn't function outside the bedroom. He got huffy about it all and stormed out, but when he tried to go back to the cousin, she told him to buzz off. He took to drinking and made a special point of telling everyone in all the bars about Isabel's bedroom habits—in great detail. In time the rest of the family hinted around that they'd all be a lot happier if she'd take up residence a long, long way from Grosse Pointe, and finally she did.''

"Don't the rich have anything better to do?"

"That's the whole point of being rich," Flood replied, turning off the freeway. "It leaves you free to pursue diversions other than money.''

"You know, I think you made all that up, Damon. I think you're putting me on.''

"Would I put you on?" Flood laughed.

"If you thought I'd swallow it, yes.''

The home of Isabel Drake was a chalet-style house set in a grove of fir trees near the shores of the lake. It was about ten-thirty when Flood's small red sports car stopped on the curving gravel drive in front of the house, and morning sun filtered down through the trees with that overripe golden quality that, more than anything, speaks of autumn.

Flood bounced from the car with unusual energy, went up the wooden steps to the wide porch that stretched across the front of the house, and rang the bell. "Come along, Raphael," he said over his shoulder.

Somewhat painfully, his muscles stiffened again from the ride, Raphael climbed from the car and started up the steps to the porch.

The door opened, and a small woman looked out inquiringly. She was short, perhaps just over five feet tall, and she wore jeans and a loose-fitting cambric shirt of the kind Raphael had seen mill workers back home wear. Her hair was quite dark and caught at the back of her neck by a red bandanna. The skin of her face and throat was very white, and her figure under the loose shirt was full. She had a smudge of pale green paint on one cheek. "Junior," she said in an exasperated tone. Her voice was rich and melodious. "You said *noon*."

"Sorry, 'Bel. We got away early." He grinned down at her.

"I'm a mess," she protested, glancing down at the front of her shirt. She was holding two long, pencillike paintbrushes in her right hand. "You always do this to me, Junior."

"This way we get to see the real you, 'Bel." Flood's grin was slightly malicious. "Let me present the Archangel Raphael," he said, turning and beckoning.

Isabel Drake's eyes widened, and she stared directly at Flood as if he had just said something totally unbelievable. Then she turned and looked at Raphael. Very clearly he could see a kind of stunned recognition cross her face. Her eyes seemed to cloud for a moment, and she looked as if she were about to say something. Then she shook her head slightly, and her face became a polite mask.

"Mrs. Drake," Raphael said rather formally, inclining his head in a sort of incipient bow.

"Please," she replied, "just 'Bel." She smiled up at him. Her eyes were large, and her lips sensual. "There's no point in being formal, since Junior arranged for you to catch me in my work clothes. Is it really Raphael?"

Raphael made a face. "My mother's idea of a joke. I'll answer to Rafe if it'd make you more comfortable."

"God no," she said. "I love it. Raphael—it's so musical." She switched the paintbrushes and offered her hand. Raphael took it.

"Oh dear," she said. "The paint. I completely forgot."

Raphael looked at his hand and laughed at the smudges on his palm.

"It's only watercolor, but I *am* sorry."

"It's nothing."

"Junior," she said sharply, "I positively *hate* you for this."

Flood, who had been watching the two of them intently, laughed sardonically.

"Come and see my little house," she invited them. "Then I'll get cleaned up and change."

The interior of the chalet smelled faintly of the woman's perfume. The walls of the living room were paneled with walnut, and there were dark, open beams at ceiling height, forming a heavy latticework overhead above which open

space soared to the peaked roof. The furniture was of dark,
waxed wood and leather, very masculine, which somehow
seemed to accentuate Mrs. Drake's femininity. The floor was
also dark, waxed wood, and fur throw rugs lay here and
there, highlighting major points in the room. The morning
sun streamed through a window high in the wall above the
beams, catching a heavy crystal service on a buffet in the
dining area beyond the couch. The gleaming cut glass filled
the room with a golden light that seemed somehow artificial,
an unreal glow that left Raphael bemused, almost powerless.
Here and there on the dark walls muted watercolors added
that touch of something indefinable that spoke of class.

"Pretty fancy, 'Bel." Flood looked around approvingly.

"It's comfortable." She shrugged. "The kitchen's through
here." She led them into a cheery kitchen with a round table
near the broad window that faced a wooden deck that overlooked the sparkling waters of the lake. An easel was set up
on the deck with a partially finished watercolor resting on it.

Raphael looked out at the painting and recognized its similarity to the ones hanging in the living room. "You do your
own, I see," he said, pointing.

"It passes the time." She said it deprecatingly, but he
could see that she was rather proud of her efforts.

"Say," Flood said, stepping out onto the deck, "that's
really pretty good, 'Bel. When did you get into this? I thought
dance was your thing."

Raphael and Isabel went out onto the deck and stood looking at the watercolor. She laughed, her voice rich. "That
was a long time ago, Junior. I found out that I'm really too
lazy for all the practice, and I'm getting a little hippy for it.
Male dancers are quite small, and it got to be embarrassing
the way their eyes bulged during the lifts." She smiled at
Raphael. "Good grief, Raphael," she said, her eyes wid-
ening, "what on earth did you do to your arm?" She pointed
at the large, dark bruise on his upper bicep, a bruise exposed
by his short-sleeved shirt.

"The Angel here is our star athlete," Flood told her.

"Yesterday afternoon he single-handedly destroyed an opposing football team."

"Really?" She sounded interested.

"He's exaggerating." Raphael was slightly embarrassed. "There were ten other people out there, too. I just got lucky a few times."

"That looks dreadfully sore." She touched the bruise lightly.

"You should see his chest and stomach." Flood shuddered. "He's a major disaster area."

"They'll fade." Raphael tried to shrug it off. "I heal fairly fast." He looked out over the lake.

"Come along now, you two," Isabel ordered. "I'll show you where the bar is, and then I *have* to get cleaned up and change." She led them back through the kitchen into the dining room. She pointed out the small portable bar to Flood and then went upstairs. A few minutes later they heard a shower start running.

"Well," Flood said, busily at work with the shaker, "what do you think of our 'Bel?"

"She's a lady," Raphael said simply.

Flood laughed. "You're naive, Raphael. 'Bel has breeding; she's got class; she's got exquisite manners and taste; but she's *not* a lady—as I'm sure you'll soon discover."

"What's that supposed to mean?" Raphael asked, a little irritated by Flood's flippancy.

"You'll find out." Flood began to rattle the shaker.

"Isn't it a little early for that?" Raphael asked, sitting carefully in one of the large chairs in front of the fireplace in the living room.

"Never too early." Flood's tone was blithe. "It'll anesthetize all your aches and pains. You're gimping around like an arthritic camel." He came into the living room, handed Raphael a glass, and then sprawled on the leather couch.

"Nice house," Raphael noted, looking around, "but isn't it sort of—well—masculine?"

"That's 'Bel for you." Flood laughed. "It's all part of her web. 'Bel's not like other women—that's why I like her so much. She's very predatory, and she usually gets exactly what she wants."

"You're a snide bastard, Flood."

"Right on." Flood laughed easily. "It's part of my charm."

A half hour later Isabel came back down in a flowered print dress that was sleeveless and cut quite low in front. Raphael found that he had difficulty keeping his eyes where they belonged. The woman was full-figured, and her arms plumply rounded. There was about her a kind of ripeness, an opulence that the firm-figured but angular girls of his own age lacked. Her every move seemed somehow suggestive, and Raphael was troubled by his reactions to her.

They passed the afternoon quietly. They had lunch and a few more drinks afterward. Isabel and Raphael talked at some length about nothing in particular while Flood sat back watching, his hard, bright eyes moving from one to the other and an indecipherable expression on his face.

In Raphael's private place he told himself that he really had no business being there. 'Bel and Flood were aliens to him—bright, beautiful, and totally meaningless. With a kind of startled perception he saw that sophisticated people are sophisticated for that very reason. Meaningless people have to be sophisticated, because they have nothing else.

When it grew dark, they changed clothes and went over to a supper club in Oswego. Raphael rode with Isabel in her sedan, and Flood followed in his Triumph.

At dinner they laughed a great deal, and Raphael could see others in the restaurant glancing at them with eyebrows raised speculatively. Isabel was wearing a low-cut black cocktail dress that set off the satiny white sheen of her skin, and her hair, dark as night, was caught in a loose roll at the back of her neck. As Raphael continued to order more drinks he saw that there was about her an air of enormous sophistication that made him feel very proud just to be seen with her.

As the evening wore on and they lingered over cocktails, Raphael became increasingly convinced that everyone else in the room was covertly watching them, and he periodically forced his laughter and assumed an expression of supercilious boredom.

They had a couple more drinks, and then Raphael knocked over a water glass while he was attempting to light Isabel's cigarette. He was filled with mortification and apologized profusely, noticing as he did that his words were beginning to slur. Isabel laughed and laid her white hand on his sleeve.

Then Flood was gone. Raphael could not remember when he had left. He forced his eyes to focus on Isabel, seeing the opulent rising mounds of creamy white flesh pressing out from the top of her dress and the enigmatic smile on her full lips.

"I'd better catch the check," he slurred, fumbling for his wallet.

"It's already been taken care of," she assured him, still smiling and once again laying her hand lingeringly on his arm. "Shall we go?" She rose to her feet before he could clamber out of his seat to hold her chair.

He offered his arm, and laughing, she took it. They went outside. Once out in the cool night air, Raphael breathed deeply several times. "That's better," he said. "Stuffy in there." He looked around. "Where the hell is Damon?"

"Junior?" She was unlocking her car. "He wanted to take a look around town. He'll be along later."

They climbed into the car and drove in silence back toward Isabel's house. The night seemed very dark outside the car, and Raphael leaned his head back on the seat.

He awoke with a start when they pulled up in the drive.

They got out of the car and went into the house. He stumbled once on the steps, but caught himself in time.

Isabel turned on a dim light in one corner of the living room, then she stood looking at him, the strange smile still on her face. Quite deliberately she reached back and loosened her hair. It tumbled down her back, and she shook her head to free it. She looked at him, still smiling, and her eyes seemed to glow.

She extended her hand to him. "Shall we go up now?"
she said.

V

The autumn proceeded. The leaves turned, the nights grew
chill, and Raphael settled into the routine of his studies. The
library became his sanctuary, a place to hide from the continuing distraction of Flood's endless conversation.

It was not that he disliked Damon Flood, but rather that
he found the lure of that sardonic flow of elaborate and rather
stilted speech too great. It was too easy to lay aside his book
and to allow himself to be swept along by the unending talk
and the sheer force of Flood's personality. And when he was
not talking, Flood was singing. It was not the music itself
that was so distracting, though Flood had an excellent singing voice. Rather it was the often obscene and always outrageous lyrics he composed, seemingly on the spur of the
moment. Flood had a natural gift for parody, and his twisting
of the content of the most familiar songs inevitably pulled
Raphael's attention from his book and usually prostrated him
with helpless laughter. It was, in short, almost impossible to
study while his roommate was around.

And so, more often than not, Raphael crossed the dark
lawn in the evenings to the soaring cathedral that was the
library; and there, in a pool of light from the study lamp, he
bent to his books in the vast main hall beneath the high vault
of the ceiling.

And sometimes he saw in another pool of light the intent
face of the girl whose voice had so stirred him during his
first few weeks on campus. They spoke once in a while,
usually of material for the class they both attended, but it
was all quite casual at first. The vibrant sound of her voice
still struck him, but not as much as it had before he had met
Isabel Drake.

If his weeks were consumed with study, his weekends
were devoted to what he chose to feel was debauchery. Isabel

Drake proved to be a woman of infinite variety and insatiable appetite. She seemed to delight in instructing and guiding him in what, a few months earlier, he would have considered perversion. He did not delude himself into believing that it was love. She was charmed by his innocence and took joy in his youthful vigor and stamina. It was so far from being love that sometimes on Sunday nights as he drove back to Portland, physically wrung out and even sore from his exertions, he felt that he had somehow been violated.

For the first few weekends Flood had accompanied him, delivering him, as it were, into Isabel's hands. Then, almost as if he had assured himself that Raphael would continue the visits without him, he stopped going down to the lake. Without Flood's presence, his knowing, sardonic eyes always watching, Isabel's demeanor changed. She became more dominant, more demanding. Raphael sometimes had nightmares about her during the week, vivid, disconnected dreams of being suffocated by the warm, perfumed pillows of her breasts or crushed between the powerful white columns of her thighs. He began to dread the weekends, but the lure of her was too strong, and helplessly he delivered himself each Friday evening to her perfumed lair by the shores of the lake, where she waited—sometimes, he almost felt, lurked—in heavy-lidded anticipation.

"Have you read the Karpinsky book yet?" It was the girl, Marilyn Hamilton, and she spoke to him as they came out of the library one evening after it closed.

"I'm nearly finished with it," he replied.

"I don't know," she said, falling into step beside him, "but it seemed to me that he evades the issue."

"He does seem a little too pat," Raphael agreed.

"Glib. Like someone who talks very fast so you don't have time to spot the holes in his argument."

They had stopped near the center of the broad lawn in front of Eliot Hall.

"Pardee seems to think a lot of him," Raphael said.

"Oh yes," the girl said, laughing slightly. The vibrance

of her voice pierced him. "Mr. Pardee studied under Karpinsky at Columbia."

"I didn't know that."

"My sister found out. She took the course a couple years ago. Mr. Pardee won't mention it in class, of course, but it's a good thing to know." She suddenly mimicked their instructor's gruff voice and deliberately antigrammatical usage. "Since he ain't about to accept no disrespect."

Raphael laughed, charmed by her.

She hesitated and then spoke without looking at him. "I saw you play in that game last month," she told him quietly.

"Oh," he said, "that. It wasn't much of a game, really."

"Not the way *you* played, it wasn't. You destroyed them."

"You think I overemphasized?" he asked, grinning.

"I'm trying to pay you a compliment, dammit." Then she grinned back.

"Thank you."

"I'm making a fool of myself, right?"

"No, not really."

"Anyway, I thought it was really spectacular—and I don't like football very much."

"It's only a game." He shrugged. "It's more fun to play than it is to watch."

"Doesn't it hurt when you get tackled like that?"

"The idea is not to get tackled."

"You're a stubborn man, Raphael Taylor," she accused. "It's almost impossible to talk to you."

"Me?"

"And *will* you stop looking at me all the time. Every time I look up, there you are, watching me. You make me feel as if I don't have any clothes on."

"I'm sorry."

"I'll start making faces at you if you don't stop it," she warned. "Then how would you feel?"

"The question is how are you going to feel when people start to think your gears aren't meshing?"

"You're impossible," she said, but her voice was not really angry. "I have to go home and study some more." She turned abruptly and strode away with a curiously leggy gait that seemed at once awkward and almost childishly feminine.

"Marilyn," he called after her.

She stopped and turned. "What?"

"I'll see you tomorrow."

"No, you won't. I'm going to hide under the table." She stuck her tongue out at him, turned, and continued across the lawn.

Raphael laughed.

Their growing friendship did not, of course, go unobserved. By the time it had progressed to the stage of going for coffee together at the Student Union Building, Flood became aware of it. "Raphael's being unfaithful to you, 'Bel," he announced on one of his now-infrequent visits to the lake.

"Get serious," Raphael told him, irritated and a little embarrassed.

"Don't be a snitch, Junior," Isabel said quite calmly. "Nobody likes a snitch."

"I just thought you ought to know, 'Bel." Flood grinned maliciously. "Since I introduced you two, I feel a certain responsibility." His eyes, however, were serious, even calculating.

"Our relationship isn't that kind." She still seemed unperturbed. "I don't have any objections if Raphael has other diversions—any more than he's upset by *my* little flings."

Raphael looked at her quickly, startled and with a sudden sinking feeling in the pit of his stomach.

"Oh, my poor Angel," she said, catching the look and laughing, "did you honestly think I was 'saving myself' for you? I have other friends, too, you know."

Raphael was sick, and at the same time ashamed to realize that he was actually jealous.

In bed that night she brought it up again. She raised up on one elbow, her heavy breast touching his arm. "How is she?" she asked. "The other girl, I mean?"

"It's not that kind of thing," he answered sulkily. "We just talk—have coffee together once in a while, that's all."

"Don't be coy," she said with a wicked little laugh, deliberately rubbing her still-erect nipple on his shoulder. "A young man who looks like you do could have the panties off half the girls in Portland inside a week."

"I don't go around taking people's panties off."

"You take *mine* off," she disagreed archly.

"That's different." He moved his shoulder away.

"Why is it different?"

"She's not that kind of a girl."

"*Every* girl is that kind of a girl." She laughed, leaning forward so that the ripe breast touched him again. "We're all alike. Is she as good as I am?"

"Oh, for God's sake, 'Bel. Why don't we just skip all this? Nothing's going on. Flood's got a dirty mind, that's all."

"Of course he has. Am I embarrassing you, sweet? We shouldn't be embarrassed by anything—not here."

"What about those other men?" he accused, trying to force her away from the subject.

"What about them?"

"I thought—well—" He broke off helplessly, not knowing how to pursue the subject.

"Are you really upset because I sleep with other men once in a while? Are you really jealous, Angel?"

"Well—no," he lied, "not really."

"We never made any promises, did we? Did you think we were 'going steady' or something?" The persistent nipple continued its stroking of his shoulder.

"I just didn't think you were—well—promiscuous is all."

"Of course I'm promiscuous." She laughed, kissing him. "I had you in bed within twelve hours of the moment I met you. Is that the sort of thing you'd expect from a nice girl? I'm not exactly a bitch in heat, but a little variety never hurt anyone, did it?"

He couldn't think of anything to say.

"Don't sulk, Angel," she said almost maternally as she pulled him to her again. "You've got my full attention at the moment. That's about the best I can promise you."

His flesh responded to her almost against his will. He'd

have liked to have been stubborn, but she was too skilled, too expert.

"You should try her, Raphael," Isabel said almost conversationally a couple of minutes later. "A little variety might be good for you, too. And who knows? Maybe she's better at it than I am." She laughed, and then the laugh trailed off into a series of little gasps and moans as she began to move feverishly under him.

vi

The idea had not been there before. In Raphael's rather unsophisticated views on such matters, girls were divided into two distinct categories—those you took to bed and those you took to school dances. It was not that he was actually naive, it was just that such classification made his relations with girls simpler, and Raphael's views on such things *were* simplistic. He had been raised in a small, remote city that had a strongly puritanical outlook; his Canadian mother had been quite firm about being "nice," a firmness in part deriving from her lurking fear that some brainless sixteen-year-old tramp might unexpectedly present her with a squalling grandchild. Raphael's football coach at high school, moreover, had taught Sunday school at the Congregational church, and his locker-room talks almost as frequently dealt with chastity as they did with the maiming of middle linebackers. Raphael's entire young life had been filled with one long sermon that concentrated almost exclusively on one of the "thou shalt nots," the only amendment having been the reluctant addition of "—with nice girls." Raphael knew, of course, that other young men did not make a distinction between "nice" girls and the other kind, but it seemed somehow unsporting to him to seduce "nice" girls when the other sort was available—something on the order of poaching a protected species—and sportsmanship had been drilled into him for so long that its sanctions had the force of religious dictum. Isabel's sly insinuations, however, had planted the idea, and in the weeks that followed he found himself frequently looking at Marilyn Hamilton in a way he would not have considered before.

His relationship with the girl passed through all the normal stages—coffee dates in the Student Union, a movie or two, the first kiss, and the first tentative gropings in the front seat of a car parked in a secluded spot. They walked together in the rain; they held hands and they talked together endlessly and very seriously about things that were not particularly significant. They studied together in the dim library, and they touched each other often. They also drove frequently to a special spot they had found outside town where they parked, and in the steamy interior of Raphael's car with the radio playing softly and the misted windows curtaining them from the outside, they partially undressed each other and clung and groped and moaned in a frenzy of desire and frustration as they approached but never quite consummated the act that was becoming more and more inevitable.

Flood, of course, watched, one eyebrow cocked quizzically, gauging the progress of the affair by Raphael's increasing irritability and the lateness of his return to their room. "No score yet, I see," he'd observe dryly upon Raphael's return on such nights.

"Why don't you mind your own damned business?" Raphael would snap, and Flood would chuckle, roll over in his bed, and go back to sleep.

In those weeks Isabel became a virtual necessity to Raphael. With her he found a release for the tensions that had built up to an almost unbearable pitch during the course of the week. She gloated over the passion he brought to her, and sent him back to Portland on Sunday nights sufficiently exhausted to keep him short of the point of no return with the girl. The knowledge that Isabel was there served as a kind of safety valve for him, making it possible for him to draw back at that last crucial instant each time.

And so autumn ground drearily on with dripping skies and the now-bare trees glistening wet and black in the rain. Isabel grew increasingly waspish, and finally announced that she was leaving for a few weeks. "I've got to get some sun," she said. "This rain's driving me up the wall."

"Where are you going?" Raphael asked her.

"Phoenix maybe. Vegas—I don't know. I haven't decided yet. I've got to get away from the rain for a while."

There was nothing he could say. He knew he had no real hold on her, and he even welcomed the idea in a way. His visits had become almost a duty, and he had begun to resent her unspoken demands upon him.

After he had seen her off at the airport outside Portland, he walked back to his car almost with the sense of having been liberated.

On his first weekend date with Marilyn he felt vaguely guilty—almost like an unfaithful husband. The weekends had always belonged to Isabel. He had not been entirely honest with Marilyn about those weekends. It was not that he had lied, exactly; rather, he had let her believe that Isabel was elderly, an old friend of his family, and that his weekly visits were in the nature of an obligation.

After the movie they drove to their special spot in the country and began the customary grappling. Perhaps because the weekends had always been denied to her and this evening was somehow stolen and therefore illicit, Marilyn responded to his caresses with unusual passion, shuddering and writhing under his hands. Finally she pulled free of him for an instant, looked at him, and spoke quite simply. "Let's," she said, her voice thick and vibrant.

And so they did.

It was awkward, since they were both quite tall, and the steering wheel was horribly in the way, but they managed.

And afterward she cried. He comforted her as best he could and later drove her home, feeling more than a little ashamed of himself. There had been some fairly convincing evidence that, until that night, Marilyn had been one of the girls one would normally take to a school dance.

The next time they used the backseat. It was more satisfactory, and this time she did not cry. Raphael, however, was still a bit ashamed and wished they had not done it. Something rather special seemed to have been lost, and he regretted it.

After several weeks Isabel returned, her fair skin slightly tanned and her temper improved.

Flood accompanied Raphael to the lake on the first weekend, his eyes bright and a knowing smile on his face.

Raphael was moody and stalked around the house, stopping now and then to stare out at the rain, and drinking more than was usual for him. It was time, he decided, to break off the affair with Isabel. She was too wise for him, too experienced, and in a way he blamed her for having planted that evil seed that had grown to its full flower that night in the front seat of his car. If it had not been for her insinuating suggestions, his relationship with Marilyn might still be relatively innocent. Beyond that, she repelled him now. Her overripe figure seemed to have taken on a faint tinge of rottenness, and the smooth sophistication that had attracted him at first seemed instead to be depravity now—even degeneracy. He continued to drink, hoping to incapacitate himself and thus avoid that inevitable and now-disgusting conclusion of the evening.

"Our Angel has fallen, I'm afraid," Flood said after dinner when they were all sitting in front of the crackling fireplace.

"Why don't you mind your own business, Damon?" Raphael said, his words slurring.

"Has he been naughty?" Isabel asked, amused.

"Repeatedly. He's been coming in with claw marks on his back from shoulder to hip."

"Why don't you keep your goddamn mouth shut?" Raphael snapped.

"Be nice, dear," Isabel chided him, "and don't try to get muscular. My furniture's too expensive for that sort of foolishness."

"I just want him to keep his mouth shut, that's all." Raphael's words sounded mushy even to him.

"All right then. *You* tell me. Was it that girl?"

He glared sulkily into the fireplace.

"This won't be much of a conversation if you won't talk to me. Did she really scratch you, Angel? Let me see." She came across the room to him and tugged at his shirt.

"Lay off, 'Bel," he warned, pushing her hands away. "I'm not in the mood for any of that."

"Oh"—she laughed—"it's *true* then. I've never liked scratching. It's unladylike."

"How the hell would *you* know?"

Her eyes narrowed slightly, and her voice took on an edge. "All the usual things, I suppose? Parked car, clumsy little gropings in the dark, the steering wheel?"

Raphael's face flamed. She saw the flush and laughed, a deep, throaty sound that made him flush even more. "You *did*!" she exulted. "In a *car seat*! My poor Angel, I thought I'd taught you better. Are motels so expensive now? Or couldn't you wait? Was she a virgin?"

"Why don't we just drop this?"

"I think the boy's in love, Junior," she said to Flood.

"Here's to love." Flood toasted, raising his glass. "And to steering wheels, of course."

"Oh, that's cute, Flood," Raphael said sarcastically. It sounded silly even to him, but he didn't care.

"Don't be nasty, dear." Isabel's tone was motherly. "It doesn't become you."

It was that note in her voice more than anything—that tolerant, amused, superior tone that finally infuriated him. "Don't patronize me, 'Bel," he told her, getting up clumsily. "I won't take that—not from you."

"I don't think I like your tone, Raphael."

"Good. At least I managed to insult you. I wasn't really sure I could."

"I've had about enough of this."

"I had enough a long time ago." He picked up his jacket.

"Where are you going?"

"Someplace where the air's a little cleaner."

"Don't be stupid. You're drunk."

"What if I am?" He started to lurch toward the door.

"Stop him, Junior."

Raphael stopped and turned toward Flood, his jaw thrust forward pugnaciously.

"Not me," Flood said, raising both hands, palms out. "If you want to go, go ahead." His eyes, however, were savage.

"That's exactly what I'm going to do." Raphael turned and stumbled out the door into the rain.

"Raphael!" Isabel called to him from the porch as he fumbled with his car keys. "Don't be ridiculous. Come back into the house."

"No thanks, 'Bel," he replied. "You cost too much for me. I can't afford you anymore." He got the door open and climbed into the car.

"Raphael," she called again.

He started the car and spun away, the rear end fishtailing and wet gravel spraying out behind him.

Because he knew that Flood might try to follow him, he avoided the freeway, sticking instead to the narrow, two-lane country roads that paralleled it. He was still angry and more than a little drunk. He drove too fast on the unfamiliar roads and skidded often—heart-stopping little drifts as he rounded curves, and wrenching, side-to-side slides as he fought to bring the car back under control.

It had all been stupid, of course—overdramatic and even childish. Despite his anger he knew that his outburst had been obviously contrived. Inwardly he almost writhed with embarrassment. It was all too pat and far too easy to attach the worst motives to. Quite bluntly, he had found someone else and had deliberately dumped Isabel. He had been bad-mannered, ungrateful, and even a little bit contemptible. He knew he should go back, but he continued to roar down the wet, winding road, stubbornly resisting even his own best impulses.

He rounded a sharp right-hand curve, and the car went almost completely out of control. In a single, lucid flash he saw directly ahead of him the large white wooden "X" on a pole at the side of the road and the glaring light bearing down on him. As he drove his foot down on the brake, he heard the roaring noise. His tires howled as the car spun and skidded broadside toward the intersection.

The locomotive klaxon bellowed at him as he skidded, tail-first now, onto the tracks in front of the train.

The world was suddenly filled with noise and light and a great stunning shock. He was thrown helplessly around inside the car as it began to tumble, disintegrating, in front of the grinding mass of the locomotive.

He was hurled against a door, felt it give, and he was partially thrown out. Then the remains of the car rolled over on top of him, and he lost consciousness.

vii

At first there was only shattering, mind-destroying pain. Though he feared the unconsciousness as a kind of death, his mind, whimpering, crept back into it gratefully each time he awoke to find the pain still there.

Later—how much later he would never know—there were drugs that stunned him into insensibility. Vacant-eyed and uncaring, he would watch the slow progression of light outside the window of the room. It grew light, and it stayed light for a while, and then it grew dark again. And always, hiding somewhere below the smooth surface, the pain twisted and heaved like some enormous beast reaching up out of the depths to drag him down out of the billowy gray indifference of the drugs and feed upon his shrieking body again. Sometimes, when the drugs were wearing off and their thick, insulating cloud was growing thin, he would cry, knowing that the beast was almost upon him once more, feeling the first feathery touches of its claws. And then they would come and give him more of the drugs, and it would be all right.

There were many bandages. At times it was almost as if the whole bed was one enormous bandage, and there seemed to be a kind of wire cage over his hips. The cage bothered him because it tented the bedclothes up in front of him, so that he could not see the foot of the bed, but when he tried to move the cage, they came and gave him more drugs and strapped his hands down.

And then his mother was there, accompanied by his uncle Harry. Harry Taylor's usually florid face blanched as he approached the bed, and Raphael vaguely wondered what could be so disturbing. It was, however, his mother's shriek that half roused him. That animal cry of insupportable loss and the look of mindless horror on her face as she entered the room reached down into the gray fog where he hid from the pain and brought him up, partially sitting, staring beyond the tented cage over his hips at the unbelievable vacancy on the left side of the bed.

It was a mistake, of course, some trick of the eye. Quite plainly, he could feel his left leg—toes, foot, ankle, knee, and thigh. He half sat, feeling the leg in exquisite detail while his eyes, sluggish and uncomprehending, told him that it was no longer there.

viii

"Taylor," the blocky, balding man in the wheelchair snapped, "get your weight off your armpits."

"I was just resting, Mr. Quillian." Raphael lifted his body with his hands.

"Don't rest on your armpits. You remember what I told you about crutch paralysis?"

"All right. Don't make a federal case out of it." He went back to his slow, stumping shuffle back and forth across the small, gymlike therapy room. "This is bullshit," he said finally, collapsing into his wheelchair near the door. "I told you people it was too early for this." He sat massaging his aching hands. "They haven't even taken the dressings off yet."

"Taylor," Quillian said coldly, "if you lie around for another two weeks, you won't be strong enough to lift your own dead ass. Try it again."

"Screw it. I'm tired."

"Do you enjoy being an invalid, Taylor?"

"Come on," Raphael objected. "This is hard work."

"Sure it is. You afraid of hard work?"

"Where's the difference? I mean, I've seen people on crutches before—sprained ankles, broken legs—stuff like that. They pick it up right away. What makes it so damned hard for me?"

"Balance, Taylor, balance. A broken leg is still there. You're a one-legged man now. You've lost nearly a fifth of your body weight. Your center of gravity is in your chest instead of your hips. You've got to learn balance all over again."

"Not all at once. I'm tired. I'm going back to my room."

"Quitting, Taylor? I thought you were an athlete. Is this the way you used to win football games?"

"I'm hurting, man. I need a shot."

"Sure you do." Quillian's voice was contemptuous. "But let's not lie to each other. Let's call it by its right name. You need a fix, don't you? You're a junkie, Taylor, and you need a fix."

Raphael spun his chair around angrily and wheeled himself out of the therapy room.

Later, in the hazy euphoria the drug always brought, Raphael lay in his bed and tried to bring his mind to bear on the problem. "Junkie," he said, trying the word out. It sounded funny to him, and he giggled. "Junkie," he said again, and giggled some more.

A day or so later a starched nurse came into his room with a brightly professional smile on her face. "You have a visitor, Mr. Taylor," she said.

Raphael, gritting his teeth at the pain that seemed to have settled in his phantom knee and knowing that it was still hours until they would give him another shot, turned irritably toward her. "Who is it?" he asked harshly.

"A Miss Hamilton."

"No! I don't want to see her. Send her away."

"Oh, come on," she coaxed. "A visit might cheer you up."

"No!" Raphael shouted. "Now get the hell out of here and leave me alone!" He turned his face toward the wall.

After the nurse had left and he was sure that he was alone, he cried.

Her name was Miss Joan Shimp, and Raphael hated her from almost the first moment he laid eyes on her. She was led into the room by the hospital chaplain, who said a few nice things about social workers and then left. Miss Shimp wore a businesslike suit. No starched white uniform for old Shimpsie. Nobody was going to ask *her* to empty a bedpan by mistake. She was a pear-shaped young woman with enormous hips, narrow shoulders, and no noticeable bosom. Her complexion was acne-ravaged, and she had dun-colored hair, an incipient mustache, a nasal voice, and what might best be described as an attitude problem. "Well now," she started briskly, "how are we doing?" The nurses on the floor had all learned rather early not to say "we" to Raphael.

"I don't know about you, lady," Raphael replied in a flat, unfriendly tone, "but *I'm* doing lousy."

"Self-pity, Mr. Taylor? We must avoid self-pity."

"Why? It's a dirty job, but somebody's got to do it."

"This just won't do," she scolded.

"We're not going to get along, lady. Why don't you just go away?"

"We can play this either way, Taylor." Her voice was sharp. "You've been assigned to me, and I *am* going to do my job. There are programs for people like you, and like it or not, you *are* going to participate."

"Really? Don't bet the farm on it."

Things deteriorated rapidly from there.

Shimpsie talked about programs as if programs were holy things that could solve all the world's problems. Raphael ignored her. His half-drugged mind was not particularly retentive, but he soon had a pile of books at his bedside, and every time Shimpsie entered his room, he would select a book at random and use it as a barrier. In one of his more outrageous moments Flood had once described social workers as representatives of a generation of bright young ladies who don't know how to type. Raphael clung to that definition. It seemed to help for some reason.

Shimpsie asked probing questions about his background and family. She liked the phrase "dysfunctional family," and she was desperately interested in his "feelings" and "relationships." Shimpsie, he felt, was queer for feelings and relationships. On one occasion she even screamed at him, "Don't think! Feel!"

"And abandon twenty-five thousand years of human development? Not very likely, Shimpsie."

"*Miss* Shimp!" she snapped.

"Whatever." He said it as insultingly as possible. "Angleworms feel, Shimpsie. So do oysters, I imagine. I don't know about you, but I hope *I've* come further than that."

Just for the sake of variety he would sometimes lie to her, inventing outrageous stories about a background as "dysfunctional" as he could concoct. She lapped it up, her eyes begging for more.

He hated her with a passion, but he began to long for her visits. In a strange sort of way Shimpsie *was* therapeutic.

"That's better, Taylor," Quillian said a week later. "You're starting to get the rhythm now. Don't stump. Make it smooth. *Set* the crutches down, don't jab at the ground with them. Try to keep from jarring your arms and shoulders."

Raphael, sweating profusely, grimly moved back and forth across the therapy room, gritting his teeth at the burning pain in his arms.

"Why are you picking on Miss Shimp?" Quillian said in a half-amused way.

"Shimpsie? I pick on her because she's an asshole."

Quillian laughed. "Never heard a woman called an asshole before."

"Would you prefer asshole-ess?"

"Asshole or not, you'd better at least *try* to get along with her, Taylor."

"Why should I bother?"

"Because you can't get out of here without her okay. She has to sign a release before they'll discharge you. Okay, enough bullshit. Get back to work."

A week or so later Uncle Harry made another trip to Portland, alone this time. "Good to see you again, Rafe," he said, shaking Raphael's hand. He glanced at the crutches leaning in the corner. "I see that you're getting around now."

Raphael looked at him through the haze of the shot he had just been given. "What brings you down here, Uncle Harry?"

"Oh . . ." his uncle replied a bit evasively, "this and that. I thought I'd stop by and see how you were doing."

"I'm coming along."

"Good for you. Have they given you any idea yet about when you'll be getting out of here?"

Raphael shifted in the bed, wincing slightly. "I imagine that it's going to be a while longer."

"You going back to school when you get out?"

"I haven't really thought about it yet."

Uncle Harry gave him a speculative look. "I'm going to give this to you straight, Rafe. I think we know each other well enough for that."

"Okay," Raphael replied, "what is it?"

"It's your mother, Rafe."

"Mom?"

"She's always been a delicate woman, you know, and I'm afraid all of this has been too much for her—your father's death, your accident, all of it. She's a little—well—disoriented. Her doctors say that she'll come out of it eventually, but it's going to take time."

"I'd better go home. I can get around now—a little. I'll see if they'll discharge me."

"Uh—that's going to be a problem, Rafe. You see, what's happened is that your mother has—well, sort of retreated. I mean, she's not catatonic or anything, but it's just that in her mind none of this has really happened. As far as she's concerned, your father's away on a business trip, and you're off at college. She's perfectly happy—talks about you both all the time. The doctors think that it might be best to keep her that way for the time being. If you came back with your—on crutches, that is—she'd have to face things she's just not ready to come to grips with yet.''

"I see.''

"I hate to have to be the one to tell you, but it's better coming from me than from somebody else. Just give her a little time, that's all. Write to her from time to time—that sort of thing. I'll keep you posted on her progress.''

"Thanks for telling me, Uncle Harry.''

"That's what family is for. If you're not too tired, there are a couple of other things I need to discuss with you.''

"I'm fine,'' Raphael told him.

"Okay, Rafe.'' Uncle Harry opened his briefcase. "Financially you're pretty well off.''

"Sir?''

"You'll have a fairly comfortable income. Edgar—your father—had a number of insurance policies. Edgar was always very interested in insurance.''

"He was a careful man.''

"That he was, Rafe. That he was. The policies will cover all your medical expenses here and give you an income besides—not very big, actually. Walking-around money is about all. You'll also be receiving Social Security disability benefits.''

"I've never had a job, Uncle Harry—not a real one. I'm not eligible for Social Security.''

"You worked for four summers at the mill back in Port Angeles.''

"That wasn't a real job, Uncle Harry. The owner hired me because of my father—and because I was a football player.''

"They withheld Social Security from your check, didn't they?''

"Yes.''

"Then you're entitled. Don't rush out and make any down

payments on any castles, though. What's really got you set up is the settlement you got from the railroad.''

''Settlement? What settlement?''

''I told you about that the last time I was here. I had you sign some papers, remember?''

''To be honest with you, Uncle Harry, there are some big gaps in what I remember. The painkillers sort of erase things.''

''I suppose they do at that. Well, to cut it short, the railroad's insurance company got in touch with me not long after your accident. They made an offer.''

''What for? It was *my* fault. I was drunk and driving too fast. It wasn't the train's fault.''

''You don't necessarily have to make an issue of that, Rafe—not that it really matters now, I guess. The railroad didn't want a messy court case. Jurors in this part of the country are a little unpredictable where railroads are concerned. It's cheaper in the long run for the railroad to make an offer in any case where there are personal injuries. Those ten-million-dollar judgments really bite into company profits. Anyway, you'll be getting a monthly check from them. I still wouldn't get my heart set on any castles, though. If you don't go hog-wild, you'll get by okay. I'll put the money—your settlement, your insurance, and your Social Security check all in the bank back home for you. You remember Anderson, don't you?''

''The banker?''

''Right. He remembers you from the football field, and he'll take care of everything for you. You'll be getting a check every month. I put a few thousand in the hospital safe for you.''

''A few *thousand*?''

''You're going to have unusual expenses when you leave the hospital, Raphael. I don't want you to run short. I'm afraid you'll find out just how little it is when you get out on the street. You're set financially, so you can just relax until you get back on your feet again.'' Harry stopped abruptly and looked away. ''I'm sorry, but you know what I mean.''

"Sure."

"I'll need your signature on a few things," his uncle went on. "Power of attorney for you and your mother—that kind of thing. That way you can concentrate on getting well and just leave everything else up to me. Okay?"

"Why not?"

"Mr. Quillian," Raphael said to his therapist a few days later while resting on his crutches.

"What is it, Taylor?" the balding man in the wheelchair asked him.

"Did you have any problems with all the drugs they give us?"

"Jesus Christ, Taylor! I've got a broken back. Of course I had a problem with drugs. I fought drugs for five years."

"How did you beat it?"

"Beat it? Beat it, boy?" Quillian exploded. "You *never* beat it. Sometimes—even now—I'd give my soul for one of those shots you get every other hour."

"All right, then. How did you stop?"

"How? You just stop, boy. You just stop. You just don't take any more."

"All right," Raphael said. "I can do that if I have to. Now, when do I get my wooden leg?"

Quillian looked at him. "What?"

"My peg leg? Whatever the hell you call it?"

"Prosthesis, Taylor. The word is prosthesis. Haven't you talked with your doctor yet?"

"He's too busy. Is there something else I'm supposed to know?"

Quillian looked away for a moment, then looked back, his face angry. "Dammit," he swore. "I'm not supposed to get mixed up in this." He spun his wheelchair away and rolled across the room to a file cabinet. "Come over here, Taylor." He jerked open a cabinet drawer and leafed through until he found a large brown envelope.

Raphael crutched across the room, his movements smoother now.

"Over to the viewer," Quillian said harshly, wheeled, and snapped the switch on the fluorescent viewer. He stuck an X-ray picture on the plate.

"What's that?" Raphael asked.

"That's you, Taylor. That's what's left of you. Full front, lower segment. You don't have a left hip socket. The left side of your pelvis is shattered. There's no way that side of you could support your weight. There won't be any prosthesis for you, Taylor. You're on crutches for the rest of your life, boy. You might as well get that down in your mind."

Raphael stood on his crutches, looking at the X ray. "All right. I can live with that if I have to."

"You still want to try to get off the dope?"

"Yes." Raphael was still looking at the X ray, a horrible suspicion growing as he looked at the savagely disrupted remains of his pelvis that the shadowy picture revealed. "I think it's time I got my head back together again."

ix

"There really wasn't any alternative, Raphael," the doctor told him. "The damage was so extensive that there just wasn't anything left to salvage. We were lucky to be able to restore normal urinary function."

"That's the reason I've got this tube?" Raphael asked.

"The catheter? Yes. That's to allow the bladder time to heal. We should be able to remove it soon. There'll be some discomfort at first, but that'll pass and the function will be normal."

"Then there was no damage to the—uh—"

"Some, but we were able to repair that—to a degree. That's a pretty tricky area to work with. My guess is that even if we'd been able to save the scrotal area and one or both testes, normal sexual function probably couldn't have been restored."

"Then I'm a eunuch."

"That's a very old-fashioned term, Raphael," the doctor said disapprovingly.

Raphael laughed bitterly. "It's an old-fashioned kind of condition. Will my voice change—all that kind of thing?"

"That's mythology. That kind of thing only happens if the removal takes place before puberty. Your voice won't change, and your beard won't fall out. You can check with an endocrinologist periodically if you like, but it won't really be necessary."

"All right," Raphael said, shifting uncomfortably in his chair. He'd begun to sweat again, and there was an unpleasant little twitching in his left hip.

"Are you all right?" the doctor asked, looking at him with concern.

"I can live with it." Raphael's left foot felt terribly cold.

"Why don't I have them increase your medication for a few days?" the doctor suggested.

"No," Raphael said sharply. He lifted himself up and got his crutches squared away.

"In time it'll begin to be less important, Raphael," the doctor said sympathetically.

"Sure. Thanks for your time. I know you're busy."

"Can you make it back to your room okay?"

"I can manage it." Raphael turned and left the doctor's office.

Without the drugs he found that he slept very little. After nine, when the visitors left, the hospital became quiet, but never wholly silent. When he found his hand twitching, reaching almost of its own volition for the bell that would summon the nurse with the needle, he would get out of bed, take his crutches, and wander around in the halls. The effort and the concentration it required to walk helped to keep his mind off his body and its craving.

His arms and shoulders were stronger now, and Quillian had given him his permanent crutches. They were called Canadian crutches, a term that seemed very funny to Raphael for some reason. They had leather cuffs that fit over his forearms, and they angled slightly at the handgrips. Using them was much less awkward, and he began to develop the smooth, almost stately pace of the one-legged man.

He haunted the halls of the hospital during the long hours of the night, listening to the murmurs and the pain-filled moans of the sick and the dying. Although he realized that it might have been merely coincidence, a series of random occurrences of an event that could happen at any time, Raphael became persuaded that most people die at night. Usually they died quietly, but not always. Sometimes, in the exhaustion with which he sandbagged his craving body to sleep toward the morning of each interminable night, he wondered if it might not somehow be *him*. It seemed almost as if his ghosting passage down the dim halls, like the turbulence in the wake of a passing ship, reached in through the doors and walls to draw out those teetering souls. Sometimes in those last moments before sleep he almost saw himself as the Angel of Death.

Once, during his restless midnight wandering, he heard a man screaming in agony. He angrily crutched his way to the nurses' station. "Why don't you give him a shot?" he demanded.

"It wouldn't do any good," the starched young nurse replied sadly. "He's an alcoholic. His liver's failed. Nothing works with that. He's dying, and there's nothing we can give him to relieve the pain."

"You didn't give him enough," Raphael told her, his voice very quiet, even deadly.

"We've given him the maximum dosage. Any more would kill him."

"So?"

She was still quite young, so her ideals had not yet been eroded away. She stared at Raphael, her face deathly white. And then the tears began to run slowly down her cheeks.

Shimpsie noted from Raphael's chart that he had been refusing the painkilling medication, and she disapproved. "You *must* take your medication, Raphael," she chided.

"Why?"

"Because the doctors know what's best for you."

He made an indelicate sound. "I've got the free run of the hospital, Shimpsie," he told her. "I've been in the doctors' lounge, and I've heard them talking. Don't bullshit me about how much doctors know. They're plumbers and pill pushers. I haven't heard an original thought from one of them since I've been here."

"Why do you go out of your way to be so difficult?"

"It's an attention-getting device, Shimpsie." He smiled at her sweetly. "I want you all to remember me. I quit taking the goddamn dope because I don't want to get hooked. I've got enough problems already."

"There are programs to help you break that habit," she assured him. Her voice was actually earnest.

"You've got a program for everything, haven't you, Shimpsie? You send a couple of orderlies to my room about nine times a week to drag me to meetings—meetings of the lame, the halt, and the blind—where we all sit around spilling our guts for you. If you want to fondle guts, go fondle somebody else's. Mine are just fine the way they are."

"*Why* can't I get through to you? I'm only trying to help."

"I don't need help, Shimpsie. Not yours, anyway."

"You want to do it 'your way'? Every client starts out singing 'My Way.' You'll come around eventually."

"Don't make any bets. As I recall, I warned you that you weren't going to enjoy this. You'd save yourself a lot of grief if you just gave up on me."

"Oh no, Taylor. I *never* give up. You'll come around—because if you don't, you'll stay here until you rot. We'll grow old together, Taylor, because you won't get out of here until *I* sign you off. Think about it." She turned to leave.

He *couldn't* let her get in the last word like that. He absolutely *couldn't*. "Oh, Shimpsie?" he said mildly.

"Yes?"

"You really shouldn't get so close to my bed, you know. I haven't gotten laid for a long time. Besides, you've got a nice big can, and I'm a compulsive fanny-patter."

She fled.

Finally, when the craving for the drugs had almost gone and the last dressings had been removed to reveal the puckered, angry red new scars on his hip and groin, when the Christmas season was upon them, Flood finally came to visit.

Their meeting was awkward, since there was very little they could really talk about. Raphael could sense in Flood that stifling unease all hospital visitors have. They talked desultorily of school, which was out for the Christmas holiday; of the weather, which was foul; and of nearly anything else except those uncomfortable subjects that by unspoken mutual consent they avoided.

"I brought your luggage and books and your other stuff," Flood said. "I decided to get an apartment off campus next semester, and I was pretty sure you wouldn't want the college to store your things. They tend to be a little careless."

"Thanks, Damon."

"Are you going to be coming back to school when you get out of here?" Flood asked, a curiously intent look in his dark eyes.

"I haven't decided yet. I think I'll wait a semester or so—get things together first."

"Probably not a bad idea. Tackle one thing at a time." Flood walked to the window and stood looking out at the rain.

"How's 'Bel?" Raphael asked, crossing that unspoken boundary.

"Fine—as far as I know, anyway. I haven't been going down there much. 'Bel gets a little tiresome after a while, and I've been studying pretty hard."

"You?" Raphael laughed. "I didn't think you knew how."

Flood turned back from the window, grinning. "I'm not much of a scholar," he admitted, "but I didn't think it'd look good to flunk out altogether. Old J.D.'d like nothing better than to find an excuse to cut off my allowance."

"Look," Raphael said uncomfortably, "I really ran my mouth that night at 'Bel's place. If you happen to see her, tell her I apologize, okay?"

"What the hell? You were drunk. Nobody takes offense at anything you say when you're drunk. Besides, you were probably right about her. I told you about that, didn't I?"

"All the same," Raphael insisted, "tell her I apologize."

"Sure"—Flood shrugged—"if I see her. You need anything?"

"No. I'm fine."

"I'd better get going then. I've got a plane to catch."

"Going home for Christmas?"

"It's expected. Scenic Grosse Pointe for the holidays. Hot spit. At least it'll pacify the old man—keep those checks coming." He looked at his watch. "I'm going to have to get cranked up. I'll look you up when I get back, okay?"

"Sure."

"Take care, Gabriel," Flood said softly, and then he left. They did not shake hands, and the inadvertent slip passed almost unnoticed.

The hospital became intolerable now that his body was mending. Raphael wanted out—away—anyplace but in the hospital. He became even more irritable, and the nurses pampered him, mistakenly believing that he was disappointed because he could not go home for Christmas. It was not the holiday, however. He simply wanted out.

Shimpsie was going to be a problem, however. On several occasions she had held her power to withhold her approval for his discharge over his head. Raphael considered it in that private place in his mind and made a decision that cost him a great deal in sacrificed pride. The next day he got "saved." He went through the entire revolting process. Once he even broke down and cried for her. Shimpsie, her eyes filled with compassion and with the thrill of victory, comforted him, taking him in her arms as he feigned racking sobs. Shimpsie's deodorant had failed her sometime earlier that day, and being comforted by her was not a particularly pleasant experience.

She began to talk brightly about "preparation for independent living." She was so happy about it that Raphael almost began to feel ashamed of himself. Almost.

He was fully ambulatory now, and so one day she drove

him to one of those halfway houses. In the world of social
workers, *everything* had a halfway house. Ex-convicts, ex-
junkies, ex–sex offenders—all of them had a halfway house—
a kind of purgatory midway between hell and freedom.
Shimpsie *really* wanted the state of Oregon to pick up Raphael's tab, but he firmly overrode that. He was running a
scam—a subterfuge—and he wanted to pay for it himself,
buying, as it were, his own freedom. He paid the deposit
and the first month's rent for a seedy, rather run-down room
in an old house on a quiet back street, and Shimpsie drove
him back to the hospital. She fervently promised to look in
on him as soon as he got settled in. Then, just before she
hurried off to one of her meetings, she hugged him, a little
misty-eyed.

"It's all right, Joanie," he said consolingly. "We'll be
seeing each other again." That had been one of the marks
of his rehabilitation. He had stopped calling her "Shimpsie"
and used "Joanie" instead. He cringed inwardly each time
he did it.

She nodded and went off down the hall, exuding her smug
sense of victory.

"So long, Shimpsie," Raphael murmured under his
breath. "I'm really going to miss you." The funny thing was
that he almost meant it. He turned and crutched his way
toward the gym. He wanted to say good-bye to Quillian.

"I see you're leaving," Quillian said, his voice harsh as
always.

Raphael nodded. "I stopped by to say thanks."

"It's all part of the job."

"Don't be a shithead. I'm not trying to embarrass you,
and I'm not talking about showing me how to use these."
He waved one of his crutches.

"All right. Did you finally quit feeling sorry for yourself?"

"No. Did you?"

Quillian laughed suddenly. "No, by God, I never did.
You're going to be okay, Taylor. Be honest with yourself,
and don't be afraid to laugh at yourself, and you'll be okay.

Watch out for booze and drugs when you get out there, though," he added seriously. "It's an easy way out, and a lot of us slip into that. It'd be particularly easy for *you*. All you'd have to do is shamble into any doctor's office in the country and walk out fifteen minutes later with a pocketful of prescriptions. You've got the perfect excuse, and Dr. Feelgood is just waiting for you."

"I'll remember that."

Quillian looked at him for a moment. "Be careful out there, Taylor. The world isn't set up for people like us. Don't fall down—not in front of strangers."

"We all fall down once in a while."

"Sure," Quillian admitted, "but those bastards out there'll just walk around you, and you can't get up again without help."

"I'll remember that, too. Take care, Quillian, and thanks again."

"Get the hell out of here, Taylor. I'm busy. I've got people around here who still need me." They shook hands, and Raphael left the therapy room for the last time.

He stored most of his things at the hospital, taking only two suitcases.

The pasty-faced man from the halfway house was waiting for him outside the main entrance, but Raphael had planned his escape very carefully. He already had his reservation at a good downtown hotel, and he had called a cab, telling the dispatcher very firmly that he wanted to be picked up at the *side* door. As his cab drove him away from the hospital, he began to laugh.

"Something funny?" the driver asked him.

"Very, very funny, old buddy," Raphael said, "but it's one of those inside kind of jokes."

He spent the first few nights in the hotel. It was a good one, and there were bellhops and elevators to make things easier. He began to refer to it in his mind as his own private halfway house. He had his meals sent up to his room, and he bathed fairly often, feeling a certain satisfaction at being able to manage getting in and out of the tub without help. After he had been in the hotel for two days, he bathed again and then lay on the bed to consider the future.

There was no reason to remain in Portland. He was not going back to Reed—not yet certainly—probably never. There were too many painful associations there. He also knew that if he stayed, sooner or later people would begin to come around—to look him up. In his mind he left it at that— "people"—even though what he really meant was Isabel and Marilyn. It was absolutely essential that he have no further contact with either of them.

He called the desk and made arrangements to have the hotel pick up the rest of his belongings from the hospital and ship them to his uncle in Port Angeles. He could send for them later, after he got settled. The sense of resolve, of having made a decision, was quite satisfying; and since it had been a big day, he slept well that night.

The next morning he called Greyhound. A plane would be faster certainly, but airlines keep records, and he could not really be sure just how far Shimpsie might go to track him down. Shimpsie had full access to the resources of the Portland Police Department, if she really wanted to push it, and Shimpsie would probably want to push it as far as it would go. Hell, as they say, hath no fury like a social worker scorned, and Raphael had not merely scorned Shimpsie, he had tricked her, deceived her, and generally made a fool of her. Right now Shimpsie would probably walk through fire to get him so that she could tear his heart out with her bare hands.

It was difficult to explain things over the phone to the man at Greyhound. It was really against policy for an interstate bus to make an unscheduled stop at a downtown street corner. Raphael waved the missing leg at him and finally got around that.

Then there was the question of destination. Raphael quickly calculated the amount of time it would take for a messenger to reach the depot with the money and return with a ticket. He concentrated more on that *time* than upon any given destination. He wanted to be gone from Portland. He wanted to go *anyplace* as long as it wasn't Portland.

Finally the man on the phone, puzzled and more than a little suspicious, ventured the information that there were still seats available on the bus that would leave for Spokane in two hours, and that the bus would actually pass Raphael's hotel. That was a good sign. Raphael had not had any good luck for so long that he had almost forgotten what it felt like. "Good," he said. "Hold one of those seats for me. I'll be outside the front door of the hotel."

"Are you sure you want to go to Spokane?" the man at Greyhound asked dubiously.

"Spokane will do just fine," Raphael said. "Everything I've always wanted is in Spokane."

Fortuna plango vulnera
stillantibus ocellis

i

It was snowing when they reached Spokane, a swirling snow-fall of tiny crystalline flakes that glittered in the streetlights and muffled the upper floors of the buildings. The traffic on the white-covered streets was sparse, and dark, ill-defined automobiles loomed, bulky and ominous, out of the swirling white with headlights like smeared eyes.

The bus pulled under the broad roof that sheltered the loading gates at the terminal and stopped. "Spokane," the driver announced, and opened the door of the bus.

The trip had been exhausting, and toward the end had become a kind of tedious nightmare under a darkening, lead-gray sky that had spat snow at them for the last hundred miles. Raphael waited until the bus emptied before attempting to rise. By the time he had struggled down the steps and reached the safety of the ground, most of the other passengers had already joined family or friends, reclaimed their luggage, and left.

The air was crisp, but not bitterly cold, and the Muzak inside the depot came faintly through the doors.

There was another sound as well. At first Raphael thought it might be a radio or a television set left playing too loudly. A man was giving an address of some kind. His words seemed to come in little spurts and snatches as the swirling wind and intermittent traffic first blurred and then disclosed what he said.

"If chance is defined as an outcome of random influence

58

produced by no sequence of causes," he was saying in an oratorical manner, "I am sure that there is no such thing as chance, and I consider that it is but an empty word."

Then Raphael saw the speaker, a tall, skinny man wearing a shabby overcoat of some kind of military origin. He was bald and unshaven, and he stood on the sidewalk at the front of the bus station talking quite loudly to the empty street, ignoring the snow that piled up on his shoulders and melted on his head and face. "For what place can be left for anything to happen at random so long as God controls everything in order? It is a true saying that nothing can come out of nothing." The speaker paused to allow his unseen audience to grasp that point.

"These your bags?" a young man in blue jeans and a heavy jacket who had been unloading suitcases from the bus asked, pointing at Raphael's luggage sitting alone on a baggage cart.

"Right," Raphael said. "What's with the prophet of God there?" He pointed at the skinny man on the sidewalk.

"He's crazy," the young man replied quite calmly. "You see him all over town makin' speeches like that."

"Why don't they pick him up?"

"He's harmless. You want me to put your bags in the station for you?"

"If you would, please. Is there a good hotel fairly close?"

"You might try the Ridpath," the young man suggested, picking up Raphael's suitcases. "It's not too far."

"Can I get a cab?"

"Right out front." The young man shouldered his way into the station and held the door open as Raphael crutched along behind him.

"If anything arises from no causes, it will appear to have arisen out of nothing," the man on the sidewalk continued. "But if this is impossible, then chance also cannot—"

The door swung shut behind Raphael, cutting off the sound of that loud voice. Somehow he wished that it had not. He wished that he might have followed the insane prophet's reasoning to its conclusion. Chance, luck—good or bad—if you

will, had been on Raphael's mind a great deal of late, and he
really wanted to hear a discussion of the subject from the
other side of sanity. His thoughts, centering, as they had, on
a long series of "what-if's," were growing tedious.

A few people sat in the bus station, isolated from each
other for the most part. Some of them slept, but most stared
at the walls with vacant-eyed disinterest.

"I'll set these over by the front door for you," the young
man with the suitcases said.

"Thanks."

The Ridpath is one of the best hotels in Spokane, and
Raphael stayed there for four days. On the first morning he
was there he took a cab to a local bank with branches in all
parts of the city and opened a checking account with the
cashier's check he had purchased in Portland. He kept a couple hundred dollars for incidentals and then returned to his
hotel. He did not venture out after that, since the snowy
streets would have been too hazardous. He spent a great deal
of time at the window of his room, looking out at the city.
While he was there he had all of his pants taken to a tailor to
have the left legs removed. The flapping cloth bothered him,
and the business of pinning the leg up each time he dressed
was a nuisance. It was much better with the leg removed and
a neat seam where it had been.

On his third day in Spokane it rained, cutting away the
snow and filling the streets with dirty brown slush. It was
when he checked his wallet before going to the dining room
for supper that a rather cold realization came to him. It was
expensive to be disabled. Since the disabled man could do
very little for himself, he had to hire other people to do them
for him. He skipped supper that night and sat instead with
pad and pencil adding a few things up. The very first conclusion he reached was that although the Ridpath was very
comfortable, staying there was eating up his funds at an
alarming rate. A man of wealth might comfortably take up
permanent residence at the Ridpath, but Raphael was far
from being a millionaire. The several thousand dollars Uncle
Harry had given him in Portland had seemed to be an enor-

mous sum, but now he saw just how small it really was. "Time to pull in the old horns," he said wryly. "I think we'd better make some other arrangements."

He took the phone book and made a list of a half dozen or so nearby hotels and apartment houses. The next morning he put on his coat and went downstairs to the cabstand at the front of the hotel.

The first hotel on his list was the St. Clair. It was totally unsuitable. Then the cab took him up Riverside to the Pedicord, which was even worse. The Pedicord Hotel was very large, and it looked as if it might at one time have had some pretensions about it. It had long since decayed, however. The lobby was filled with stained and broken couches, and each couch was filled. The men were old for the most part, and they smoked and spat and stared vacant-eyed at a flickering television set. There were crutches and metal-frame walkers everywhere. Each time one of the old men rose to go to the bathroom, a querulous squabble broke out among those who stood along the walls over who would get the vacant seat. The smell was unbelievable.

Raphael fled.

"Just what are you lookin' for, man?" the cabdriver asked when Raphael climbed, shaken, back into the cab again.

"A place to live."

"You sure as hell don't wanna move in to *that* dump."

"How can they live that way?" Raphael looked at the front of the Pedicord and shuddered.

"Winos," the driver replied. "All they want is a place that's cheap and gets 'em in outta the cold." He stopped and then turned and looked at Raphael. "Look. I could drive you all over this downtown area—run up a helluva fare—and you're not gonna find anyplace you'd wanna keep a pig in—not if you thought anything about the pig. You're gonna have to get out a ways—outta this sewer. I'm not supposed to do this, but I think I know a place that might be more what you're lookin' for. How much do you wanna pay?"

Raphael had decided what he could afford the previous night. He rather hesitantly named the figure.

"That sounds pretty close to the place I got in mind. You wanna try it?"

"Anything. Just get me away from here."

"Right." The driver started his motor again. They drove on back down Riverside. It was raining again, a misty, winter kind of rain that blurred the outlines of things. The windshield wiper clicked, and the two-way radio in the front seat crackled and hissed.

"You lose the leg in 'Nam?" the driver asked.

"No," Raphael replied. "I had a misunderstanding with a train." He was surprised to find that he could talk about it calmly.

"Ooog!" The driver shuddered. "That's messy. You're lucky you're still around at all. I saw a wreck like that out in the valley once. Took 'em two hours to pick the guy up. He was scattered half a mile down the tracks."

"How far is this place?"

"Not much farther. Lemme handle it when we get there, okay? I know the guy. You want a place where you can cook?"

"No. Not right away."

"That'll make it easier. There's a pretty good little restaurant just down the street. You'll wanna be on the main floor. The place don't have an elevator."

The cab pulled up in front of a brick building on a side street. The sign out front said, THE BARTON. WEEKLY-MONTHLY RATES. An elderly man in a well-pressed suit was coming out the front door.

"Sit tight," the driver said, climbed out of the cab, and went inside.

About ten minutes later he came back. "Okay," he said. "He's got a room. It's in the back, so there's no view at all, unless you like lookin' at alleys and garbage cans. He's askin' 'bout thirty-five a month more than what you wanted to pay, but the place is quiet, pretty clean, and like I said, there's that restaurant just down the street where they ain't gonna charge you no ten bucks for a hamburger. You wanna look at it?"

"All right," Raphael said, and got out of the cab.

The room was not large, but it had a good bed and an armchair and a sturdy oak table with a few magazines on it. There was a sink and a mirror, and the bathroom was right next door. The walls were green—every rented room in the world is painted green—and the carpet was old but not too badly worn.

"Looks good," Raphael decided. "I'll take it." He paid the landlord a month's rent and then went back to the Ridpath to get his luggage and check out. When they returned to the Barton, the driver carried his bags into the room and set them down.

"I owe you," Raphael said.

"Just what's on the meter, man. I might need a hand myself someday, right?"

"All right. Thanks."

"Anytime," the driver said, and left. Raphael realized that he hadn't even gotten his name.

The weather stayed wet for several weeks, and Raphael walked a little farther each day. Quillian had told him that it would be months before his arms and shoulders would develop sufficient strength to make any extensive walking possible, but Raphael made a special point of extending himself a little more every day, and he was soon able to cover a mile or so without exhausting himself too much.

By the end of the month he could, if he rested periodically, cover most of the downtown area. He considered sending for the rest of his things, but decided against it. The room was too small.

Spokane is not a particularly pretty city, especially in the winter. Its setting is attractive—a kind of basin on the banks of the Spokane River, which plunges down a twisted basalt chute in the center of town. The violence of the falls is spectacular, and an effort was made following the World's Fair in 1974 to convert the fairgrounds into a vast municipal park. The buildings of the downtown area, however, are for the most part very old and very shabby. Because the city is small, the worst elements lie side by side with the best.

Raphael became accustomed to the sight of drunken old men stumbling through the downtown streets and of sodden Indians, their eyes a poached yellow, swaying in bleary confusion on street corners. The taverns were crowded and noisy, and a sour reek exhaled from them each time their doors opened. In the evenings hard-faced girls in tight sweaters loitered on street corners, and loud cars filled with raucous adolescents toured an endless circuit of the downtown area, their windows open and the mindless noise of rock music blasting from them at full volume. There were fights in front of the taverns sometimes and unconscious winos curled up in doorways. There were adult bookstores on shabby streets and an X-rated movie house on Riverside.

And then it snowed again, and Raphael was confined, going out only to get his meals. He had three or four books with him, and he read them several times. Then he played endless games of solitaire with a greasy deck of cards he'd found in the drawer of the table. By the end of the week he was nearly ready to scream with boredom.

Finally the weather broke again, and he was able to go out. His very first stop was at a bookstore. He was determined that another sudden change in the weather was *not* going to catch him without something to read. Solitaire, he decided, was the pastime of the mentally deficient. He came out of the bookstore with his coat pockets and the front of his shirt stuffed with paperback books and crutched his way on down the street. The exercise was exhilarating, and he walked farther than he ever had before. Toward the end of the day he was nearly exhausted, and he went into a small, gloomy pawnshop, more to rest and to get in out of the chill rain than for any other reason. The place was filled with the usual pawnshop junk, and Raphael browsed without much interest.

It was the tiny, winking red lights that caught his eye first. "What's that thing?" he asked the pawnbroker, pointing.

"Police scanner," the unshaven man replied, looking up from his newspaper. "It picks up all the police channels—fire department, ambulances, stuff like that."

"How does it work?"

"It scans—moves up and down the dial. Keeps hittin' each one of the channels until somebody starts talkin'. Then it locks in on 'em. When they stop, it starts to scan again. Here, I'll turn it up." The unshaven man reached over and turned up the volume.

"District One," the scanner said, "juvenile fifty-four at the Crescent security office."

"What's a fifty-four?" Raphael asked.

"It's a code," the man behind the counter explained. "I got a sheet around here someplace." He rummaged through a drawer and came up with a smudged and tattered mimeographed sheet. "Yeah, this is it. A fifty-four's a shoplifter." He handed Raphael the sheet.

"Three-Eighteen," the scanner said. The row of little red lights stopped winking when someone spoke, and only the single light over the channel in use stayed on.

"This is Three-Eighteen," another voice responded.

"We have a man down in the alley behind the Pedicord Hotel. Possible DOA. Complainant reports that he's been there all day."

"I'll drift over that way."

"DOA?" Raphael asked.

"Dead on arrival."

"Oh."

The lights went on winking.

"This is Three-Eighteen," the scanner said after a few minutes. "It's Wilmerding. He's in pretty bad shape. Better send the wagon—get him out to detox."

Raphael listened for a half an hour to the pulse that had existed beneath the surface without his knowing it, and then he bought the scanner. Even though it was secondhand, it was expensive, but the fascination of the winking flow of lights and the laconic voices was too great. He had to have it.

He took a cab back to his hotel, hurried to his room, dumped his books on the bed, and plugged the scanner in.

Then, not even bothering to turn on the lights, he sat and
listened to the city.

"District Four."

"Four."

"Report of a fifty at the Maxwell House Tavern. Refuses
to leave."

"Spokane Ambulance running code to Monroe and Francis. Possible heart."

"Stand by for a fire. We have a house on fire at the corner
of Boone and Chestnut. Time out eighteen-forty-seven."

Raphael did not sleep that night. The scanner twinkled at
him and spoke, bringing into his room all the misery and
folly of the city. People had automobile accidents; they went
to hospitals; they fought with each other; they held up gas
stations and all-night grocery stores. Women were raped in
secluded places, and purses were snatched. Men collapsed
and died in the street, and other men were beaten and robbed.

The scanner became almost an addiction in the days that
followed. Raphael found that he had to tear himself from the
room in order to eat. He wolfed down his food in the small
restaurant nearby and hurried back to the winking red lights
and the secret world that seethed below the gloomy surface
of the city.

Had it lasted much longer, that fascination might have so
drugged him that he would no longer have had the will to
break the pattern. Late one evening, however, a crippled old
man was robbed in a downtown alley. When he attempted to
resist, his assailants knifed him repeatedly and then fled. He
died on the way to the hospital, and Raphael suddenly felt
the cold constriction of fear in his stomach as he listened.

He had believed that his infirmity somehow exempted him
from the senseless violence of the streets, that having endured and survived, he was beyond the reach of even the
most vicious. He had assumed that his one-leggedness would
be a kind of badge, a safe-conduct, as it were, that would
permit him to pass safely where others might be open to
attack. The sportsmanship that had so dominated his own
youth had made it inconceivable to him that there might be

any significant danger to anyone as maimed as he. Now, however, he perceived that far from being a guarantee of relative safety, his condition was virtually an open invitation to the jackals who hid in alleys and avoided the light. He didn't really carry that much cash on him, but he was not sure how much money would be considered "a lot." The crippled old man in the alley had probably not been carrying more than a few dollars.

Raphael was unused to fear, and it made him sick and angry. In the days that followed he became wary. He had to go out; hunger alone drove him from the safety of his room. He took care, however, always to go in the daylight and at times when the streets were most crowded.

In time it became intolerable. He realized that even his room was not an absolute sanctuary. It was, after all, on the ground floor and in the back. The front door of the building was not that secure, and his window faced on an unlighted alley. The night was filled with noises—small sounds he had not heard before and that now seemed unspeakably menacing. He slept fitfully and dreamed of the feel of the knives going in. It was not pain that he feared, since for Raphael pain was no longer relevant. It was the indignity of being defenseless, of being forced to submit to violation simply because he would not be able to protect himself that he feared.

It could not go on. He could not continue to let this fear so dominate him that it became the overriding consideration of his life. And so he decided to move, to take himself out of the battle zone, to flee even as Christian had fled from the City of Dreadful Night. And ultimately it was for much the same reason—to save his soul.

There were apartments to be had; the want ads were full of them. He bought a city map and rode the buses, seeking a location, a neighborhood that could offer both convenience and greater security. The newer apartment houses were all too expensive. The insurance settlement and his disability income from Social Security and the policy his father had carried for him provided him with enough to live on if he

was careful with his money, but there was not really enough
for extravagance. He began to concentrate his search on the
north side, beyond the churning turbulence of the river, as if
that barrier might somehow hold off the predators who
roamed the downtown streets.

It was luck, really, when he found it. The apartment was
not listed in the paper, but there was a discreet sign in a
downstairs window. The bus he customarily rode had passed
it a half-dozen times before he realized that the sign was
there. He got off at the next stop and went back, his paces
long and measured, and his crutches creaking with each
stride.

The building had been a store at one time, wooden-framed,
and with living quarters for the owner upstairs. There was a
large screened porch across the front of the second floor and
five mailboxes beside the bayed-in downstairs door that had
at one time been the entrance to the business. The entire
structure was somewhat bigger than a large house, and it sat
on a corner facing two quiet streets with older houses and
bare trees poking up stiffly at the gray winter sky. The roof
was flat, and there was a small building up there, windowed
on three sides.

"I saw your sign," Raphael said to the T-shirted man who
came in answer to his ring. "Do you suppose I could look
at the apartment?"

The man scratched his chin doubtfully, looking at the
crutches and the single leg. "I don't know, buddy. It's that
place up on the roof. Those stairs might give you a problem."

"One way to find out," Raphael said to him.

"You working?" the man asked, and then went on quickly:
"Don't get me wrong. I'm not trying to be a shithead, but if
you got behind in your rent, I'd look like a real son of a bitch
if I tried to kick you out. I had a woman on welfare in here
last year who stopped paying her rent. Took me six months
to get her out. I had social workers all over me like a rug—
called me every dirty name in the book."

"I've got an income," Raphael replied patiently. "Social

Security and disability from an insurance policy. They bring in enough to get me by. Could I look at it?'' He had decided not to mention the railroad settlement to strangers.

The man shrugged. ''I'll get the key. The stairway's around on the side.''

The stairway was covered, a kind of long, slanting hallway attached to the side of the house. There was a solid handrail, and Raphael went up easily.

''You get around pretty good,'' the man in the T-shirt commented as he came up and unlocked the door at the top of the stairs.

''Practice.'' Raphael shrugged.

''It's not much of an apartment,'' the man apologized, leading the way across the roof to a structure that looked much like a small, square cottage. ''There sure as hell ain't room in there for more than one guy.''

''That much less to take care of.''

It was small and musty, and the dust lay thick everywhere. There was a moderate-sized living-room/dining-room combination and a Pullman kitchen in the back with a sink, small stove, and tiny refrigerator. Beside the door sat a table with two chairs. A long sofa sat against the front wall, and an armchair angled back against one of the side walls. There were the usual end table and lamps, and solid-looking but somewhat rough bookcases under the windows.

''The bedroom and bath are through there,'' the man in the T-shirt said, pointing at a door beside the kitchen.

Raphael crutched to the door and looked in. There was a three-quarter-size bed, a chair, and a freestanding wardrobe in the bedroom. The bathroom was small but fairly clean.

''Hotter'n a bitch up here in the summer,'' the man warned him.

''Do all these windows open?'' Raphael asked.

''You might have to take a screwdriver to some of them, but they're all supposed to open. It's got baseboard electric heat—you pay your own utilities.'' He quoted a number that was actually twenty-five dollars a month less than what

Raphael had been paying at the Barton. "You'll roast your ass off up here in July, though."

Raphael, however, was looking out the window at the top of the stairs. The slanting enclosure that protected the stairs had a solid-looking door at the top. "Is there a key to that door?" he asked.

"Sure." The man seemed to have some second thoughts. "This won't work for you," he declared. "You got those stairs, and what the hell are you gonna do when it snows and you gotta wade your way to the top of the stairway?"

"I'll manage," Raphael said, looking around at the dusty furniture and the dirty curtains over the windows. "This is what I've been looking for. It'll do just fine. I'll write you a check."

ii

The landlord's name was Ferguson, and Raphael made arrangements with him to have someone come in and clean the apartment and wash the dusty windows. He also asked Ferguson to get in touch with the phone company for him. Telephones are absolute necessities for the disabled. Back at his hotel he sat down and drew up a careful list of the things he would need—sheets, blankets, towels, dishes, silverware. He estimated the cost and checked the balance in his checkbook. There was enough to carry him through until the first of the month when his checks would begin to arrive from home. Then he went to the pay phone down the hall, called his uncle in Port Angeles to ask him to ship his things to his new address.

"You doing all right, Rafe?" Harry Taylor asked him.

"Fine," Raphael replied, trying to sound convincing. "This downtown area's a little grubby and depressing, but the new place is in a lot nicer neighborhood. How's Mom?"

"About the same."

"Look, Uncle Harry, I've got to run. I've got a lot of

things to take care of before I move. You know how that goes.''

"Lord yes." Harry Taylor laughed. "I'd rather take a beating than move. Take care of yourself, Rafe."

"You too, Uncle Harry."

The last few nights in the hotel were not so bad. At least he was getting away. The scanner did not seem as menacing now. There was a kind of excitement about it all, and he felt a sense of genuine anticipation for the first time in months.

He moved on a Friday and stopped only briefly at the apartment to have the cabdriver carry up his bags and turn on the heat. Then he had the cab take him to the shopping center at Shadle Park, where there were a number of stores, a branch of his bank, and a supermarket.

The shopping was tiring, but he went at it methodically, leaving packages with his name on them at each store. His last stop was at the supermarket, where he bought such food as he thought he would need to last him out the month. The prices shocked him a bit, but he reasoned that in the long run it would be cheaper than eating in restaurants.

At last, when the afternoon was graying over into evening, he called another cab and waited impatiently in the backseat as the driver picked up each of his purchases.

After the patient cabdriver had carried up the last of the packages and come back down, Raphael climbed to the top of the stairs, stepped out onto the roof, and locked the door behind him with an immense feeling of relief.

"There, you little bastards," he said softly to the city in general, "try to get me now." And then, because the night air was chilly, he hurried inside to the warm brightness that was home. He locked the apartment door and closed all the drapes.

He put a few things away and made the bed. He fixed himself some supper and was pleased to discover that he wasn't that bad a cook, although working in the tiny kitchen was awkward with the crutches. After dinner he unpacked his suitcases and hung his clothes carefully in the wardrobe. It was important to get that done right away. It was all right

to live out of a suitcase in a hotel, but this was his home now.
Then he bathed and sat finally at his ease in his small living
room, secure and warm and very pleased with himself, listening to the scanner murmuring endlessly about the terrors
from which he was now safe.

For the first few days there was an enormous satisfaction
with being truly independent for the first time in his life. At
home and at college there had always been someone else in
charge, someone to prepare his meals and to look after him.
The hospital, and to a lesser degree the hotels where he had
stayed, had been staffed. Now he was alone for the first time
and able to make his own decisions and to care for himself.

He puttered a great deal, setting things first here, then
there, arranging and rearranging his cupboards and his refrigerator. When his belongings finally arrived from Port Angeles, he dived into them with enthusiasm. He hung up the
rest of his clothes and spent hours meticulously sorting and
placing his books and the cassettes for his small but quite
good tape player in the low bookcases. He rather lovingly
ran his fingers over his cassettes—the usual Bach, Beethoven,
and Brahms and the later Romantics, as well as a few
twentieth-century compositions. He worked to music after
that. He kept very busy, and the days seemed hardly long
enough for everything he wanted to accomplish. The apartment was small enough so that he could move around quite
easily in it, and he felt very comfortable knowing that the
door at the top of the stairs was locked and that he had the
only key.

And then, after a week, it was done. Everything was arranged to his satisfaction, and he was quite content.

He stood in the center of the room and looked around.
"Okay, baby," he said quietly to himself, "what now?" His
independence was all very fine, but he finally realized that
he didn't have the faintest idea what he was going to do with
it. His life suddenly loomed ahead of him in arid and unending emptiness.

To be doing something—anything—he crutched outside
onto the roof, although the air was biting and the leaden skies

were threatening. It was only midafternoon, but the day seemed already to be fading into a gloom that matched his mood.

A light in the upstairs of the house next door caught his eye, and he glanced at the window. The man in the room was talking animatedly, gesturing with his hands. Several cats sat about the room watching him. He did not appear to be talking to the cats. Something about the man's face seemed strange. Curious, Raphael watched him.

The man turned toward the window, and Raphael looked away quickly, not wanting to be caught watching. He feigned interest in something down over the railing that encircled the roof. The man in the lighted window turned back to the room and continued to talk. Raphael watched him.

After several minutes the iron-cold air began to make him shiver and he went back inside. When he had been about nine, he had developed an interest in birds, and his mother had bought him a pair of binoculars. The interest had waned after a summer, and the seldom-used binoculars had become merely an adjunct, a possession to be moved from place to place. He went into the bedroom and took them down from the top shelf of the wardrobe. He turned out the lights so that he would not be obvious, sat by the window, and focused the glasses on the face of the man next door.

It was a curious face. The mouth was a ruin of missing teeth, and the nose and chin jutted forward as if protecting that puckered vacancy. The eyes were wary, fearful, and moved constantly. It was the hair, however, that began to provide some clue. The man was not bald, at least not entirely. Rather, his head was shaved, but not neatly. There were razor nicks here and there among the short bristles. Two unevenly placed patches of sparse, pale whiskers covered his cheeks. They were not sideburns or any recognizable beard style, but were simply unshaven places.

The strange man suddenly froze, his eyes cast upward, listening. He nodded several times and tried once to speak, but the voice that only he could hear seemed to override him.

He nodded again, reached up with both hands, and ran searching fingers over his scalp and face.

"Crazy," Raphael said with almost startled realization. "This whole goddamn town is filled with crazies."

The man in the house next door got out a shaving mug and brush and began stirring up a lather, his face intent. Then he started to slap the lather on his head and face, stopping now and then to listen raptly to instructions or urgings from that private voice. Then he picked up a razor and began to scrape at his head and face. He did not use a mirror, nor did he rinse his razor. He simply shook the scraped-off lather and stubble onto the floor and walls. The cats avoided those flying white globs with expressions of distaste. Lather ran down the man's neck to soak his shirt collar, but he ignored that and kept on scraping. Little rivulets of blood ran from cuts on his scalp and face, but he smiled beatifically and continued.

Raphael watched until his eyes began to burn from the strain of the binoculars. The name "Crazy Charlie" leaped unbidden into his mind, and he watched each new antic with delight. He sat in the dark with the scanner twinkling at him and watched the strange, involved rituals by which Crazy Charlie ordered his life.

Later that night when Charlie had gone to his bed, leaving the lights on, Raphael sat in the dark on his couch listening to the scanner and musing, trying to probe out the reason for each of those ritual acts he had just witnessed. The despair that had fallen over him that afternoon had vanished, and he felt good—even buoyant—though he could not have explained exactly why.

iii

And then there were two weeks of snow again, and Raphael was housebound once more. He listened to the scanner, played his music, and read. As Quillian had told him he would, he had reached a certain competence with his crutches and then had leveled off. He could get around, but he was still awkward. Fixing a meal was a major effort, and cleaning his tiny apartment was a two-day project.

"That's when you need to get your ass back to a therapist," Quillian had said. "If you don't, you'll stay right at that point. You'll be a cripple all your life, instead of a guy who happens to have only one leg."

"There's a difference?" Raphael had asked.

"You bet your sweet ass there is, Taylor."

He considered it now. He could put it into the future since there was no way he could go out and wade around in knee-deep snow. It seemed that it would be a great deal of trouble, and he got around well enough to get by. But in his mind he could hear Quillian's contemptuous verdict, "Cripple," and he set his jaw. He was damned if he'd accept that. He decided that he would look up a therapist and start work again—as soon as the snow was gone.

Most of the time he sat and watched Crazy Charlie next door. He had no desire to know the man's real name or background. His imagination had provided, along with the nickname, a background, a personal history, far richer than mundane reality could ever have been. Crazy Charlie had obviously once been a somebody—nobody could have gotten *that* crazy without a certain amount of inspiration. Raphael tried to imagine the kind of pressures that might drive a man to take refuge in the demon-haunted jungles of insanity, and he continued to struggle with the problem of the rituals. There was a haunting kind of justification for each of them, the shaving of the head and face, the avoidance of a certain spot on the floor, the peculiar eating habits, and all the rest. Raphael felt that if he could just make his mind passive enough and merely watch as Charlie expended his days in those ritual acts, sooner or later it would all click together and he would be able to see the logic that linked them all together and, behind that logic, the single thing that had driven poor Charlie mad.

It was enough during those snowy days to sit where it was warm and secure, to listen to music and the scanner with an

open book in front of him on the table, and to watch Crazy
Charlie. It kept his mind occupied enough to prevent a sudden upsurge of memories. It was very important not to have
memories, but simply to live in endless now. Memories were
the little knives that could cut him to pieces and the little axes
that could chop his orderly existence into rubble and engulf
him in a howling, grieving, despairing madness that would
make the antics of Crazy Charlie appear to be profoundest
sanity by comparison.

In time the snow disappeared. It did not, as it all too frequently does, linger in sodden, stubborn, dirty-white patches
in yards and on sidewalks, but rather was cut away in a single
night by a warm, wet chinook wind.

There were physical therapists listed in Raphael's phone
book, but most of them accepted patients by medical referral
only, so he called and made an appointment with an ortho-
pedic surgeon.

It was raw and windy on the day of his appointment, and
Raphael turned up the collar of his coat as he waited for the
bus. A burly old man strode past, his face grimly determined. He walked very fast, as if he had an important en-
gagement somewhere. Raphael wondered what could be of
such significance to a man of that age.

The receptionist at the doctor's office was a motherly sort
of lady, and she asked the usual questions, took the name of
Raphael's insurance company, and finally raised a point
Raphael had not considered. "You're a resident of this state,
aren't you, Mr. Taylor?" she asked him. She had beautiful
silver-white hair and a down-to-earth sort of face.

"I *think* so," Raphael replied. "I was born in Port Angeles. I was going to college in Oregon when the accident
happened, though."

"I'm sure that doesn't change your residency. Most people
who come to see the doctor are on one of the social programs. As a matter of fact I think there are all kinds of programs you're eligible for. I know a few of the people at
various agencies. Would you like to have me call around for
you?"

"I hadn't even thought about that," he admitted.

"You're a taxpayer, Mr. Taylor. You're entitled."

He laughed. "The state didn't make all that much in taxes from me."

"It did from your parents, though. I'll call around and see what I can find out. I can give you a call later, if you'd like."

"I'd appreciate that. Thank you." He signed the forms she handed him and sat down to wait for the doctor. It was good to get out. He had not realized how circumscribed his life had been for the past several weeks.

The doctor examined him and made the usual encouraging remarks about how well he was coming along. Then he made arrangements to enroll him in a program of physical therapy.

Because he still felt good, and because it was still early when he came out of the doctor's office, Raphael rode buses for the rest of the day, looking at the city. Toward late afternoon, miles from where he had first seen him, he saw the burly old man again. The old man's face still had that grimly determined expression, and his pace had not slowed.

In the days that followed, because the scanner and the books and Crazy Charlie were no longer quite enough, Raphael rode buses. For the most part it was simply to be riding—to be doing something, going somewhere. For that reason rather than out of any sense of real need, he called the helpful receptionist.

"I was meaning to get in touch with you, Mr. Taylor," she said. "The people at social services are *very* interested in you."

"Oh?"

"You're eligible for all sorts of things, did you know that? Food stamps, vocational guidance—they'll even pay for your schooling to train you in a new trade."

"I was a student," he told her dryly. "Are they going to make a teacher out of me instead?"

"It's possible—if you want to get a degree in education." Her voice took on a slightly confidential note. "Do you want to know the *real* reason they're so interested in you?" she asked.

"Why's that?"

"Your particular case is complicated enough to provide full-time work for three social workers. I don't really care for those people. Wouldn't it make more sense to just give the money to the people who need it rather than have some girl who's making thousands and thousands of dollars a year dole it out to them in nickels and dimes?"

"A lot more sense, but the girl can't type, so she can't get an honest job."

"I don't quite follow that," she admitted.

"A friend of mine once described a social worker as a girl who can't type."

She laughed. "Would you like to have me give you a few names and phone numbers?"

"I think we might as well drop it," he decided. "It's a little awkward for me to get around."

"Raphael," she said quite firmly, asserting her most motherly authority, "*we* don't go to *them*. *They* come to *us*."

"We?"

"You probably didn't notice because I was sitting down when you came in. I'm profoundly arthritic. I've got so many bone spurs that my X rays look like pictures of a cactus. You just call these people, and they'll fall all over themselves to come to your house—at *your* convenience."

"They make house calls?" He laughed.

"They almost have to, Raphael. They can't type, remember?"

"I think I'm in love with you," he joked.

"We might want to talk about that sometime."

Raphael made some calls, being careful not to commit himself. He remembered Shimpsie and wondered if she had somehow put out the social-worker equivalent of an all-points bulletin on him. He was fairly sure that escaping from a social worker was not an extraditable offense, however.

He was certain that the various social agencies could have saved a great deal of time and expense had they sent one caseworker with plenipotentiary powers to deal with one Taylor, Raphael—cripple. He even suggested it a couple of times, but they ignored him. Each agency, it appeared, wanted to hook him and reel him in all on its own.

He began to have a great deal of fun. Social workers are always very careful to conceal the fact, but as a group they have a very low opinion of the intelligence of those whom they call "clients," and no one in this world is easier to deceive and mislead than someone who thinks that he, or in this case, she, is smarter than you are.

They were all young—social workers who get sent out of the office to make initial contacts are usually fairly far down on the seniority scale. They did not, however, appear to have all attended the same school, and each of them appeared to reflect the orientation of her teachers. A couple of them were very keen on "support groups," gatherings of people with similar problems. One very earnest young lady who insisted that he call her Norma even went so far as to pick him up one evening in her own car and take him to a meeting of recent amputees. The amputees spent most of the evening telling horror stories about greater or lesser degrees of addiction to prescription drugs. Raphael felt a chill, remembering Quillian's warning about Dr. Feelgood.

"Well?" Norma said, after the meeting was over and she was driving him home.

"I don't know, Norma," Raphael said with a feigned dubiousness. "I just couldn't seem to relate to those people." (He was already picking up the jargon.) "I don't seem to have that much in common with a guy who got drunk and whacked off his own arm with a chain saw. Now, if you could find a dozen or so one-legged eunuchs—"

Norma refused to speak to him the rest of the way home, and he never saw her again.

Once, just to see how far he could push it, he collected a number of empty wine bottles from the garbage can of two old drunks who lived across the street. He scattered the bottles around on the floor of his apartment for the edification of a new caseworker. *That* particular ploy earned him a week of closely supervised trips to Alcoholics Anonymous meetings.

It stopped being fun at that point. He remembered the club Shimpsie had held over his head at the hospital, and realized just how much danger his innocent-seeming pastime placed him in. Because they had nearly total power over something the client wanted or needed, the caseworkers had equally total power over the client's life. They could—and usually did—use that power to twist and mold and hammer the client into a slot that fit their theories—no matter how half-baked or unrealistic. The client who wanted—needed—the thing the social worker controlled usually went along, in effect becoming a trained ape who could use the jargon to manipulate the caseworker even as she manipulated him. It was all a game, and Raphael decided that he didn't want to play. He didn't really need their benefits, and that effectively placed him beyond their power. He made himself unavailable to them after that.

One, however, was persistent. She was young enough to refuse to accept defeat. She could not be philosophical enough to conclude that some few clients would inevitably escape her. She lurked at odd times on the street where Raphael lived and accosted him when he came home. Her name was Frankie—probably short for Frances—and she was a cute little button. She was short, petite, and her dark hair was becomingly bobbed. She had large, dark eyes and a soft, vulnerable mouth that quivered slightly when someone went counter to her wishes.

"We can't go on meeting this way, Frankie," Raphael said to her one afternoon when he was returning from physical therapy. "The neighbors are beginning to talk."

"Why are you picking on me, Raphael?" she asked, her lip trembling.

"I'm not picking on *you*, Frankie. Actually, I rather like you. It's your profession I despise."

"We're only trying to help."

"I don't need help. Isn't independence one of the big goals? Okay, I've got it. You've succeeded. Would you like to have me paste a gold star on your fanny?"

"Stop that. I'm your caseworker, not some brainless girl you picked up in a bar."

"I don't need a caseworker, Frankie."

"Everybody needs a caseworker."

"Have you got one?"

"But I'm not—" She faltered at that point.

"Neither am I." He had maneuvered her around until her back was against the wall and had unobtrusively shifted his crutches so that they had her blocked more or less in place. It was outrageous and grossly chauvinistic, but Frankie really had it coming. He bent forward slightly and kissed her on top of the head.

Her face flamed, and she fled.

"Always nice talking to you, Frankie," he called after her. "Write if you get honest work."

His therapy consisted largely of physical exercises designed to improve his balance and agility, and swimming to improve his muscle tone. The sessions were tiring, but he persisted. They were conducted in an office building on the near north side of Spokane, and he did his swimming at the YMCA. Both buildings had heavy doors that opened outward and swung shut when they were released. Usually someone was either going in or coming out, and the door would be held open for him. Sometimes, however, he was forced to try to deal with them himself. He learned to swing the door open while shuffling awkwardly backward and then to stop the seemingly malicious closing with the tip of his crutch. Then he would hop through the doorway and try to wrench the crutch free.

Once the crutch was so tightly wedged that he could not free it, and, overbalanced, he fell.

He did not go out again for several days.

He called the grim-faced old man "Willie the Walker," and he saw him in all parts of the city. The walking seemed to be an obsession with Willie. It was what he did to fill his days. He moved very fast and seldom spoke to anyone. Raphael rather liked him.

Then, one day in late March, the letter from Marilyn came. It had been forwarded to him by his uncle Harry. It was quite short, as such letters usually are.

Dear Raphael,
There isn't any easy way to say this, and I'm sorry for that. After your accident I tried to visit you several times, but you wouldn't see me. I wanted to tell you that what had happened to you didn't make any difference to me, but you wouldn't even give me the chance. Then you left town, and I hadn't even had the chance to talk to you at all.

The only thing I could think was that I wasn't very important to you anymore—maybe I never really was. I'm not very smart about such things, and maybe all you really wanted from me was what happened those few times. No matter what, though, it can't go on this way anymore. I can't tie myself to the hope that someday you'll come back.

What it all gets down to, dear Raphael, is that I've met someone else. He's not really very much like you—but then, who could be? He's just a nice, ordinary person, and I think I love him. I hope you can find it in your heart to forgive me and wish me happiness—as I do you.

I'll always remember you—and love you—but I just can't go on hoping anymore.

Please don't forget me,
Marilyn

When he finished the letter, he sat waiting for the pain to begin, for the memories with their little knives to begin on him; but they did not. It was past now. Not even this had any power to hurt him.

His apartment, however, was intolerable suddenly, and although it was raining hard outside, he pulled on his coat and prepared to go down to the bus stop.

For only a moment, just before he went out, there was a racking sense of unspeakable loss, but it passed quickly as he stepped out onto the rain-swept rooftop.

Willie the Walker, grimly determined, strode past the bus stop, the beaded rain glistening on his coat and dripping from the brim of his hat. Raphael smiled as he went by.

Across the street there was another walker, a tall, thin-faced young Indian moving slowly but with no less purpose. The Indian's gait was measured, almost fluidly graceful, and in perhaps a vague gesture toward ethnic pride, he wore moccasins, silent on the pavement. His dark face was somber, even savagely melancholy. His long black hair gleamed wetly in the rain, and he wore a black patch over his left eye.

Raphael watched him pass. The Indian moved on down to the end of the block, turned the corner, and was gone.

It kept on raining.

iv

By mid-April, the weather had broken. It was still chilly at night and occasionally there was frost; but the afternoons were warm, and the winter-browned grass began to show patches of green. There was a tree in the yard of the house where Crazy Charlie lived, and Raphael watched the leaf buds swell and then, like tight little green fists, slowly un-curl.

He began walking again—largely at the insistence of his therapist. His shirts were growing tight across the chest and shoulders as the muscles developed from the exercises at his therapy sessions and the continuing effort of walking. His stamina improved along with his strength and agility, and he soon found that he was able to walk what before would have seemed incredible distances. While he was out he would often see Willie the Walker and less frequently the patch-eyed Indian. He might have welcomed conversation with either of them, but Willie walked too fast, and Patch, the Indian, was too elusive.

On a sunny afternoon when the air was cool and the trees had almost all leafed out, he was returning home and passed the cluttered yard of a house just up the block from his apartment building. A stout, florid-faced man wheeled up on a bicycle and into the yard.

"Hey," he called to someone in the house, "come and get this stuff."

A worn-looking woman came out of the house and stood looking at him without much interest.

"I got some pretty good stuff," the stout man said with a bubbling enthusiasm. "Buncha cheese at half price—it's only a little moldy—and all these dented cans of soup at ten cents each. Here." He handed the woman the bag from the carrier on the bicycle. "I gotta hurry," he said. "They put out the markdown stuff at the Safeway today, an' I wanna get there first before it's all picked over." He turned the bicycle around and rode off. The woman looked after him, her expression unchanged.

Raphael moved on. His own supply of food was low, he knew that, and there was a Safeway store only a few blocks away. He crutched along in the direction the man on the bicycle had gone.

The store was not very large, but it was handy, and the people seemed friendly. The stout man's bicycle was parked out front when Raphael got there.

It was not particularly busy inside as Raphael had feared that it might be, and so he got a shopping cart and, nudging it along the aisles ahead of him with his crutches, he began picking up the items he knew he needed.

Back near the bread department the stout man was pawing through a large basket filled with dented cans and taped-up boxes of cereal. His florid face was intent, and his eyes brightened each time he picked up something that seemed particularly good to him. A couple of old ladies were shame-facedly loitering nearby, waiting for him to finish so that they might have their turns.

Raphael finished his shopping and got into line behind the stout man with his cartful of damaged merchandise. The man paid for his purchases with food stamps and triumphantly carried them out to his bicycle.

"Does he come in often?" Raphael asked the clerk at the cash register.

"Bennie the Bicycler?" the clerk said with an amused look. "All the time. He makes the rounds of every store in this part of town every day. If he'd spend half as much time looking for work as he does looking for bargains, his family could have gotten off welfare years ago." The clerk was a tall man in his mid-thirties with a constantly amused expression on his face.

"Why do you call him that?" Raphael asked, almost startled by the similarity to the little name tags he himself used to describe the people on his block.

The clerk shrugged. "It's a personal quirk," he said, starting to ring up Raphael's groceries. "There's a bunch of regulars who come in here. I don't know their names, so I just call them whatever pops into my mind." He looked around, noting that no one else was in line or standing nearby. "This place is a zoo," he said to Raphael in a confidential tone. "All the weirdos come creeping out of Welfare City over there." He gestured vaguely off in the direction of the large area of run-down housing that lay to the west of the store. "We get 'em all—all the screwballs in town. I've been trying to get a transfer out of this rattrap for two years."

"I imagine it gets depressing after a while."

"That just begins to describe it," the clerk replied, rolling his eyes comically. "Need anything else?"

"No," Raphael replied, paying for his groceries. "Is there someplace where I can call a cab?"

"I'll have the girl do it for you." The clerk turned and called down to the express lane. "Joanie, you want to call a cab?"

"Thanks," Raphael said.

"No biggie. It'll be here in a couple of minutes. Have a good one, okay?"

Raphael nudged his cart over near the door and waited. It felt good to be able to talk with people again. When he had first come out of the hospital, his entire attention had been riveted upon the missing leg, and he had naturally assumed that everyone who saw him was concentrating on the same thing. He began to realize now that after the initial reaction, people were not really that obsessed by it. The clerk had taken no particular notice of it, and the two of them had talked like normal people.

A cab pulled up, and the driver got out, wincing in obvious pain. He limped around the cab as Raphael pushed his cart out of the store. The driver's left foot was in a slipper, and there was an elastic bandage around his grotesquely swollen ankle.

"Oh, man," the driver said, looking at Raphael in obvious dismay. "I *told* that half-wit at dispatch that I couldn't handle any grocery-store calls today."

"What's the problem?"

"I sprained my damn ankle. I can drive okay, but there's no way I could carry your stuff in for you when we get you home. Lemme get on the radio and have 'em send another cab." He hobbled back around the cab again and picked up his microphone. After a couple minutes he came back. "What a screwed-up outfit. Everybody else is tied up. Be at least three quarters of an hour before anybody else could get here. You got stairs to climb?"

"Third floor."

"Figures. Would you believe I did this on a goddamn *skateboard*? Would you *believe* that shit? My kid was showin' me how to ride the damn thing." He shook his head and then looked across the parking lot at a group of children passing on the sidewalk. "Tell you what. School just let out. I'll knock a buck off the fare, and we'll give the buck to a kid to haul your stuff up for you."

"I could wait," Raphael offered, starting to feel ashamed of his helplessness.

"Naw, you don't wanna stand around for three quarters of an hour. Let's go see if we can find a kid."

They put Raphael's two bags of groceries in the cab and then both got in.

"You know," the driver said, wheeling out of the lot, "if I'd been smart, I'd have called in sick this morning, but I can't afford to lose the time. I wish to hell the bastard who invented skateboards had one shoved up his ass."

Raphael laughed. He still felt good.

They pulled up in front of the apartment house, and the driver looked around. "There's one," he said, looking in the rearview mirror.

The boy was about fourteen, and he wore a ragged denim vest gaudy with embroidery and metal studs. He had long, greasy hair and a smart-sullen sneer on his face. They waited until he had swaggered along the sidewalk to where the cab sat.

"Hey, kid," the driver called to him.

"What?" the boy asked insolently.

"You wanna make a buck?"

"Doin' what?"

"Haul a couple sacks of groceries upstairs."

"Maybe I'm busy."

"Sure you are. Skip it then. There's another kid just up the street."

The boy looked quickly over his shoulder and saw another boy on a bicycle. "Okay. Gimme the dollar."

"*After* the groceries are upstairs."

The boy glowered at him.

Raphael paid the driver and got out of the cab. The boy got the groceries. "These are *heavy,* man," he complained.

"It's just up those stairs." Raphael pointed.

The cab drove off, and the boy looked at Raphael, his eyes narrowing.

"I'll go up first," Raphael told him. "I'll have to unlock the door at the top."

"Let's go, man. I ain't got all day."

Raphael went to the stairs and started up. Halfway to the top, he realized that the boy was not behind him. He turned and went back down as quickly as he could.

The boy was already across the street, walking fast, with the two bags of groceries hugged in his arms.

"Hey!" Raphael shouted at him.

The boy looked back and cackled a high-pitched laugh.

"Come back here!" Raphael shouted, suddenly consumed with an overwhelming fury as he realized how completely helpless he was.

The boy laughed again and kept on going.

"You dirty little son of a bitch!" a harsh voice rasped from the porch of the house directly across the street from Raphael's apartment. A small, wizened man stumbled down the steps from the porch and staggered out to the sidewalk. "You come back here or I'll kick the shit outta ya!"

The boy began to run.

"Goddamn little bastard!" the small man roared in a huge voice. He started to run after the boy, but after a couple dozen steps he staggered again and fell down. Raphael stood grinding his teeth in frustrated anger as he watched the boy disappear around the corner.

The small man lay helplessly on the sidewalk, bellowing drunken obscenities in his huge rasping voice.

V

After several minutes the wizened little man regained his feet and staggered over to where Raphael stood. "I'm sorry, old buddy," he said in his foghorn voice. "I'da caught the little bastard for ya, but I'm just too goddamn drunk."

"It's all right," Raphael said, still trying to control the helpless fury he felt.

"I seen the little sumbitch around here before," the small man said, weaving back and forth. "He's always creepin' up an' down the alleys, lookin' to steal stuff. I'll lay fer 'im—catch 'im one day an' stomp the piss outta the little shit." The small man's face was brown and wrinkled, and there was dirt ingrained in the wrinkles. He had a large, purplish wen on one cheek and a sparse, straggly mustache, pale red—although his short-cropped hair was brown. His eyes had long since gone beyond bloodshot, and his entire body exuded an almost overpoweringly acrid reek of stale wine. His clothes were filthy, and his fly was unzipped. In many ways he resembled a very dirty, very drunk banty rooster.

"Them was your groceries, wasn't they?" the small man demanded.

Raphael drew in a deep breath and let it out slowly. He realized that he was trembling, and that angered him even more. "It doesn't matter," he said, even though it did.

"Was that the last of your money?"

"No."

"I got a idea. I'll go get my truck, an' we'll go look fer that little bastard."

Raphael shook his head. "I think it's too late. We'd never catch him now."

The little man swore.

"I'll have to go back to the store, I guess."

"I'll take you in my truck, an' me'n Sam'll take your groceries upstairs for ya."

"You don't have to do that."

"I know I don't hafta." The little man's voice was almost pugnacious. "I *wanna* do it. You come along with me." He grabbed at Raphael's arm, almost jerking him off balance. "We're neighbors, goddammit, an' neighbors oughta help each other out."

At that moment Raphael would have preferred to have been alone. He felt soiled—even ashamed—as a result of the theft, but there was no withstanding the drunken little man's belligerent hospitality. Almost helplessly he allowed himself to be drawn into the ramshackle house across the street.

"My name's Tobe Benson," the small man said as they went up on the creaking porch.

"Rafe Taylor."

They went inside and were met by a furnace blast of heat. The inside of the house was unbelievably filthy. Battered furniture sat in the small, linoleum-floored living room, and the stale wine reek was overwhelming. They went on through to the dining room, which seemed to be the central living area of the house. An old iron heating stove shimmered off heat that seemed nearly solid. The floor was sticky with spilled wine and food, and a yellow dog lay under the table, gnawing on a raw bone. Other bones lay in the corners of the room, the meat clinging to them black with age.

A large gray-haired man sat at the table with a bottle of wine in front of him. He wore dirty bib overalls and a stupefied expression. He looked up, smiling vaguely through his smudged glasses.

"That there's Sam," Tobe said in his foghorn voice. "Sam, this here's Rafe. Lives across the street. Some little punk bastard just stole all his groceries. It's a goddamn shame when a poor crippled fella like Rafe here ain't safe from all the goddamn little thieves in this town."

The man in the overalls smiled stupidly at Raphael, his eyes unfocused. "Hi, buddy," he said, his voice tiny and squeaking.

"Sit down, Rafe," Tobe said, and lurched across to a rumpled bed that sat against the wall opposite the table. He collapsed on the bed, picked up the wine bottle sitting on the floor near it, and took a long pull at it. "You want a drink?" he asked, offering the bottle.

"No. Thanks all the same." Raphael was trying to think of a way to leave without aggravating the little man.

"Hi, buddy," Sam said again, still smiling.

"Hi, Sam," Raphael replied.

Tobe fished around in a water glass he used as an ashtray and found a partially burned cigarette. He straightened it out between his knobby fingers and lit it. Then he looked around the room. "Ain't much of a place," he half apologized, "but we're just a couple ol' bachelors, an' we live the way we want." He slapped the bed he half lay on. "We put this here for when we get too drunk to make it up the stairs to go to bed."

Raphael nodded.

"Hi, buddy," Sam said.

"Don't pay no mind t' ol' Sam there," Tobe said. "He's been on a toot fer three weeks. I'm gonna have t' sober 'im up pretty quick. He's been sittin' right there fer four days now."

Sam smiled owlishly at Raphael. "I'm drunk, buddy," he said.

"He can see that, Sam," Tobe snorted. "Anybody can see that you're drunk." He turned back to Raphael. "We do okay. We both got our pensions, an' we ain't got no bills." He took another drink from his bottle. "Soon's it gets dark, I'll get my truck, an' we'll go on back over to the Safeway so's you can buy more groceries. They took my license away from me eight years ago, so I gotta be kinda careful when I drive."

They sat in the stinking room for an hour or more while Tobe talked on endlessly in his raucous voice. Raphael was able to piece together a few facts about them. They were both retired from the military and had worked for the railroad when they'd gotten out. At one time, perhaps, they had been men like other men, with dreams and ambitions—meaningful men—but now they were old and drunk and very dirty. Their days slid by in an endless stream, blurred by cheap wine. The ambition had long since burned out, and they slid at night not into sleep but into that unconsciousness in which there are no dreams. When they spoke, it was of the past rather than of the future, but they had each other. They were not alone, so it was all right.

After it grew dark, Tobe went out to the garage in back and got out his battered truck. Then he erratically drove Raphael to the supermarket. Raphael did his shopping again, and Tobe bought more wine. Then the little man drove slowly back to their street and, with wobbly steps, carried Raphael's groceries up the stairs.

Raphael thanked him.

"Aw, don't think nothin' about it," Tobe said. "A man ain't no damn good at all if he don't help his neighbors. Anytime you wanna use my truck, ol' buddy, you just lemme know. Anytime at all." Then, stumbling, half falling, he clumped back down the stairs.

Raphael stood on the rooftop, looking over the railing as Tobe weavingly drove his clattering truck around to the alley behind the house across the street to hide it in the garage again.

Alone, with the cool air of the night washing the stench of the two old men from his nostrils, Raphael was suddenly struck with an almost crushing loneliness. The light was on in the upstairs of the house next door, but he did not want to watch Crazy Charlie anymore.

On the street below, alone under the streetlight, Patch, the one-eyed Indian, walked by, his feet making no sound on the sidewalk. Raphael stood on his rooftop and watched him pass, wishing that he might be able to call out to the solitary figure below, but that, of course, was impossible, and so he only watched until the silent Indian was gone.

vi

Sadie the Sitter was an enormously fat woman who lived diagonally across the intersection from Raphael's apartment house. He had seen her a few times during the winter months, but as the weather turned warmer she emerged from her house to survey her domain.

Sadie was a professional sitter; she also sat by inclination. Her throne was a large porch swing suspended from two heavy chains bolted to the ceiling. Each morning, quite early, she waddled onto the porch and plunked her vast bulk into the creaking swing. And there she sat, her piggish little eyes taking in everything that happened on the street, her beet-red face sullen and discontented.

The young parents who were her customers were polite, even deferential, as they delivered their children into her custody each morning. Sadie's power was awesome; and like all power it was economic. If offended, she could simply refuse to accept the child, thus quite effectively eliminating the offending mother's wages for the day. It was a power Sadie used often, sometimes capriciously—just for the sake of using it.

Her hair was a bright, artificial red and quite frizzy, since it was of a texture that accepted neither the dye nor the permanent very well. Her voice was loud and assertive, and could be heard clearly all over the neighborhood. She had, it seemed, no neck, and her head swiveled with difficulty atop her massive shoulders. She ate continually with both hands, stuffing the food into her mouth.

Sadie's husband was a barber, a thin man with a gray face and a shuffling, painful gait. The feelings that existed between them had long since passed silent loathing and verged now on open hostility. Their arguments were long and savage and were usually conducted at full volume. Their single child, a scrawny girl of about twelve, was severely retarded, physically as well as mentally, and she was kept in a child's playpen on the porch, where she drooled and twitched and made wounded-animal noises in a bull-like voice.

Sadie's mother lived several houses up the street from her, and in good weather she waddled each morning about ten down the sidewalk in slapping bedroom slippers and a tent-like housecoat to visit. Sadie's mother was also a gross woman, and she lived entirely for her grandchildren, a raucous mob of bad-mannered youngsters who gathered in her front yard each afternoon when school let out to engage in interminable games of football or tag or hide-and-seek with no regard for flower beds or hedges while Granny sat on her rocker in bloated contentment like a mother spider, ready to pounce ferociously upon any neighbor with the temerity to protest the rampant destruction of his property.

At first Raphael found the entire group wholly repugnant, then gradually, almost against his will, he began to develop a certain fascination. The greed, the gluttony, and the naked, spiteful envy of Sadie and her mother were so undisguised that they seemed not so much to be human, but were rather vast, primal forces—embodiments of those qualities—allegorical distillations of all that is meanest in others.

"She thinks she's so much," Sadie sneered to her mother. "She has all them delivery trucks come to her house like that on purpose—just to spite her neighbors. I could buy new furniture, too, if I wanted, but I got better things to do with my money.''

"Are you Granny's little love?" Sadie's mother cooed at the idiot.

The child drooled and bellowed at her hoarsely.

"Don't get her started, for God's sake," Sadie said irritably. "It takes all day to quiet her down again." She glanced quickly at her mother with a sly look of malice. "She's gettin' too hard to handle. I think it's time we put her in a home."

"Oh no," her mother protested, her face suddenly assuming a helplessly hurt look, "not Granny's little darling. You couldn't *really* do that."

"She'd be better off," Sadie said smugly, satisfied that she had injured her mother's most vulnerable spot once again. The threat appeared to be a standard ploy, since it came up nearly every time they visited together.

"How's *he* doing?" Sadie's mother asked quickly, changing the subject in the hope of diverting her daughter's mind from the horrid notion of committing the idiot to custodial care. As always, the "he" referred to Sadie's husband. They never used his name.

"His veins are breakin' down," Sadie replied, gloating. "His feet and hands are cold all the time, and sometimes he has trouble gettin' his breath."

"It's a pity." Her mother sighed.

Sadie snorted a savage laugh, reaching for another fistful of potato chips. "Don't worry," she said. "I keep his insurance premiums all paid up. I'll be a rich woman one of these days real soon."

"I imagine it's a terrible strain on him—standing all the time like that."

Sadie nodded, contentedly munching. "All his arteries are clogged almost shut," she said smugly. "His doctor says that it's just a question of time until one of them blows out or a clot of that gunk breaks loose and stops his heart. He could go at any time."

"Poor man," her mother said sadly.

"Soon as it happens, I'm gonna buy *me* a whole buncha new furniture." Sadie's tone was dreamy. "An' I'm gonna have all them delivery trucks pullin' up in fronta *my* house. *Then* watch them people down the street just wither up an' blow away. Sometimes I just can't hardly wait."

Raphael turned and went back into his little apartment. Walking was not so bad, but simply standing grew tiring after a while, and the phantom ache in the knee and foot that were no longer there began to gnaw at him.

He sat on the couch and turned on the scanner, more to cover the penetrating sound of Sadie's voice than out of any real interest in morning police calls. A little bit of Sadie went a long way.

It was a problem. As the summer progressed the interior of the apartment was likely to become intolerably hot. He knew that. He would be driven out onto the roof for relief. The standing would simply bring on the pain, and the pain would drive him back into the apartment again. He needed something to sit on, a bench, or a chair or something like Sadie's swing.

He checked his phone book, made some calls, and then went down to catch a bus.

The Goodwill store was a large building with the usual musty-smelling clothes hanging on pipe racks and the usual battered furniture, stained mattresses, and scarred appliances. It had about it that unmistakable odor of poverty that all such places have.

"You've come about the job," a pale girl with one dwarfed arm said as he crutched across toward the furniture.

"No," he replied. "Actually, I came to buy a chair."

"I'm sorry. I just assumed—" She glanced at his crutches and blushed furiously.

"What kind of a job is it?" he asked, more to help her out of her embarrassment than out of any real curiosity.

"Shoe repair. Our regular man is moving away."

"I wouldn't be much good at that."

"You never know until you try." She smiled shyly at him.

Her face seemed somehow radiant when she smiled. "If you're really looking for something to do, it might not hurt to talk with Mrs. Kiernan."

"I don't really need a job. I've got insurance and Social Security." It was easy to talk with her. He hadn't really talked with one of his own kind since the last time he'd spoken with Quillian.

"Most of us *do* have some kind of coverage," she said with a certain amount of spirit. "Working here makes us at least semiuseful. It's a matter of dignity—not money."

Because he liked her, and because her unspoken criticism stung a little, he let her lead him back to the small office where a harassed-looking woman interviewed him.

"We don't pay very much," she apologized, "and we can't guarantee you any set number of hours a week or anything like that."

"That's all right," Raphael told her. "I just need something to do, that's all."

She nodded and had him fill out some forms. "I'll have to get it cleared," she said, "but I don't think there'll be any problem. Suppose I call you in about a week."

He thanked her and went back out into the barnlike salesroom. The girl with the dwarfed arm was waiting for him. "Well?" she asked.

"She's going to call me," Raphael told her.

"Did she have you fill out any forms?"

He nodded.

"You're in then," she said with a great deal of satisfaction.

"Do you suppose I could look at some chairs now?" Raphael asked, smiling.

vii

His world quite suddenly expanded enormously. The advent of the chair enabled him to see the entire neighborhood in a way he had not been able to see it before. Because standing had been awkward and painful, he had not watched before, but the chair made it easier—made it almost simpler to watch than not to watch. It was a most serviceable chair—an old office chair of gray metal mounted on a squat, four-footed pedestal with casters on the bottom. It had sturdy arms and a solid back, and there were heavy springs under the seat that enabled him to rock back to alter his position often enough to remain comfortable. The addition of a pillow provided the padding necessary to protect the still-sensitive remains of his left hip. The great thing about it was that it rolled. With his crutches and his right leg, he could easily propel himself to any spot on the roof and could watch the wonderful world expanding on the streets below.

Always before they had seemed to be quiet streets of somewhat run-down houses only in need of a nail here, a board there, some paint and a general squaring away. Now that winter had passed, however, and the first warm days of spring had come, the people who lived on the two streets that intersected at the corner of the house where he lived opened their doors and began to bring their lives outside where he could watch them.

Winter is a particularly difficult time for the poor. Heat is expensive, but more than that, the bitter cold drives them inside, although their natural habitat is outside. Given the opportunity, the poor will conduct most of the business of their lives out-of-doors, and with the arrival of spring they come out almost with gusto.

"Fuckin' bastard." It was an Indian girl who might have been twenty-three but already looked closer to forty. Her face was a ruin, and her arms and shoulders were covered with crudely done tattoos. She cursed loudly but without inflection, without even much interest, as if she already knew what the outcome of the meeting was going to be. There was a kind of resignation about her swearing. She stood swaying drunkenly on the porch of the large house two doors up from Tobe and Sam's place, speaking to the big, tense-looking man on the sidewalk.

"That's fine," the tense man said. "You just be out of here by tomorrow morning, that's all."

"Fuckin' bastard," she said again.

"I'll be back with the sheriff. He'll by God *put* you out. I've had it with you, Doreen. You haven't paid your rent in three months. That's it. Get out."

"Fuckin' bastard."

A tall, thin Negro pushed out of the house and stood behind the girl. He wore pants and a T-shirt, but no shoes. "Look here, man," he blustered. "You can't just kick somebody out in the street without no place to go."

"Watch me. You got till tomorrow morning. You better sober her up and get her ass out of here." He turned and started back toward his car.

"You're in trouble, man," the Negro threatened. "I got some real mean friends."

"Whoopee," the tense man said flatly. He got into the car.

The Indian girl glowered at him, straining to find some insult sufficient for the occasion. Finally she gave up.

"Fuckin' bastard," she said.

"Oh, my God!" the fat woman trundling down the sidewalk exclaimed. "Oh, my God!" She was very fair-skinned and was nearly as big as Sadie the Sitter. Her hair was blond and had been stirred into some kind of scrambled arrangement at the back of her head. The hair and her clothes were covered with flecks of lint, making her look as if she had slept in a chicken coop.

She clutched a tabloid paper in her hand and had an expression of unspeakable horror on her face. "Oh, my God!" she said again to no one in particular. "Did you see this?" she demanded of Sadie the Sitter, waving the paper.

"What is it?" Sadie asked without much interest.

"Oh, my God!" the woman Raphael had immediately tagged "Chicken Coop Annie" said. "It's just awful! Poor Farrah's losin' her hair!"

"Really?" Sadie said with a faint glint of malicious interest. Sadie was able to bear the misfortunes of others with great fortitude.

"It says so right here," Chicken Coop Annie said, waving the paper again. "I ain't had time to read it yet, but it says right here in the headline that she's losin' her hair. I just hadda bring it out to show to everybody. Poor Farrah! Oh, poor, poor Farrah!"

"I seen it already," Sadie told her.

"Oh." Annie's face fell. She stood on the sidewalk, sweating with disappointment. "Me 'n her got the same color hair, you know," she ventured, putting one pudgy hand to her tangled hairdo.

"That so?" Sadie sounded unconvinced.

"I gotta go tell Violet."

"Sure." Sadie looked away.

Annie started off down the street.

"Oh, my God!" she said.

Their cars broke down continually, and there were always a half dozen or so grimy young men tinkering with stubbornly exhausted iron brutes at the curbs or in the alleys. And when the cars did finally run, it was at best haltingly with a great deal of noise and smoke, and they left telltale blood trails of oil and transmission fluid on the streets behind them.

They lost their money or their food stamps, and most of the men were in trouble of one kind or another. Each time a police car cruised through the neighborhood, back doors slammed all up and down the street, and furtive young men dashed from the houses to run down the alleys or jump fences and flee through littered backyards.

Raphael watched, and gradually he began to understand them. At first it was not even a theory, but rather a kind of intuition. He found that he could look at any one of them and almost smell the impending crisis. That was the key word— crisis. At first it seemed too dramatic a term to apply to situations resulting from their bumbling mismanagement of their lives or deliberate wrongheaded stupidity, but they themselves reacted as if these situations were in fact crises.

If, for example, a live-in boyfriend packed up and moved out while the girl in question was off at the grocery store, it provided her with an irresistible opportunity to play the role of the tragic heroine. Like a Greek chorus, her friends would dutifully gather around her, expressing shock and dismay. The young men would swagger and bluster and leap into their cars to go importantly off in search of the runaway, forming up like a posse and shouting instructions to each other over the clatter of their sick engines. The women would gather about the bereaved one, commiserating with her, supporting her, and admiring her performance. After a suitable display of grand emotion—cries, shrieks, uncontrollable sobbing, or whatever she considered her most dramatic response—the heroine would lapse into a stoic silence, her head nobly lifted, and her face ravaged by the unspeakable agony she was suffering. Her friends would caution each other wisely that several of them at least would have to stay with her until all danger of suicide was past. Such situations usually provided several days of entertainment for all concerned.

Tobe was roaring drunk again. He staggered out into the yard bellowing curses and waving his wine bottle. Sam came out of the house and stood blearily on the porch wringing his hands and pleading with the little man to come back inside.

Tobe turned and cursed him savagely, then collapsed facedown in the unmowed grass and began to snore.

Sam stumbled down off the porch, and with an almost maternal tenderness, he picked up the sleeping little man and bore him back into the house.

Mousy Mary lived in the house on the corner directly opposite Raphael's apartment and right beside Tobe and Sam's house. She was a slight girl with runny eyes and a red nose and a timid, almost furtive walk. She had two children, a girl of twelve or so and a boy about ten. Quite frequently she would lock herself and her children in the house and not come out for several days. Her telephone would ring unanswered, sometimes for hours.

And then a woman Raphael assumed was her mother would show up. Mousy Mary's mother was a small, dumpy woman with a squinting, suspicious face. She would creep around Mary's house trying all the doors and windows. Then she would return to her car and drive slowly up and down the streets and alleys, stopping to jot down the license numbers of all the cars in the neighborhood. Once she had accomplished that, she would find a suitable spot and stake out the house, sometimes for as long as a day and a night. The blinds in Mousy Mary's house would move furtively from time to time, but other than that there would be no sign that anyone was inside. When it grew dark, no lights would come on, and Raphael could imagine Mary crouching in the dark with her children, hiding from her mother.

"I wonder if I might use your telephone," Mousy Mary's mother said to Sadie one afternoon.

"What's the problem?" Sadie asked.

"I have to call the police," the old woman said in a calm voice that seemed to indicate that she had to call the police quite frequently. "Somebody's holding my daughter and her children hostage in her house there."

"How do you know?" Sadie sounded interested.

"I've checked all the evidence," Mousy Mary's mother said in a professional tone. "There's some tiny little scratch marks around the keyhole of the back door. It's obvious that the lock's been picked."

"That so?"

"Happens all the time. They'll probably have to call out the SWAT team." Mousy Mary's mother's voice was dry, unemotional.

In time the police arrived, and after they talked with Mousy Mary's mother for a few minutes, one of them went up on the front porch and knocked. Mousy Mary answered the door immediately and let them in, but she closed the door quite firmly in her mother's face. In a fury the dumpy little woman scurried around the house, trying to look in the windows.

After a while the police came out and drove away. Mousy

Mary's mother stomped up onto the front porch and began pounding on the door, but Mary refused to open it.

Eventually, the dumpy woman returned to her car and continued her surveillance.

"Couldn't you at least look into it, Raphael—for me?" Frankie's lower lip trembled.

Raphael, sitting in his chair on the roof where they were talking, rather thought he might like to nibble on that lip for a while. He pushed that thought away. "I was a student, Frankie," he said. "I can still do that. I don't need both legs to study."

"Our records show that you were a worker in a lumber mill."

"That was a summer job back home when I was in high school and junior college. It wasn't a lifelong career."

"I'm really going to get yelled at if I don't get you into vocational rehabilitation," she told him. "And there are support groups—people to see and to talk to."

"I've got a whole street full of people to see, Frankie." He waved his hand at the intersection. "And if I want to talk with somebody, I can talk with Tobe and Sam."

"But they're just a couple of old alcoholics. We gave up on them years ago."

"I'll bet they appreciated that."

"Couldn't you at least *consider* vocational rehab, Raphael?"

"Tell you what, Frankie." He smiled at her. "Go back to the office and tell them that I've already chosen a new career and that I'm already working at it."

Her eyes brightened. "What kind of career are we talking about here, Raphael?"

"I'm going to be a philosopher. The pay isn't too good, but it's a very stimulating line of work."

"Oh, *you*," she said, and then she laughed. "You're impossible." She looked out over the seedy street. "It's nice up here." She sighed. "You've got a nice breeze."

"I sort of like it."

"Wouldn't you consider the possibility of shoe repair?" she asked him.

That was startling. He remembered the Goodwill store and the girl with the dwarfed arm. Coincidence, perhaps? Some twist of chance? But the prophet on the downtown street had said that there was no such thing as chance. But what had made the words "shoe repair" cross Frankie's trembling lips? It was something to ponder.

It was not that they were really afraid of him. It was merely that there was something so lost, so melancholy about his dark face as he walked with measured pace and slow down the shabby streets that all sound ceased as he passed. They did not mention it to each other or remark about it, but each time Patch, the one-eyed Indian, walked by, there was an eerie hush on the street. They watched him and said nothing. Even the children were still, suspended, as it were, by the silent, moccasin-footed passage of the dark, long-haired man with the black patch over one eye.

Raphael watched also, and was also silent.

And then in a troop, a large, rowdy group of more or less young men and, with a couple of exceptions, younger women moved into the big old house from which the tattooed Indian girl and her black boyfriend had been evicted.

They were nearly a week moving in, and their furniture seemed to consist largely of mattresses and bedding. They arrived in battered cars from several different directions, unloaded, and then drove off for more. They were all, for the most part, careful to be away when the large, tense-appearing man who owned the house stopped by. Only the oldest woman and her five children—ranging in age from nine or ten up to the oldest boy who was perhaps twenty—remained.

After the landlord left, however, they would return and continue moving in. When they were settled, the motorcycles arrived. In the lead was a huge man with a great, shaggy beard who wore a purple-painted German helmet. The front wheel of his bike was angled radically out forward, and his handlebars were so high that he had to reach up to hold them. Two other motorcycles followed him, one similarly constructed and ridden by a skinny, dark-haired man in a leather vest, and the other a three-wheeled affair with a wide leather bench for a seat and ridden by another thin fellow, this one with frizzy blond hair and wearing incredibly filthy denims. None of the motorcycles appeared to be equipped with anything remotely resembling a muffler, and so the noise of their passage was deafening.

After they dismounted, they swaggered around in front of the house for a while, glowering at the neighborhood as if daring any comment or objection, then they all went inside. One of the young men was sent out in his clattering car and came back with beer. Then they settled down to party.

Their motorcycles, Raphael observed in the next several days, were as unreliable as were most of the cars on the block. They bled oil onto the lawn of the big old house, and at least one of them was usually partially or wholly dismantled.

With the exception of the big, bearded man in the German helmet, whom they respectfully called Heintz, the bikers for the most part appeared to be a scrawny bunch, more bluster than real meanness. In his mental catalog Raphael dubbed the group "Heck's Angels."

At his ease, sitting in his chair on the roof, Raphael watched them. From watching he learned of the emotions and turmoil that produced the dry, laconic descriptions that came over the police radio. He learned that a family fight was not merely some mild domestic squabble, but involved actual physical violence. He learned that a drunk was not simply a slightly tipsy gentleman, but someone who had either lapsed into a coma or who was so totally disoriented that he was a danger to himself or to others. He learned that a fight was not just a couple of people exchanging a few quick punches, but usually involved clubs, chains, knives, and not infrequently axes.

As his understanding, his intuition, broadened and deepened—as he grew to know them better—he realized that they were losers, habitual and chronic.

Their problems were not the result of temporary setbacks or some mild personality defect, but seemed rather to derive from some syndrome—a kind of social grand mal with which they were afflicted and which led them periodically to smash up their lives in a kind of ecstatic seizure of deliberate self-destruction.

And then they were taken over by the professional care-takers society hires to pick up the pieces of such shattered lives. Inevitably, the first to arrive were the police. It seemed that the police were charged with the responsibility for making on-the-spot decisions about which agency was then to take charge—social services, mental health, the detoxification center, child protective services, the courts, or on occasion the coroner. Society was quite efficient in dealing with its losers. It was all very cut and dried, and everyone seemed quite comfortable with the system. Only occasionally did one of the losers object, and then it was at best a weak and futile protest—a last feeble attempt at self-assertion before he relaxed and permitted himself to be taken in hand.

Raphael was quite pleased with his theory. It provided him with a convenient handle with which to grasp what would have otherwise been a seething and incomprehensible chaos on the streets below.

And then Patch went by again, followed by that strange hush that seemed always to fall over the neighborhood with his passage, and Raphael was not so sure of the theory. Into which category did Patch fit? He was totally unlike the others—an enigma whose dark, melancholy presence seemed somehow to disturb the losers as much as it did Raphael. Sometimes, after he had passed, Raphael felt that if he could only talk with the man—however briefly—it might all fit together, the whole thing might somehow fall into place. But Patch never stopped, never looked up, and was always gone before Raphael could call to him or do anything more than note his silent passage.

Omnia Sol temperat puris et subtilis

In the end Raphael took the job at Goodwill Industries more because he could find no reason not to than out of any real desire to work. The sour hunchback who was moving to Seattle to live with his sister taught him the rudiments of shoe repair and then, without a word, got up and left.

"Don't worry about Freddie," the pale girl with the dwarfed right arm said to him. "He's been like that ever since his family ganged up on him and made him agree to move to Seattle."

The girl seemed always to be hovering near the bench where Raphael worked, and her concern for him seemed at times almost motherly. She was a very fair young woman with long, ash-blond hair and a face that was almost, but not quite, pretty. Her name was Denise, and Raphael forced himself to think of her as Denise to avoid attaching a tag name to her as he had to all the sad losers on his block. A nickname for Denise would be too obvious and too cruel. Denise was a real person with real dignity, and she was not a loser. She deserved to be recognized as a person, not over-simplified into a grotesque by being called "Flipper," even in the hidden silences of his mind.

The dwarfed arm bothered him at first, but he soon came to accept it. Although it was somewhat misshapen and awkward, and the tiny knuckles and fingers seemed always chapped and raw as if it had been brutally windburned, it was not a totally useless appendage. Denise wrote with it and was able to hold things with it, although she could not carry much weight on that side.

There were others who worked at Goodwill also, assorted defectives, the maimed, the halt, the marginally sighted, dwarves, and some who seemed quite normal until you spoke with them and realized that anything more than the simplest tasks was beyond their capabilities. They were not, however, losers. Common among them was that stubborn resolve to be independent and useful. Raphael admired them for that, and wished at times that he could be more like them. His own work record, he realized, was spotty. There were days when he had to go to therapy, of course, but there were other days as well, bad days when the phantom ache in thigh and knee and foot made work impossible, and other days when he deliberately malingered simply to avoid the tedium of the long bus ride to work.

On one such day, a fine, bright day in late April when the trees were dusting the streets with pale green pollen and the air was inconceivably bright and clear, he called in with his lame apologies and then crutched out to his chair and his roof to watch the teeming losers on the streets below.

"Try the son of a bitch again," Jimmy, one of the scruffier of Heck's Angels, called from under the hood of a battered Chevy convertible parked on the lawn of the house up the street.

The car's starter ground spitefully, but the engine refused to turn over.

"Ain't no use, man," Marvin, the frizzy-haired blond one sitting in the car, said. "The bastard ain't gonna start."

"Just a minute." Jimmy crawled a little farther into the engine compartment. "Okay, now try it."

The starter ground again, sounding weaker.

Big Heintz came out on the porch holding a can of beer. "You're just runnin' down the battery," he told them. "Give it up. The fucker's gutted."

Jimmy came out from under the hood, his face desperate. "It's *gotta* run, man. I *gotta* have wheels. A guy ain't shit if he ain't got no fuckin' wheels."

"The fucker's gutted," Heintz said again with a note of finality.

"What am I gonna *do*, man?" Jimmy's voice was anguished. "I *gotta* have wheels."

"Start savin' your nickels," Heintz suggested, and laughed.

"Dirty useless son of a bitch!" Jimmy yelled at his car in helpless fury. He kicked savagely at one of the tires, winced, and then began to pound on one of the front fenders with a wrench. "Bastard! Bastard! Bastard!" he raged.

Marvin went up and joined Heintz on the porch, and the two of them stood watching Jimmy pound on his car with the wrench. Finally he gave up and threw the wrench down. There were tears on his face when he turned toward the two men on the porch. "What am I gonna *do*, man?" he demanded. "I *gotta* have wheels. Maybe Leon can fix it."

Big Heintz shook his head and belched. "Forget it, man. Nobody can fix that pig. The fucker's gutted."

Jimmy's shoulders slumped in defeat. "I *gotta* have wheels. I just *gotta*."

The idea had not really occurred to Raphael before. His injury had seemed too final, too total, and he had resigned himself to using public transportation, but now he began to consider the possibility. Driving, after all, was *not* really impossible. You only needed one leg to drive. The memory of the crash was still there, of course, but it was not something insurmountable. The more he thought about it, the more possible it all seemed.

He went back into his apartment and methodically began to draw up a list. The amount he would spend on buses and taxi fare in the course of a year surprised him, and when he added to that the wages he would lose on those days when the decision to go to work or not was weighted by his distaste for the bus ride, the number began to approach a figure he might reasonably expect to pay for reliable transportation.

He decided to think about it some more, but that evening he bought a newspaper and checked the used-car section of the want ads.

More than anything, what he wanted was a sense of independence. He had not particularly missed it before because he had not even considered the possibility of driving again, but now it became a matter of urgent necessity. "I *gotta* have wheels," he said to himself in a wry imitation of Jimmy's anguished voice. "I just *gotta.*"

The car was adequate—not fancy, certainly—but it had been well maintained, and the price was right. He was startled to discover how nervous he was when he test-drove it. By the time he had gone three blocks, he was sweating, and his hands were shaking. He had not thought that he would be so afraid. He set his teeth together and forced himself to continue driving.

After he had paid for it and brought it home, he went out onto his roof quite often to look down at it. He did not drive it to work or to his therapy sessions yet, but concentrated on growing accustomed to it and to driving in traffic again. The fear was still there, but he drove a little farther every day and inserted himself carefully into heavier and heavier traffic. His accident had made a cautious driver of him, but he managed to get around, and he finally worked up enough nerve to drive it to work.

Because Denise lived on the same bus route as he, they had usually ridden together when they got off work. On that first night, however, realizing that he was showing off his new toy, he gave her a lift home.

"Why don't you come up?" she suggested hesitantly when he pulled up in front of her apartment house. "I'll make a pot of coffee." She blushed and turned her face away.

"Could I take a raincheck on it? I have to go grocery shopping tonight, and it takes me hours."

"Oh," she said quickly, "sure. Maybe next time."

"You can count on it."

She got out of the car. "See you in the morning, then. Thanks for the ride." She closed the door and hurried across the sidewalk to her apartment building.

The shopping had been a lie, of course, but Raphael had

not wanted to become involved in anything just yet. The implication of the invitation might have been wholly imaginary, but it was the kind of thing that he had to avoid at all costs. Still, he was just a bit ashamed of himself as he drove home.

Flood was waiting for him when he got there. "Where the hell have you been?" he demanded, leaning against the rear fender of his little red sports car with his arms crossed, "and what the hell are you doing in Spokane, for God's sake?" His tone was matter-of-fact, as if they had seen each other only the week before.

Raphael crutched toward him, feeling a sudden surge of elation. He had not realized until that moment how desperately lonely he had been. "Damon! What are you doing here?"

Flood shrugged, his eyes strangely hard and his smile ambiguous. "The world is wide, my Angel," he said, "but there are only a few places in it where my face is welcome." The rich baritone voice, so well remembered, with all its power to sway him, to persuade, to manipulate him, had lost none of its force. Raphael immediately felt its pull upon him.

One of Heck's Angels roared by, his motorcycle sputtering and coughing. "Come on upstairs." Raphael was suddenly aware of the curious eyes of the people on the street, and he did not want to share Flood with any of them. He led the way to the stairs at the side of the house, and they went up.

"A penthouse, no less," Flood noted when they reached the roof.

"Hardly that." Raphael laughed. "More like a pigeon loft." They went on inside. "Sit down," Raphael told him. "I'll make some coffee." He needed something to do to cover his confusion, to get him past that first stiff awkwardness that was always there when he met someone again after a long time. He was quite suddenly painfully aware of his one-leggedness and particularly anxious that Flood should not think of him as a cripple, so he made a special show of his competence, even though he was aware at the time that it was childish to do so.

Flood had not changed much. His skin was a bit sallower, and there were circles under his eyes that had not been there before. His grin was still sardonic, and his eyes still had that same hard glitter, but he seemed less sure of himself, almost ill at ease, as if he had somehow lost control of his life or something important had gotten away from him.

"Why aren't you in school?" Raphael asked, filling his coffeepot at the sink.

"I dropped out at midterm," Flood replied, sitting on the couch. "The Reed experience got to be a bit overpowering. Scholarship was never one of my strong points."

"How did your father take that?"

"He was moderately unenthusiastic—until I assured him that I wasn't coming home to dear old Grosse Pointe. We struck a bargain. The old pirate will keep those checks coming as long as I stay west of the Mississippi. It's a pretty good working arrangement."

Raphael put the pot on and then crutched over to the armchair. "How did you find me?"

Flood shrugged. "It wasn't that hard. I stopped by the hospital after Christmas vacation, but you'd already left. I talked with some of the nurses and that bald guy in the wheelchair."

"Quillian?"

Flood nodded. "There's a man with all the charm of a nesting rattlesnake."

"He's rough," Raphael agreed, suddenly remembering all the sweating hours in therapy under the lash of Quillian's contemptuous voice, "but he's damn good at his job. You might not want to walk when he starts on you, but you're damn well walking when he gets done."

"If only to get away from him. Anyway, I finally wound up in the administration office. I seduced the name of your uncle in Port Angeles out of one of the file clerks—blew in her ear, that sort of thing. You really don't want all the sordid details, do you?"

"Spare me."

"Sure. Anyhow, I filed Port Angeles away for future reference, and then after I hung it up at Reed, I drifted on up to Seattle. There was a girl who got fed up with the Reed experience about the same time I did. We got along—for a while, anyway. I was thinking about San Francisco, but she convinced me that we'd have a ball in Boeing City. We went on up and set up housekeeping for a month or so. It didn't work out, so I pulled the plug on her.''

"You're still all heart, Damon."

"I improved her life. I taught her that there are more important things in the world than rock concerts and political theory. Now she's got a deep and tragic affair in her past. It'll make her more interesting for the next guy. God knows she bored the hell out of me." Flood had been speaking in a dry, almost monotonous tone with few of the flashes of that flowery extravagance Raphael remembered from the days when they had roomed together. The feeling was still there that something had gone out of him somehow, or that he had suffered some obscure and hidden injury that still gnawed at him. "I knocked around Seattle for a while," he went on, "and then I decided to take a quick run up to Port Angeles to see how you were doing."

"What made you think I'd be there?"

Flood shrugged. "It just seemed reasonable. That's your home. I just had it in my mind that you were there. It seemed quite logical at the time."

"You should have called first."

"You know, your uncle Harry told me exactly the same thing. Anyway, after I found out that I was wrong and got your address here from him, I took a quick turn around Port Angeles and then bombed on over. Once I set out to do something, I by God do it. I'd have followed you all the way to hell, my friend."

"What did you think of Port Angeles?"

"Would you accept picturesque?"

"You were unimpressed."

"Moderately. I don't want to offend you, but that is one of the gloomiest places I've ever had the misfortune to visit."

"It was raining, I take it."

"It was, and you can. I get the impression that it rains there about ninety percent of the time."

Raphael got up and poured two cups of coffee. Flood came over to him and took one. "I don't imagine you've got anything to drink?" he asked.

"Water."

"I'm thirsty, Raphael, not dirty. I'll go pick something up in a bit." He went back to the couch. "So much for the expedition of J. D. Flood, Junior. How are *you* doing? And what the hell are you doing in Spokane, of all places?"

"I'm adjusting. I suppose that answers both questions, really. I had to get away from Portland, so I took the first bus to anyplace. I wound up here. It's as good as anyplace for what I have to do at the present time."

"This is just temporary then?" Flood was looking intently at Raphael.

"Everything's temporary, Damon. Nothing's permanent."

"Have you been reading Kierkegaard again?"

Raphael grinned at him. "Sorry about that. Quillian told me that I had a choice between being a cripple or a man who happened to only have one leg. I decided not to be a cripple. I'm in physical therapy right now, but it takes a while to get it all put together. Spokane's a good place to do that. There aren't many distractions."

"You can say that again. From what I've seen this is the *least* distracting place in the whole damned world."

"What's got you so down, Damon?" Raphael asked bluntly, trying to get past that seeming reserve.

"I don't know, Raphael." Flood leaned back and looked at the ceiling. "I'm at sixes and sevens, I guess. I haven't really decided what to do with myself. I think I need a diversion of some kind."

"Have you thought of work?"

"Don't be insulting."

"How long are you planning to be in town?"

"Who knows? Who knows?" Flood spread his hands. "I've got a motel room downtown—if I can ever find it again.

I'm paid up for a week. I don't have to make any decisions until then.'' He got up quickly. "Goddammit, I need a drink. I'm going to go find a boozeria. You'll be here?''

"Until the end of the month at least. My rent's paid up, too.''

"Don't be snide. I'll be back in a little bit.'' He crossed the small room and went out.

It was strange—even unreal. Even with the sound of Flood's footsteps going down the stairs, it seemed almost as if he had not really been there. Something had happened to Flood since they had last talked. Something had somehow shaken that enormous self-confidence of his. Even his presence here had seemed in some way tentative, as if he were not really sure that he would be welcome. And why had he come at all? His motives were unclear.

Raphael crutched out onto the roof and to the railing at the front of the house. Flood's little red car was pulling away from the curb, its engine snarling, and across the street Patch stood watching with a strange expression on his somber face.

ii

By the end of the week Raphael had become accustomed to Flood's presence again, and Flood's moody abstraction seemed to be letting up a bit. There was no pattern to his visits. He simply appeared without warning, stayed for a time and talked, and then left. From his conversation Raphael gathered that he was out exploring the city and the surrounding countryside.

On Friday, the day when Flood's rent ran out at his downtown motel, he did not show up, and Raphael began to think that he had checked out and left town without even saying good-bye. He knew it was foolish, but he was hurt by it, and was suddenly plunged into a loneliness so deep that it seemed almost palpable.

He called Flood's motel.

"I'm sorry," the woman at the motel said, "but Mr. Flood checked out just before ten this morning."

"I see," Raphael said. "Thank you." He hung up slowly.

"Well," he told himself, "that's that, then." The loneliness fell on him like a great weight, and the small room seemed suddenly very silent, very empty.

To be doing something, to fill up that silence, he made out a meticulous grocery list and went shopping.

When he returned, it was just growing dusk. He parked in front of the house and started to get out of his car. Across the street Patch walked by on silent feet, crossed over, and went on up past the houses of Sadie the Sitter and Spider Granny, her mother. On an impulse Raphael took out his crutches, closed the car door, and followed the melancholy Indian.

At the corner he had to wait while a couple of cars passed. He looked at the cars with impatience, and when he looked back up the street, Patch was gone. Raphael knew that he had not looked away for more than a second or so, and yet the silent man he had intended to follow had vanished.

He crutched on up past Sadie's house and then past Spider Granny's. Maybe Patch had gone down an alley. But there was no alley, and the yards in that part of the street where he had last seen Patch were all fenced.

Troubled, Raphael went slowly back down the street toward his apartment in the gathering darkness.

Flood had just pulled up behind Raphael's car and was getting out. "Training for the Olympics?" he asked sardonically as Raphael came up.

"Damon," Raphael said with a sudden sense of enormous relief, "where have you been all day? I tried to call you, but they said you'd checked out."

"I've been moving," Flood explained. "I found a place so grossly misnamed that I *had* to live there for a while."

"What place is that?"

"Peaceful Valley," Flood said, drawing the words out. "Isn't that a marvelous name?"

"Sounds moderately bucolic. Where is it?"

"Down at the bottom of the river gorge. Actually, it's almost in the middle of town, but it might as well be a thousand miles away. There's only one street that goes down there. The banks of the gorge are too steep to build on, so they've just let them go to scrub brush and brambles. There's a flat area along the sides of the river, and that's Peaceful Valley. The whole place is a rabbit warren of broken-down housing, tarpaper shacks, and dirt streets that don't go anyplace. The only sounds are the river and the traffic on the Maple Street Bridge about fifty feet overhead. It's absolutely isolated—sort of like a leper colony. Out at the end of the street there's an area called People's Park. I guess all the hippies and junk freaks camped there during the World's Fair. It's still a sort of loitering place for undesirables."

"Are you sure you want to live in a place like that?" Raphael asked doubtfully. "There are new apartment houses all over town."

"It's perfect. Peaceful Valley's a waste disposal for human beings—a sort of unsanitary landfill."

"All right." Raphael was a little irritated. "It's picturesque, but what are *you* doing down there? I know you can afford better."

"I've never lived in a place like that," Flood explained. "I've never seen the lower depths before. I suppose I'm curious."

"That kind of superior attitude can get a jack handle wrapped around your head. These people are touchy, and they've got short fuses. Give me a hand with the groceries in the car, and I'll fix us some supper."

"Do you cook?" Flood asked, almost surprised.

"I've found that it improves the flavor. You can have yours raw if you'd like."

"Smart-ass."

They went upstairs, and Flood nosed around while Raphael stood in the kitchen preparing their supper.

"What's this thing?" he demanded.

"Scanner," Raphael replied. "If you want to know what Spokane is *really* like, turn it on."

"I've heard about them. Never saw one before, though."
He snapped it on. "Is that all it does? Twinkle at you?"

"District Four," the dispatcher said.

"Four."

"We have a forty-two at the intersection of Boone and
Maple."

"Okay. Do you have an ambulance on the way?"

"What's a forty-two?" Flood demanded.

"Auto accident," Raphael told him, "with injuries."

"Terrific." Flood's tone was sarcastic. "They talk in
numbers—'I've got a seventeen and a ninety-three on my
hundred and two. I think they're going to twelve all over the
eighty-seven.' I don't get much out of all that."

"It's not quite that complicated. There's a sheet right there
on top of the bookcase. It's got the numbers on it."

Flood grunted, picked up the sheet, and sat on the couch
with it.

"Attention all units," another dispatcher said. "We have
an armed robbery at the Fas-Gas station at Wellesley and
Division. Suspect described as a white male, approximately
five-foot-seven. One hundred and forty pounds, wearing blue
jeans and an olive-green jacket—possibly an army field
jacket. Suspect wore a red ski mask and displayed a small-
caliber handgun. Last seen running south on Division."

"Well now." Flood's eyes brightened. "That's a bit more
interesting."

"Sticking up gas stations is a cottage industry in Spokane," Raphael explained.

While they ate they listened to the pursuit of the suspect
in the ski mask. When he was finally cornered in an alley,
the anticlimactic "suspect is in custody" call went out, and
the city returned to normal.

"That's all you get?" Flood objected. "Don't they report
or something? How did they catch him?"

"Either they ran him down and tackled him or flushed him
out of somebody's garage."

Flood shook his head. "You never get any of the details,"
he protested.

"It's not a radio program, Damon. Once he's in custody, that's the end of it. They take him back for identification and then haul him downtown."

"Will it be in the paper tomorrow?"

"I doubt it. If it is, it'll be four or five lines on page thirty-five or something. Nobody got hurt; it was probably only about fifty or sixty dollars; and they caught him within a half hour. He's not important enough to make headlines."

"Shit," Flood swore, flinging himself down on the couch. "That's frustrating as hell."

"Truth and justice have prevailed," Raphael said, piling their dishes into the sink. "The world is safe for gas stations again. Isn't it enough for you to know that all the little gas stations can come home from school without being afraid anymore?"

"You know, you're growing up to be a real smartmouth."

Raphael went back to his armchair. "So you've decided to stay in Spokane for a while."

"Obviously. The town intrigues me."

"Good God, why? The place is a vacuum."

"Why are *you* staying here then?"

"I told you. I need some time to get it all together again. This is a good place for it."

"All right." Flood's eyes were suddenly intent. "I can accept that. But what about afterward—after you get it together? You're not going to stay here, are you? Are you going back to school?"

"I don't know."

"You'll feel better about it later. Sure, it's going to take a while to get squared away, but you ought to make some plans—set some goals. If you don't, you're just going to drift. The longer you stay here, the harder it's going to be to pull yourself away."

"Damon." Raphael laughed. "You sound like you just dug out your freshman psychology text and did some brushing up."

"Well, dammit, it's true," Flood said hotly, getting to his

feet. "If you stay here, you're going to get so comfortable that nobody's going to be able to blast you loose."

"We'll see."

"Promise you'll think about it."

"Sure, Damon."

"I'm serious." For some reason it seemed terribly important to him.

"All right. I'll think about it."

They looked at each other for a moment, and then let it drop.

Flood leaned down and looked out the window. "What the hell?" he said, startled. "What in God's name is he doing?" He pointed.

Raphael glanced out the window. "Oh, that's just Crazy Charlie. He's shaving his head again."

"What does he do that for?"

"Hard to say. I think God tells him to—or maybe one of his cats."

"Is he really crazy?"

"What do you think? He hears voices, he shaves his head like that once a week or so, and he's got a whole set of rituals he lives by. Doesn't that sound sort of schizophrenic?"

"Is that his real name—Charlie?"

"I don't know what his real name is. That's just what I call him."

"What's he doing now?"

Raphael glanced out the window again. "That's where he keeps his towel. He always wipes his head down with the same towel after he shaves. He has to lean way over like that because he's not allowed to step on that spot in front of the cupboard—either there's a big hole that goes straight down to hell or there's a dragon sleeping there, I haven't quite figured out which yet."

"Why don't they haul him off to the place with the rubber rooms?"

"He's harmless. I don't see any reason to discriminate against somebody just because he's crazy. He's just one of the losers, that's all."

"The losers?" Flood turned and looked at him.

"You're not very observant, Damon. This whole street is filled with losers."

"The whole town's a loser, baby." Flood went back to the couch and sprawled on it. "Wall-to-wall zilch."

"Not exactly. It's a little provincial—sort of a cultural backwater—but there are people here who make it all right. The real hard-core loser is something altogether different. Sometimes I think it's a disease."

Flood continued to look at him thoughtfully. "Let's define our terms," he suggested.

"There's the real Reed approach."

"Maybe that's a disease, too," Flood agreed ruefully. "Okay, exactly what do you mean when you say 'loser'?"

"I don't think I can really define it yet." Raphael frowned. "It's a kind of syndrome. After you watch them for a while, it's almost as if they had big signs on their foreheads—'loser.' You can spot them a mile off."

"Give me some examples."

"Sure, Winnie the Wino, Sadie the Sitter, Chicken Coop Annie, Freddie the Fruit, Heck's Angels—"

"Hold it," Flood said, raising both his hands. "Crazy Charlie I understand. Who are all these others?"

"Winnie the Wino lives on the floor beneath Crazy Charlie. She puts away a couple gallons of cheap wine a day. She's bombed out all the time. Sadie the Sitter lives on the other street there. She baby-sits. She plops her big, fat can in a swing on her porch and watches the neighborhood while she stuffs her face—with both hands. She's consumed by greed and envy. Chicken Coop Annie is a blonde—big as a house, dirty as a pig, and congenitally lazy. She makes a career of sponging. She knows the ins and outs of every charity in Spokane. She's convinced that her hair's the same color as Farrah's, and every so often she tries to duplicate that hairdo—the results are usually grotesque. Freddie the Fruit is a flaming queen. He lives with a very tough girl who won't let him go near any boys. He has to do what she tells him to because her name's the one on the welfare checks.

Heck's Angels are a third-rate motorcycle gang. There are eight or ten of them, and they've got three motorcycles that are broken-down most of the time. They swagger a lot and try to look tough, but basically they're only vicious and stupid. They've lumped together the welfare checks of their wives and girlfriends and rented the house up the street. They peddle dope for walking-around money, and they sneak around at night siphoning gas to keep their cars and motorcycles running.''

"And you can see all this from your rooftop?''

Raphael nodded. ''For some reason they don't look up. All you have to do is sit still and watch and listen. You can see them in full flower every day. Their lives are hopelessly screwed up. For the most part they're already in the hands of one or two social agencies. They're the raw material of the whole social-service industry. Without a hard-core population of losers, you could lay off half the police force, ninety percent of the social workers, most of the custodians of the insane, and probably a third of the hospital staffs and coroners' assistants.''

"They're violent?'' Flood asked, startled.

"Of course. They're at the bottom. They've missed out on all the goodies of life. The goodies are all around, but they can't have them. They live in filth and squalor and continual noise. Their normal conversational tone is a scream—they shriek for emphasis. Their cars are all junkers that break down if you even look at them. Their TV sets don't work, and they steal from each other as a matter of habit. Their kids all have juvenile records and are failing in school. They live in continual frustration and on the borderline of rage all the time. A chance remark can trigger homicidal fury. Five blocks from here last month a woman beat her husband's brains out with a crowbar after an argument about what program they were going to watch on TV.''

"No *shit*?'' Flood sat looking at Raphael, his dark eyes suddenly burning. "What are you doing in this sewer, Raphael?''

Raphael shrugged. "Let's call it research. I think there's

one single common symptom that they all have that makes them losers. I'm trying to isolate it.''

''How much consideration have you given to sheer stupidity?''

''That contributes, probably,'' Raphael admitted, ''but stupid people *do* occasionally succeed in life. I think it's something else.''

''And when you do isolate it, what then? Are you going to cure the world?''

Raphael laughed. ''God, no. I'm just curious, that's all. In the meantime there's enormous entertainment in watching them. They're all alike, but each one is infinitely unique. Let's just say that they're a hobby.''

The expression on Flood's face was strange as he listened to Raphael talk, and his eyes seemed to burn in the faint red glow of the winking scanner. It might have been Raphael's imagination or a trick of the light, but it was as if a great weight had suddenly been lifted from the dark-faced young man's shoulders—that a problem that had been plaguing him for months had just been solved.

iii

Raphael worked only a half day on Wednesday, since he was just about to the bottom of the pile of repairable shoes that lay to one side of his worktable.

About eleven-thirty Denise brought him a cup of coffee, and they talked. ''You've changed in the last week or so, Rafe.''

''What do you mean, 'changed'?''

''I don't know, you just seem different, that's all.''

''It's probably Flood. He's enough to alter anybody.''

''Who?''

''Damon Flood. He was my roommate at college. His family has money, and he's developed a strange personality over the years. He came to Spokane a couple weeks ago— I'm not really sure why.''

"I don't think I like him."

"Come on, Denise." Raphael laughed. "You've never met him."

"I just don't like him," she repeated stubbornly, pushing a stray lock of hair out of her face. "I don't like what he's doing to you."

"He hasn't done anything to me."

"Oh yes, he has. You're not the same. You're flippant. You say things that are meant to be funny, but aren't. The humor around here needs to be very gentle. We're all terribly vulnerable. We can't be flip or smart aleck or sarcastic with each other. Don't put us down, Rafe. Don't be condescending. We can smell that on people the way you can smell wine on a drunk. If this Damon Flood of yours makes you feel that way about us, you'd better stay away from here, because nobody'll have anything to do with you."

Raphael looked at her for a moment, and she blushed furiously. "Has it seemed that way?" he asked her finally. "Have I really seemed that bad?"

"I don't know," she wailed. "I don't know anything anymore. All I know is that I'm not going to let anyone hurt any of my friends here."

"Neither am I, Denise," Raphael said softly. "Neither am I. Flood makes me defensive, that's all."

"You don't have to be defensive with *us*." She made a little move toward him, almost as if she were going to embrace him impulsively, but she caught herself and blushed again.

"Okay, Denise. I'll hang it on the hook before I come to work, okay?"

"You're mad at me, aren't you?"

"No. I wasn't paying attention to how I was treating people. Somebody needed to tell me. That's what friends are for, right?"

It troubled him, though. After he left work, he drove around for a while, thinking about what she had said. There was no question that Flood could influence people—manipulate them. Raphael had seen it too many times to have any doubts. He had, however, thought that *he* was immune to that kind of thing. He had somehow believed that Flood would not try his skills on him, but apparently Flood could not resist manipulation, and it was so very subtle that it was not even evident to someone who knew Flood as well as he did.

When he pulled up in front of his apartment, Sadie the Sitter and Spider Granny were in full voice. "Just wait," Sadie boomed. "As soon as I collect his insurance, I'll show her a thing or two. I'll be able to spend money on fancy clothes, too—*and* a new car—*and* new furniture."

It was evident by now that Sadie regarded the insurance money on her husband as already hers. The fact that he was still alive was merely an inconvenience. She counted the money over and over in her mind, her piggish little eyes aflame and her pudgy, hairy-knuckled hands twitching. When her husband came home at night, walking slowly on feet that obviously hurt him, she would glare at him as if his continued existence were somehow a deliberate affront.

Spider Granny, of course, cared only about the bellowing-idiot grandchild, and hurriedly agreed to anything Sadie said simply to prevent the horrid subject of commitment from arising again.

Raphael shook his head and checked his mailbox. There was some junk mail and an envelope from his uncle Harry. Harry Taylor forwarded Raphael's mail, but he never followed the simple expedient of scribbling a forwarding address on the original envelope.

Raphael went on upstairs. He dumped the junk mail in the wastebasket without even looking at it and opened Uncle Harry's envelope.

There was a letter from Isabel Drake inside. The envelope was slightly perfumed. Raphael stood at the table holding the envelope for a long time, looking out the window without really seeing anything. Once he almost turned to pitch the unopened letter into the wastebasket. Then he turned instead and took it to the bookcase and slipped it between the pages of his copy of the collected works of Shakespeare, where

Marilyn's letter was. Then he went out onto the roof. He made a special point of not thinking about the two letters.

Flood arrived five minutes later. He was in high good humor and at his sardonic best. "What a wonderful little town this is," he said ebulliently after he had bounded up the stairs and come over to where Raphael sat in the sun beside the railing. "Do you realize that you managed to find perhaps the one place in the whole country that's an absolute intellectual vacuum?"

"What's got you so wound up?" Raphael asked, amused in spite of himself. When Flood was in good spirits, he was virtually overpowering, and Raphael needed that at the moment.

"I've been out examining this pigsty," Flood told him. "Were you aware that the engineering marvel of the entire city—the thing they're proudest of—is the sewage-treatment plant?"

Raphael laughed. "No, I didn't know that."

"Absolutely. They all invite you to go out and have a look at it. They all talk about it. It's terribly important to them. I suppose it's only natural, though."

"Oh? Why's that?"

"Old people, Raphael, old, old, old, *old* people. Spokane has more hospitals and doctors per square inch than cities five times its size because it's full of old people, and old people get sick a lot. Spokane is positively overwhelmed by its sewage-treatment plant because old people are obsessed with the functioning of their bowels. They gloat over their latest defecation the way young people gloat over their most recent sexual conquest. This place is the prune-juice and toilet-paper capital of America. It's got more old people than any place this side of Miami Beach. And the whole town has a sort of geriatric artsy-craftsy air about it. They do macramé and ceramics and little plaster figurines they pop out of ready-made rubber molds so they can call themselves sculptors. They crank out menopausal religious verse by the ream and print it up in self-congratulatory little mimeographed booklets and then sit around smugly convinced that they're poets."

"Come on." Raphael laughed.

"And the biggest thing on their educational TV station is the annual fund-raising drive. There's an enormous perverted logic there. They hustle money to keep the station on the air so that it can broadcast pictures of them hustling money to keep the station on the air. It's sort of self-perpetuating."

"There are some colleges here," Raphael objected. "The place isn't a total void."

Flood snorted with laughter. "Sure, baby. I've looked into them—a couple of junior colleges where the big majors are sheet metal, auto mechanics, and bedpan repair, and a big Catholic university where they pee their pants over basketball and theology. I love Catholic towns, don't you? Wall-to-wall mongoloids. That's what comes of having a celibate priesthood making sure that their parishioners are punished for enjoying sex. A good Catholic woman can have six mongoloids in a row before it begins to dawn on her that something might be wrong with her reproductive system."

"You're positively dazzling today, Damon. You must be in a good humor."

"I am, babes, I am. I'm always delighted to discover elementals—things that seem to be a distillation of an ideal. I think I'm a Platonist—I like to contemplate concepts in their pure state, and Spokane is the perfect place to contemplate such concepts as mongolism, senility, perversion, and bad breath in all their naked, blinding glory."

"Bad breath?"

"It must be something in the water. Everybody in town has breath that could peel paint at forty yards. I could stand that, though, if they weren't all about three quarters 'round the bend."

"It's not quite *that* bad."

"Really? The biggest growth industry in the area is the loony bin out at Medical Lake. The whole town is crawling with maniacs. I saw a man on the sidewalk giving a speech to a fifty-seven Chevy this morning."

"Tall?" Raphael asked. "Skinny? Bald and with a big, booming voice?"

"You've seen him?"

"He was in front of the bus station when I first got into town. Is he still talking about the nonexistence of chance?"

"No. The old bastard was lecturing on Hegel as close as I could tell—thesis, antithesis, synthesis, all that shit."

"Did it make any sense?"

"Not to *me* it didn't, but that doesn't mean anything. Even the original didn't make sense to me."

"It's nice to know that he's still around." Raphael smiled. "It gives the place a sort of continuity."

Flood looked at him, one eyebrow raised. "*That's* the sort of continuity you like? You sure you don't want me to reserve you one of those rubber rooms out at Medical Lake?"

"Not just yet. What else have you been up to? I haven't seen much of you in the last few days."

Flood leaned out over the railing, looking down into the streets.

"Careful," Raphael warned.

"It's solid enough," Flood said negligently. "I've been playing your game, Angel."

"What game is that?"

"Watching people—examining loserhood in all its elemental purity. You picked the wrong place, Raphael. Come on down to Peaceful Valley. *That's* the natural and native habitat of the archetypal loser. Did you know that people throw things off the Maple Street Bridge down onto the roofs of the houses down there? It's the only place in the world where it rains beer cans. A couple years back a drunken old woman got her head caved in when somebody chucked a potted plant over the side up there. Can you imagine being *geraniumed* into eternity? Now that's a real, honest-to-God loser for you."

"You're not serious."

"May the great and eternal flyswatter of God squash me flat right here if I'm not. Who's that?" He pointed down at the street.

Raphael glanced over the rail. "That's Patch."

"Another one of your losers?"

"No, I don't think so. He doesn't look like a loser, and he doesn't act like one. I haven't figured him out yet."

"Gloomy-looking bastard, isn't he? He's got a face that could curdle milk." Flood walked away from the railing as if the sight of Patch were some kind of personal affront. "Anyway," he went on quickly as if trying to recapture his mood, "I've started collecting losers, too. We got a whole 'nother class down in Peaceful Valley. Take Bob the Buggerer, for example. He's been busted four or five times for molesting little boys. One more time and he goes off to the slammer for the rest of his natural life plus about seventy-five years. Every time a kid goes by on a bicycle, he gets that same desperately longing look on his face you see on the old geeks downtown when a wine truck passes. It's just a matter of time until it'll get to be too much for him. And then there's Paul the Pusher. He's got stashes of dope all over the valley down there. The cops shake him down every time they go through—just to keep in practice—so he's afraid to keep the stuff in his house. He buries it in tin cans under logs and behind trees up on the hillside. He's worried that somebody's going to find it, so he's always digging it up to make sure it's still there. Every night you can see him scurrying out of his house with a shovel and a panic-stricken look on his face. Freddie the Flasher creeps around exposing himself to little girls. Polly the Punchboard is a raging nymphomaniac. She frequents some of the raunchier taverns and brings home horny drunks by the busload."

Flood's tone was harsh, contemptuous, and his descriptions were a kind of savage parody of Raphael's earlier observations. It was almost as if the silent passage of Patch had somehow set him off, somehow made him so angry that he went beyond the bounds of what he might normally have said. Raphael watched him and listened closely, trying to detect the note of personal ridicule he knew must be there, but Flood was too smooth, too glib, even in his anger, and the flow of his description moved too fast to be able to pin him down.

It had been private before, a kind of passive observing that hadn't harmed anyone, but he had made the mistake of telling Flood. He should have known that the dark young man with the obsidian eyes would twist it, pervert it for his own amusement. Raphael began to wish that he had kept his mouth shut.

iv

Raphael had been swimming, and he had spent an hour in the weight room at the YMCA. The car made getting around much easier, but it had definitely disrupted his exercise routine. Since Flood had arrived in Spokane, Raphael's life had suddenly become so full that he no longer had time for everything. All in all, though, he preferred it that way. He thought back to those long, empty hours he had spent when he had first arrived in Spokane, and shuddered.

Frankie was waiting for him again when he got home. She stood on the sidewalk wearing a sleeveless blouse. It had been warm for the past week, and Frankie had started to work on her tan. Her arms and shoulders were golden. Her eyes, however, were flashing, and her lips were no longer tremulous. Her raven's-wing eyebrows were drawn down, and she looked very much like a small volcano about to erupt.

Raphael crossed the sidewalk. "Hi, babe." He leered at her. "You wanna go upstairs and fool around?" He had begun to use innuendo and off-color remarks to keep her off balance.

Frankie, however, was not off balance this time. " 'Sfacim!'" she almost spat at him.

He blinked. He had a sort of an idea what the word meant, and it was not the sort of word he expected from Frankie. Then she said a few other things as well.

"I didn't know you spoke Italian," he said mildly.

"Bastard!"

"Frankie!"

"Get up those goddamn stairs!" She pointed dramatically. This was *not* the Frankie he knew.

He went around to the side of the building and started up the stairs. He could hear her coming up behind him, bubbling curses like a small, angry teapot.

"What's got you so wound up?" he asked her when they reached the roof.

"You got me in trouble, you son of a bitch!"

"Come on, Frankie, calm down. We're not going to get anywhere if all you're going to do is swear at me." He went over and sat down in his chair.

"Why didn't you *tell* me that you'd gone to work?"

"I didn't think it was particularly important. It's not much of a job."

"You're supposed to report *any* kind of a job. You've got a hole in your progress chart you could drive a truck through. You didn't even go to vocational rehab. What were you *thinking* of?"

"You didn't tell me the rules. How was I supposed to know?"

"You stupid, inconsiderate bastard!"

"If you feel like swearing, Frankie, you can probably handle it without having me around."

"Cabrone!"

"Spanish, too? You *are* gifted."

"We had Spick neighbors when I was a kid." She drew in a long, shuddering breath and seemed to get control of herself. "We have to fill out reports, Raphael," she told him, her dark eyes still flashing. "Am I going too fast for you?"

"Be nice."

She made a somewhat elaborate obscene gesture that involved both hands. "There's a procedure, Raphael. First we discuss various occupations and decide what sort of job's compatible with your disability. Then you go to vocational rehab to get the training you need to qualify you for the job. Then *we* set up the interviews for you. You didn't do any of that. Now I'm going to have to fake all kinds of reports. My supervisor thinks I'm incompetent."

"I'm sorry, Frankie. Why didn't you tell me?"

"Because you were too busy trying to talk dirty to me to

see if you could embarrass me." She laughed derisively. "Fat chance. I'm what's known as a tough little broad. You couldn't embarrass me no matter *what* you said."

"What was all that puppy-dog stuff about then?"

"You use what you've got, Raphael. It makes other people feel superior, and then they go out of their way to help you. It makes my job easier. I thought I had you all tied up with a neat little bow, and then you turn around and stab me in the back. Now we've got to fix it."

"Why don't you start at the beginning, Frankie?"

"All right. You've been assigned a number."

"Who's idea was that?" His voice was cold.

"My supervisor's. She's queer for numbers. She even assigns numbers to the pencils on her desk. You can be sure it wasn't *me*. I know how you feel about us, so I thought I'd handle you sort of informally. Then Goodwill sent in their quarterly report, and guess who's name was right at the top of the list of new hires. My supervisor got all over my case for not reporting your progress. I told her that I hadn't had time to fill out all the reports."

"You lied," he accused.

"Of course I lied. I had to cover my ass."

"You're gonna burn in hell, Frankie."

"Whatever. How did you learn to repair shoes without any training?"

He shrugged. "Something I picked up."

"It takes *weeks*."

"Not if you don't spend the first twelve sessions having somebody explain to you how a sewing machine works. I ruined a few pair of shoes when I started, but what the hell? They were throwaways to begin with anyway. I'm getting better at it now. Would you like a leather brassiere? I'll make you one if you'll model it for me."

Her hands went to the neck of her blouse. "Do you want to check the size? My left boob's a little bigger than the right one."

He almost choked on that. This was *definitely* not the Frankie he'd known.

"Do you still want to play?" she said. "Or should we get down to business?"

"Sorry, Frankie."

"Let's get to work then. I'm going to need to put down dates and names for the progress reports—all the usual dog doo-doo. Nobody's ever going to read the reports anyway, but we have to have them in your file."

"You're a fraud, Frankie."

"Of course I am, but I'm a very good fraud." She started asking questions and taking notes. "If anybody ever asks, tell them that I sort of guided you through all this. I'll put in enough comments about your initiative to keep our asses out of the soup, but you're going to have to cooperate."

"It'll cost you."

"Anytime, Raphael, but you might just be biting off more than you can chew." Frankie knew about his condition, of course, but for some reason she chose not to let that knowledge modify her comments. Raphael rather ruefully admitted to himself that *he* had been the one who had started it, and this new Frankie he had just discovered beneath the disarming, little-girl exterior would not back away from *anything*.

She sighed. "Why do you have to be so different, Raphael? Why do you insist on not fitting into any of the compartments?"

"It's a gift."

"It's a pain in the ass. And *why* do you have to be so damn good-looking? Those cute remarks you've been making came very close to getting you in all kinds of trouble."

He thought of something he'd been meaning to ask. "Frankie—is that short for Frances?"

"Sort of." She said it evasively.

"Sort of?"

"All right, smart-ass, it's Francesca. Francesca Dellamara. Happy now?"

"That's gorgeous, Frankie. Why don't you tell people?"

"I don't want them to know I'm a wop."

"You ashamed of bein' a wop?"

"Blow it out your ass."

When she had finished taking notes, she looked around, her soft lower lip pushed out in a kind of thoughtful pout. Her dark eyes, however, were twinkling mischievously. "This is a very nice roof you've got up here," she said. "A girl could get an all-over tan up here if she wanted one. I could tan places that don't usually get tanned, and I wouldn't even get arrested for it." She looked at him archly. "You could watch, if you'd like," she offered.

Raphael suddenly blushed. He couldn't help it.

"*Gotcha!*" she squealed delightedly.

"You're a naughty girl, Frankie."

"Do you want to spank me?" She opened her eyes very wide with a little-girl eagerness.

"Stop that." Somehow she'd shifted the whole thing around, and now *he* was on the receiving end.

Then Flood arrived. Raphael made the introductions, and Frankie told them that she had to go back to work and left.

"She looks good enough to eat." Flood smirked.

"Don't pick on my caseworker," Raphael told him.

"Your *what*?"

"My caseworker. I made a mistake when I got here, and now I'm in the toils of the Department of Human Resources. Frankie comes by now and then to make sure that I don't cheat—sprout a new leg while they're not looking or something."

"You actually let those leeches get their hands on you?" Flood seemed amazed.

"Frankie's not hard to manage. She's young and pliable. I'm molding her character—making a closet dissident out of her." In the light of what he had just discovered, that might not have been entirely true.

"Why in hell did you ever go near those people?"

"I was playing games with them, and the games got out of hand. Social workers are notoriously devoid of any kind of sense of humor—except for Frankie. There might be some hope for that one."

"Don't ever bet on that," Flood said darkly. "Social science was my first major. You knew that, didn't you?"

"You don't seem the type."

"You've got *that* right, baby. The smell drove me off."

"The smell?"

"Haven't you ever noticed? Social workers all smell like rotting flesh—the same way vultures do, and probably for the same reason. Do you know what their ultimate goal is, Raphael?"

"To tend the wounds of the casualties of life—or so they say."

"Bullshit! Their goal is to take over—to take over everything and everybody—to make us live *their* way, and to make us pay for it, of course. It's all money and power, Raphael, the same as everything else. Once a social worker gets her hooks into you, you never get well, because you're a renewable resource. Anytime they need more money, they screw around with you until you have to go back into some kind of therapy—at so much an hour. They never let you get free, because someday they might want to squeeze some more money out of you or out of your insurance company. And power? What greater power can you have than to be able to make somebody not only *do* what you tell him to but *think* what you tell him to as well?"

"Aren't you exaggerating a bit?"

"Grow up, Raphael. Their magic word is 'programs.' They've got programs for everything, and every program is based on thought control. They've already taken over the schools. Every teacher in the public schools has a de facto degree in social work. I doubt if you could find a real English teacher or a real history teacher anywhere in America. Johnny can't read because his teachers are too worried about his 'relationships,' and their major tool is 'the group.' Modern Americans are sheep. They herd up by instinct. You won't find no Lone Rangers out there no more, Kimo Sabee. Peer pressure, baybee, peer pressure. That's the club they use. Americans would sooner die than do anything that runs counter to the wishes of the peer group. Before I finally threw the whole thing over, I spent *hours* taking notes in those group meetings. If I ever hear anybody say the words 'y'know' again, I'll throw up right on the spot.''

Raphael remembered the endless, monotonous repetition of the 'y'knows' during his enforced attendance at AA meetings when he'd tried playing games with a new caseworker. ''They *are* sort of fond of that, aren't they?''

''It's the Ave Maria and Paternoster of the groupie. It's a part of the recognition system, the badge of membership in the cult.''

''Cult?''

''God, yes. They're all cults, Raphael. They're based on the mind-destroying success of AA. You can cure somebody of *anything* if you put him in a cult and grind off all his individuality and alienate him from such distractions as friends, families, wives—little things like that. Be glad you're not married, my friend, because the very first thing your cute little caseworker would have done would have been to poison your wife because your marriage hadn't been approved by the group—whatever group it is she's hustling for.'' Flood's expression was strange, intent, and he seemed almost to have his teeth clenched together. ''Have you ever noticed how much they all want you to 'talk about it'?''

''Of course. That's what they do—talk.''

''Do you want to know why? Social workers are almost all women, and women *talk* about problems. They don't *do* things about them. If John and Marsha's house catches on fire, John wants to put the fire out. Marsha wants to sit down and discuss it—to find out why the fire feels hostility toward them.''

''Get serious.''

''I am. Most social workers are women, and they know that they can control women by talking to them. It doesn't work that well with men, so the first thing a social worker does to a man is castrate him.''

Raphael stiffened. How much did Flood know?

Flood, however, didn't seem to notice. ''Social workers have to castrate their male clients so that they can turn them into women so that they'll be willing to sit around and *talk* about their problems rather than *do* something about them. If somebody actually *does* something about his problems, he doesn't need a social worker anymore. That's the *real* purpose of all the programs. They want to keep the poor sucker from really addressing his problem. If he does that, he'll probably solve it, and then he gets away. They won't have the chance to leech off his bank account or his emotions anymore. The bitches are vampires, Raphael. Stay away from them. The content of any social-science course is about fifty-percent vocabulary list—the jargon—and about fifty-percent B. F. Skinner behavior-modification shit. And as I said, the whole idea is to get everybody in the whole goddamn world into a program. They've probably even got a program for normal people—a support group for people who don't need a support group—a group to screw up their minds enough to make them eligible for the really *interesting* programs. Give those bastards a few years, and ninety percent of the people in the United States will be social workers. They'll have to start branching out then—spread the joy to other species. Guide dogs and cats through the trauma of divorce. Death counseling for beef cattle—so that we can all get happy hamburgers at the supermarket. Eventually they'll probably have to start exhuming the dead just to have enough customers to keep them all working. How about 'Aftercare for the Afterlife'? Ten social workers to dig up your uncle Norton to find out how he's doing? 'How's it going, Nort?' ' 'Bout the same—still dead.' 'Would you like to talk about it?' ''

"Aren't you reaching just a bit, Damon?"

"Of course I am. I'm doing this off the top of my head. You didn't give me any time to prepare. I'd still like to tumble your little caseworker, though."

"Tumble?"

"It's an old-fashioned term. It means—"

"I know what it means. You keep your hands off Frankie. I'm raising her as a pet." That was not really true anymore, but he decided that it might be better for all concerned if he kept what he'd just found out to himself.

"*Sure* you are, baby. Next time she comes around though, check real close to find out which one of you is wearing the dog collar."

V

In mid-May the weather turned foul. Denise told Raphael that this was normal for Spokane. "April and the first half of May are beautiful. Then it starts raining and keeps it up until the end of June. Then it gets hot."

"You mean it's going to do this for six weeks?"

"Off and on. It makes the lilacs bloom."

"Why does everybody in Spokane pronounce that word ly-*lock*?" he demanded irritably. "The word is ly-*lack*."

"Don't get grumpy with *me*, Blue Eyes," she told him tartly. "It's not *my* fault it's raining."

"Oh, go sell a refrigerator or something." He faked a scowl to let her know that he was not angry with her so much as with the weather.

"Why don't you go back to your little bench," she suggested, "and take that nice stout little machine of yours and sew all your fingers together? That way you'll have something to worry about besides the weather or how I pronounce the word 'lilac.' "

"You did it again. You said ly-*lock*."

"So beat me."

He made a threatening move toward her, and she scampered away, laughing.

That afternoon he sat in his apartment drinking coffee and staring dispiritedly out at the dirty gray clouds scudding by overhead. He had the scanner on—more for company than out of any interest.

"District Four," the scanner said.

"Four."

"Nineteen-nineteen West Dalton," the dispatcher said. Raphael looked quickly at the scanner. The address was on his block.

''Check on the welfare of the Berry children. Complainant is the children's grandmother—states that the children may be abused or neglected. Child Protective Services is dispatching a caseworker.''

''You want me to check it out or just back up the caseworker?'' District Four asked.

''See what the situation requires first. We've had calls from this complainant before. There might be some kind of custody dispute involved.''

''Okay,'' District Four said.

Raphael realized that it was Mousy Mary that they were descending upon. The dumpy woman with the pinched-in face had finally figured out a way to get into Mary's house.

He reached for his crutches and went out on the roof. The rain had stopped, at least for the moment, and the gusty wind blew ripples across the surface of a puddle of water standing in a low spot on the roof. Raphael crutched over to the front railing and stood looking down at the soggy street.

The police car, followed closely by a gray car from the state motor pool, drove up slowly and stopped. The policeman got out and put on his cap. A very nervous young woman got out of the gray car and hurried over to him, carrying her briefcase self-consciously. They spoke together briefly and then went up onto Mousy Mary's porch.

Across the street, in front of Sadie the Sitter's house, Mousy Mary's mother stood watching, her face gripped with an expression of unspeakable triumph.

The policeman and the nervous young caseworker went inside, and the dumpy little woman scurried across the street to stand directly in front of the house.

After a few moments the screaming started. Raphael could hear the anguish and the outrage in Mary's shrieks, but not the words. Then they all came out onto the porch, the caseworker holding protectively on to the arms of Mary's two confused-looking children, and the policeman interposing himself between her and the now-hysterical Mary.

''It's *her*!'' Mary shrieked, leveling a shaking finger at her mother. ''Why don't you make her leave me alone?''

The caseworker said something to her in a low voice, but Mary continued to scream at her smug-faced mother.

The policeman removed the small portable radio unit from his belt. "This is District Four." The voice came from the scanner inside Raphael's apartment. "You'd better respond Mental Health to this nineteen-nineteen West Dalton address. There's a female subject here who's pretty hysterical."

The caseworker led the two wide-eyed, crying children down to the sidewalk.

"I'll take them," Mousy Mary's mother declared in an authoritative voice. "I'm a personal friend of Sergeant Green's, and he said that I'd get custody."

"I'm very sorry," the young social worker told her firmly, her voice louder now, "but custody is a matter for the courts to decide."

"Don't let her take them," Mary screamed. "She'll never let me see them again. She's been trying to take them away from me for five years now. Don't let the old bitch have them."

"Don't you *dare* call me that in front of the babies!" her mother scolded. Then she turned back to the caseworker. "I'm *taking* those children," she announced.

"Officer," the caseworker called.

"All right, ma'am," the policeman said to Mary's mother, "you're going to have to stand aside."

"But I have custody," Mary's mother insisted.

"At the moment Child Protective Services has custody," the caseworker said, leading the children around the old woman toward her car.

"You come back here!" the dumpy woman screamed. "Sergeant Green said I could have custody."

"Go ahead and take off, miss," the officer on the porch said.

"What are you talking about? She can't take those children. I have custody."

The social worker got into her car with Mary's children and pulled away from the curb.

"You come back here! You come back here!" Mary's mother shrieked.

Then the car was gone, and she spun to confront the officer who had come down off the porch. "What's your badge number?" she demanded. "You're in a great deal of trouble, young man. Sergeant Green will take care of you."

"Just calm down, ma'am," the policeman said to her. "We'll get this all sorted out, but we're not going to get anywhere if we all stand around yelling at each other."

Then Mary said something, and the two women began screaming again.

Raphael turned and went back inside. The wind was brisk, and he had begun to feel chilled.

An hour later, after the affair across the street had quieted down, Flood arrived with a pizza. He had been drinking and was in high spirits. "Bob the Buggerer got busted today," he announced gleefully. "The temptation of budding boyish buttocks finally got to him, I guess."

"What's with the alliteration?" Raphael asked. He was not really in the mood for Flood. The weather and the incident across the street had soured him.

"Purely unintentional." Flood grinned. "To alliterate or not to alliterate—that's the question," he declaimed. "Whether 'tis fancier to consonantize constantly or to rhyme in time."

"Consonantize?"

"Poetic license—number forty-seven eighteen. Anyhow, poor old bumbling Bob nailed a paperboy on his morning route this A.M., and then he made his getaway—or at least he thought so. But the fuzz showed the rapee a bunch of mug shots, and the kid fingered Bob. About two this afternoon three squad cars came roaring down the hill into Peaceful Valley. Hey, baybee, that's like throwing a brick into a hornet's nest. You absolutely wouldn't *believe* what happens in Peaceful Valley when the pigs come down there in force. It looked like an impromptu track meet. There were people running every which way. Two guys came running out of Polly the Punchboard's house stark-ass naked and bailed into the river. Last I saw of them they were being swept around the bend. Guys I'd never even *seen* before came out of some of those houses. It looked like a convention of jackrabbits there for a while. Poor old Bob tried to run, too, but he's a little too old and a little too fat, so the cops caught up with him about fifty yards up the side hill. He tried to fight, and they literally kicked the shit out of him—I mean, they flat stomped a mud puddle in his ass right there on the spot. You've got some real unfriendly cops in this town."

"Was he hurt?" Raphael asked, not knowing whether to believe Flood or not. In his present mood Flood could expand and embellish a simple incident into an extended narrative that would be related to the truth only by implication.

"Hard to say. He looked pretty comfortable—lying there."

"Damon," Raphael said irritably, "I don't think I believe one single word of all this."

"Would I lie to you?"

"Yes, I think you would—just to see if I'd swallow all this crap."

"May the motor scooter of the Almighty run over my bare toes if it didn't happen just the way I described it."

"I think you're missing the whole point, Damon. I'm just not *too* entertained by this unsympathetic attitude of yours."

"Unsympathetic? *Me?* What about you, Raphael? What's your excuse for *your* attitude?"

"What about my attitude?"

"You're playing God. You sit in splendid isolation on top of your grubby little Mount Zion here, using your injury as an excuse not to come down among the real people. You've created a little fantasy world instead and peopled it with these losers of yours—'and whatsoever the God Raphael called them, so were they named.' But let me tell you something, Archangel, old buddy. You can sit brooding on your lonely mountaintop here with those seraphic wings outspread to shade these rickety streets, but your cute little fantasy names have no relationship whatsoever to these people and who they *really* are. Those are *real* people down there with real emotions and real problems, and you did *not* create them."

"I've never said I did." Raphael was startled by the sudden intensity of Flood's words.

Flood stood up and began pacing in the small apartment, his eyes burning. "Okay, so you had a little accident—you've got a certain disability. Big goddamn deal! What if it had been your *eyes*, baby? Think about that."

Raphael flinched, the sudden horrid picture of a world of total darkness coming over him so palpably that he could almost feel the anguish of it.

"You've created this little dreamworld of yours so you can hide." Flood jabbed at him. "You want to sit up here where it's safe, wallowing in self-pity and dreaming away the rest of your life. Well, I've got a flash for you, Rafe, baby. Jake Flood is here, and he's goddamned if he's going to let you just vegetate your life away like this—doped out on melancholy musings, drunk on mournful little fantasies. If you're so damned interested in these shitty little people, get *involved*, for Chrissake. Go out and meet them. Find out who they *really* are."

"Why don't you mind your own business, Flood?" Raphael was getting angry. "Why don't we just forget all this. Just go away and leave me alone. Go back to Portland—go back to Grosse Pointe—go to hell for all I care. Just get off my back."

Flood stopped, turned sharply, and stared at Raphael. Then he grinned broadly. *"Gotcha!"* he said exultantly. "By God, you're alive after all! For a while there I was starting to have some doubts. You're going to make it after all, baby. It may be in spite of yourself, but you're going to make it. If you can get mad, at least it proves you're not dead."

"Oh, go to hell!"

"Anyplace, baby, anyplace." Flood laughed. "I finally got a rise out of you. Have you got any idea how I've been busting my ass to do just that?"

"Flood," Raphael said, feeling suddenly sheepish, "don't play games with me. Exactly what are you up to now?"

"What's necessary, Raphael, what's necessary. I'll set fire

to your crutches if I have to, but I'll be a son of a bitch if
I'm going to sit back and let you lie down and play dead."

It sounded very convincing, but the look in Flood's eyes
was too familiar. Raphael remembered it, and it stirred
doubts. It was all very complicated. Flood almost never
did things for the apparent or obvious reason; his motives
were usually obscure. It would be easy—even flattering—to
accept this protestation of hardheaded friendship at face
value, but the agatelike eyes and that faintest shadow of a
sardonic smile that flickered at the corners of his mouth made
Raphael cautious, uncertain. As always with Flood, he decided, it might be better to wait and see.

vi

The next day when he was coming home from his therapist's
office, Raphael stopped by the grocery store to pick up a few
things, and as he usually did, he stopped to talk with the
blond clerk. The man had a dry wit Raphael liked and an
open, friendly manner that was a relief from the deviousness
of Flood or the tart touchiness he sometimes encountered in
the people with whom he worked.

"Hey, Rafe," the clerk said, looking up from the milk
case he was filling, "what's shakin', baby?"

"Just passin' through, Darrel."

"That friend of yours was in a while ago."

"Damon?"

"Is that his name?" the clerk asked, straightening. "I
thought it was Jake."

"It is. The other is a name he used to use at school."

"Whatever turns him on, I guess," Darrel said. "I don't
want to hurt your feelings or anything, Rafe, but I'm not *too*
partial to that young man. I think a lesson or two in manners
wouldn't hurt him all that much."

"His family's got money. Sometimes he lets that go to his
head a little."

"You might suggest to him that he's using up his welcome

in here pretty fast. If he bad-mouths one of the girls about one more time, he and I are going to tangle assholes—definitively.''

''Was he offensive?''

''That gets pretty close to it. He had one of the girls in tears before he left.''

''I'm sorry, Darrel. I'll have a talk with him about it.''

''I'd appreciate it, Rafe.'' The clerk started to return to the milk case, but stopped and turned back suddenly. ''Hey, you live over there on the same street with Tobe and Sam, don't you?''

''Yeah, right across the street. Why?''

''Have you seen them lately?''

''I haven't really paid that much attention.''

''They're usually in here two or three times a day to buy wine, but I haven't seen them all week.''

''Maybe I'd better stop by and see if they're okay.''

''Might not hurt. They're a couple of likable old bastards. They don't *smell* too good sometimes, but they're good-natured old farts. I'd hate to see anything happen to them.''

''I'll look in on them,'' Raphael promised, starting off down one of the aisles. ''Later, Darrel.''

''I'll be here,'' the clerk said wryly, ''unless I can figure out a way to get fired.''

Raphael laughed perfunctorily and finished his shopping.

It was curious, he thought, sitting in his car at the stoplight on Boone Avenue. This store was a long way from Peaceful Valley. The only reason Flood would be over here would be to visit him, but he hadn't seen him that morning. ''What the hell is he up to?'' Raphael was puzzled.

The light turned green, and he drove on home. Several weeks before, he had picked up a canvas bag of the type used by newspaper boys. It provided an excellent means for carrying groceries up to his apartment since it left both of his hands free for the business of locomotion. At the moment, however, it was neatly rolled and tucked in the cupboard under the sink.

''Damn,'' he swore, and got out of the car.

He was halfway across the sidewalk when, on an impulse, he turned and went back, crossed the street, and climbed up onto the sagging porch of Tobe and Sam's house.

He knocked, but there was no answer. He knocked again and listened. There was no sound from inside.

"Hey, Tobe?" he called, his face close to the door.

There was still no sound.

He tried the door. It was unlocked, and he opened it an inch or two. Their yellow dog started to bark.

"Tobe?" he called again. "Sam? Are you guys okay?"

The dog kept on barking, and the sour stink of the house exhaled out through the partially open door.

"Tobe? It's Rafe. You guys all right in there?" He did not want to go into their house uninvited.

"Hi, buddy," Sam's wheezy little voice said weakly from inside. "Come on in an' have a drink."

The dog kept on barking.

Raphael steeled himself and shoved the door open.

The yellow dog stood and barked at him, his tail wagging.

"Shut up, Rudy," Raphael told the dog.

The dog barked a couple more times dispiritedly, came over to sniff Raphael's leg, and then padded on into the dining room, his nails clicking on the linoleum.

Sam sat at the table, a half-full bottle of wine in front of him. He looked up, smiling blearily. "Hi, buddy," he said in his wispy voice.

Tobe lay on the floor, his wiry little body twisted grotesquely. His mouth was agape, and his eyes, half-open, were glazed. A piece of grayish lint was stuck to one of his eyeballs, and he did not move. He had fouled himself, and a filthy brown puddle had oozed through his pants and dried on the floor under his scrawny haunches. The stink was overpowering.

"All right, Sam," Raphael said disgustedly. "What happened?"

"Hi, buddy," Sam said happily.

"Never mind the 'hi, buddy' crap. What's the matter with Tobe?"

Sam slowly moved his head to look at the man lying on the floor. He took a long drink.

"Come on, Sam," Raphael insisted. "What happened to Tobe?"

"Poor old Tobe," Sam said, shaking his head. "He had the fits. You wanna drink, buddy?" He offered the bottle.

"No, I don't want a goddamned drink. How long has he been like this?"

"Two—maybe three days. I dunno. I forget."

"Jesus Christ! You said he had fits. What kind of fits?"

"He took to jerkin' an' twitchin'. Then he fell down an' started bangin' his head on the floor. Then he kinda stiffened up a little, an' then he went all limp, kinda. That's when he shit his pants like that. You sure you don't want a drink, buddy?" He held up the bottle and squinted at it. "I could get you a glass, if you like."

Raphael took a deep breath. "No thanks, Sam," he said in a gentler tone. "Not right now." He braced himself, reached out, and touched Tobe gently with the tip of his crutch. The body seemed soft, yielding.

He pushed a little harder, and Tobe moved loosely on the floor.

The yellow dog growled at him from under the table.

"Have you got a telephone, Sam?" Raphael asked.

"Why would we want a phone, buddy? Ain't nobody gonna call us."

"Just sit tight," Raphael said, and then realized how stupid a thing that was to say. He turned and crutched on out.

Flood's car was parked behind his own, and Flood was coming back down the outside stairway, his face puzzled.

"Damon," Raphael called, "I need some help."

"What's up?" Flood came quickly across to the shabby little house.

"I think there's a dead man in here."

"No shit? Who is he?" Flood's eyes narrowed, and his face grew wary.

"Tobe Benson," Raphael told him. "He lives here."

"Maybe we shouldn't get involved."

"Flood, this isn't a dead dog we're talking about."

Flood looked at him. "All right, Raphael," he said finally. "It's going to be a pain in the ass, but if it's that damned important, let's see what we can do." He came on into the house. "Jesus! What the hell is that stink?"

"They drink. Old men who drink don't smell very good." Raphael stumped on into the dining room, and the yellow dog started to bark again.

"Rudy," Raphael snapped, "will you shut your goddamn mouth and lay down?"

The dog glowered at him and slunk back under the table.

"Hi, buddy," Sam said.

Flood looked quickly at Raphael.

"He's bombed," Raphael explained. "Ignore him." He pointed at Tobe with his crutch. "What do you think? Is he dead?"

"Christ, how the hell should I know?"

"See if he's breathing. I couldn't get down there to find out."

Flood's face was a pale green. "I wouldn't do this for just anybody." He knelt beside Tobe and put a hesitant hand on the little man's chest. "He's still warm, and I think I'm getting a beat. It looks like he's still alive—if you want to call it that. What the hell zonked him out like this?"

"Booze. They drink a lot."

"Hi, buddy," Sam said to Flood. "You wanna drink?"

"How long's he been down like this?" Flood asked.

"Two or three days, I guess. It's a little hard to get specifics out of Sam there. He doesn't know Tuesday from Saturday."

"Really," Flood agreed. "What do you think?"

"Here's my keys." Raphael dug them out of his pocket. "They don't have a phone. Why don't you go over to my place and get hold of the police?"

"Shouldn't we call an ambulance?"

"Let the police handle that. It'll save time in the long run."

"I'll be right back."

Five minutes later the house was filled with the official stomping of two policemen. "What made you think there might be a problem here, Mr. Taylor?" the one who had come to Mousy Mary's house the day before asked Raphael.

"I was at the grocery store over on Boone," Raphael replied. "One of the clerks there—Darrel—said that he hadn't seen them in several days. I came by to see if they were okay."

"Not many people would have taken the trouble."

"Mr. Taylor has a unique concern for his fellow man," Flood said dryly from the rickety chair across from Sam. "Will the old man live?"

The policeman shrugged. "Hard to say. He's not in very good shape—neither one of them is, really. We're going to send them both to the hospital and then out to the detoxification center—see if they can't dry them out a little."

"You don't sound very optimistic."

"They're both in their sixties, Mr. Flood, and they've been drunk for ten or fifteen years now. Their brains are pickled, and their livers are shot. I don't see too much to hope for, do you? Is there somebody who can take care of the dog?"

"The backyard's fenced," Raphael told him. "Put him out there. I'll see to it that he gets fed."

"I don't think there's any need for you gentlemen to hang around," the officer decided. "We know these two. We know what has to be done."

"It's happened before?" Flood asked.

"They haven't been any problem since we took the gun away from them."

"The gun?" Raphael was startled.

The policeman laughed shortly. "They got all boozed up one night here four, maybe five years back. The fat one there shot the little one in the belly with a twenty-two."

"*Sam?*" Raphael exclaimed. "Sam wouldn't hurt anybody—least of all Tobe. He loves the little old guy."

"He had a pretty good head of steam that night."

"What happened?"

"The little one wouldn't press charges. Claimed it was an

accident. All we could do was take the gun away.'' He looked at Raphael. ''I'm glad you came by when you did, Mr. Taylor. It's messy if somebody dies in a situation like this. There are always questions and not too many answers. Thanks.''

Later, on the roof, as they watched the ambulance carry off the two old men, Flood started laughing.

''What's so funny now?'' Raphael demanded.

''It just goes to prove what I said last night, Gabriel. Your two old drunks had a big shoot-out. God only knows what else is happening on this block.''

As always when Flood made that strange slip, Raphael felt a peculiar chill in the pit of his stomach. He knew that Flood was not even aware of the fact that he had used that name. He also knew that the name had a much deeper significance. He somehow felt that if he could only find out exactly who this mysterious Gabriel was, he would have the key to Flood's entire personality.

''Reality, Angel, reality,'' Flood went on. ''Reality is infinitely more interesting than fantasy. Look at the real world. Look at the real people. Come down from Zion. Fold your wings and walk among us. I'll show you a world your wildest imaginings could never approach.'' And he threw back his head and laughed. But the laugh sounded hollow somehow and savagely mocking.

In taberna quando sumus

i

Toward the end of May the weather broke, and there were five or six days of sunshine. Raphael moved outside to luxuriate in the warmth, coming in off his rooftop only to eat and sleep or to go to work.

Quite early one morning he saw Crazy Charlie coming furtively out of the house next door. Charlie always tried to attend to those things that required him to leave the safety of his apartment early in the day when there were few people on the streets and in the stores. He avoided contact with people as much as possible, even crossing the street when he saw someone coming up the sidewalk toward him in order to make chance meetings or the possibility of conversation impossible.

This morning, however, Flood was waiting for him. The small red car came down the street a moment or so after Charlie emerged, pulled into its usual parking place behind Raphael's car, and Flood bounded out. Without any preliminary word, he came around the back of his car and placed himself on the sidewalk directly in front of Crazy Charlie. " 'Morning, friend," he said with a breezy cheerfulness.

Charlie mumbled something, his head down, and tried to cringe back off the sidewalk onto the grass.

"I wonder if you could give me some information," Flood pressed. "I seem to be lost. Could you tell me how to get back to Interstate 90?"

Charlie pointed south mutely.

150

"I go *that* way?" Flood assumed an expression of enormous perplexity. "Man, I'm completely turned around. I could have sworn that I had to go *that* way." He pointed north.

Charlie shook his head and gave more specific directions in a nasal, almost trembling voice.

"Man," Flood said with an ingenuousness so obviously faked that Raphael, watching from his rooftop, cringed. "I sure do want to thank you." Without warning, he reached out, grabbed Charlie's hand, and shook it vigorously.

Charlie looked as if he were ready to faint. Having someone talk to him was bad enough, but to have someone actually *touch* him—

"Beautiful morning, isn't it?" Flood went on in the same breezy tone, releasing Charlie's hand.

Charlie looked around, confused. In all probability he had not paid any attention to the weather for several years now. "Yes," he said in the same hesitant voice, "it seems pretty . . . nice."

"All that rain was starting to destroy me."

Charlie had begun sidling away, moving up the sidewalk away from Flood's car, but Flood kept talking, walking along beside him.

Raphael watched the two of them move slowly up toward the end of the block, Flood talking animatedly and Charlie appearing to grow less apprehensive as they went. By the time they reached the corner they were talking and laughing together like old friends.

They stood on the corner for almost ten minutes in the slanting, golden light of the early-morning sun, and when they parted, they shook hands again. Charlie seemed almost wistful as he looked at Flood's retreating back, then his shoulders slumped again into their usual slouch, and he crossed the street to pursue his early-morning errand.

Flood was buoyant when he came up the stairs and onto the roof. "How 'bout that?" he crowed. "Were you watching?"

"Of course. Wasn't I supposed to be?"

Flood ignored that. ''I've been laying for that silly bastard for four days now. I knew he'd have to come out sooner or later.''

''Why don't you just leave him alone?''

''Don't be ungrateful. Look at all the sleep I've missed for your benefit.''

''Mine?''

''Of course. *You're* the one who's so damned interested in him. His name's Henry, not Charlie, and he gets a disability pension because he's nervous—that's the way he put it—'I get nervous.' He's supposed to be in therapy of some kind, but he doesn't go. He has seven cats—he told me their names, but I forget what they are—and he used to have a little dog named Rags, but Rags ran away. Sometimes, late at night when everybody's asleep, he goes out and looks for Rags. He calls him—very softly so that he won't wake anybody up—but Rags never comes. Henry misses him terribly. He didn't tell me the name of the dragon who sleeps on the floor in front of that cupboard—as a matter of fact, we didn't get into the question of the dragon at all.''

''Jesus,'' Raphael said, feeling a sudden wrenching pity for Crazy Charlie and the abysmal emptiness of his life.

''Sad as hell, isn't it?'' Flood agreed. ''A couple times there I almost broke down and cried while he was talking.''

''You?''

''Come on,'' Flood protested, ''I'm not *totally* insensitive, you know.''

''You could have fooled me.''

Later, when they had gone inside to have coffee, Charlie returned to his apartment. He put down his packages and began to talk animatedly.

Flood watched him intently through Raphael's binoculars. ''I think he's going through the whole conversation again, word for word.''

''Why don't you leave him alone?'' Raphael said disgustedly, realizing that he had said it before.

''I didn't hurt him.'' Flood was still watching through the binoculars. ''For all I know, I might have done him some good. God knows how long it's been since he actually talked to somebody.''

"That's not the point. You're *using* him—that's the point.''

"Everybody uses people, Raphael.'' Flood still had the binoculars to his eyes. "That's what we're here for. You used him for months and never even talked to him—didn't even take the trouble to find out his real name. At least when I used him, he got something out of it. Here.'' He shoved the binoculars at Raphael. "Go on and take a look at him. He's genuinely happy. When did you ever do anything like that for him?''

Helplessly, feeling somehow furtive, Raphael took the binoculars and looked across the intervening space at Crazy Charlie's broadly smiling face. He knew that what Flood had done was wrong, but he could not put his finger on exactly what it was that had made it wrong. And so he watched, and for the first time he began to feel ashamed.

Chicken Coop Annie had waddled out of her house to yell at her kids. Flood came down the street and stopped to talk with her.

On his rooftop Raphael knew that the meeting was once again deliberate and that it had been carefully staged for his benefit. He had even seen the brief flicker of Flood's eyes as he had thrown a quick glance up to be sure that he was sitting there.

Chicken Coop Annie was wearing a tentlike wrapper that somehow accentuated rather than concealed the enormous nudity that lay beneath it. She giggled often as she spoke with Flood, her pudgy hands going nervously to the tangled wrack of her hair.

Flood eyed her boldly as they spoke, an insinuating smile playing about his lips, and Annie glowed, her eyes sly and her expression and gestures grossly coquettish.

They talked for quite a long while as Raphael watched helplessly from his rooftop. As Flood left, Annie raised her arms, ran all ten fat fingers through her hair, and shook her head with a movement that was somehow enormously sensual. When she walked back toward her house, her waddle seemed to become almost a conscious strut.

"Her name's Opal," Flood announced when he reached the rooftop.

"Really?"

"She has urges," Flood said, leaning against the railing.

"I noticed. Are you two going steady?"

"Interesting idea. Maybe if she was a little cleaner . . ."

"Why let that bother you? If you're going to wallow, why not go all the way?"

"Don't be crude." Flood suddenly laughed. "My God, she's a big woman! You don't realize it until you get up close to her. She's like a monument. A woman like that could scare a whole generation of young men into monasteries."

"Aren't you getting tired of this game?"

"No, not just yet. The street still has enormous possibilities."

And again, in bright and vivid morning air, Flood strode step for step with grim-faced Willie the Walker, deep in conversation, their words chopped and measured by the steady rhythm of their feet upon the sidewalk.

Sitting, Raphael watched them pass and turned away in disgust.

"Name's George," Flood informed Raphael later. "He had a heart attack ten years ago. His doctor advised him to get more exercise—suggested walking. That might have been the wrong thing to say to George."

"How much longer are you going to keep this up?"

"The old boy covers fifteen miles a day," Flood said, ignoring the question. "His doctor dropped dead three years ago, but old George keeps on walking. The only trouble with it is that it's the only thing he's got to talk about. He's a walking city map. He talked at me for a solid half hour, reciting the street names from the river to the North Division Y." He stopped and winced, shaking one foot. "Goddamn, my feet hurt."

"Good."

* * *

And again as Mousy Mary struggled down the street with two huge sacks of groceries, the ever-present Flood came to her aid with overwhelming gallantry. Suspicious at first and even apprehensive, she finally permitted him to carry one, then both. By the time they reached her porch, they were chatting together as if they had been neighbors for years. Her runny eyes brightened, and her slack mouth trembled now and then into a fleeting and tenuous smile. They talked together for almost half an hour before Flood came back across the street and up the stairs to the roof.

"Would you believe that her name really *is* Mary?" he told Raphael.

"Whoopee."

"They're going to give her kids back this weekend. Somebody finally got smart enough to really sit down and *listen* to that mother of hers. I guess the old bag's genuinely certifiable. They ought to fit her for a straitjacket."

"I could have told you that. So, what are you proving by all of this?"

"Just verifying your theory. You know—scientific method, empirical data, independent observer, all that shit. A theory isn't worth much if it isn't subject to verification, right?"

"I think there's also some question about the presence of the observer as a factor in the validity of the tests, isn't there?"

"Shit!" Flood said disgustedly. "Next you'll be talking about the noise in the woods."

"Why not? It'd be a damn sight more useful than all these fun and games."

"Oh no, Raphael. You're not going to put me off the track *that* easy. I'm going to run down each and every one of your losers before I'm through. We're going to have a good hard look at the face of reality—warts, pimples, and all—and nothing less than getting run down by a garbage truck is going to stop me."

"That's an interesting thought."

"Be nice."

* * *

And again, in conversation with Freddie the Fruit under the hard and watchful eye of Freddie's girlfriend. Freddie, almost girlish, wriggled under the full impact of Flood's charm. Even the girl thawed a bit, though her expression was still suspicious.

"Harold and Wanda," Flood told Raphael. "He's Harold, she's Wanda."

"Obviously."

"Not entirely. A very tough broad, that one. She had a boyfriend named Douglas once. She's got his name tattooed on her shoulder—D-U-G. Can you imagine carrying an illiteracy to your grave like that? Anyway, they've completely reversed the traditional male-female roles, and they're really quite happy. He flirts with men to make her jealous, but he's probably not very serious about it. It's all part of a very elaborate game they play. Your original theory was an oversimplification this time. That's a very subtle and complex relationship."

"So?"

"I just thought you'd like to know, is all. After all, they're your losers, not mine." And Flood grinned, his dark eyes glittering in the sunlight.

And again on the porch with Sadie the Sitter, both of them lounging at their ease. "He drinks, of course," Sadie told Flood.

"I didn't know that."

"Oh, sure. He has for years now. Sometimes when he comes home, it's all he can do to make it into the house, he's so drunk."

"Then why does *she* act as if they were so special?" Flood asked, playing the straight man.

Sadie smiled knowingly. "Her family had money. They're the ones who set him up in business—and she never lets him forget it, let me tell you. That's why he drinks, naturally."

"Naturally."

"And the one next to her," Sadie went on, pointing.

"*She's* always bustin' a gut tryin' to keep up. They spend all their time tryin' to out-uppity each other. It makes me sick."

"I don't know why people have to be like that."

"That's all right. *I'll* be comin' into some money pretty soon. *Then* we'll see who's gonna outfancy who."

"Good for you," Flood approved.

Sadie nodded smugly and stuffed another handful of potato chips into her mouth. "Get the hell away from that rosebush, you little bastard!" she bellowed at one of the children she was watching.

"That woman is an abomination," Flood told Raphael later. "I'm moderately immoral myself, but she's not even human. She hates *everything*. Talking to her is like crawling into a sewer."

"It was your idea," Raphael pointed out. "Had enough yet?"

"What keeps her *alive*?" Flood exclaimed. "What keeps her from exploding from all that sheer, overwhelming envy? Oh, by the way, her name's Rita. They call her husband Bob the Barber."

"So?"

Flood shrugged. "I just thought you'd be interested."

"What made you think I'd be interested? I could see what she is from here. I didn't have to sit on her porch and let her spew on me to find out everything I needed to know about her."

"I don't see how she fits into your theory, though."

"She's a loser. You can smell it from here. There's a catastrophe just around the corner—something crouching, waiting to pounce on her."

"That'd be one helluva pounce." Flood laughed. "Maybe it's Jamesean—'Beast in the Jungle' and all that crap. Maybe her catastrophe is going to be the fact that no catastrophe ever happens to her."

"Aren't we getting a little far afield? How much longer are you planning to play this little game?"

"Only as long as necessary, Angel," Flood said with an infuriating blandness. "Only as long as necessary."

* * *

Jimmy and Marvin were on the lawn of the house up the street laboring with Jimmy's new car—a battered Ford in only slightly better shape than his old one. They had brought speakers out of the house and connected them to the car's radio and had turned the volume all the way up. The mindless bawling they called music bounced and echoed off the front of the houses and shook windows from one end of the block to the other. As they worked they had to scream at each other to be heard over the noise, but that was not as important as the fact that the music attracted attention—that everyone knew that they were out there doing something important.

And then, inevitably, Flood came sauntering down the street, hands in his pockets and a cigarette dangling from one corner of his mouth, though Flood rarely smoked. "Hey, man," he said to Jimmy, who had just come out from under the gaping hood of the Ford to stare at him truculently, "what's happening?"

Jimmy answered shortly, his face still suspicious, but his words were lost in a fresh blare of noise from the radio. Flood walked a few steps toward him, his face questioning, and Jimmy nervously backed up a step or two. Raphael had noticed that Jimmy's mouth often got him into more trouble than he could handle.

"What'd you say, man?" Flood asked pleasantly. "I didn't quite catch it." He spoke quite loudly.

Jimmy mumbled something, his eyes down.

"I'm sorry," Flood said over the music. "I still can't hear you." He went closer to Jimmy, who backed up a little farther.

"What's the matter with it, man?" Flood asked Marvin, who was struggling under the hood with the stubborn guts of the sick car.

Marvin answered shortly and then began to swear as his wrench slipped and his knuckles smashed against the solidity of the engine block.

"Ouch," Flood said, "I'll bet that hurts like a son of a bitch. Did you check the coil?" He pointed at something under the hood and murmured some instructions.

"Jimmy," Marvin shouted exasperatedly, "will you turn that fuckin' radio *down*?"

"What for?" Jimmy's tone was still belligerent.

"Because I can't hear myself think, for Chrissake."

Jimmy glowered at him.

Flood reached into the engine compartment and carefully disconnected a wire. The music stopped abruptly in mid-squawl. The sudden silence was stunning.

"Sorry," Flood said. "Wrong wire."

"What the hell you think you're *doin'*, man?" Jimmy screamed at him. He went to the side of the car and started to bang on one of the speakers.

Flood reattached the wire, and naked noise erupted into Jimmy's face. The pasty-faced young man flinched visibly and stepped back a few paces. "Jesus!"

The music stopped again.

"Hang on," Flood said. "I'll get it."

Jimmy approached the car again, and once again the full volume blasted into his face. "Aw, for Chrissake!" He climbed into the car and turned the radio off. "Hey, man," he said to Flood, "quit fuckin' around with my car, huh?"

"Shut up, Jimmy," Marvin told him, still leaning into the engine compartment.

"What the fuck you talkin' about?" Jimmy demanded. "It's my goddamn car, ain't it?"

"Okay." Marvin straightened up. "*You* fix the bastard then." He threw down his wrench.

"Come on, Marv," Jimmy pleaded, "you know more about this than I do."

"What's the problem with it?" Flood asked.

"Son of a bitch runs like a thrashin' machine," Marvin replied. "Half the time it won't start at all; and when it does, it sounds like it's tryin' to shake itself to pieces."

"Timing," Flood diagnosed. "You got a timing strobe?"

Marvin shook his head.

"Leon's got one," Jimmy offered hopefully. "You think you could fix it, man?" He looked at Flood with an almost sick yearning on his face.

"Shouldn't be too tough. I'll need that strobe, though."

"Lemme use your car, Marv," Jimmy said. "I'll go get it."

"Why not?" Marvin gave Jimmy his keys and then turned back to Flood. "Hey, man, what's your name?"

"Jake."

"I'm Marvin. This is Jimmy. Let's have a beer while we're waitin' for him to get back."

"Don't drink up all the beer, man," Jimmy protested.

"Get some more. Pick up the strobe and go over to the store an' get some more."

"I ain't got no money."

"Here." Flood took out his wallet and pulled out a bill. "Why don't you pick up a case?"

"Hey, Darla," Marvin yelled at the house, "bring out a couple beers, huh?"

Jimmy went to the curb and climbed into Marvin's car. Flood and Marvin went up on the porch and sat down as he pulled away. One of the girls, a blonde with stringy hair, brought out some beer, and they sat around on the porch, talking.

On the roof Raphael watched. He wished that Flood would get away from them. He felt strangely angered by the easy way Flood had insinuated himself into the rowdy, clannish group up the street. He was startled to suddenly realize that he was actually jealous. In disgust he pushed his chair away from that side of the house, rolled himself across the roof, and sat staring moodily into the alley at the back of the house.

He could still hear their voices, however, laughing and talking. Then they turned the radio on again, and some bawling half-wit began to sing at the top of his lungs about true love in a voice quavering with technically augmented emotion.

Raphael got up and stumped into his apartment. In part it was anger with Flood, but it was more than that, really. Raphael had never been particularly attracted to rock music. In the first place it was normally played at a volume about two decibels below the pain level, and in the second place he found the lyrics and the actual musical quality of the stuff absurdly juvenile—even simpleminded. He was quite convinced that most adolescents listened to it not so much out of preference, but rather so that other adolescents could *see* them listening to it. It was a kind of badge, a signal to other members of the tribe. There was something beyond that, however. Since his accident Raphael had rather carefully kept himself in an emotional vacuum. The extent of his injury had made that necessary. There were thoughts and feelings that he simply could not permit if he were to retain his sanity.

Even inside, however, the blaring music penetrated, and Raphael grew angrier. "The hell with that." He crutched to the bookcase and ran a finger across the backs of his tape cassettes. It was childish, but he was too irritated to care. "Let's see how they like *this*." He pulled out a cassette and clicked it into the player. Then he turned the volume up and opened the doors and windows.

The tape he played was a pyrotechnic work by Orff, an obscure German composer of the early twentieth century. It was quite satisfyingly loud, and the choral lyrics, in Low German and corrupt Latin, were suitably cynical and of course quite beyond the comprehension of the cretins up the street.

Raphael waited in the maze of naked sound.

After several minutes the phone rang.

"Yes?" he answered it.

"Don't you think that's a little loud?" Flood asked acidly.

"Not particularly. Sounds just about right to me. It pretty well covers certain undesirable noises in the community."

"Don't get shitty. Other people don't want to listen to that crap."

"What's the matter, baby? All your taste in your mouth?"

"Grow up. Turn the goddamn thing down."

"Just as soon as you persuade your new friends down there to turn down that garbage they're listening to."

"We aren't hurting anybody."

"Neither am I."

"Just turn it down."

"Stuff it." Raphael hung up.

The tape played through, and Raphael turned it off and went back outside.

Flood and Marvin were leaning under the hood of the car while Jimmy hovered anxiously behind them. The speakers were gone, and the neighborhood was silent.

"I think that's got it," Flood announced, straightening. "Give it a try."

Jimmy got into the car and started it. "Hey, wow!" he exulted. "Listen to that baby purr!"

There was a racking snarl up the street, and two of the motorcycles came down to the house, bumped up over the curb, and stopped on the lawn. Big Heintz and the skinny one Raphael had named Little Hitler dismounted and swaggered over to the car.

"You still fuckin' around with that pig?" Heintz demanded.

"Hey, Heintz," Jimmy said proudly, "listen to her now." He revved his engine.

Heintz cocked one ear toward the car. "Not bad," he admitted. "What was wrong with it?"

"Timing," Marvin told him. "Jake here spotted it right off."

"Jake?" Heintz looked suspiciously at Flood as if the inclusion of someone new into the group without his express permission was a violation of some obscure ethic.

"This is Jake," Marvin introduced him. "We got Leon's timing light, and he fixed the bitch in no time at all."

Jimmy backed his car into the street and roared off, tires squealing.

"You a mechanic?" Heintz asked Flood.

"I tinker a little now and then." Flood shrugged, wiping his scarcely dirty hands on a rag.

"Know anything about bikes?"

Flood shook his head. "I'm not into bikes."

"Where you from?"

"Detroit."

"Never been there."

"I wouldn't make a special trip just to see it."

"Let's have a beer," Heintz suggested, his manner relaxing a bit.

"You bet, Heintz," Marvin said quickly. "We got a whole case. Jake bought it." He hurried up onto the porch and yelled into the house. "Hey, Darla, bring out some beer, huh?"

Heintz draped a meaty arm over Flood's shoulders as they went up onto the porch. "What brings you way out here, Jake?" he asked in a friendlier tone.

"I'm on the run." Flood laughed shortly.

Heintz gave him a startled look.

"I don't get along with my family," Flood explained. "We all decided it'd be better if I kept about a thousand miles distance between us."

Heintz laughed harshly. "I *know* that feeling."

They gathered on the porch, and the women came out of the house. The sun was just going down, and they all sat around talking and drinking beer.

Jimmy roared up and down the street several times, showing off, then parked at the curb in front of the house.

The talk grew louder, more boisterous, and more people arrived or came out of the house. Raphael had never been able to determine exactly how many people actually lived in the big house, since the population seemed to fluctuate from week to week. Their relationships were casual, and it was difficult to determine at any one time just who was sleeping with whom. Sourly he sat on his rooftop and watched Flood insinuate himself into the clan. By the time it had grown dark, he had been totally accepted, and his voice was as rowdy and boisterous as any.

The party continued, growing louder and more raucous, until about eleven-thirty when two police cars arrived and the officers got out to break it up.

Flood came down the street, got into his car, and drove away. He did not even glance up at the rooftop where Raphael sat watching.

ii

The first of June fell on a Wednesday, and Raphael went in to work early. Normally he waited until about ten in order to avoid the rush of traffic, but the first of the month was different.

Heavy traffic still made him jumpy, and he was in a bad humor when he reached the store. Denise was inside, and she unlocked the door to let him in. "You're early."

"Mother's Day," Raphael replied shortly, crutching into the barnlike building. "I have to get home early to guard the mailbox."

"I don't follow that." She locked the door again.

"The welfare checks come today. It's also the day when I get a check from my bank in Port Angeles. The kids over there in Welfare City find unwatched mailboxes enormously fascinating on Mother's Day."

"Why don't you move out of that place?"

He shrugged. "It's not that big a thing. You just have to be careful is all."

"You want some coffee?"

"I thought you'd never ask."

They went back through the dimly lighted store to the cluttered workroom in the rear. It was very quiet in the big building, and shadows filled the corners and crouched behind the endless racks of secondhand clothes that reeked of mothballs and disinfectant.

"Is your friend still in town?" Denise asked as she poured coffee.

"Flood?" Raphael lowered himself into a chair. "Oh yes. The pride of Grosse Pointe still lurks in Fun City."

"Now that's exactly what I mean," she said angrily, bending slightly to bang down his coffee cup with her dwarfed arm.

"That's what you mean about what? Come on, Denise,

164

it's too early in the morning to be cryptic. I'm not even awake yet.''

''All those cute little remarks. You never used to talk that way before he came. When is he going to go away and leave us alone?''

''Us?''

''You know what I mean.''

Raphael smiled briefly. ''Sorry. I'm grumpy today. It's always a hassle on the day when the checks come. I'm not looking forward to it, that's all.''

''Why don't you just have your bank in Port Angeles transfer the money directly to your bank here?'' she asked him, sitting on the edge of the table. ''That way you wouldn't have to worry about it.''

Raphael looked up, startled. ''I never thought of that.''

''I think you need a keeper, Rafe. You're a hopeless incompetent when it comes to anything practical. What's he up to now?''

''Who? Oh, Flood? I'm not sure. He's playing games. He's going around introducing himself to all my neighbors. It's all very obscure and not particularly attractive. He says he's doing it to 'bring me out of my shell,' but I'm sure there's something else behind it as well. Jake Flood is a very devious young man.''

''I hate him.'' She said it flatly.

''You've never met him.''

''I never met Hitler, either—or Attila the Hun.''

''You're a very opinionated person, Denise.'' He smiled at her.

''He's going to hurt you, Rafe. I can see it coming, and I hate him for it.''

''No. He's not going to hurt me. Flood likes to manipulate people, that's all. I know him, and I know what he's up to. I can take care of myself.''

''*Sure* you can.''

''Little mother of the world,'' Raphael said fondly, reaching out and taking her misshapen little hand, ''you're going to rub raw spots on your soul if you don't stop worrying about all of us.''

"Well, I *care*, dammit!" She did not pull her hand away.

"You're cold," he noted, feeling the tiny, gnarled bones in the dwarfed hand.

"It's always cold. The other one's fine, see?" She reached out to put her other hand briefly on his wrist.

"Well." Raphael released her and reached for his crutches. "I guess I'd better get to work."

She sighed. "Me too, I suppose."

Raphael rose and crutched smoothly through the dim light to his bench and the pile of battered and broken shoes that awaited him.

He went home about eleven, and Flood was waiting for him. The top was down on the little red sports car, and Flood half lay in the front seat, his feet propped up on the opposite door.

"Loitering, Damon?" Raphael asked, coming up beside the car.

"Just watching your people. They're all out today, aren't they?"

"Mother's Day. They're waiting for the mailman."

"Mother's Day?"

"The day the welfare checks arrive. Big party night tonight. Let's go upstairs."

"Right." Flood climbed out of the car. "Is that why all the kids are out of school?"

"Sure. It's sort of like Christmas—very exciting. Lots of money and goodies and stuff."

"Nigger rich," Flood said as they climbed the stairs.

"That's one way to put it."

Later they sat by the railing, watching the street.

"Who's that kid belong to?" Flood asked, pointing at a long-haired fourteen-year-old with a permanent sneer on his face lounging against the light pole on the corner. "I don't think I've seen him before."

"He's a thief. He's probably looking for the chance to steal somebody's welfare check."

"You've seen him before?"

"I sure have. He stole my groceries once."

"He did *what*?" Flood was outraged.

Raphael told him about the incident with the cabdriver and the two bags of groceries.

"Slimy little bastard," Flood growled.

"That he is."

"Can I use your phone for a minute?" Flood asked, his eyes narrowing.

"You know where it is."

Flood went inside and then came back in a few minutes, a malicious smile on his dark face. He sat down again and watched the street.

"What are you up to now?" Raphael asked him.

"That'd spoil it. Just keep your eyes open."

Up the street at the house of Heck's Angels, Jimmy and Marvin came out and began tossing a Frisbee back and forth, casually walking down toward the corner where the kid stood.

Raphael suddenly had a horrid suspicion. "Look out, kid!" he shouted.

But it was too late. Jimmy and Marvin pounced on the kid and held him, laughingly avoiding his desperate kicks.

"What do you guys want?" the kid yelled at them. "Lemme go."

Marvin held the kid's skinny arms, and Jimmy squared off in front of him.

"Help!" the kid screamed. "Somebody help me!"

Jimmy hit him in the mouth.

"Help!" the kid cried.

Jimmy hit him again.

They pounded him for several minutes, and after he fell to the sidewalk, they kicked him in the stomach and face for a while. Then they sauntered across the street and glanced up at the rooftop.

"Good job!" Flood called down to them. "Thanks."

"Anytime, Jake," Marvin called back up, grinning. They went on back up the street, talking and laughing.

On the corner the kid pulled himself up, using the light

pole. His mouth and nose streamed blood, and his eyes were swollen nearly shut. "Dirty bastards!" he sobbed at the backs of the two who had just beaten him.

They turned and started back, and the kid ran, half crouched over, holding his stomach with both hands.

"Quite satisfying, wasn't it?" Flood said to Raphael, his eyes burning.

"It was disgusting. Sickening."

"Of course it was, but satisfying all the same. Right? I liked that little touch—the warning you gave him—just a moment too late. Nicely done, Raphael. Perfect timing. You get all the satisfaction out of watching the little bastard get the shit stomped out of him with no guilt attached to it at all, because you *did* try to warn him."

"You're contemptible."

"Of course I am." Flood laughed. "We're *all* contemptible. We all have these base, vile, disgusting little urges—revenge, hate, spite, malice. Each man's soul is a seething sewer. I just bring it out into the open, that's all. I take a certain pride in my disinterestedness, though."

"In your *what*?"

"That was for you, Raphael. I didn't give a shit about that kid one way or the other. You're the one who had a hard-on for him. Look upon me as an instrument of a vengeful God. The Archangel proposes, and Jake Flood disposes. Just be careful about the things you wish for while I'm around, though, because you'll probably get exactly what you want." His eyes were very bright now. "Admit it. Deep down in that part of your mind nobody likes to look into, you really enjoyed that, didn't you?"

Raphael started to say something, but suddenly could not, because it was true. He *had* enjoyed it.

Flood saw his hesitation and laughed, a long, almost bell-like peal of pure mirth.

And then the mailman came, and the streets below exploded with people. Impatiently, they waited on the sidewalk for him and literally grabbed the checks out of his hands as he approached. As soon as they had the checks, they dashed to their cars and raced away in a frenzy, as if the world might suddenly run out of money before they could convert the checks into spendable cash. "Get in the car! Get in the car!" mothers screamed urgently at their children, and their men hovered closely, even anxiously, over the women who held, each in her own two tightly clenched hands, that ultimate reality in their lives—the welfare check. For those brief, ecstatic hours between the time when the checks arrived and the time when they all watched in anguish as the seemingly vast wealth dwindled down to the last few paltry dollars that were surplus, the women were supreme. The boyfriends who had beaten them and sworn at them, ridiculed and cheated on them, were suddenly docile, even fawning, in the presence of the awful power represented by the checks. As the day wore on and so much went for rent, so much for the light bill, and so much for payments on this or this or that, the faces of the men became more desperate. Mentally, each man watched that huge stack of tens and twenties melt away like frost in the sun, and since he knew that he could only wheedle a third or even a quarter of what was left, his eyes grew wide with near panic.

But first there was the orgy of shopping, of filling the house with food. An hour or two after the checks arrived, the cars began to return, clattering and smoking as always, but filled with boxes and sacks of groceries. The children screamed and squabbled and ran up and down the sidewalks almost hysterical with excitement. They gorged themselves on candy and potato chips and swilled soda pop as fast as they could drink it, knowing that what they could not eat or drink today would be lost forever.

And then, when the food was in and the money orders for the bills were all bought and safely in the mail, the men took their women inside and, each in his own fashion, cajoled a share of the loot. It was only then that the parties started.

"My God!" Flood said, watching. "It's a circus down there. Does this happen every month?"

"Every month," Raphael told him. "It's Christmas and

New Year's Eve and the Fourth of July all rolled into one—
and it happens on the first of every month.''

The all-powerful women emerged from their houses,
contented and enormously satisfied that they had once again
provided bountifully for their dependents. The scrimping and
borrowing and hunger of the last week were forgotten in an
orgy of generosity and openhanded benevolence. For the
moment at least, they were all rich.

"Let's cruise around a bit," Flood suggested.

"What for?"

"Because you're taking root in that chair. It's unhealthy
to sit in one spot for so long. Let's away, my Angel, and
behold the wonders of Welfare City on payday. Call it research if you like—an observation of the loser at play.''

As he almost always did, Raphael succumbed in the end
to Flood's badgering. It was not so much that he accepted
his friend's feeble excuses, but rather that he, too, felt the
contagious excitement from the streets below. The thought
of remaining stationary while so much was going on became
unbearable under Flood's prodding.

And so they cruised in Flood's small red car, drifting
slowly up and down the streets of shabby houses with junked
cars sitting up on blocks in the yards and broken-down appliances and boxes of junk piled on the porches. The streets
were alive with people, and they sat on porches and lawns
drinking and laughing. Music blasted from a dozen radios
and record players, and packs of kids on bicycles rode wildly
up and down the streets.

"A good old-fashioned truant officer could have a ball
today," Flood observed.

"They don't seem to pay that much attention in Spokane.''

"Sure. After all, how much education do you need to be
able to sign a welfare check?''

They pulled up in front of a tavern on Broadway.

"Now what?" Raphael asked.

"Let's have a beer and take a look at party time in the
poor man's social club.''

"Why not?" Raphael dug his crutches out from behind the seat and they went in.

The first thing that struck them was the noise. The place seethed with people, most of them already drunk and all of them shouting.

Flood found a small table near the corner, got Raphael seated, and then went to the bar for beer. "Loud, huh?" he said when he came back.

"You noticed."

"What time do the fights start?"

Raphael looked around. "Hard to say."

An Indian shambled by their table with his mouth gaping open and a sappy look of bludgeoned drunkenness on his face.

"The old-timers were right," Flood observed. "They can't hold their liquor, can they?"

"He doesn't seem much drunker than anybody else."

"Really? I'd give him another five minutes before he passes out."

"He could surprise you."

"Let's get up a pool on which way he falls. I'd bet on north—that's the side of the tree the moss grows on."

"What's that got to do with it?"

"You know—child of nature, all that crap."

"Why not south then—the way the geese fly? Or east to west—with the rotation of the earth? Or west to east—with the prevailing winds?"

"Interesting problem. There he goes."

Raphael turned in his seat. The Indian had reeled against a wall and was sliding slowly to the floor, his eyes glazed.

"No bet," Flood said. "The son of a bitch passed out vertically."

An argument broke out at the pool table, and two drunken young men threatened each other with pool cues until they were separated.

Everyone was a big shot today, and loud arguments erupted about who was going to pay for the next round. The noise was stunning, and Raphael began to get a headache. "Had about enough?" he asked Flood.

"Let's have one more." Flood got up quickly and went back to the bar. As he turned, a glass in each hand, a tall black man with graying hair lurched into him, knocking one of the glasses to the floor.

"Hey, man," the black man apologized quickly, "I'm sorry."

Flood's eyes were flat and his expression cold.

"Let me buy you another."

"Forget it."

"No, man—I mean, it was me that spilled it."

"I said to forget it." Flood deliberately turned his back on the man to return to the bar.

The black man's eyes froze, and his face went stiff. He drew himself up as if about to say something, then looked around as if suddenly realizing how many whites were in the bar and where their sympathies would lie in the event of an argument. "Shit," he muttered, and cautiously made his way to the door, his face still carrying that stiff, defensive expression.

Flood returned to the table and put down the two beers.

"You could have let him buy," Raphael said.

"I don't like niggers. I don't like the way they look; I don't like the way they smell; and I don't like the way they're trying to niggerize the whole country."

"The man was only trying to be polite. You didn't have to shit on him."

"That's what they're *for,* Gabriel. The only reason they exist is to be shit on."

Once again Raphael felt that strange shock that always came when Flood let the other name slip.

"Look around out there," Flood went on, obviously unaware that he had called Raphael by the wrong name. "You've got a whole generation of white kids trying to wear Afros and speak in fluent ghetto. Something's radically wrong when white kids knock themselves out trying to look and sound like niggers."

"Ship 'em all back to Africa, huh?"

Flood grinned at him. *"Gotcha!"*

"Damon," Raphael said in exasperation, "quit that."

Flood laughed. "You're still as innocent as ever, Raphael. You still believe everything anybody says to you. You ought to know me better than that by now."

"May all your toenails fall out. Let's get out of this rattrap. I'm starting to get a headache."

"Right on." Flood drained his glass.

They got up and made their way through the seething crowd of half-drunk people between them and the door.

Outside, the sun had gone down and the streetlights were just coming on. They got into Flood's car and sat for a few moments, letting the silence wash over them.

"Great group," Flood said.

"Letting off steam. They build up a lot of pressure during the course of a month."

"Doing what?"

"Living, Damon. Just living—and waiting for the next check."

Flood started his car, and they wound slowly through the streets. "Haven't you had about enough of this sewer?" he asked finally.

"What's that supposed to mean?"

"Let's find some other town. Let's pack up and go on down to San Francisco—or Denver, maybe."

"What brought all that on?"

"The place is starting to irritate me, that's all." Flood's voice was harsh, almost angry. "You can only take so much of a place like Spokane. It's called Spokanitis. That's when you get sick of Spokane."

"I'm settled. I don't feel like moving just yet."

"Okay, Raphael." Flood's voice was strangely light. "It was just a thought."

"Look, Damon," Raphael said seriously. "I appreciate your coming here and all. You've pulled me through some pretty rough times; but if the town bothers you all that much, maybe you ought to cut out. We can keep in touch. Maybe by the end of the summer I'll want to try something new, but right now I'm just not ready to take on that much change. You can understand that.''

"Sure," Flood said, his voice still light. "Forget I said anything."

"When do you think you'll be leaving?"

"Oh no." Flood laughed. "I can stand it as long as you can.''

They pulled up in front of Raphael's apartment.

Across the street the light was on in Tobe and Sam's place, and Flood looked speculatively at the house. "Let's go see how the old boys are doing," he suggested, and bounded out of the car before Raphael could answer.

Uncertain of what he was up to, Raphael crutched along behind him toward the shabby little house.

The two old men had made some effort to clean the place, and they themselves were clean for the first time since Raphael had known them. There was still caked dirt in the corners, but the floors had been mopped and the woodwork wiped down.

They had been playing cribbage at the table in the dining room, and their cups held coffee. They were a little embarrassed by company and stood around, not knowing exactly what to say. Finally Tobe offered coffee.

"Wait one," Flood said quickly, and dashed out of the house again. He came back a moment later with a brown-bagged bottle of whiskey and set it down on the table. "Why don't we all have a drink instead?" he suggested, his eyes very bright.

Tobe and Sam sat at the table, looking at the bottle with a terrible longing on their faces.

"What do you think, Sam?" Tobe asked hesitantly.

"I don't know," Sam said, still looking at the bottle. "Maybe one won't hurt."

"I'll get some glasses." Tobe got up quickly.

In a fury, almost sick with rage, Raphael stood up, took his crutches, and stumped out of the house. Blindly, he went down the steps, jabbing down hard with the tips of his crutches. For a moment he actually hated Flood.

On the corner, in the pale glow of the streetlight, Patch stood watching him as he came out of the house. Then, after a moment when they had looked wordlessly at each other, he turned and went on silent feet out of the light and into the darkness, and then he was gone.

iii

Flood was in a foul humor when he came by a few days later, and he'd only been at Raphael's apartment for a few minutes before they were snapping at each other.

"Maybe!" Flood said. "Don't be so goddamn wishy-washy. Give me a date—some kind of approximation."

"I don't *know*. I told you before I'm just not ready for that kind of change yet. If this place bothers you so much, go ahead and take off."

"How can you stand this town? There's absolutely nothing to do here."

"All right." Raphael said it flatly. "I'm going to explain this once more. Maybe you'll listen this time. I've got some pretty damned big adjustments to make, and this is a good place to make them. The fact that there's nothing to do makes it all the better."

"Come *on*. You're fine. You're not going to adjust by just sitting still."

"I'm not sitting still. I'm in therapy. I'm still learning how to walk, and you want to drag me off to a town that's wall-to-wall hills. Have you got any idea how far I'd bounce if I happened to fall down in San Francisco?" It was the first time either of them had directly mentioned Raphael's injury, and it made him uncomfortable. It also made him angry that it was finally necessary. It was because of the anger that he went on. "That's the one thing you just can't understand, Damon—falling down. If *you* trip or stumble, you can catch yourself. I can't. And even if you *do* happen to fall, you can get up again. I can't. Once I'm down, I'm *down,* baby—until somebody comes along and helps me get back up again. I can't even bend over to pick up my crutches. I have nightmares about it. I fall down in the street, and people just keep on walking around me. Have you got the faintest idea how degrading it is to have to ask somebody to help you get up? I have to lie there and *beg* strangers for help."

Flood's face was sober. "I didn't realize. I'm sorry, Raphael. I guess I wasn't thinking. You *have,* I suppose?"

"Have what?"

"Fallen."

"What the hell do you think I've been talking about? Christ, yes, I've fallen—a dozen times. I've fallen in the street, I've fallen in hallways, I've fallen down stairs. Once I fell down in a men's room and had to lie there for a half hour before some guy came in and helped me up. Don't beat me over the head about moving until I get to the point where I can get back on my feet without help. *Then* we'll talk about it. Until then I'm going to stay right where I am, and no amount of badgering is going to move me. Now, can we talk about something else?"

"Sure. Sorry I brought it up."

They talked for a while longer, but Raphael's mood had turned as sour as Flood's, and both of them were unnecessarily curt with each other.

"I'll catch you later," Flood said finally, standing up. "All we're going to do is snipe at each other today."

"All right." Raphael also got up and crutched out onto the roof behind Flood.

At the railing he looked down into the street and watched Flood come out at the bottom of the stairs.

Next door Crazy Charlie was furtively putting out his garbage. His face brightened when he saw Flood. "Hi, Jake," he offered timidly.

Flood turned, changing direction in midstride without changing his pace. He bore down on Crazy Charlie and stopped only a few inches from the nervously quailing man.

"Henry," he said, his voice harsh, "I've been meaning to talk to you—for your own good."

Charlie's head swiveled this way and that, his eyes darting, looking for a way to escape.

"How come you shave your head like that, Henry?" Flood demanded. "It looks silly as hell, you know. And you missed a place—just over your left ear."

Horror-stricken, Charlie reached up and felt his head.

"And why don't you take a bath? You stink like cat piss all the time. If you can't keep the cats from pissing on your clothes, get rid of the goddamn things. And just who the hell are you talking to all the time? I've seen you talk for hours when there's nobody there. Do you know what they call you around here? Crazy Charlie, that's what they call you. They watch you through the windows and laugh at you because you're so crazy. You'd better straighten up, Henry, or they're going to come after you with the butterfly net and lock you up in the crazy house." Flood's voice was ruthless, and he kept advancing on the helpless man in front of him.

Quite suddenly Charlie broke and ran, stumbling up the stairs, almost falling.

"Nice talking to you, Henry," Flood called after him, and then he laughed mockingly.

Charlie's door slammed, and Flood, still laughing, went to his car.

Upstairs, Raphael caught one quick glimpse of Crazy Charlie's haunted face before the shades came down.

They did not go up again.

iv

Several afternoons later they were in the tavern again. Some need drove Flood to such places occasionally. They hadn't spoken of the incident with Crazy Charlie, nor had Flood raised again the issue of leaving Spokane.

The tavern was quieter this time and less crowded. The orgy of drunken conviviality that always accompanied Mother's Day had passed when the money ran out, and the losers had settled down to the grim business of grinding out the days until the next check came. The ones in the tavern spaced their drinks, making them last.

The only exception was the large table where Heck's Angels sat in full regalia—creaking leather and greasy denim. They drank boisterously with much raucous laughter and bellowed obscene jests. They all tried, with varying degrees of success, to look burly and dangerous.

Big Heintz, his purple helmet pulled low over his eyes, bulked large and surly at the head of the table like some medieval warlord surrounded by his soldiers, and drank and glowered around the tavern, looking for some real or imagined slight—some excuse to start a brawl. The others—Marvin, Jimmy, Little Hitler, and two or three more Raphael had seen but never bothered to put names to—glanced quickly at him after each joke or remark, looking for some hint of a laugh or expression of approval, but Big Heintz remained morose and pugnacious.

"Hey Jake," Marvin said to Flood, "why don't you two join us?"

Flood raised his glass in mock salute, but made no move to shift around from the table at which he and Raphael sat.

"Maybe he don't want to," Big Heintz rumbled, staring hard at Flood. Suddenly he turned irritably on Little Hitler, who had just punched the same song on the jukebox that he had already played three times in succession. "For Chrissake, Lonnie, ain't there no other fuckin' songs on that sumbitch?"

"I like it," Little Hitler said defensively.

The song was a maudlin lament by some half-witted cracker over his recently deceased girlfriend. Little Hitler sat misty-eyed, his thin, pimply face mournful as the lugubrious caterwauling continued.

"Shit!" Heintz snorted contemptuously when the song ended.

"I think he left out the last verse," Flood said, grinning.

"I never heard no other verses." Little Hitler sounded a bit truculent.

"I thought everybody knew the last verse. It's the point of the whole song."

"Well, I never heard it. How does it go?"

Flood looked up at the ceiling. "Let's see if I can remember it." And then he started to sing in his rich voice. The impromptu verse he added was cynical and grossly obscene. There was an almost shocked silence when he finished.

"Hey, *man*!" Little Hitler said in the almost strangled tone of someone mortally offended.

Suddenly Heintz burst out with a roar of laughter, pounding on the table with glee.

The other Angels, always quick to follow, also began to laugh.

Big Heintz's laughter was gargantuan. He kept pounding on the table and stomping his feet, his beefy face red and contorted. "You slay me, Jake," he finally gasped, wiping at his eyes. "You absolutely fuckin' slay me." And he roared off into another peal of laughter.

Flood's impromptu parody changed the tone of the afternoon. Big Heintz was suddenly in better spirits, and the Angels quickly became gleeful and sunny-tempered. Raphael had almost forgotten Flood's gift for parody, which had so amused him when they were in school. The Angels still swaggered back and forth to the bar for more beer or to the men's room to relieve themselves with their cycle chains and chukka sticks dangling from their belts and their eyes flat and menacing, but their mood was no longer one of incipient riot.

Flood pulled their table closer to that of the Angels and introduced Raphael as Rafe, casting one quick apologetic glance at him as he did.

Big Heintz watched Raphael hitch his chair around to the newly positioned table.

"Hey, Rafe," he said good-humoredly, "how'd you lose the pin?"

"Hit a train." Raphael shrugged.

''Hurt it much?'' Big Heintz asked, grinning.

''Scared it pretty bad.''

This sent Heintz off into another gale of table-pounding, foot-stomping laughter. ''You guys absolutely fuckin' *slay* me. Fuckin' absolutely *waste* my ass.''

The party went on for another half hour or so. Raphael watched and listened, but didn't say anything more. Finally he turned to Flood. ''I think I'll cut out.''

''Stick around,'' Flood urged. ''We'll go in a little bit.''

''That's okay. It's not too far, and I need some exercise anyway.''

''Don't be stupid.''

''I'm serious. I really want to walk for a bit. I've been riding so much lately that I'm starting to get out of practice.''

Flood looked at him for a moment. ''Suit yourself. I'll stop by later.''

''Sure.'' Raphael pushed himself up. Carefully, avoiding the tables and chairs, he crutched out of the tavern into the pale, late-afternoon sunlight.

It had rained that morning, and the streets all had that just-washed look. The air was clean, and it was just cool enough to make the exertion of walking pleasant.

The houses here were all turn-of-the-century style, and many of them had a kind of balcony or sitting porch on the second floor. Raphael thought that those porches might have been used quite frequently when the houses were new, but he had not seen anyone on one of them since he had come to Spokane.

Bennie the Bicycler rode past on his way to the grocery store.

Raphael kept walking, consciously trying to make his pace as smooth as possible. It was important to measure the stride. Too short and he stumped; too long and he had to heave with his shoulders. The idea was to kind of flow along.

It was farther back to his apartment than he had thought, and about halfway there he stopped to rest. He had not walked much since he'd bought the car, and he was surprised to discover that his arms and shoulders were tired.

The snarling roar of the motorcycles was several blocks away when he first heard it. He leaned against a tree and waited.

The three bikes, with Big Heintz in the lead, came charging down the street, popping and smoking as always. Oddly, or perhaps not, Flood was mounted on one of the bikes, and he didn't seem to be having much difficulty with it. Big Heintz had a vicious grin on his face as they roared by. Trailing behind the bikes were two of the Angels' clattering cars, and behind them Marvin was driving Flood's little red sports car. They toured the neighborhood slowly, letting themselves be seen.

Bennie the Bicycler came peddling back with two sacks of groceries balanced in the basket on his handlebars. The Angels came sputtering back and spotted him.

The original intention, if it had even fully formulated itself in Heintz's thick skull, was probably simply to buzz Bennie once and then go on, but Flood was aboard one of the bikes, and that was not enough for him. As he passed Bennie he suddenly cramped his front wheel over hard and drove in a tight circle around the man on the bicycle. Bennie wobbled, trying to avoid the snarling motorcycle. Big Heintz and Little Hitler, already halfway up the block, turned, came back, and followed Flood in the circling of the wobbling bicycle. Bennie's eyes grew wide, and his course grew more erratic as he tried to maintain control of his bicycle. The noise was deafening, and Bennie began to panic. With a despairing lunge he drove his bicycle toward the comparative safety of the sidewalk, but in his haste he misjudged it and smashed headlong into the rear of a parked car. With a clatter he pitched over the handlebars of his bicycle onto the car's trunk and then rolled off.

The front wheel of his bicycle was twisted into a rubber-tired pretzel, and the bags fell to the street and broke. Dented cans rolled out, and a gallon container of milk gushed white into the gutter.

With jackal-like laughter the Angels roared away, leaving Bennie sprawled in the street in the midst of his bargains. As he passed, Flood flickered one quick glance at Raphael, but his expression did not change.

Slowly, painfully, Bennie got up. Grunting, he began to gather the dented cans and moldy cheese and wilted produce. Then he saw the bicycle. With a low cry he dropped his groceries again and picked up the bike. He took hold of the wheel and tried to straighten it with his hands, but it was obviously hopeless.

Raphael wished that he might do something, but there was nothing he could do. Slowly he crutched on past the spot where Bennie stood in the midst of the garbage that had been his whole reason for existence, staring at the ruin of his bicycle. His lip was cut and oozed blood down onto his chin, and his eyes were filled with tears.

Raphael went by and said nothing.

When he got home, he went up the stairs and locked the door at the top.

Up the street the Angels were partying again, their voices loud and raucous. Flood was with them, and his red car was parked at the curb among theirs. Raphael went inside and pulled his curtains.

The party up the street ground on, growing louder and louder until about midnight, when somebody on the block called the police.

V

Toward the end of June the rainy weather finally broke, and it turned warm. The stunning heat of July had not yet arrived, and it was perhaps the most pleasant part of the year in Spokane.

Raphael found that the mornings were particularly fine. He began to arise earlier, often getting up with the first steely light long before the sun rose. The streets below were quiet then, and he could sit on his rooftop undisturbed and watch the delicate shadings of colors in the morning sky as the sun came up. By seven the slanting light was golden as it came down through the trees and lay gently on the streets almost like a benediction.

Flood came by infrequently now, although he often visited with Heck's Angels just up the street until the early hours of the morning. A kind of unspoken constraint had come between Raphael and Flood. It was as if some unacknowledged affront had taken place that neither of them could exactly remember but that both responded to. They were studiously correct with each other, but no more than that.

Raphael considered this on one splendid morning as he sat with his third cup of coffee, looking down over the railing into the sunlit street. He had placed his scanner in an open window, but it merely winked and twinkled at him as the city lay silent in sleep, with yesterday's passion and violence and stupidity finished and today's not yet begun. He felt strange about Flood now. Weeks before he had even experienced a sharp pang of jealousy when Flood had first begun to hang around with the Angels, but now he was indifferent. He noticed Flood's comings and goings at the crowded house up the street without much interest.

A movement caught his eye, and he turned slightly to watch.

Spider Granny, housecoat-wrapped and slapping-slipper shod, trundled down the other street on her morning pilgrimage to the porch where Sadie was already enthroned in ponderous splendor.

Ruthie, the retarded child, recognized her and bellowed a bull-like greeting from the playpen where she spent her days.

"There's Granny's little darling," Sadie's mother cooed. She bustled up onto the porch and fussed over the drooling idiot in the pen.

Sadie said nothing, but sat stolidly, her head sunk in the rolls of fat around her neck, and her face set in its usual expression of petulant discontent.

"She seems more alert today," Spider Granny observed hopefully. "She recognized me right off—didn't you, love?"

The idiot bellowed at her.

Sadie still said nothing.

"Are you all right, Rita?" Sadie's mother asked her. "You sure are quiet this morning. I'll fix us some coffee, and you can tell Mother all about it." She patted the idiot's head fondly and bustled on into the house. A few minutes later she came out with two steaming cups and offered one to her daughter.

Sadie did not move, and her face did not change expression.

"Will you take this?" her mother demanded irritably, bending over with the coffee.

Sadie sat, mountainlike in her gross immobility.

"Rita," Spider Granny said sharply. "Snap out of it." She set the coffee cups down on the porch railing and turned back to her daughter. "Aren't you feeling well, dear?" She reached out and touched the sitting woman.

The scream was enormous, a sound at once so vast and so shocking that it seemed to lie palpably in the street. Even the birds were stunned into silence by it.

Spider Granny backed away, her hands to the sides of her face, and screamed again, another window-shaking shriek.

The idiot in the playpen began to bellow a deep-throated bass accompaniment to her grandmother's screams.

Doors began to bang open up and down the street, and the losers all came flooding out in response to the primal call of Granny's screams. Mostly they stood watching, but a few went down to Sadie's house.

Sadie, sitting in vast and splendid silence, neither moved nor spoke, and her expression remained imperially aloof.

"District Four," the scanner said.

"Four."

"Fourteen-hundred block of North Birch. We have a report of a possible DOA on a front porch."

"Have you got an exact address?" District Four asked.

"The complainant stated that there were several people there already," the dispatcher said. "Didn't know the exact house number."

"Okay," Four said.

Spider Granny had finally stopped screaming and now

stood in vacant-eyed horror, staring at the solid immensity of her daughter. The idiot in the playpen, however, continued to bellow and drool.

More of the neighbors came down to stand on the lawn. The children came running to gape in silent awe. Chicken Coop Annie waddled down, and Mousy Mary scurried across the street.

Queenlike Sadie, sat to death, received in silence this final tribute.

Then the police arrived, and shortly thereafter the ambulance.

Bob the Barber drove up and pushed his way through the crowd on his front lawn. He spoke with the policemen and the ambulance drivers on the porch, but he did not touch his wife or even seem to look at her.

They struggled with Sadie's vast bulk, and it took two policemen as well as the two attendants to carry the perilously bending stretcher to the back of the ambulance.

The crowd on the front lawn lingered after the ambulance drove off, murmuring among themselves as if reluctant to leave. Two of the women led Spider Granny, weeping now, back up the street to her house, and the rest of the crowd slowly, reluctantly broke up. The children hung around longer, hoping to see something else, but it was over.

Bob the Barber sank into Sadie's vacant swing and sat, his gray face seemingly impassive, but Raphael could quite clearly see the tears that ran slowly down his cheeks.

The idiot in the playpen drooled and bellowed, but otherwise the street was quiet again.

From up the street, his black hair glistening in the sun, Patch came. Somber-faced, he passed the house where the idiot bellowed and the thin, gray-faced man mourned. He crossed the street and walked on past Mousy Mary's house. He glanced up at Raphael once. There seemed for an instant a kind of brief flicker of recognition, but his face did not really change, and as silently as always he passed on up the street and was gone.

Ave formosissima, gemma pretiosa, ave decus virginum, virgo gloriosa

i

They broke for lunch at noon as they usually did, and Raphael and Denise sought out a quiet place in the storeroom to eat. "You seem to be down lately," she said. "Is something bothering you?"

"Not really. A woman died on my block last week. That's always sort of depressing."

"A friend of yours?" she asked, her voice neutral.

"Not hardly. She was a monster."

"Why the concern then?"

"Her husband took it pretty hard. I didn't think he would."

"What did she die from?"

"She sat herself to death."

"She *what?*"

Raphael told her about Sadie the Sitter, and Denise sat listening. It was easy to talk to Denise. There was about her a kind of calmness, a tranquillity that seemed to promise acceptance of whatever he said. She was sitting in a patch of sunlight that streamed through a dusty window. He noticed for the first time as he spoke with her that her skin was not pale so much as it was translucent, and her sunlit hair was not really limp and dun-colored but was really quite thick and shaded through all the hues of blond from palest gold to deep ash. In repose, as it was now, her face was Madonna-like.

She looked up and caught him watching her. "Please don't stare at me, Rafe," she said, blushing slightly. Her tone, however, was matter-of-fact. "We don't do that to each other. We don't *avoid* looking at each other, but we don't stare. I thought you knew that." She turned slightly so that the dwarfed arm was hidden from him.

"I wasn't staring at that. Did you know that your hair isn't all the same color?"

"Thanks a lot. Now I've got something else to worry about."

"Don't be silly. Everybody's hair has different colors in places. Mine's darker at the neck and sides than it is on top, but you're seventeen different shades of blond."

"I'll get it all cut off," she threatened, "and start wearing a wig—bright red, maybe."

"Bite your tongue."

"Is what's-his-name still around?"

"Who? Flood? Yes, he's still here. I haven't seen much of him lately, though. He's found other diversions."

"Good. Let's hope it's a sign that he's getting bored and won't stay much longer."

"Be nice."

"No. I don't want to. I want to be spiteful and bitchy about him. I'd like to spit in his eye."

"Sweet child." He shifted around in his chair.

"There's something else, isn't there, Rafe?"

He grunted. "My caseworker's been on my case lately." It was an outrageous pun, but he rather liked it.

"I didn't know you had one."

"It's sort of semiofficial. I pick on her a lot, but she keeps coming back for more."

"You have to be very careful with those people, Rafe."

"If I could handle Shimpsie, I can sure as hell deal with Frankie."

"Who's Shimpsie?"

"She was the social worker in the hospital where they modified me." He told her the story of Shimpsie and of his daring escape from her clutches. "Frankie's definitely not in Shimpsie's league," he added.

"That's where you're making your mistake, Rafe. You won

once. You got away from this Shimpsie person, and now you've got a caseworker who seems to be no more than a cute little bubblehead. You're overconfident, and they'll eat you alive.''

"Frankie's hardly dangerous.''

"Don't kid yourself.'' Her pale face was deadly serious. "They're *all* dangerous.''

"Only if you want something from them. I'm more or less independent, so I don't have any handles on me. It makes Frankie crazy.''

"Their power goes a lot further than that, Rafe. The whole system is on their side. They have the police, the courts—everything—on their side. They can *make* you do what they tell you to do. They can put you in jail, they can tear your family apart, they can have you committed to an asylum. There's almost nothing they can't do to you. Isn't it a comfort to know that some little froth-head who spent her college years on her back and graduated with a solid C-minus average has absolute power over your life?''

"Frankie's not like that. She's more like a puppy.''

"Puppies have very sharp teeth, Rafe.''

"You've had bad experiences, I take it.''

"We've *all* had bad experiences. Caseworkers are our natural enemies. They're the cats and we're the mice. You want another cup of coffee?''

"That'd be nice,'' he said, smiling at her.

She got up and started to squeeze past him. There was a warm, almost sweet fragrance about her. When she was behind him, she touched his hair. "It *is* darker in places, isn't it?'' Her hand lingered on his head.

"Careful. It takes a week to untangle it.''

"I'd give my soul for curly hair like that.''

"It's vastly overrated.''

"Why don't you let it grow a little longer?''

"I prefer not to look like a dust mop.''

"You're impossible.'' She laughingly mussed his hair and scampered away.

"Rat!'' he called after her.

He felt good. For the first time in weeks he actually felt good. After work he ran a couple of errands and drove on home, still feeling in good spirits. The sun was warm, and the sky was bright. Ever since his accident he had become accustomed to a kind of dormancy, settling for the most part for a simple absence of pain, but now he began to perceive that somewhere—maybe a long way down the road yet, but someday certainly and inevitably—he would actually be happy again. It was a good feeling to know that.

A young woman he did not recognize was standing at the row of mailboxes at the front of the apartment. For an instant his chest seemed to constrict almost with fear. From a particular angle she almost exactly resembled Marilyn Hamilton. Then she turned, and it was all right. The similarity was not that great.

He got out of his car slowly in order to give her time to get her mail and go back inside, but she did not move. Instead, she stood looking somewhat distracted, one hand to her stomach, and her face turning suddenly very pale.

"Are you all right?" he asked.

She looked sharply at him with quick, hard suspicion. Then she saw the crutches and relaxed. "I think I'm going to faint," she announced quite calmly.

"Around here," Raphael said, loping toward her with his long, one-legged stride. "Hang on to the building." He led her around the corner to the stairs that went up to his rooftop. "Sit down. Put your head between your knees."

Gratefully, she sank down onto the bottom step and put her head down.

"Breathe deeply," he instructed.

"I know."

"Are you sick? I mean, do you want me to take you to a hospital or anything?"

"No. I'm just pregnant," she said wryly, lifting her head. "There's no cure for that except time—or a quick trip to a non-Catholic doctor."

"Is it—" He faltered. "I mean, it's not time or anything, is it?"

She grinned at him suddenly, her face still pale. "Either you aren't very observant, or you haven't been around very many pregnant women. You swell up like a balloon before you get to the point of the trip to the hospital. I'm getting a little hippy, but my tummy hasn't started to pooch out that much yet. I've still got months of this to look forward to."

"Are you feeling better now?"

"I'll be all right. It's a family trait. My mother used to faint all the time when she was carrying Brian—that's my kid brother." She got up slowly.

"Maybe you ought to sit still for a little longer."

"It's all passed now. Thanks for the help."

"You sure you're going to be all right?"

"I'll be fine. Do you live here?"

"Up there." He nodded his head at the steps.

"The penthouse? I wondered who lived there. Isn't it a little . . ." She glanced at the crutches.

"It's no particular problem."

"Well, I guess I'd better get back to cleaning my apartment. I think that whoever lived there before kept goats or something." She smiled at him. "See you." She went back around to the front of the building again.

Later, on his rooftop, Raphael thought about the girl. In some ways she seemed to be much like Marilyn, but there were differences. Her voice was lighter, and the expressions were different. And this girl seemed wiser, less vulnerable than Marilyn had been.

It surprised him that he could think about Marilyn now without pain or even the fear of pain that had locked away that part of his memory for so long. He found that he could even remember Isabel without discomfort. He experimented with the memories—trying consciously to stir some of the old responses, wondering almost clinically if there might be some vestigial remnants of virility left. But there were not, of course. Finally, disgusted with himself, he thought about other things.

Flood drove by late that afternoon and came up to the rooftop instead of stopping at the house where Heck's Angels lounged belligerently on the lawn, daring the neighbors to complain. Raphael resisted the temptation to make some clever remark about Flood's new friends. Things were uncomfortable enough between them already.

Flood leaned negligently against the railing as always. His face seemed strained, and his complexion was more sallow. There was something tense about him, almost as if somehow, in some obscure fashion, things were going wrong, and he was losing control—not only of the situation, but of himself as well. He smoked almost continually now, flipping the butts out to arc down into the street below and almost immediately lighting another. "I *hate* this goddamned town," he said finally with more passion than he'd probably intended.

"You don't have to stay."

Flood grunted and stared moodily down at the street. "It doesn't *mean* anything. This is the most pointless place in the whole damned universe. What the hell is it doing here, for Chrissake? What possessed them to build a town here in the first place?"

"Who knows? The railroad, probably."

"And the people are just as pointless as the town," Flood went on. "Empty, empty, empty—like the residents of a graveyard. They have no meaning, no significance. I'm not just talking about your losers—I'm talking about all of them. Good God, the vacancy of the place! How the hell can you stand it?"

"I grew up in a pretty vacant place, remember?"

"You're wrong. I saw Port Angeles. At the end of his life a man there can say, 'I cut down some trees and made some lumber. They took the lumber and built some houses with it.' That's *something*, for God's sake! What the hell can a man say about his life here? 'I buried my grandpa in 1958, my mother in seventy-two, and my old man in eighty-five; I contributed about eight tons of shit to the sewage-treatment plant; and they're going to bury me right over there in that dandy little graveyard on the other side of the river.' Fertilizer—that's all they're good for, fertilizer." He turned to

Raphael suddenly. "Well, by God, I decline to be a fertilizer factory for the greater glory of the shit capital of America. I've had it with this place."

"When do you think you'll be leaving?" Raphael asked, his voice neutral.

Flood grinned at him suddenly. "Gotcha again," he said.

"Damon," Raphael said in annoyance, "quit playing games."

"Oh no, Raphael," Flood declaimed. "You won't escape me so easily. I will hound you; I will dog your footsteps; I will harry you out of this vacuum and deliver your soul to the Prince of Darkness, who sits expectant in steamy hell. Double-dipped in vilest corruption shall I send you to the eternal fire and the loathsome embrace of the Emperor of the Inferno."

"Oh, that's good," Raphael said admiringly. "I thought you'd lost your touch for a while there. That was particularly fine."

"I rather liked it," Flood admitted modestly, and then he laughed, the mocking laughter that Raphael remembered so well, and his eyes glittered in the ruddy glow of the dying sun.

ii

And then in mid-July it turned suddenly hot. With no apparent transition from pleasant to unbearable, the temperature soared to the one-hundred-degree mark and stuck there. The streets shimmered like the tops of stoves, and lawns that were not constantly watered wilted and browned under the blasting weight of the swollen sun.

Sleep was impossible, of course. Even long past midnight the interiors of the houses on Raphael's block were like ovens. The losers sat on their porches or on their lawns in the dark, and the children ran in screaming packs up and down the streets. Fights broke out with monotonous regularity. Since they lived in continual frustration anyway, always on the verge of rage, the added aggravation of the stunning heat made the smallest irritation a *casus belli*.

Raphael's tiny apartment on the roof was unprotected from the sun for the largest part of the day, and the interior heated up like a blast furnace. The rooftop was unbearable under the direct weight of the sun. He lingered at work, finding refuge in the dim coolness of the barnlike store, and he helped Denise with the volumes of paperwork that were a part of her job.

The heat added a new dimension to his discomfort. Perspiration irritated the relatively new scar tissue on his hip, and he sometimes writhed from the phantom pain of the missing leg. The swimming that was a part of his therapy helped, but ten minutes after he had pulled himself out of the pool, he was sweltering again.

Only at night, when there was sometimes a slight breeze, could he find any kind of comfort. He would sit on his rooftop stupefied by lack of sleep and watch the streets below.

"Hello? Are you up there?" It was the girl from downstairs. She stood one midnight on the sidewalk in front of the house, looking up at the roof.

"Yes," Raphael said, looking over the railing.

"Would it be all right if I came up? I'm suffocating in there."

"Sure. The stairs are on the side."

"I'll be right up." She disappeared around the corner of the house. He heard her light step on the stairs, and then she came out onto the roof. "It's like a stove in my apartment," she said, coming over to where he sat.

"I know. Mine's the same way."

"I've got a fan, but all it does is move the hot air around. If I take off any more clothes, I'll get arrested for indecent exposure." She wore a light housecoat and kept her arms crossed tightly in front of her body.

"It's brutal," Raphael agreed, "and it's probably not going to get any better for a while."

Up the street one of Heck's Angels was fighting with his

girlfriend. They stood on the lawn, screaming obscenities at each other.

"Does that go on all the time?" the girl asked.

"More or less."

"Aren't there an awful lot of them living in that house?"

"Fifteen or twenty. It varies from week to week."

The young man up the street got into his car, slammed the door, and roared away. The girl on the lawn screamed at him until he turned the corner. Then it was quiet again.

The girl from downstairs sank down onto the small bench Flood had brought up to the roof a few weeks ago and laid her arm on the railing. "This is a fun neighborhood," she said dryly.

"That it is." Raphael thought briefly of telling her about the losers—simply to pass the long hours until things cooled down enough to allow two or three hours of sleep just before dawn—but he decided not to. He didn't know her that well, and he didn't want to take the chance of offending her.

They sat in the silent darkness on the roof, watching the children loitering on corners or creeping furtively around the houses.

"Is your husband out of town?" Raphael asked finally.

"I'm not married."

"I'm sorry. I just assumed—" He stopped, embarrassed.

"Because I'm pregnant? You don't have to be married to get pregnant. It happens in the best of families these days."

"I'm not being nosy. It's none of my business."

She laughed. "In a few months it'll be *everybody's* business. It's a condition that's pretty hard to conceal."

"Things'll work out."

"*Sure* they will. Nothing like a little unwed pregnancy to add spice to a girl's life."

A police car cruised by, and there was the usual scramble out the back doors of the neighborhood.

The night wound on, still hot and close, and, as the losers began to seek their beds for a few hours of restless sleep, the crickets and tree frogs began to sing the raspy song of summer.

Lulled by their song, Raphael caught himself half dozing in his chair a few times.

The girl talked about many things—mostly about the little town near the Canadian border where she had grown up. Her voice was soft, almost dreamy, and in his weariness Raphael listened not so much to her words as to the soft murmur of her voice.

"It's all so trite," she said. "It's almost like a bad soap opera. Poor little girl from Metalline Falls comes to the big city to go to college. Girl meets boy. Boy seduces girl. Girl gets pregnant. Boy runs away. I feel like the heroine in one of those gloomy nineteenth-century novels we used to have to read in high school. I guess I'm supposed to drown myself or something."

"I don't particularly recommend it. That river over there's got a fierce current to it. You could get yourself pretty thoroughly beaten up by all the rocks in the process."

"You've got a point there." She laughed. "Drowning yourself in the Spokane River could be a pretty hectic experience. I checked out a couple of those homes they have, but I don't think I'd like that. The girls all looked kind of pale and morning-sicky, and the nuns are very kind and maternal, but you can see that they disapprove. I just don't feel like being disapproved of right now."

"Do you plan to keep the baby?"

"Of course. I'm not going to go through all of this and then not have anything to show for it." She fell silent again.

Quite clearly, almost like the obvious plot of a piece of bad fiction, Raphael could see the girl's life stretched out in front of her. The baby would come at its appointed time; and because there was no alternative and a baby must be clothed and fed and suitably housed, the girl would turn to those social agencies that even now lurked on the horizon waiting for her. The agencies were very kind, very understanding, but they demanded of their clients a certain attitude. First of all there must be no pride, no dignity. The girl would have to learn to grovel. Groveling is one of the most important qualifications for welfare recipients. Once she had been taught to grovel in front of the desks of superior young ladies with minimal degrees in social science, she would almost be ready to join the ranks of the losers. With her pride and self-respect gone, she would be ready to accept the attentions of one of the horde of indolent young men who can smell a welfare check the way a shark smells blood. Her situation would quickly become hopeless, and her humor and intelligence would erode. She would begin to court crisis out of sheer boredom, and any chance for meaning or improvement would be blown away like dry leaves in the first blast of winter.

"Not *this* one," Raphael murmured more to himself than to any blind, impish gods of mischance.

"What?" the girl asked.

"Nothing. Do you have to stay here—in Spokane, I mean?"

She shrugged, and Raphael almost ground his teeth at the futility of the gesture. Indifference was the first symptom of that all-prevalent disease that infested the streets below. If she was to be salvaged, that would have to be attacked first.

"The hospitals are good," she said, "and I'm going to need a hospital before the year's out."

"There are hospitals everyplace, and it's not like you were going to be going in for brain surgery, you know."

She shrugged again. "Spokane's as good as any place—certainly better than Metalline Falls. I couldn't go back there."

"Why not?"

"I just couldn't. You don't know small towns."

"I know big ones," he said grimly.

The night was still warm, and the hot reek of dust still rose from the sun-blasted street below, and the crickets and tree frogs sang endlessly of summer as Raphael for the first time began carefully to attack the disease that until now he had only observed.

One night, several evenings later, Flood came by with some beer, and he sat on the rooftop with Raphael, talking dispiritedly.

"I thought you were a martini man," Raphael observed.

"I've fallen in with evil companions. Most of these cretins don't know a martini from a manhattan. Besides, it's too hot. Unless you swill it right down, a martini turns lukewarm on you in this kind of weather."

"Nothing like a belt of warm gin to fix you right up."

Flood shuddered.

Down at the corner a motorcycle snarled and popped as Big Heintz made his appearance. He pulled up onto the lawn of the house up the street and stepped off his bike. "The Dragons are in town," he announced to the Angels and their women, who lounged in wilted discomfort on the porch.

"Dragons?" Raphael murmured. "What's that big clown been smoking?"

"It's a rival gang," Flood told him, his voice tensing slightly. "They're from Seattle. They come over here every so often, and there's always a big fight."

"Whoopee," Raphael said flatly.

On the lawn Heck's Angels gathered around Big Heintz, all talking excitedly. "Who seen 'em?" Jimmy demanded.

"Leon was at the Savage House." Heintz flexed his beefy shoulders. "He seen a couple of 'em come in flyin' their colors. The Mongol was one of 'em."

"Wow!" Jimmy said. "They mean business, then. The Mongol is one bad motherfucker. I seen 'im a couple years ago. He absolutely *creamed* Otto."

"I ain't afraid of that fuckin' Mongol," Heintz declared belligerently.

"Anybody know where they're hangin' out?" Little Hitler asked.

"We'll find 'em." Heintz said it grimly.

Jimmy ran into the house and came back out with a length of heavy chain. He swung it whistling around his head.

"This is it," Big Heintz announced solemnly. "This is really it—the last and final war. Them fuckers been comin' over here every summer. They find one or two of our guys and stomp 'em, and then they all run back to Seattle. This time it's gonna be different. This is gonna be the last and final war." He strode up and down in front of the Angels, his beard bristling and his helmet pulled low over his eyes. "I sent out the word," he went on. "Everybody's comin', and I mean *everybody*. This time them fuckers ain't gonna find just one or two of us. They're gonna find *all* of us, and it's gonna be a *war!*"

They were all talking at once now, their voices shrill and excited. Several of the others ran into the house for chains and lengths of pipe and nail-studded baseball bats.

"You gonna take the Mongol, Heintz?" Jimmy asked breathlessly.

Heintz struck a dangerous pose. "Yeah. I'm gonna take that fuckin' Mongol. I'm gonna *waste* that motherfucker. Somebody get my gear." He tucked his thumbs into his belt and puffed out his chest. "Anybody that ain't got the guts for real war better split now, 'cause there's gonna be blood, man, *blood!*"

Flood was breathing rapidly. Suddenly he stood up.

"Where are *you* going?" Raphael demanded.

"I thought I—" Flood broke off.

"What in God's name is the matter with you, Damon? You don't really *care*, do you? All they're going to do is ride around looking tough, and then they'll all get drunk and spend the rest of the night telling each other how mean they would have been. Don't be childish."

Flood stared at him, hard-faced, and then he suddenly laughed. "Shit," he said, sitting back down. "This goddamn place is turning me into a ding-a-ling. You know? I was actually going down there. We've got to get out of this town, Raphael. It's starting to percolate our goddamn brains."

Two of the women came out of the house carrying Heintz's implements of combat. He stood very straight while they solemnly put his nail-studded leather vest on him. Then they wrapped his thick waist several times around with a long length of heavy, tinkling chain. One of the women knelt reverently and tucked a long, sheathed knife into his right boot while the other attached a heavy length of taped pipe to the chain around his waist.

"I want you women to take the kids inside and bolt all the doors," Heintz instructed. "Put stuff in front of the windows and don't turn on no lights. Them bastards might try to come here an' mess you up while we're gone."

With mute, almost worshipful respect Jimmy handed Big Heintz a can of beer. The big man tipped back his head, drained the can, and then threw it away.

"All right!" he roared. "Let's *go*!"

With a clatter of chains and clubs the Angels piled into their battered cars or aboard their motorcycles. Their engines roared to life, and with smoking exhausts and screeching tires they blasted off, grim-faced, to that last and final war their leader had promised them. Their women, equally grim-faced, gathered the shouting children and retreated to the house, slamming the door behind them.

Big Heintz, his meaty arms proudly crossed, stood in splendid solitude on the now-deserted front lawn. Then slowly, majestically, girt in steel and leather, he strode to his bike, mounted, and tromped savagely down on the starter crank.

Nothing happened.

He tromped again—and again—and yet again. The big Harley wheezed.

"Come on, you bastard," Big Heintz rasped hoarsely. "Come on, *start*!"

For ten minutes Big Heintz tromped, and for ten minutes the big Harley stubbornly refused to start. "Son of a bitch!" Heintz gasped, sweat pouring down his face. "Come on, *please* start!"

Finally, in desperation, he grasped the handlebars and

pushed the heavy machine into the street. Running along-side, he pushed the balky bike along the empty street in the long-vanished wake of his departed warriors. At the end of the block he pushed it around the corner and was gone.

The street was silent again except for the strangled sound of Flood's muffled laughter drifting down from the rooftop.

iv

"I'm not the least bit sorry for her," Denise said. "It's her own fault."

"Come on, Denise," Raphael objected.

"Come on, my foot. There's a little pill, remember? If a girl gets pregnant these days, it's because she *wants* to get pregnant. It's just a cheap ticket to an early wedding. I'm glad it didn't work. Next time she'll know better."

"She isn't that kind of girl."

"Really? Then how come she's got a big belly?"

"Don't be coarse."

"Oh, grow up, Rafe," she said angrily, slapping her dwarfed hand down on the table in irritation. "If she's such a nice girl, why didn't she keep her legs crossed? Why are *you* so concerned about what happens to some dim-witted trollop?"

"She's not a trollop. That kind of thing can happen. Young men can be very persuasive sometimes. Don't be so Victorian."

"You haven't answered my question." Her pale face was flushed. "Why are you so interested in her?"

Raphael took a deep breath. "All right," he said finally. "There's a disease on my street. It's a combination of poverty, indifference, stupidity, and an erosion of the will. You could call it the welfare syndrome, I suppose. The people are cared for—they get a welfare check and food stamps. After a while that welfare check is the only important thing to them. They live lives of aimless futility—without meaning, without dignity. Society feeds them and puts them in minimal housing, and then it quite studiously tries to ignore the fact that they exist. But people are more than cattle. They need more than a bale of hay and a warm stall in some barn. The people on my street turn to violence—to crisis—in an effort to say to the world, 'Look at me. I'm here. I exist.' I'd like to salvage just one of them, that's all. I'd like to beat the system just once. I'd like to keep one of them—just one—out of the soft claws of all those bright young ladies you warned me about—the ones who smother lives with welfare checks like you'd smother unwanted kittens with a wet pillow. *That's* what my interest is.''

''You're trying to save the world,'' she said with heavy sarcasm.

''No. Not the world—just one life. If I can't salvage just one life, I don't see much hope for any of us. The social workers will get us all. That's what they want, of course—to get us all—to bury us all with that one universal welfare check—to turn us into cattle.''

''And she's pretty, of course,'' Denise said acidly.

''I hadn't really paid that much attention.'' That was not entirely true. ''She's a human being. Frankly, I wouldn't give a damn if she looked like Frankenstein.''

''But she *doesn't* look like Frankenstein, does she?'' Denise bored in.

''I didn't notice any bolts sticking out of her neck.'' Raphael was starting to get tired of it.

''Why don't you *marry* her then?'' she suggested. ''That'd solve everything, wouldn't it?''

''Don't be silly.''

''It's a perfect solution. You can marry her, and you can save her from the goblin social workers. You legitimize her bastard, and then you can spend the rest of your life looking for the bolts. I wouldn't worry too much about that—'' She pointed at his missing leg. ''After all, a girl in her situation can't afford to be *too* choosy, can she?''

''Why don't we just drop this?''

''Why don't we just drop the whole damned thing?'' she said hotly. ''Why don't you get back to work? We're not paying you to sit around and drink coffee and philosophize about saving the world; we're paying you to fix shoes."

His face tightened, and he got up without saying anything. He grabbed his crutches and stumped back toward his workbench.

"Rafe!" Her voice was stricken. He heard her feet, quick and light on the floor behind him, and then she had her arms around him and her face buried in his chest. He fought to keep his balance. "I'm sorry," she wailed. The tiny hand, twisted and misshapen, clutched the fabric of his shirt at the shoulder, kneading, grasping, trying to hold on. He was surprised at how strong it was.

Denise cried into his chest for a few moments, and then she turned and fled, her face covered with her normal hand.

Raphael stood, still shifting his weight to regain his balance, and stared after her, his face troubled and a hollow feeling in his stomach.

He was still profoundly troubled when he got home that afternoon. He sat for several minutes in his car, staring vacantly out the window.

Hesitantly, old Tobe came out of the house across the street and walked over to Raphael's car. For once he did not seem particularly drunk. "Hello, Rafe," he said, his foghorn voice subdued.

"Tobe."

"You think you could come over to the place for a minute, Rafe?" Tobe asked, his tone almost pleading. "Old Sam's took sick, an' I'm awful worried about him. I don't know what the hell to do."

"How do you mean sick?" Raphael asked, getting out of his car.

"He's just layin' on that couch in the dinin' room there," Tobe said. "He can't get up, an' he talks funny—like he can't quite get the words put together right."

"Let's go." Raphael started across the street.

"I don't think it's nothin' very serious," Tobe said hopefully. "Old Sam's as strong as a horse. He just needs some medicine or somethin' to get him back on his feet."

"You guys drinking again?" Raphael asked, carefully going up the steps onto the porch.

"Not like before. We cut way back. We don't even really get drunk no more."

The little house was almost as filthy as it had been the first time Raphael had seen it. The yellow dog stood in the center of the living room and barked as Raphael entered.

"Shut up, Rudy," Raphael said.

"Go lay down," Tobe ordered the dog.

Rudy gave one last disinterested bark and went back into the dining room.

Sam lay on the rumpled daybed in the dining room partially covered by a filthy quilt. He recognized Raphael and tried to smile. "Hi, buddy," he said weakly in his wheezy voice. His left eye was half-closed, and the left corner of his mouth hung down slackly.

"Hi there, Sam." Raphael steeled himself against the smell and went to the side of the bed. "How you feeling?"

"Funny, kinda." Sam's words were slurred.

Raphael reached down and took hold of the old man's left hand. "Squeeze my hand, Sam."

"Sure, buddy."

The hand in Raphael's grasp did not move or even tremble.

"How's that?" Sam asked.

"That's fine, Sam." Raphael gently laid the hand back down.

"All right?" Sam slurred. " 'M I gonna be all right?"

"Sure, Sam." Raphael turned and crutched toward the living room, motioning with his head for Tobe to follow.

"You come back—real soon now, buddy," Sam said haltingly, and his head fell back on the pillow.

"Can you figure what's wrong with 'im?" Tobe asked anxiously in a low voice.

"We'd better call an ambulance."

"No!" Tobe shook his head. "He don't want no more hospitals. He told me that when we come outta that detox place after I got sick that time."

"This is different."

"No," Tobe said stubbornly. "He said no more hospitals."

"Tobe, I think he's had a stroke. He could *die* in there if we don't get him to a hospital. His whole left side's paralyzed."

Tobe stared at him for a moment. "Oh God," he said. "I was afraid that's what it was. Poor old Sam. What are we gonna do, Rafe?"

"We're going to call an ambulance. Sam's got to see a doctor right away."

"All right, Rafe." Tobe's narrow shoulders slumped. "Anything you say. You think he's gonna die?"

"I don't know, Tobe. I'm not a doctor. I'll go call an ambulance."

"Okay, Rafe." Tobe's voice was broken. Tears had begun to fill his eyes and spilled over, plowing dirty furrows down his cheeks.

Raphael went out quickly and crutched across the street to call the ambulance.

V

It was early, very early, even before the first faint hint of dawn. Raphael had endured the heat until about two in the morning when the breeze had finally turned cool, and then he had gone to bed. It seemed that he had only slept for a few minutes when he heard the faint, muffled banging on the locked door at the top of the stairs. Groggily, almost sick with the heat and the lack of sleep, he fumbled his way into his pants and reached for his crutches. The leather cuffs that fit around his forearms seemed cold, even clammy, and he shivered slightly at their touch.

"Who's there?" he asked when he reached the locked door.

"It's me." Flood's voice came from the other side. "Unlock the goddamn door." His words seemed mushy, thick.

"Damn!" Raphael muttered, slipping the latch. "Come

on, Damon," he said, opening the door, "I'm tired, and I've got to get some sleep."

Flood was bent slightly, and his hands were pressed against his ribs. Raphael could not see his face in the dark stairwell. "Let me in, dammit." He moved into the light, and Raphael could see the blood on his face.

"What happened, Damon?"

"I got hit with a chain," Flood said thickly, "and kicked in the ribs for good measure. Can I sit down?"

"Come on in." Raphael stepped back awkwardly. "Let me have a look at that cut."

Flood lurched across the roof to the apartment, went in, and sank carefully on the couch. There was a long, bruised cut on one side of his forehead, just above the eye, and his lip was cut and swollen. The blood had run down the side of his face and dried there. His olive skin was greenish, and little beads of perspiration stood out on his face. His breathing was shallow, and he kept his hands pressed to his ribs on the right side.

"Let me get some things and clean you up," Raphael said. He turned and went into the bathroom. He got a washcloth and a small bottle of antiseptic. He juggled them around until he could hold them between his fingers and then crutched back out to the kitchen. "What happened?" he asked from the sink where he ran cold water on the cloth.

"We went out to visit scenic Hillyard—a very unfriendly part of town. We found the Dragons, and Big Heintz got his last and final war. Jimmy and Marvin are in the hospital, and Heintzie's bleeding out of his ears. A most unsavory group, the Dragons." He laughed slightly and winced. "I think I've got a couple of cracked ribs."

"Why are you running with that bunch anyway?" Raphael demanded, going to the couch and beginning to carefully wash away the caked blood on Flood's face.

"For laughs. All that bully-boy bravado is sort of amusing." Flood's voice was muted and quavered with shock.

"How much fun are you having right now?"

"Not much." Flood winced and stifled a groan.

"This is going to hurt." Raphael carefully started to clean the cut.

"You're right." Flood said it through his clenched teeth.

"That's going to need some stitches," Raphael said, looking at the cut. "You want me to take you to the hospital?"

"You're going to have to, Raphael," Flood said shakily. "I damn near passed out a couple times on my way down here. I dropped Heintzie off up the street, and this was as far as I could make it. The big clown bled all over my front seat. They got him down and kicked him in the head a time or twelve. Jesus!" Flood doubled over, holding his side. "That hurts like hell."

"Don't move around too much. If those ribs are broken, you could puncture a lung."

"You're a little bundle of good news, aren't you?"

"Let me throw on a shirt and a shoe." Raphael went into the bedroom.

"I need a gun," Flood said through the door. "The bastards wouldn't have gotten me if I'd had a gun."

"That's a real sensible approach you've got there." Raphael was lacing up his shoe. "You shoot somebody, and they'll lock you up forever. Why don't you just stay away from those half-wits instead?"

"Nobody's going to run Jake Flood off. I'll go where I damn well please and with whoever I damn well please, and the next time some greasy punk comes at me with a chain, I'll make him eat the damned thing."

"You're getting as bad as they are." Raphael came out into the living room again.

"Nobody's going to run me off. I'll get a gun and then I'll make it my personal business to obliterate every one of those bastards."

"Damon," Raphael said firmly, "knock off this bullshit about guns. You don't know anything about them in the first place—and do you actually think you could deliberately pull the trigger on a man? I had to shoot a sick cat once, and I couldn't even do *that*."

"You're different from me, Raphael."

"Not *that* different. It takes a special kind of sickness to shoot a fellow human being, and you're not that sick."

Flood coughed and then he groaned slightly. "I'm pretty sick right now." He was holding his ribs tightly. "All I'll need is a little practice—a bit of plinking."

"Plinking beer cans and shooting people are altogether different, Damon."

"I wasn't thinking of beer cans." Flood's eyes were flat.

It was useless to talk with him. Raphael could see that. Maybe later, when he had calmed down, there might be some hope of getting through to him, but right now he was too angry, too hurt, too affronted and outraged by the beating even to be rational.

"Can you make it downstairs?" Raphael asked. "There's no way I can help you."

"I'll make it." Flood got up from the couch carefully and went back out, still half bent over.

Raphael followed him. "Get into my car," he said when they reached the street. "You aren't going to do those ribs any good trying to fold yourself into that sports car, and I can't work the clutch anyway."

"All right." Flood slowly got into Raphael's car.

Raphael went around to the other side, got in, and started the motor.

Flood was still holding his ribs, and he had his head laid back on the seat. "I've got to get a gun," he said.

vi

After work on Thursday, Raphael gave Denise a lift home as he usually did when he worked late. Things had been a bit strained between them since her outburst the week before, even though they both tried to behave as if the incident had not happened.

"Would you like to come up for coffee?" she asked routinely when he pulled up in front of her apartment house.

She did not look at him, and her tone indicated that she did not expect him to accept the invitation.

But because he genuinely liked her and wanted to bury the uneasiness between them, he did not, as usual, start looking for some excuse to beg off. "Sure. For once I don't have a thing to do when I get home."

She looked at him quickly, almost surprised. "Let's go then, before you have time to change your mind."

Her apartment was on the second floor in the back. The building was clean, although the carpeting in the hallway was slightly worn. Denise seemed nervous as she unlocked her door. "The place is a mess," she apologized as they went in. "I haven't had time to clean this week."

It was cool and dim inside, the drapes drawn against the blast of the summer sun. The air was faintly scented with the light fragrance she wore—a virginal, almost little-girl perfume that he noticed only when he was very close to her. The apartment was small and very clean. Probably every woman alive has declared that "the place is a mess" before escorting someone into her living quarters for the first time. Denise had a surprising number of books, Raphael saw, and they ranged from light fiction to philosophy with a fair smattering of poetry thrown in. She also had a small record player, and he saw a record jacket. Rather strangely, Denise seemed to have a taste for opera—Puccini in this case.

She led the way into the small kitchen, turned on the light, and pulled a chair out from the table for him. "Sit down. I'll put the pot on."

Raphael eased himself down into the chair and set his crutches against the wall behind him.

At the sink Denise was nervously rinsing out her coffeepot, holding it in her left hand and leaning far forward to reach the faucet handle with the dwarfed hand. She dropped the pot with a clatter and stepped back quickly to avoid the splash. "Damn. Please don't watch me. I'm not very good at this. I don't get much company."

He looked away, smiling.

She put the pot on the stove, came over, and sat down at

the table across from him. She carefully turned so that her right arm was hidden. "I'm going to say something. Don't try to stop me, because this is hard enough to say without being interrupted."

"Okay," he said, still smiling at her.

"I want to apologize for last week. I was being bitchy and there wasn't any excuse for it."

"Forget it. Everybody's cranky right now. It's the heat."

"The heat didn't have anything to do with it. I was jealous—it was just that simple."

"Jealous?"

"Are you blind, Rafe? Of course I was jealous. As soon as you started talking about that girl, I turned bright green all over—I know, there's never been any reason—I mean, there's nothing—no hint or anything that gives me any excuse to feel that way, but I did. I can't help it. It's the way I am."

"Denise—" he started.

"Don't patronize me, Raphael. In spite of everything I'm a woman. I'm not experienced at it or anything, but I *am* a woman, and I *do* get jealous."

"There's no reason to feel that way. There's nothing like that involved. There couldn't be, of course."

"Don't be stupid. Do you think that"—she gestured vaguely at his crutches—"really makes any difference at all? You're intelligent; you're gentle; and you're the most beautiful person I've ever seen." She stopped quickly. "I'm making a fool of myself again, aren't I?"

On the stove the coffeepot started to percolate.

Raphael took a deep breath. It had been bound to happen, of course—someday. It was one of the risks he had taken when he had decided to try to live as normally as possible. Sooner or later it had been bound to happen. "Denise." He tried to keep his voice as neutral as possible.

"Don't try to smooth it over. It's your life, after all. I was stupid even to build up any hopes or anything. Look at me. I'm a freak." Her tone was harsh. She was punishing herself. She turned and laid the tiny hand on the table in plain sight. "Like I say, it's your life. If that girl's attractive to you, go ahead. It's none of my business. I just hope we can still be friends after all my stupidity.''

"Denise, there's no real point to all of this. In the first place you're not a freak, and I don't want to hear any more of that kind of crap. In the second place I'll be your friend no matter what. You're stuck with me. You're one of the few people in the world I care anything about. If it hadn't been for you, I'd still be hiding from the world in that apartment of mine. Before I met you, I'd managed to cut myself off from everybody. I was pretty well down the road toward becoming one of those bitter, reclusive cripples you see once in a while. At least I've managed to get past that part of it.''

"All right, that's something, I suppose. Now that you realize that a leg more or less doesn't have anything to do with what you really are, you ought to be able to pick up your life where you left off before the accident. Why don't you go back to school? I'm sure you don't plan to spend the rest of your life fixing shoes. You'll be able to have a career, a wife, a family—the whole bit.''

"Denise—''

"No. Let me finish. I knew from the start that you'd get over it—adjust to it—and I knew that when you did, you'd go back to being normal again. I just let myself get carried away, that's all. I had you all to myself. A girl like me can't really compete with normal girls—I know that. I've never even tried. Do you know that I've never had a date?—not once in my whole life? No one has ever taken me to the movies or out to dinner or any of it. Anyhow, I began to think that because we were both—well, special—that somehow, when you got over it all, you'd look around and there I'd be. It was foolish of me, of course. If you really like this girl you met, *do* something about it. Just please don't stop being my friend is all.''

"Denise, I don't think you understand. I'm not going to go back to being what you call 'normal' again. There was never any question about that part of it. I lost more than just a leg in that accident, so all the things you've been talking about just aren't really relevant. I'm interested in that girl for exactly the reasons I said I was—I want to salvage one human life. I don't want her to become a loser. And I'll always be your friend—but that's all. Maybe I should have told you earlier, but it's not exactly the sort of thing you go around bragging about.''

She was staring at him, her face stricken and pale. Suddenly she was out of her chair and was cradling his head in her arms, pressing him tightly against her body. ''Oh, my poor Angel,'' she sobbed.

Why was it always ''Angel''? Why was that always the first word that came to people's lips? Why that and not something else?

She held him for a long time, crying, and then she turned and fled into her bedroom, slamming the door behind her. He could hear her still crying in there.

After a few minutes he took his crutches, got up, and went to the closed door. ''Denise?''

''Go away. Just go away, Rafe.''

He went back into the kitchen, turned off the coffeepot, and then quietly left her apartment.

When he got home, old Tobe was sitting on the porch of the shabby little house across the street. A half-full wine bottle sat beside him, but he did not seem to be all that drunk. More than anything right now Raphael did not want to be alone. He went across to the little man. ''How's Sam?'' he asked.

''He's dyin', Rafe. Ol' Sam's dyin'. They found out he's got the lung cancer, too.''

''Aw, no. I'm sorry, Tobe.''

''They got 'im in a nursin' home out in the valley,'' Tobe went on quietly. ''I went out there an' seen 'im today. He told me he don't want me comin' to see 'im no more. We been together for damn near twenty years now, an' now he says he don't wanna see me no more.'' The little man shook his head.

''I'm really sorry, Tobe.''

Tobe looked up, his eyes filled with tears. ''How come he

done that, Rafe? How come ol' Sam said a thing like that to me after all these years?''

''I don't know, Tobe.''

And then Tobe bowed his face into his gnarled hands and began to cry.

Raphael gently laid his hand on the little man's shaking shoulder, and then, because there was nothing else he could do, he turned and started toward the street.

Patch stood at the corner in the twilight watching him, his dark face set in that impenetrable expression of stony melancholy.

Raphael looked at the solitary figure for a moment and then crutched slowly across the street to his apartment house.

By the time he reached the roof, Patch was gone.

vii

Frankie's tan was progressing nicely, and she seemed quite proud of it.

''You're beginning to look like an old saddle,'' Raphael told her as she came out on the roof.

''Thinking about taking a ride?'' she asked archly.

''Knock it off, Frankie. That sort of remark makes you sound like a hooker.''

''You're the one who started all the cute stuff. I can be just as tough as you can, Raphael. I know all sorts of dirty words in Italian.''

''I'll bet. Am I in trouble again?''

''Not that I know of. Have you been naughty lately?''

''That's why you usually come by—to chew me out for something.''

''That's not altogether true, Raphael.'' She sat on the little bench. ''Sometimes I come by just to visit—and to get away from all those losers I have to deal with day in and day out.''

Her use of the word startled him. As closely as he could remember, he had never discussed his theory with her.

''You're one of my few successes,'' she went on moodily.

"And you did it all by yourself. You didn't enroll in any programs, you didn't go to vocational rehab, you don't have a support group, and you haven't once cried on my shoulder. You cheated, Raphael. You're a dirty rotten cheater. According to all the statistics, you should be a basket case by now. Do you have any idea how many hours I spent studying statistics in school? I *hated* that course. I passed it, though. You have to if you want your degree."

"Anomalies, Frankie. Your course didn't teach you about anomalies—probably because they shoot statistical theory in the butt."

"Explain."

"An anomaly is an unpredictable event."

"I know what it means."

"Groovy—or is that gravy? We're way ahead then. Statistics are used to predict things. Your profession is almost totally dependent on an ability to predict what's going to happen to people, isn't it?"

"Well—sort of."

"I'm not a basket case because I'm an anomaly. I beat the odds."

"But the question is *how*. If I could find out how you did it, maybe I could use it to help other people."

"How does sheer, pigheaded stubbornness grab you?"

"That depends on what you're being stubborn about. I like a certain amount of persistence." She rolled her eyes wickedly.

"Never mind that. It's too hot right now." He thought of something then. He hadn't really intended to tell anybody about it—not Flood certainly—but Frankie was a professional, and professionally she was one of the enemy. He liked her, though, and he felt that she deserved a sporting chance. It wouldn't really be sportsmanlike to potshoot Frankie off a fence rail when she wasn't looking. "I met a girl," he told her.

"Are you being unfaithful to me, Raphael?"

"No. You more than satisfy my lust, twinkie butt."

"Twinkie-butt?" she objected.

"You've got an adorable fanny."

She stood up, thrust out her bottom, and looked back over her shoulder at it. "Do you really like it?" she asked, actually sounding pleased.

"It's dandy. Anyhow, there's this girl—"

"A *relationship*?"

"That's bullshit, Frankie. Say what you mean. Don't babble about people having a 'relationship.' Use the right term. They're shacking up."

"That's crude."

"Isn't that what they're really doing?"

"Well—yes, I suppose so, but it's still a crude way to put it."

"So beat me."

"You want me to? Really?"

"Quit. I met a girl and she's pregnant—without benefit of clergy. She's right on the verge of going down to your office to apply for welfare."

Frankie took out her notebook. "What's her name?" She was suddenly all business.

"Jane Doe."

She almost started to write it down. "Raphael, this is serious. Don't kid around."

"I'm not kidding, Frankie. I'm dead serious about it. I won't tell you her name, and I won't tell you where she lives."

"Why?"

"Because I'm not going to let you ruin her life."

"She needs us, Raphael."

"Statistically? I'm going to make another anomaly out of her, Frankie. I'm going to train her to make it on her own—without you."

She threw her notebook across the roof, jumped to her feet, and began yelling at him in snarling, spitting Italian, waving her arms and shaking her fingers in his face. It was fairly obvious that she was not talking about the weather.

He sat grinning impudently at her.

"You dirty, rotten, miserable son of a bitch!"

"Why, *Francesca*," he said, "I'm shocked at you. Don't you love me anymore?"

She stormed across the roof, picked up her notebook, and bolted down the stairs, slamming the door behind her.

He didn't even think. The fact that his crutches were leaning against the railing fifteen feet away did not even cross his mind. He had meant to irritate Frankie—to make her think. He had not meant to hurt her.

It was the most natural thing in the world to do. He stood up, intending to follow her, to call her back.

And of course he fell.

His stomach suddenly constricted in a moment of icy terror. He was completely alone on this roof. It might be days before anyone came up those stairs.

"Frankie! Help me!" His voice had that shrill note of panic in it that more than anything else strikes at the ears of others.

He heard her running back up the stairs. "Raphael!" She was there then, kneeling beside him, turning him over. She was surprisingly strong. "Are you all right?"

"A little scared is all. I have nightmares about this."

"You idiot! What the hell were you thinking?" She cradled his head in her arms, pulled his face tightly against her breast, and rocked back and forth with him. If there had ever been any doubts, they vanished. Frankie was definitely a girl. She exuded an almost overpowering girlness.

Raphael began to feel very uncomfortable. "I'm all right, Frankie," he assured her, his words muffled by her body. "I just panicked, that's all. I could have managed—crawled inside to the phone or something."

"What the hell were you *doing*? You *know* you can't get around without your crutches."

"Maybe I was hoping for a miracle—spontaneous regeneration or something." He wished that she would let him take his face away from her body. He laughed a muffled little laugh. "I just didn't think, Frankie," he admitted. "Would you believe that I actually forgot that I don't have a left leg anymore? What a dumb thing."

"What did you think you were going to do?"

"I was going after you. I got cute and hurt your feelings. I had to try to fix that."

She pulled him tighter and nestled her cheek in his hair. Then he felt the quiver of a strange little laugh run through her.

"What's so funny?"

"I've *really* got you now, Raphael." Her voice was strangely vibrant. "You're completely helpless, do you know that? I can do anything to you I want to do—and you've got no idea of the kinds of things I'd like to do to you."

"Quit kidding around, Frankie."

"Who's kidding?" Then she sighed and let him come up for air. "I'm sorry, Raphael," she apologized. "That was a rotten thing to say, wasn't it? Here." She pulled his chair closer and helped him into it. Then she went after his crutches. "Are you all right now?" she asked him.

"Yes. Thanks, Frankie."

"Good." Then her eyes narrowed. "I'm still pissed off at you, Raphael. Don't start thinking that you're off the hook just because my hormones got the best of me there for a minute." She stormed back to the door and opened it. Then she slammed it shut. Then she slammed it again. And again. "I get a kick out of doing that," she said in an almost clinical tone. Then she gave him an impish little grin. "See ya," she said, went through the door, and slammed it behind her.

viii

And then, early one evening, there was a crashing, gutter-flooding thunderstorm, and the heat wave was broken. For several days the storm fronts that had stacked up in the western Pacific crossed in successive waves. The sky glowered and dripped, and the burned grass began to turn green again.

Flood came by one afternoon, still moving stiffly from the tape on his ribs and with his forehead still bandaged. Raphael had not seen him since the night of the brawl in Hillyard.

"What are you up to?" he asked, coming into Raphael's apartment.

"Nothing much," Raphael replied. "Reading."

"You ought to get yourself a TV set." Flood sprawled on the couch.

"What for? So I can watch soap operas?"

"The great American pastime. How do you expect the economy to expand if you don't give all those hucksters out there in TV land a chance at your bank account?"

"You're in an odd mood today."

"Edgy. I'm bored—God, I'm bored. This is a singularly unattractive town when it rains. I wandered around downtown for a while this morning. What a dump!"

"I could have told you that."

"When are we going to get out of here? Haven't you had about enough? Tell you what. Why don't we throw a few clothes in a bag and run down and see 'Bel? Get out of here for a couple days."

Raphael shook his head. "No. 'Bel and I didn't exactly part friends last time. I don't think it'd be a good idea to stir all that up again." He had not told Flood about the letter from Isabel. He had almost forgotten that he had it in fact, and for the first time he wondered what she had said in it.

"Oh hell," Flood scoffed. " 'Bel doesn't hold grudges. Forget it then. It was just a thought."

"Why don't you go ahead?" Raphael suggested. "Maybe if you get away for a while, it'll clear your head. You're starting to vegetate, Damon. This place is all right for me, but it's not doing you much good."

"I can stand it as long as you can. Oh, hey, I saw your friend again this morning."

"Which friend is that?"

"The public speaker. He was standing on a corner downtown delivering a sermon."

"It's nice to know he's still around. What was he talking about?"

"It was a sermon. He preaches rather well, actually—a bit

hellfire and brimstone for my tastes, but impressive. You could hear him for a block and a half.''

Raphael laughed. ''I'll bet he scares hell out of the tourists.''

''Really,'' Flood agreed. He looked out the window with distaste. ''It's going to rain again.''

''Probably.''

''Well, now that we've exhausted *that* particular topic of conversation, what'll we do? Shall we go out and get drunk?''

''I'll pass.''

''Goddammit, *do* something!'' Flood exploded in sudden exasperation. ''All you ever want to do is sit. Let's go pick up some girls—get laid or something.''

''I don't know that I'm ready for that yet,'' Raphael said carefully. He had never discussed that particular issue with Flood.

''You're a regular ball of fire. I think I'll go down and see how Heintzie's doing.''

''Didn't you get enough last time? It looks to me as if Heintzie's parties usually wind up filling the emergency rooms at the hospitals.''

''Oh, Heintzie's not so bad. He isn't very bright, but he's good to his friends.''

''Why don't you tell that to Jimmy and Marvin? Look, Damon, you're getting in over your head with that bunch. Why don't you stay away from them?''

''They amuse me.''

''It's contagious, you know.''

''What's contagious?''

''Being a loser. If you hang around with them long enough, it's going to rub off.''

''Bullshit! You're getting all hung up on that theory of yours. There's no such thing as a class of losers. It's not a disease, and it's not a syndrome. It's simply a matter of economics and intelligence. People get *off* welfare, too, you know. They smarten up a little, get a job, and boom! End of theory.''

''I don't think so. There's more to it than economics. It's

the whole business of crisis, disaster, turmoil. Right now you're just itching to go out and get into trouble.''

"I'm *bored,* for Chrissake!"

"Sure. That's part of it too.''

"Bullshit! Anything at all is a symptom the way you look at it. I've got a hangnail. How does that fit in, Herr Professor?''

"Don't be silly.''

"Shit!'' Flood snorted. "I'll come back when you've got your head together. Right now you're just babbling.'' He got up and stamped out of the apartment.

Raphael watched out through the window as Flood crossed the rooftop to the door at the top of the stairs and disappeared.

ix

After a few days of rain the sun came out again, but the temperatures were no longer as extreme as they had been in July. Raphael noticed that the sun came up later and that evening came earlier as the summer wound down into those last dusty, overripe days of mid-August. It was an unusual period for him. For the first time since his childhood, late summer was not accompanied by the anticipation of a return to school. There was a certain pang involved in the fact that the turn of the seasons would not be matched by that ritual return from vacation. The stately, ordered progress of the year seemed somehow disrupted. It was as if he had been cast into some timeless world of endless now with nothing to distinguish August from November except the weather. He even considered enrolling for a few classes in one of the local colleges simply to maintain some kind of continuity with the past, but he dropped that idea. He was not quite ready for that yet.

Very early one morning, almost before the sun came up, Flood came by. His eyes were very bright, and he seemed enormously keyed up.

"What are you doing out of bed so early?" Raphael asked him a bit sourly. The mornings were his, and he rather resented Flood's intrusion.

"I haven't been to bed yet," Flood replied. He had obviously been drinking, but his excitement seemed to have nothing to do with that. Without asking, he went over and turned on the scanner.

"There's not much doing in the morning," Raphael told him. "The assorted perpetrators tend to sleep late."

"That's all right." Flood grinned broadly. "You never know what daylight might turn up." He lit a cigarette, and Raphael was startled to see that his hands were actually shaking.

"You want some breakfast?" he asked.

"God, no. You know I never eat breakfast."

"Coffee then?"

"Why not?"

Raphael went toward the tiny kitchen.

"District One," the scanner said.

"One," came the curt reply.

"We have a report of a man down in the alley behind the Pedicord. Possible DOA."

"I'll check it out."

"You'll have to come and get this," Raphael said after he had poured Flood a cup of coffee.

"Yeah," Flood replied tensely. "In a minute." He was staring intently at the scanner.

Raphael shrugged and went to the small refrigerator for a couple of eggs. "You sure you don't want any breakfast?"

"What? No, none for me, thanks." Flood was still concentrating on the scanner.

"This is District One," the tinny voice came from the small speaker. "You'd better have the coroner come down here to the alley behind the Pedicord. We've got a DOA here. Gunshot wound to the head—at close range."

"Any ID on the subject?"

"I don't want to disturb the scene until the detectives get

here, but the subject's pockets are all turned inside out, and he doesn't have any shoes.''

Flood suddenly laughed. "Picked clean. Vultures couldn't have done it any better.''

"You're in a charming frame of mind this morning.'' Raphael put a frying pan on the stove and turned back to the refrigerator for bacon.

"God's in his heaven, and all's right with the world,'' Flood said expansively. "Where's that coffee?''

"Sitting on the counter there.''

Flood came to the kitchen, picked up the coffee cup, and returned to the scanner. Raphael continued to make his breakfast as his friend listened to the progress of the investigation. Predictably, there was no immediate identification of the dead man in the alley behind the Pedicord.

"Funny that nobody heard the shot,'' Raphael said, sitting down to eat.

"A gun doesn't make that much noise when you hold it right up against something before you pull the trigger,'' Flood told him. "Just a little pop, that's all.''

"How did you find that out?''

"Read it someplace.'' Flood shrugged.

Raphael frowned. "A wino like that couldn't have had more than a few dollars on him. Doesn't seem like much of a reason to shoot him.''

"Not to you, maybe—or to me either, for that matter, but there are strange passions out there in the garbage dump, Raphael. There could be all kinds of reasons for putting the muzzle of a gun against a sleeping wino's head and sending him on to his reward.''

"How do you know he was asleep when it happened?''

"Deduction, Raphael, pure deduction. Put a gun to a man's head, and he's going to shy away—it's instinctive.''

"How do you know he didn't?''

"No report of a shot, remember? Somebody just walked through the alley, saw him sleeping in a doorway, and blew him away—just for the hell of it.'' He laughed again and stuck out his finger, imitating the shape of a pistol. "*Plink.*

Just like that, and there's one less sodden derelict stumbling through the downtown streets. No reason. No motive. Nothing. Somebody just plinked him like a beer can.''

"That's a shitty attitude."

"Does anybody really care about what happens to a drunken bum? Basically, what happened to him was nothing more than a form of street cleaning. If the street cleaner hadn't got him, cirrhosis of the liver would have in another year or two.''

"He was still a human being.''

"Bullshit. He was garbage.''

"That's no reason to blow his brains out.''

"It's as good a reason as any.'' Flood stood up. "I'm going to split. Thanks for the coffee.'' And without saying anything more, he left.

X

Although the worst of the heat had broken, the girl from downstairs still came up to the rooftop occasionally. They would sit and talk through the long, idle hours of evening, watching the people in the streets below. Often, for no reason other than the simple need to talk, they sat until long after midnight, their conversations drowsy and their voices blurring on the edge of sleep. Perhaps it was chance, perhaps not, but not once during any of her visits did Flood appear. Raphael was apprehensive about that. For some reason it was quite important to keep Flood and the girl apart.

"Have you thought any more about going back home?'' he asked her late one evening when the tree frogs and crickets sang monotonously from nearby lawns and the cars had thinned out in the streets.

"Not really. I'm settled in now. I don't feel like going through the hassle of moving—facing family and friends and all that.''

"And it's easier to sit?'' He probed at her, trying to test her will.

"Bodies at rest tend to remain at rest." She said it glibly. "As time goes on and I get progressively bigger, I suspect I'll tend to remain at rest more and more."

"You hardly even show yet, and that's all the more reason to do something now—before you get cemented in."

"I show," she disagreed wryly. "My clothes are starting to get just a teensy bit snug. Besides, what's all this to you? Are you secretly working for the Metalline Falls tourist bureau?"

"Have you looked around you lately—at the people on this street?"

"It's just a street, and they're just people."

"Not exactly. This is Welfare City, kid. These people make a career out of what my father used to call 'being on the dole.' That's a corrosive kind of thing. It eats away at the ambition, the will. After a while it becomes a kind of disease."

"They're just down on their luck. It's only temporary."

"Eighteen years? That's your idea of temporary?"

"Eighteen years? Where did you get that number?"

"That's how long you're eligible for welfare—Aid to Families with Dependent Children. What the hell do you do when you're thirty-eight years old and the check stops coming? You don't have any skills, any trade or profession, and you've been a welfairy for eighteen years—just sitting. What happens then?"

She frowned.

"Most of the girls down there have come up with a fairly simple answer to the problem," Raphael went on. "Another baby, and you're back in business again. With luck you could stretch it out until you're in your early sixties, but what then? What have you done with your life? You've sat for forty or forty-five years collecting a welfare check every month. You've lived in these run-down hovels scrounging around at the end of the month for enough pennies or pop bottles you can cash in so you can buy a loaf of bread or a package of cigarettes. And at the end of it all you have nothing, and you are nothing. You've existed, and that's all."

"It doesn't *have* to be that way."

"But it is. Like you say, bodies at rest tend to remain at rest. That's a physical law, isn't it?"

"That's about objects—things, not people."

"Maybe that's the point. At what point do people stop being people and start being things—objects."

"It's not the same."

"Are you sure? Are you willing to bet your life on it? You said you didn't feel like going through the hassle of moving. Are you going to feel any more like it after the baby comes?"

"I'll think about it." Her voice was troubled.

"Do that."

"It's late." She stood up. "I guess I'll go to bed. See you." Her tone was abrupt, but that was all right. At least he had gotten through to her.

After she was gone and he was alone, Raphael sat for a long time in the silent darkness on the rooftop. Maybe it was time to give some consideration to *his* situation as well. Flood was probably right. Perhaps it was time to give some serious thought to moving on. It was too easy to sit, and the longer he remained, the more difficult it would be to uproot himself. His own arguments came back to gnaw at him.

"All right," he promised himself. "Just as soon as I get the girl squared away. *Then* I'll think about it."

The sense of having made a decision was somehow satisfying, and so he went to bed and slept very soundly.

Estuans interius ira vehementi in amaritudine loquor me menti

i

By late August the worst of the summer heat was past, and there was a faint haze in the air in Spokane. The evenings were cooler now, and sometimes Raphael even wore a light jacket when he sat up late.

Flood visited seldom now. His time seemed mostly taken up by his growing attachment to Heck's Angels. Raphael could not exactly put his finger on what caused the attraction. The Angels were stupid, vicious, and not very clean. None of those qualities would normally attract Flood. Although they blustered a great deal, they were not really very brave. Their idea of a good fight appeared to be when three or preferably four of them could assault one lone opponent. They talked about fighting much of the time, and each of them attempted to exude menace, but with the possible exception of Big Heintz, they were hardly frightening.

Flood's status among them was also puzzling. At no time did he assume the clothing or the manner of the Angels. He did not wear leather, and he did not swagger. His speech was sprinkled with "man" and "What's happening?" and other identification words, but it was not larded with the casual obscenity that characterized the everyday conversation of the Angels and their women.

Big Heintz clearly respected Flood's intelligence and laughed uproariously at his jokes and his parodies of popular songs. But although Flood was not a full-fledged member, neither was he a court jester or simple hanger-on.

One evening they sat on the porch of their big house up
the street, drinking beer and talking. Raphael, sitting on his
rooftop, could hear them quite clearly.

"They ain't left town yet," Big Heintz was saying. "You
can fuckin' take that to the bank."

"Nobody's seen any of 'em," Jimmy ventured.

"The Dragons are still around," Heintz insisted. "You
can fuckin' take that to the bank. They know fuckin' well
that this ain't over yet. Me 'n that fuckin' Mongol still got
somethin' to settle between us, and he ain't gonna leave this
fuckin' town till we do." He belched authoritatively and
opened another can of beer.

"Unless you can come up with more attractive odds, I
think I'll pass next time," Flood said wryly. "I didn't get
too much entertainment out of having two of them hold me
down while another one kicked me in the ribs."

"Shit, man." Marvin laughed. "At least they was only
kickin' you in the *ribs*. They was kickin' me 'n Jimmy and
Heintz in the fuckin' *head*, man. I still hear bells ringin'
sometimes."

"Them was just games." Heintz dismissed it. "Just
playin'—sorta to let us know they was in town. Next time it
won't be no fuckin' games—it's gonna be fuckin' war, man.
I mean fuckin' *war*!"

They continued to drink and talk about the impending
battle, working themselves up gradually until their need for
action of some kind sent them into the secret hiding places
in the house where they kept their weapons. In half-drunken
frenzy each of them in unself-conscious display moved to a
separate quarter of the lawn and began to swing his favorite
implement of war.

Chains whistled in the air and thudded solidly against the
ground, churning up the grass. Spike-studded clubs sang savagely. Knives were brandished and flourished. The air re-
sounded with hoarse grunts and snarls as Heck's Angels
bravely assaulted the phantom Dragons they had conjured up
with beer and bravado to meekly accept the mayhem inflicted
upon their airy and insubstantial bodies.

"District Four," the scanner said.

"Four."

"We have a report of a seventy-six at 1914 West Dalton. Several bikers threatening each other with knives and chains."

Raphael smiled. A seventy-six was a riot, and the police usually attended such affairs in groups.

"District One," the scanner said.

"One."

"Back up Four at 1914 West Dalton. Report of a seventy-six."

"Right," District One said.

"Three-Eighteen," the scanner said.

"Three-Eighteen," the car responded.

Raphael waited.

On the lawn Heck's Angels continued their war with their unseen enemies until five carloads of police converged upon them. The police spoke with the Angels at some length and then methodically and quite systematically confiscated all their toys.

ii

A couple days later, after supper, Raphael went out onto the roof to watch the sunset. He felt strangely contented. His life, though it was circumscribed, was interesting enough. The vague ambitions he'd had before seemed unrealistic now. Probably they always had been. He idly wondered what his life might have been like if it all hadn't happened. It seemed somehow as if what had happened to him had been the result of sheer, blind chance—rotten bad luck. That was very easy to believe, and like most easy things, it was wrong. There had been a definite cause-and-effect sequence operating that night. He had been drunk, for one thing, and he had been drinking hard to incapacitate himself—to keep himself out of Isabel Drake's clutches, and he had done that because it had been Isabel's suggestions that had led to the events in the front seat of his car, and on, and on, and on. It had *not* been sheer blind chance. Of course the appearance of the train had not been all that predictable, but considering the way he had been driving when he had fled from Isabel's house, if it hadn't been the train, it would have been another car or even a tree. Trees are very unforgiving when automobiles run into them. The train had maimed him; a tree most probably would have killed him outright. He sat for quite a while, thinking about it.

"Hey up there, can I come up?"

Raphael leaned over the railing and looked down. It was the girl from downstairs. She stood on the sidewalk below in the early-evening dusk, her face turned up toward him. "Come ahead," he told her.

A minute or two later she came out on the roof. "Oh my," she said, pointing.

Raphael turned. The last touches of color from the sunset lingered along the western horizon, and the contrail from a passing jet formed a bright pink line high overhead where the sun was still shining.

The girl came over and sat on the bench near his chair. "You've got the best view in town up here."

"If you like sunsets. Otherwise it's not too much. On a clear day you can almost see to the sewage-treatment plant."

She laughed and then crossed her arms on the railing, leaned her chin on them, and looked down into the street below. "You were right, you know?"

"About what?"

"That street—those people. I've been watching them since we talked that time. All they do is exist. They don't really live at all, do they?"

"Not noticeably."

"You scared me, do you know that? I saw myself at forty—a welfairy—screaming like a fishwife and with a whole tribe of grubby little kids hanging on to me. You really scared me."

"I was trying hard enough."

"What for? Why did you bother? And why me?" She looked straight at him.

"Let's just say it's a bet I've got with myself."

"You want to run that past me again? You can be infuriatingly obscure at times."

He looked at her for a moment. In the faint light on the rooftop she seemed somehow very much like Marilyn. "It's not really that complicated. I've lived here for six or seven months now, and I've been watching these poor, sorry misfits living out their garbage-can lives for all that time. I just wondered about the possibility of beating the system. I thought that maybe—just maybe—if I could catch somebody before the habits had set in, I might be able to turn things around. Let's call it a private war between me and that street down there."

"Then it isn't anything personal?"

"Not really."

"I just happened along?"

"It's not exactly that. I like you well enough to care what happens to you. It's not just a random experiment, if that's what you mean."

"Thanks for that anyway." She laughed. "For a minute there I was starting to feel like a white rat."

"No danger."

"You don't even know my name."

"Of course I do. You're the girl on the roof."

"That's a hell of a thing to call somebody."

"It keeps things anonymous—impersonal." He smiled. "That way I can beat that thing down there with no strings attached. It can't come back and say I was out to get something for myself."

"Okay, I think it's a little nuts, but I won't tell you my name. You can keep on calling me the girl on the roof. I know your name, though. You're Raphael Taylor—it's on your mailbox. That doesn't spoil it, does it?"

"No. No problem."

"All right, Raphael Taylor, you can chalk one up for our side. The girl on the roof is going back to Metalline Falls."

"Well, good *enough*!"

"I don't know if I'd go *that* far. When the girl on the roof shows up back home with a big tummy, tongues are going to wag all over town. My father might send me back out into the snow—and let me tell *you*, Raphael Taylor, we get a *lot* of snow in Metalline Falls—whole bunches of snow."

"You'll be all right. It might be a little rough, but at least the street didn't get you."

"It almost did, you know. I was ashamed. Girls from small towns are like that. You're ashamed to go home because everybody knows you, and you know they'll all be talking about you. It's easier to hide on some street like this—to pull it around you and hide. I'll just bet that if you went down there and asked them, you'd find out that most of those poor welfary girls down there come from small towns, and that they first came here just to hide."

"It's possible," he admitted.

"And now what about you, Raphael Taylor? Since you've saved me from a fate worse than death, the least I can do is return the favor. Nobody's going to accuse the girl on the roof of being ungrateful."

"I'm fine."

"*Sure* you are," she said sarcastically. "Are you sure that street hasn't got its hooks into *you*?"

"I don't think there's much danger of that."

"Can you be sure?" she persisted. "I mean *really* sure? Except for that first day I've never seen you anyplace but up here. Are you really sure you're not just settling in? You made me think about it; now I'm going to make you think about it, too. I'd hate to remember you just sitting up here, growing old, watching that lousy street down there."

"I won't grow old up here," he told her. "I had some things to sort out, and I needed a quiet place to do that in."

"You'll be leaving then?"

"Before long."

"Before the snow flies?"

"All right."

"Promise?"

"Before the snow flies," he said.

They sat quietly then. The streetlights came on, and the crickets began their drowsy drone.

"This is the only part of it all that I'll miss," she said finally. "I only wish we'd met each other before—before a lot of things." She stood up suddenly, her movements abrupt as always. "I have to pack. I'm going to be leaving first thing in the morning."

"Good luck."

"We make our own luck, Raphael Taylor." She said it firmly. "Or somebody else makes it for us—the way you did for me. How did you know exactly what to say to me to keep the street from getting me?"

He shrugged. "Experience," he suggested. "Intuition maybe. How does divine intervention grab you?"

"God's not all that interested in me. He's too busy watching sparrows fall." She paused. "It's not really the same because the word usually means something so totally different, but I want you to know that the girl on the roof loves you, Raphael Taylor. I wanted to say that before I left." And then she came over, kissed him lightly, and was gone.

For a long time after that Raphael sat alone in the darkness. Then about midnight it turned chilly, and he went inside to bed.

iii

Two days later when Raphael came home from work, old Tobe was standing in the middle of the street. He was roaring drunk and a wine bottle hung loosely in his hand.

"Tobe!" Raphael called to him as he parked. "For Christ's sake get out of the street! You're going to get yourself killed!"

"Who says so?" Tobe demanded belligerently in his foghorn voice, swaying and squinting at Raphael.

"*I* say so." Raphael got out of his car and pulled his crutches out of the backseat.

"Oh." Tobe squinted and tottered toward Raphael's car. "It's you, ol' buddy. I didn't reconnize ya. How's it goin'?"

"What the hell are you doing out in the middle of the street, Tobe?"

"I was goin' someplace." Tobe swayed back and forth. "I forget now just where."

"The way some of these kids drive around here, that's a real bad place to stand. If one of them came ripping around that corner, you'd be inlaid right into his grille before he could stop."

"Maybe it'd be better that way."

"Don't be stupid."

"Sam's dyin'. He's got the lung cancer. Y'know that?"

"You told me. Let's get you off the street, okay?"

"I'm goin' someplace."

"Where?"

Tobe thought about it. "I forget." His face was almost purple, and his eyes were yellowish and puffed nearly shut. The stale wine reek of his breath was so sharp and acrid that it was close to being overpowering.

"Why don't we go over there and talk?" Raphael suggested, pointing at Tobe's lawn.

"Sure, ol' buddy."

They crossed the street.

"They got ol' Sam so doped up he don't even know what he's sayin' no more," Tobe said. "You know, he even tol' me he didn't want me comin' out to see 'im no more. Can you imagine that?"

"Those drugs can do funny things to you." A sudden cold, sharp memory of the endless, foggy days in the hospital came back to Raphael as if it had been only yesterday.

"That wasn't ol' Sam talkin'." Tobe stumbled over the curb. "That was all that dope he's got in 'im. Ol' Sam, he wouldn't say nothin' like that to *me,* would he?"

"Of course not."

"Poor ol' Sam. Helluva damn thing, him dyin' on me like this. We been together twenty years now, I ever tell you that?"

"Once, I think."

"I'd rather lose a wife than lose my ol' buddy like this."

"I've got to run. I've got a lot to do this afternoon. You think you can remember to stay out of the street?"

"What the hell difference does it make?"

"If the cops come by and catch you, they'll call the wagon and haul you out to detox again."

"Can they do that?" Tobe looked frightened.

"You bet your ass they can."

"That's a terrible place out there." Tobe shuddered.

"Stay out of the street then, okay?"

"Sure, buddy. Hey, if you wanna use my truck anytime, you just lemme know, okay?"

"Sure, Tobe." Raphael turned.

Across the street Patch moved silently by, his face dark and mournful. At the corner he stopped and looked back at Raphael and Tobe.

"Who is he?" Raphael asked.

"Who?"

"That fellow on the corner there."

Tobe squinted, swaying back and forth. "I don't see nobody."

Raphael turned back quickly.

The Indian was gone.

"Anytime you wanna use my truck, you jus' lemme know, ol' buddy," Tobe said. "Anytime at all. Night or day, don't make no difference to me. You jus' lemme know."

"Okay, Tobe. I'll do that." He crutched on across the street.

"Anytime at all," Tobe called after him.

iv

"Very well, Mr. Taylor," Frankie said briskly. "This is just a periodic report. We need to know what kind of progress you're making." She was very businesslike, even abrupt.

"Getting by," he replied laconically, leaning his chair back and looking down at the street.

"You know better than that, Raphael. I can't just put 'getting by' in an official report."

"I'm getting better at repairing shoes, Francesca. It only takes me about fifteen minutes a pair now. Of course they pay me by the hour, so it doesn't really make any difference. Put down 'job satisfaction.' That makes them pee their pants. The defective is so resigned to his lot that he even enjoys it. I see you're still pissed off at me—about Jane Doe, I mean."

"You're a stubborn, inconsiderate asshole, Raphael." She waved her hands at him. It was a cliché, but Frankie couldn't talk without waving her hands. "Your poor Jane Doe is going through a pregnancy without any prenatal care. Does that make you happy?"

"You're wrong, Francesca."

"Don't call me that."

"I think I will. I like it. It's a beautiful name. You're still wrong, though. Jane Doe went back home. Her family's taking care of her now—prenatal care, support, love—all the goodies, and no strings attached. I guess that means that I won, Francesca. I beat your system—again. I saved her from you. You'll never be able to assign her a number, you'll never be able to control her life, and you'll never get your hands on her baby. She got away. It's not much of a victory, but a man in my position has to take what he can get. I'm sort of proud of it, actually."

She stared at him, her huge soft eyes very wide and her lower lip trembling. Then with a wail she turned and fled.

V

On the first of September Raphael went in to work early again. His mailbox was still vulnerable, and although he had the best of intentions, he forgot each month to request the banks involved to make the transfer of funds automatic.

It was very early. The streets of Spokane were quiet, and

the morning sunlight was bright in the clear air. Later, of course, when the exhaust fumes began to collect, it would begin to grow murky.

Denise let him in, speaking only briefly. Since that terrible evening they had, as if by mutual consent, limited their conversations to business or the weather or other totally neutral subjects. Frequently they passed each other in the store without even speaking. The other employees, those who had watched their growing friendship that summer, were convinced that they had had some kind of fight—a lovers' quarrel. At first, of course, neither had spoken to the other because of the lacerating embarrassment over the things they'd had to reveal to each other. Then, as time went on and their taciturnity had become habitual, they became embarrassed at the thought of breaking the pattern, of intruding upon each other. And so they were silent, each wishing that the other would speak first, and each afraid to say anything to break the long silence.

Raphael went to his bench, switched on the light, and sat down. He turned on his machine and began to repair shoes. Always before he had rather liked coming to work. Now the job seemed suddenly tedious and boring. After a while of bending over the machine, his hip and back began to ache, and faint flickers of phantom pain began skittering like spiders up and down the thigh and knee of the leg that was no longer there.

He kept at it doggedly. There were not that many shoes in the bin, and he wanted to finish them all before he left. They piled up quickly, since shoes are the kind of thing that everyone throws away, and to leave even one pair would mean that he would start his next day's work in the hole. He began to take shortcuts, and some of the work was not entirely the sort that he took any pride in, but he managed to finish by nine.

He signed out, nodded briefly to Denise, and left.

As soon as he reached the street the depression that had settled on him and the vague ache that had begun in the missing leg vanished, and he felt good again. It was still early, and he drove to a small restaurant he knew and treated himself to breakfast. He was still puzzled by Frankie's re-action when he had told her of the escape of the girl on the roof. Irritation or anger or another outburst of lyric Italian swearing he could have understood. Frankie was sometimes a bit volcanic, but *tears*? That was not at all like Frankie. He wondered how the girl on the roof was doing back in Met-alline Falls. Then he sighed, got his crutches together, and left the restaurant.

It was almost eleven by the time he got home, and his arrival only moments before the mailman came down the street earned him a savage scowl from a greasy-haired ado-lescent loitering on the corner.

It was quite warm by the time he reached the roof, and so he sat in his chair on the roof watching the frenzy of Mother's Day in the streets below. A car pulled up in front of the house where Heck's Angels lived, and a man got out. He seemed tense, as if he had been working himself up to do something unpleasant. The man seemed familiar, and Raphael tried to remember where he had seen him before. Flood was sitting on the front porch with Marvin and Little Hitler as the man came up the walk. "I'd like to speak with Mrs. Collins."

"She ain't here," Marvin said flatly.

"When do you expect her back?"

"Beats me."

"Look, friend," the tense man said, "I don't have time for the kind of games you people like to play. I told her last week that today was the deadline. Now, either she comes up with the back rent by midnight tonight, or you're going to have to move out—all of you."

Little Hitler stood up and swaggered down the steps. "And what if we don't?" he demanded.

"Then I'll put you out." The tense man's voice tightened even more.

"Now *that* I'd like to see," Little Hitler said. "Hey, Marv, did you hear that? This shithead says he's gonna put us out. You, me, Jimmy, Heintz, Jake—all of us. All by himself he's gonna fuckin' *put* us out."

"Maybe he'd like to start right now," Marvin said, also coming down the stairs. "Maybe he'd like to try to put you and me out."

"I won't be the one who'll be moving you out," the man on the walk told them. "That's what the sheriff gets paid for."

"Too chickenshit to do it yourself, huh?" Little Hitler sneered. "Gotta run to the fuckin' pigs."

"Friend, I'm too busy to be bothered with all this happy horseshit. You tell Mrs. Collins to get that money to me by tonight, or I'll go to the sheriff tomorrow. That's it."

Flood ambled to the front of the porch and stood leaning against one of the pillars. "I don't think you can do that without due process, sport," he said pleasantly.

"Watch me, sport. I've been in this business for fifteen years, and I've bounced a hundred of you welfare bums out of one house or another. Believe me, I know exactly how it's done—who to see and which papers to have signed. If I say you're going to move, you might as well start packing, because you *are* going to move."

"Who you callin' a bum," Little Hitler demanded hotly.

The man on the walk looked him up and down. "Are you working, boy?"

"None of your fuckin' business."

"That's what I figured. I won't apologize then. You just tell Mrs. Collins what I said."

"And what if we don't?"

"You're making me tired, boy. You can tell her or not—it doesn't make diddly-squat to me—but if I don't get that money by tonight, I go to the sheriff tomorrow, and you'll be in the street by the end of the week." He turned and went back to his car.

"Chickenshit bastard," Little Hitler called after him.

The man at the car looked at him for a moment, then got in and drove off.

"Why didn't you take 'im?" Marvin asked Little Hitler.

"Shit!" Little Hitler stomped back up onto the porch. "The fucker had a piece."

"Oh?" Flood said. "I didn't see it."

"You can take my word for it. All them fuckers carry a piece when they come down here. You seen 'im, didn't you, Jake? I mean, he stood right up to us. There was three of us, an' he didn't back down an inch. Take my word for it, the fucker had a piece."

Big Heintz roared up, his motorcycle popping and sputtering. "Where's the girls?" he demanded. "I need some bread. This hog's gotta go into the shop."

"They're out buyin' groceries," Marvin replied, "an' we got a problem. Powell was just here, an' he says we gotta pay 'im the back rent or he's gonna call the sheriff—have us evicted."

"Fuck 'im. My bike's gotta go in the shop."

"He means it," Little Hitler warned. "We ain't gonna be able to put 'im off no more."

"Fuck 'im. There was three of you. Why didn't you take 'im?"

"The fucker had a piece," Little Hitler said without much conviction. "You can take my word for it, the fucker had a piece."

Heintz grunted. "How much does he want?" He went up onto the porch.

"All of it, man," Marvin replied. "Every fuckin' nickel."

"Bullshit! That'd flat wipe us out for the whole month, an' my bike's gotta go in the shop. The bastard's gonna have to wait. We'll give 'im a few bucks and put 'im off till next month."

Flood looked at the big man. "I don't think it'll work, Heintzie. I think the man's made up his mind. If you don't settle up with him, he'll call in the pigs and you'll be picking deputy sheriffs out of your hair for a solid week."

"Fuck 'im," Heintz burst out with a worried frown on his face. "My bike's *gotta* go in the shop."

"Christ, man," Marvin said. "We sure as shit don't want no cops pokin' around in the house there. We got coke in there, man. We could lose our whole goddamn stash."

Jimmy's battered car came squealing around the corner,

made a sharp right, and drove up onto the lawn. "I seen 'em," he said breathlessly, getting out. "I seen the mother-fuckers."

"Who?" Heintz demanded.

"The fuckin' Dragons. They're camped out down in Peo-ple's Park. Must be thirty or forty of the bastards down there. Bikes all over the fuckin' place."

"I *knew* the bastards hadn't left," Heintz exulted.

"What are we gonna do?" Marvin asked, his voice also excited.

"We're gonna pass the word. Get hold of Leon. All the guys stop by that gas station of his, an' he can get the word out. Tell 'em we'll all get together tomorrow night in that big field out toward Newport where we had the party last month. We'll put this thing together, and then we'll fuckin' move, man. We'll *waste* them fuckin' Dragons once and for all, man—I mean once and for fuckin' all."

"You want just our guys, Heintz?" Jimmy demanded breathlessly.

"Yeah. No, wait a minute. Have 'im pass the word to Occult, too. Them guys got a hard-on for the Dragons same as us. With us and Occult, we oughta be able to raise sixty, seventy guys. We'll flat *waste* them fuckin' Dragons. They won't *never* come back to fuckin' Spokane after we get done with 'em."

"What about Powell?" Marvin asked him.

"Fuck Powell! We ain't got no time to mess with that shithead now. We got a fuckin' *war* on our hands. Crank up your ass, Jimmy. Get to Leon an' pass the word."

"Yeah!" Jimmy dived back into his car.

Like some general marshaling his troops, Big Heintz be-gan barking orders. Marvin and Little Hitler scurried away on errands, and Heintz stood spread-legged on the porch, his chest expanded and his beefy arms crossed. "War, Jake," he said, savoring the word. "It's gonna be a fuckin' war. We're gonna cream them fuckin' Dragons once and for fuckin' all."

" 'Seek out the enemy and destroy him,' " Flood quoted.

"What?"

"Von Clausewitz on war," Flood explained. "That's what it's all about."

"Yeah," Big Heintz growled enthusiastically. "Seek and destroy. Seek and fuckin' destroy. I like that kinda shit, don't you?"

"It's got a nice ring to it." Flood grinned tightly.

"You comin' tomorrow night?"

"I might tag along. I think the Dragons still owe me for a few broken ribs, and I always collect what people owe me."

"That's the stuff." Heintz slapped Flood's shoulder.

"I'll see you tomorrow then." Flood walked down onto the street in the bright glare of noon. His shoulders were braced, and there was a slight swagger to his walk.

A couple of minutes later he came up onto Raphael's rooftop.

"Well, well," Raphael said dryly, "if it isn't the newest recruit in Big Heintzie's limp-brained little army."

"You were listening," Flood accused.

"Obviously. You're not seriously going to participate in this shindig, are you?"

"Only as an observer, Angel." Flood laughed. "*You're* the physical one in this little group. I *do* anticipate a certain satisfaction out of watching the punks who kicked in my ribs get theirs, however."

"That's stupid. Either you're going to get yourself arrested, or you're going to get the crap stomped out of you again."

Flood leaned over the rail to look down at the street. "Not this time, Angel," he said in a quiet voice.

Raphael looked at him sharply. Almost casually Flood raised the back of his jacket to let his friend see the polished black butt of an automatic pistol protruding from his waistband at the back.

"Have you completely lost your mind? If you get picked up with that thing, they'll put you away forever."

"I'm not going to get picked up with it, Raphael. I've been

carrying it for several weeks now, and nobody even notices that it's there.''

"You wouldn't actually *use* it."

"Oh?" Flood replied in that same calm voice. "It holds fifteen, Raphael. That gives me plenty of time to make up my mind, wouldn't you say?''

"You're starting to sound just like those morons up the block. Get rid of that goddamn thing.''

"I don't think so." Flood's eyes were flat.

Raphael stared at him and suddenly realized that he had not really been looking at Flood lately, but rather at some remembered image. Certain subtle changes had taken place sometime in the last month or so—a tightening around the lips, a kind of agate-hard compulsion to violence in the eyes, an expression that seemed to imply that Flood had somehow been pushed into a corner and would explode at the next nudge—no matter what the consequences. It was, Raphael realized, the look of the loser.

It was a certainty now. Flood was gone. The street had claimed him.

vi

After Flood left, Raphael sat staring sourly down into the teeming street. The Mother's Day hysteria was upon the losers. The children ran shrieking up and down the sidewalks, and the men who lived off the women and their welfare checks brushed up on their technique for wheedling just a few extra dollars.

Raphael had always been able to watch this monthly outburst objectively before, even with a certain amusement, but today he found it all enormously irritating. He realized quite suddenly that he was totally alone now—even more alone than he had been before Flood's arrival last spring.

"District One," the scanner said.

"One. Go ahead."

"We have a report of a possible suicide attempt on the east side of the Monroe Street Bridge."

"Is the subject still there?"

"The witness advised us that the subject has already jumped."

"I'll check it out."

Raphael shook his head. The Monroe Street Bridge was the most surely lethal place in town. It was not that it was so high, for it was not. A leap into the water from that height would prove fatal only if the jumper suffered from extremely bad luck. The bridge, however, overlooked the foot of the falls of the Spokane River. The riverbed broke there, and the water hurtled savagely down a polished basalt chute. It was not a straight drop where the force of the water is broken by the impact at the bottom, but rather was a steeply angled and twisting descent where the water picked up terrific speed and built up seething, tearing currents that swirled with ripping force around the jumble of house-sized boulders in the pool at the bottom of the falls. To jump there quite frequently meant not only death, but total obliteration as well. Bodies often were not found for a year or more, and sometimes not at all.

"District One," the scanner said.

"One."

"Are you at the scene?"

"Right. There are several citizens here who state that the subject definitely did go over the side."

"Any possibility of an ID?"

"There was a jacket draped over the rail. One of the citizens states that the subject took it off before he jumped. Wait one. I'll look through it." There was a silence while the red lights of the scanner tracked endlessly, searching for a voice. "This is District One. There's a card in this jacket—identifies the subject as Henry P. Kingsford, 1926 West Dalton. He appears to be an outpatient from Eastern State Hospital."

Numbly, Raphael got up and went over to the scanner. He switched it off, then went slowly to the railing and looked across at the tightly drawn shades in Crazy Charlie's apartment—the shades that had been drawn ever since that day when Flood had so savagely turned on the strange little man. Raphael turned and went into his apartment, feeling a pang of something almost akin to personal grief. Of all the losers, he had been watching Crazy Charlie the longest, and his apparent suicide left a sudden gaping vacancy in Raphael's conception of the street upon which he lived.

Finally, after several minutes, he picked up the phone and dialed the number of the police.

"Crime Check," the voice came back.

"I live on the 1900 block of West Dalton," Raphael said. "I've got a police scanner."

"Yes, sir?" The voice was neutral.

"I just heard a report that one of my neighbors, Mr. Henry Kingsford, has committed suicide."

"We're not really allowed to discuss things like that over the phone, sir."

"I'm not asking you to discuss it," Raphael said. "All I wanted to do was to tell you that Mr. Kingsford was a recluse and that he's got six or eight cats in his apartment."

"Yes, sir?"

"Don't you think it might be a good idea to notify the Humane Society?" Raphael said, trying to control his temper.

"I'm not sure we're authorized to do that, sir. Maybe a neighbor—or a friend—"

"The man's a recluse—a crazy. He doesn't have any friends, and none of the neighbors here even know he exists."

"How about you, sir? Maybe you could—"

"I'm a cripple," Raphael said bluntly. "It's all I can do to take care of myself. Tell you what—either you can get hold of the Humane Society in the next day or so, or you can wait for a couple of weeks and then get hold of the health department. It doesn't really matter to me which." He slammed down the phone.

The apartment was suddenly stifling, and the thought of looking at the street anymore was unbearable. He felt an insistent nagging compulsion to do *something*. To simply sit passively listening to the scanner was no longer possible. Although he had used the word "cripple" in describing himself to the officer he'd just talked with, he realized that it was probably no longer true. Somehow, somewhere during the last summer, he had without realizing it crossed that line Quillian had told him about. He was no longer a cripple, but rather was simply a man who happened to have only one leg. "All right," he said, facing it squarely. "That takes care of that then. Now what?"

A dozen ideas occurred to him at once, but the most important was to get out, to go someplace, do something. He pulled on a light jacket because the evenings were cool and he was not sure just how long he would be out. Then he crutched smoothly out of the apartment and across the rooftop, conscious of the grace and flow of his long, one-legged stride. The stairs had become simplicity itself, and even the once-awkward shuffle into the front seat of his car was a smooth, continuous motion now.

He drove then, aimlessly, with no goal or purpose in mind, simply looking at the city in which he had lived for more than half a year but had never considered home.

The Spokane River passes east to west through the center of town and then swings north on its way to meet the Columbia. The gorge of the Spokane on its northward course ends the city in that quarter. The streets do not dwindle or the houses grow farther apart. Everything is very paved and neat, landscaped and mowed right to the edge of that single, abrupt gash that cuts off the city like the stroke of a surgeon's knife. Raphael had never seen a place where the transition from city to woods was so instantaneous.

The rock face of the gorge on the far side of the river was a brownish black, curiously crumbled looking because of the square fracture lines of the volcanic basalt that formed the elemental foundation of the entire region.

And then, of course, he looked at the river, and that was a mistake, really. It seemed more like a mountain stream than some docile, slow-moving urban river. The water thundered and ripped at its twisted rock bed. Somewhere down there Crazy Charlie, broken and dead, turned and rolled in the tearing current, his shaved head white—almost luminous—in the dark water. The dragon on his floor would no longer threaten him, and the voices were now forever silent.

Raphael turned away from the river and drove back through the sunny early-autumn afternoon toward town.

Sadie the Sitter was dead, old Sam was dying, and now Crazy Charlie had killed himself. Bennie the Bicycler rode no more, and Willie the Walker had not strode by since early summer. Chicken Coop Annie and Freddie the Fruit had moved away, playing that game of musical houses that seemed part of the endless life of Welfare City, where moving from shabby rented house to shabby rented house was the normal thing to do. Everything was temporary; everything was transitory; nothing about their lives had any permanence. They were almost all gone now, and his street had been depopulated as if a plague had run through it. There were others living in some of those houses now, probably also losers, but they were strangers, and he did not want to know them.

Raphael suddenly realized even more sharply that he was absolutely alone. There was no one to whom he could talk. There were not even familiar faces around him. The victory that he had only just realized had been won sometime during the summer was meaningless. The fact that he was no longer a cripple but rather was a one-legged man was a fact that interested not one single living soul in the entire town.

It was at that point that he found himself parked in front of the apartment house where Denise lived. He could not be sure how deep the break between them was, but she was the only one in the whole sorry town who might possibly still be his friend. He got out of his car, went up the steps to the front of the building, and rang the bell over her mailbox.

"Who's there?" Her voice sounded tinny coming out of the small speaker.

"It's me—Rafe. I have to talk with you."

There was a momentary pause, and Raphael felt himself

shrivel inside as he considered the possibility of refusal—some easy, offhand excuse. But she said, "All right," and the latch on the door clicked.

She was waiting warily at the door to her apartment. Mutely, she stood to one side and let him in.

"I think it's time we got this squared away," he said as soon as he was inside, knowing that if they started with vague pleasantries, the whole issue would slide away and they would never really come to grips with it.

"There's no problem, really." Her voice had that injured brightness about it with which people attempt to conceal a deep hurt.

"Yes, there is. We know each other too well to start lying to each other at this point."

"Really, Rafe—" she started, but then she glanced up and saw that he was looking very intently at her, and she faltered. "All right," she said then, "let's go into the kitchen, and I'll make some coffee."

They went in, she put the pot on, and they sat down.

"I made a fool of myself that night," she told him, "and I'm sorry. I was stupid and thoughtless. My silly little jealousy forced you to tell me something no man ought to be forced to admit."

"Have you got that out of your system now?"

She looked at him sharply.

"Why do you continually beat yourself over the head? There's no need for it. We had a misunderstanding—that's all. It's no big thing. We were both embarrassed by it, but nobody dies from embarrassment, and it's not important enough to make the two of us spend the rest of our lives not talking to each other, is it?"

"I wanted to speak," she objected, "but you wouldn't even look at me."

"Okay. I'm looking at you right now—right straight at you. Speak, Denise, speak."

"Woof-woof," she said flatly. And then she smiled, and everything was suddenly all right.

And then the words that had been dammed up in those

weeks of silence came pouring out. They talked until very late, their hands frequently touching across the table.

About eleven she reached across the table and took his hand. "Stay with me tonight," she said simply.

"All right." He didn't even hesitate.

And so they got up and turned out the lights and went to bed.

Raphael woke early the next morning, coming from sleep into wakefulness without moving. Denise lay quietly beside him, her arm across his chest and her face burrowed into her pillow. Her skin was pale and very soft, and she smelled faintly of wildflowers.

In the close and friendly darkness of the night before, they had lain very close together and had talked drowsily until long after midnight. There had been no hint of sexuality in their contact, merely comfort and the sense of being together. They had said things to each other in the darkness that would have been impossible to say in the light, and Raphael was content.

In the steely, dim light of dawn filtering through the curtains, he was surprised to discover how content he really was. The closeness, the simple thing of holding each other, the affection, had produced in him an aftermath of feeling not significantly unlike that which he remembered from times before his accident when the other had been involved also. Idly, he wondered how much of the afterglow of sex was related to sex itself and how much was merely this warm euphoria of closeness—and naturally, in all honesty, he realized that he was to some degree rationalizing away his incapacity; but he felt much too good to worry about it all that much.

She stirred in her sleep and nestled closer to him. Then, startled, she awoke. "Oh, my goodness," she said, blushing furiously and covering herself quickly with the blanket.

" 'Oh, my goodness'?"

"Don't look at me." She blushed even more.

"What?"

"Don't look at me."

He laughed and lay looking at the ceiling.

"Rafe," she said finally, "you don't think I'm terrible or cheap or anything because of this, do you?"

"Of course not. Are you sorry?"

In answer she reached out and pulled him to her, making small, contented noises into his shoulder. Her tiny, misshapen hand gently caressed his neck. "Oh dear," she said after a moment.

"What?"

"We have a problem."

"What's that?"

"Do you realize that we're both stark naked?"

"So?"

"So who gets up first?"

He laughed.

"It's not funny."

"It's like a cold shower. After the initial jolt it's not so bad."

"Oh, no. You're not going to catch *me* parading around in the altogether. My whole body would go into shock. I'd absolutely *die*. I'd blush myself to death right on the spot."

"I think you're exaggerating."

"Come on, Rafe," she pleaded. "We have to get up. I have to be at work."

"All right," he relented. "I'll turn over and cover my head with a pillow. Would that be okay?"

"You won't peek?"

"Would I do that?"

"How should I know what you'd do? If you peek, I'll die."

"You won't die, but I won't peek."

"Promise?"

"Promise."

He rolled over and pulled the pillow over his head. He felt the bed quiver as she slipped out and then heard the quick scurrying as she gathered up her clothes and dashed into the bathroom.

Later, over breakfast, she would not look at him.

"Hey," he said finally.

"What?" She still did not look at him.

"I'm here."

"I know that."

He reached across the table and lifted her chin with his hand. "If you don't look at me, I'll tell everybody at work that we slept together last night."

"You *wouldn't*!"

"Oh yes, I would." And then he laughed.

"You're not a nice person," she accused, and then she also laughed, and everything was all right again.

Before they left for work, he kissed her, and she sighed deeply. "I love you, Rafe," she said. "It's stupid and useless and probably a little grotesque, but I love you anyway."

"And I love you, Denise, and that's even stupider and probably a whole lot more grotesque, but that's the way it is."

"We'll work it out." She squeezed his hand. "What we feel about each other is *our* business, right?"

"Right," he agreed, kissing her again. And then they opened the door and went out together into the hallway and down the stairs and on out into the bright morning sunlight.

Raphael finished work about noon, turned off his machine, and went over to the desk where Denise was intent on some papers. "Hey you."

"What, hey?" She looked up at him. Her eyes seemed to sparkle, and her face glowed. He was startled to realize how pretty she was, and wondered why he had never seen it before.

"I'm going to take off now. I'll give you a call when you get off work."

"Do." She smiled at him.

"Maybe we can go to dinner or something."

"Are you asking?"

"All right, I'm asking."

"Let me check my appointment schedule—see if I can fit you in."

"Funny."

Billy, a retarded boy, was standing nearby, concentrating very hard on some clothing he was unfolding and putting on hangers. He looked up at them. "Rafe," he said, his thick tongue slurring the word.

"Yes, Billy?"

"You an' Denise ain't mad at each other no more, huh?"

"No, Billy," Raphael said gently. "We're not mad at each other anymore."

"I'm real glad. I din't like it when you was mad at each other. It made me real sad."

"It made us sad, too, Billy. That's why we decided not to be mad anymore."

"I'm real glad," Billy said again. "Please don't be mad at each other no more."

"We won't, Billy," Raphael promised.

Denise reached out and squeezed his hand.

Raphael went outside, crossed the street to the graveled parking lot, and opened his car doors to let the blast-furnace heat out. After a few minutes he climbed in, opened the front windows, and started the car.

He drove down to Sprague, went west to Lincoln, and then over to Main. He followed Main along behind the Chamber of Commerce and the Masonic Temple and then down the hill into Peaceful Valley. If he could catch Flood before he went over to the house on Dalton, before, by his arrival and his presence, he committed himself to another of Heintzie's "last and final wars," he might be able to talk him out of the ultimate idiocy.

But Flood was gone. The shabby house where he had a second-floor apartment sagged on its patch of sun-destroyed grass, its paint peeling and its cracked windows patched with cardboard and masking tape, and Flood's red sports car was nowhere in sight.

The little red car was not parked in front of the house where Heck's Angels lived either, and Raphael wondered if perhaps Flood had perceived on his own how truly stupid the whole affair was and had found other diversions to fill his day.

Raphael parked his car and went up to his apartment. He bathed and shaved and put on clean clothes. He set the scanner in the window and went out onto the rooftop.

"District One," the scanner said.

"One."

"We have a report of a subject sleeping in a Dumpster in the alley behind the Saint Cloud Hotel."

"I'll drop by and wake him up."

Raphael looked down at his street. It seemed somehow alien now. The familiar faces were all gone, and he realized that there was no longer any real reason to stay. For the first time since he had come here, he began to think about moving.

"This is District One," the scanner said. "This subject in the Dumpster is DOA. Gunshot wound to the head."

Raphael felt suddenly very cold. He had heard about it. Everyone hears stories about gangsters and the like. The Mafia is as much a preoccupation of Americans as are cowboys and Indians. Someone had once told him that young men of Sicilian background who aspire to membership in the family test their nerve in this precise manner. Nobody really investigates the death of a wino in an alley. It is a safe way for a young hoodlum to get his first killing behind him so that his nerve won't falter when the *real* shooting starts. Almost without realizing what he was doing, he went over to the window and turned off the scanner. He did not want to hear any more, and he did not want to think about it. He returned to his chair and sat in silence, looking down at the shabby street.

Up the block Big Heintz sat alone on the porch, his booted feet up on the rail and his purple helmet pulled down low over his eyes.

Marvin drove up in his car, closely followed by Little Hitler on his motorcycle. They stopped in front of the house and pulled several bags and blanket-wrapped objects from

the backseat of Marvin's car. They went up onto the porch.
"We got 'em," Marvin said, "lotsa good stuff—chains,
baseball bats, stuff like that."

"Baseball bats?" Heintz scoffed.

"We took 'em over an' had Leon drill 'em out for us,"
Little Hitler explained. "Then he poured lead in 'em."

"*Now* you're talkin'." Heintz grinned. "Where's that
fuckin' Jimmy?"

"He's over talkin' to Occult," Marvin replied, "seein' if
they wanna go with us when we go to have it out with the
Dragons."

"Goddamn that little shithead!" Heintz exploded. "He's
gonna screw it up. Occult ain't gonna take a scrawny little
bastard like Jimmy serious. They're gonna just think he's
runnin' his fuckin' mouth. That's the kinda thing *I* oughta
handle myself—*me*—or maybe Jake. Fuckin' Jimmy ain't got
no sense."

"Have you seen Jake?" Little Hitler asked.

"He'll be here," Heintz assured them. "Ain't *nothin'*
gonna keep ol' Jake away from what's goin' down."

Marvin had pulled one of the baseball bats out of a blanket
and was tapping it solidly on the porch railing.

"Don't be wavin' that fuckin' thing around," Heintz ordered. "Like Jake says, we gotta cool it. One of the neighbors sees it, and they'll call the pigs on us again. We don't
want no hassles with the fuckin' pigs today."

"Sorry." Marvin quickly wrapped the bat again.

"Better lug all that shit inside," Heintz told him. "Get it
outta sight. Like I say, we don't want no hassles with the
fuckin' pigs today."

Marvin and Little Hitler took their bundles into the house,
and Big Heintz sat in menacing splendor on the porch, glowering at the street.

About four o'clock Jimmy arrived, breathless as always.
"They're in!" he announced excitedly as he got out of his
car.

"Who's in?" Heintz demanded.

"Occult. I talked to the Hog, an' he says to count 'em in."

"Jesus Christ! You ain't got no fuckin' sense at all, Jimmy."

"What's the matter?"

"It ain't *done* like that, you dumb little fucker. You don't just go runnin' off to somebody like the Hog and spillin' your guts like that. This ain't no fuckin' tea party we're talkin' about—it's a fuckin' war."

"I don't see what the difference is," Jimmy objected.

"If you're too dumb to understand, I sure as shit ain't gonna try to explain it to you. It's *courtesy,* you dumb shit. You ain't got no fuckin' manners, Jimmy. *Me.*" Heintz stabbed himself in the chest with his thumb. "*Me—I'm* the one that shoulda talked with the Hog. That way he's got my word it ain't no setup—that we ain't gonna be waitin' out there to jump *them.* But you ain't smart enough to see that, are you?"

"Sorry," Jimmy said sullenly.

"Sorry don't cut it, shithead. Now I'm gonna have to apologize to the fuckin' Hog. This is *serious,* man—serious. *You* don't invite fuckin' Occult to a war, *I* do. That's somethin' that's gotta be settled between the *leaders*—me an' the Hog. From now on you keep your fuckin' nose outta stuff like this. You just do what I tell you to, an' don't get fuckin' *creative* on me. You got it?"

Jimmy sulked into the house, once again leaving Heintz sitting in sour imperial solitude on the front porch.

At five Flood showed up, and Raphael felt suddenly sick.

"Hey, Jake," Heintz called in a relieved tone. He got up and swaggered down off the porch. "Where you been all day?"

"Here and there," Flood said with a shrug. "I drifted down to People's Park to get the lay of the land."

"Shit, man!" Heintz stared at him. "That's dangerous. Were the Dragons there?"

"Some of them."

"They mighta jumped you."

"Why would they do that? Look at me, Heintzie. Do I look like a biker?"

"Well . . ." Heintz still looked dubious.

"I look like a tourist. They didn't even pay any attention to me."

"You got balls, Jake—real balls."

Flood shrugged. "I wanted to see the ground, that's all. Now I know the way in and the way out. There won't be any surprises—not for me, anyway. The Dragons might be in for a shock or two, though."

Heintz gurgled with laughter. "You slay me, Jake. You absolutely fuckin' slay me."

"Are we all set for tonight?" Flood asked.

"All set. Fuckin' Jimmy even went and talked to Occult. The Hog musta been drunk or stoned outta his mind to take the little fucker serious, but Occult's in."

"Good enough."

Raphael was stunned. The plan had obviously changed. He had thought that he would have more time. Tonight was supposed to be the council-of-war-cum-beer-bust out on the Newport highway, but those festivities appeared to have been scratched. Talking to Flood had been something fairly serious before, but now it was a matter of urgency.

Raphael swore and went back inside to the telephone to call Denise.

"Where have you been?" she demanded. "I've been waiting for your call."

"I've got a problem," he told her.

"What?"

"It's Flood. He's been running with a motorcycle gang, and they're getting geared up for a war with a rival gang. I'm going to have to see if I can't get him off to one side and try to talk him into staying out of it."

"Why?" She said it flatly.

"Come on, Denise. The man's a friend of mine."

"Some friend." There was a long pause. "It's not Flood at all," she accused him. "It's that girl again, isn't it?"

"What are you talking about?"

"That girl—the one with the big belly. It's *her* you want to be with, isn't it?"

He was stunned. He'd never expected *this*. "Denise." He said it very calmly.

"What?"

"Stop and think for a minute. Think about me and then about what you just said."

There was another long pause and then a slightly embarrassed laugh. "I've never been jealous of anyone before," she admitted. "I'm not very good at it, huh?"

"Would you accept incompetent?"

"All right. I'm sorry. What's her name?"

"She's the girl on the roof."

"That's all? You don't even know her name?"

"Why would I want to know her name? She's not here anymore anyway. She went home to Metalline Falls. I persuaded her to make a run for it before the social workers got her. My caseworker broke down and cried when I told her that the girl on the roof made a getaway."

"The puppy?"

"That's the one. She probably went home and chewed up a pair of slippers after I told her about it. The problem really *is* Flood, Denise. Look, why don't you come over here? Why don't I come and get you? I could fix dinner for us here."

"No thanks, Rafe. That might not be a good idea. I've never met this wonderful friend of yours, and I'd like to keep it that way."

"Look. Let me see if I can get him squared away, and then I'll call you back."

There was a long, slightly sulky silence. "I'm sorry, Rafe," she said finally, her voice contrite. "I was being selfish. I'm just disappointed, that's all. I've never been stood up before. You do what you have to and call me back, okay?"

"Thanks, dear."

"Dear?"

"Would you prefer 'sweetie'?"

"You ever call me sweetie, I'll steal your crutches."

"Love you," he said.
"Me too."

vii

It was all very well to speak of talking Flood out of the
evening's insanity, but the question was how to go about it.
He knew that the woman who rented the house was named
Collins, and that the phone would be in her name, but would
a phone call pull Flood away from the tense excitement that
was erasing his brain at the moment? Perhaps some false
emergency would do it—some personal appeal for help. At
this point, however, Raphael was not sure that Flood would
even respond to that. Perhaps the answer was simply to drive
slowly by, stop, and call Flood over to the car. The problem
with that, of course, was that Flood would be directly under
the jealous gaze of Big Heintz, and there would be no way
that he could get out of his commitment to the Angels, even
if Raphael could talk some sense into him.

From up the street there came a roar of engines, and Raphael hurried out onto the roof. It was too late. He had been
sure that they would not leave until after dark, but the tension
apparently had built up to such a pitch that they were not
able to sit anymore, or perhaps the gathering of the clans was
going to involve a great deal of driving around looking tough.
The motorcycles pulled slowly into the street, with Big Heintz
in the lead and Little Hitler and Marvin flanking him. Flood's
sports car was behind them, and the battered, smoking cars
of the rest of the Angels were strung out to the rear.

They pulled down in front of Raphael's apartment house,
grim-faced and girt for war. Flood glanced up once as they
passed and waved at Raphael with a cryptic smile on his face.
The street had claimed him. The thing that Raphael had
feared had happened. There would be no reasoning with him
now. Somehow, in spite of everything, Flood had become a
loser.

Raphael watched helplessly from his rooftop. The caravan

rounded the corner and was gone, leaving the late-afternoon street filled with silence and the stench of exhaust fumes.

Raphael went back into his apartment and switched on the scanner. Then he went to the telephone.

"Crime Check."

"I'm not sure exactly how to put this," Raphael apologized, "but would you be interested in something I heard about a gang fight in the making?"

"Could I have your name, sir?" It was the same officer Raphael had spoken with about Crazy Charlie's cats.

"I don't think that's important. I overheard a conversation. There's a motorcycle gang camped out down in People's Park. I heard some members of another gang talking about them. The plan is to go down there in force for a confrontation. From what I gather they aren't planning to make it just a fistfight. There was quite a bit of talking about knives, clubs, and chains." He hesitated, then decided to mention it. A week or two in jail would be far better for Flood than twenty years to life for second-degree murder. "I think one of them has a gun," he added.

The other end of the line seemed to crackle with a sudden alertness. The word "gun" seems to do that to policemen. "Were you able to get any kind of notion about when this is supposed to happen, sir?" the officer asked.

"Sometime tonight, I think. Bikers tend to be a little vague about things like time. This group was pretty well fired up about it, though, and they looked very determined when they took off."

"We'll check it out, sir."

Raphael slipped the receiver back into its cradle. He had just violated a fairly elemental rule; he had snitched. Under the circumstances, however, he felt no particular guilt about it. He watched the winking red lights of the scanner and listened intently.

It was fully twenty minutes before the call went out. "Three-Eighteen," the dispatcher said. Three-Eighteen was one of the downtown units, the one who usually got the messy calls. Raphael knew that Three-Eighteen was a *very* tough cop.

"Three-Eighteen." The man even sounded bored.

"We have a citizen's report that wasn't really very specific. The citizen told us that there's the possibility of a fight between two rival motorcycle gangs down in People's Park sometime this evening. Do you want to take a swing down there and have a look around?"

"I'll check it out."

Raphael waited.

"This is Three-Eighteen."

"Go ahead."

"I'm down here in People's Park. There are some people camped down here, all right. They *could* be bikers, I suppose. It's mostly the women, though. I didn't see any bikes around. Maybe the fight's been called off. There's nothing going on now. I'll keep an eye on the place."

Raphael almost howled in frustration. The Dragons had obviously made a beer-and-burger run. They'd be back, and Heintzie would get his war. "Dumb cops!" Raphael almost shouted.

The sun went down lingeringly, staining the sky off to the west.

Raphael listened to the scanner and waited. By nine o'clock his nerves were wound up like springs. He felt himself actually start at each new voice on the scanner. He called Denise and told her what was happening. Her tone was still disappointed, but they talked for a while and smoothed that over.

Raphael fixed himself a sandwich and continued to listen.

"All downtown units," the dispatcher said, "we have a report of a disturbance in People's Park. Complainant states that several dozen bikers are involved."

Raphael's stomach tightened. He waited, almost holding his breath as the scanner winked its tiny red lights, reaching out in search of a voice.

"This is Three-Eighteen," a tense voice came through after several minutes. "This thing down here in People's

Park is completely out of hand. There are nearly a hundred of them—knives, clubs, and chains. We're going to need a lot of help."

"All units," the dispatcher said, his normally calm voice edging up a notch, "we have a seventy-six in People's Park." Rapidly he began diverting cars and reassigning areas to provide minimal coverage of the rest of the city while releasing every possible car to the troubled area.

"This is Three-Eleven," a new voice, crackling with authority, came on. "Advise all units that I want a lot of lights and sirens down here. I want these people to know we're here."

"Yes, sir," the dispatcher said.

"Also, contact Spokane County Sheriff's Department and Washington State Patrol. We're going to need every unit they can spare."

"Yes, sir."

"Come *on*, people!" Raphael said. "Come *on*!"

"All units responding to the seventy-six situation in the People's Park area," the dispatcher said, "be advised that the situation is *not*—repeat *not*—under control. Approach with caution. Three-Eleven requests the use of lights and sirens. All other units go to channel two. Channel one is restricted to emergency traffic until further notice."

"This is Three-Eleven."

"Yes, sir?"

"Alert the hospitals and respond ambulances to this location. We have numerous injured subjects. Also respond the fire department. Ask the battalion chief if he can get a pumper truck down here. We might have to use fire hoses to break this up." In the background behind his voice Raphael could hear shouts and curses.

"Spokane PD," another voice came in.

"Unit calling?" the dispatcher said.

"WSP. Advise Three-Eleven that we have four cars responding to his location. ETA approximately two minutes. Find out where he wants us."

"Stand by. Three-Eleven?"

"Go ahead."

"Washington State Patrol is responding four cars to your location. They should be there in approximately two minutes. Where do you want them deployed?"

"Have them move to the extreme left end of the line of cars. I want to—" A faint popping sound came over the shouts in the background.

"We have shots fired!" Three-Eleven said sharply.

"Shots fired!" the dispatcher repeated. "All units responding to the People's Park area, be advised that shots have been fired!"

Raphael stared helplessly at the blinking scanner.

For the next few minutes the transmissions were a garbled mishmash of confused and contradictory calls. Then Three-Eleven's voice cut in sharply. "Has anyone got a positive on the subject with the gun?"

"This is District Four. The subject crossed to the other side of this creek that runs into the river here. He had a car over there."

"Can he get out through that way?"

"He can go out through the cemetery, Lieutenant," another voice cut in. "Once he hits Government Way, he can go just about anyplace."

"Did we get a make on the car?"

"A red Triumph," District Four said. "Out-of-state plates. I couldn't make them out."

Raphael felt suddenly hollow. There was no question now. It was Flood. The voices of the policemen coming over the air were very excited, and there was still shouting in the background. Raphael found himself quite suddenly on the other side of the law. It was probably very natural, but it seemed strange to be rooting *against* the police. It was still possible that Flood might escape entirely. Without a license-plate number to identify the red Triumph, the police had very little to go on; and despite their other faults Heintz and his cohorts would absolutely refuse to reveal Flood's name. It all depended on his getting his car out of sight.

"Three-Eleven," the dispatcher said.

"Go ahead."

"We've had a report by a citizen that a red Triumph has been seen westbound on Driscoll Boulevard at a high rate of speed."

Raphael quickly opened his city map.

"It must be a different car," Three-Eleven said. "There's no way to get across the river between here and there, is there?"

But Raphael saw a way, and so did the dispatcher. "Yes, sir, there is. He could have gone down through the junior-college campus and across the Fort Wright Bridge."

"Do we have any cars up there?"

"This is District Nine," another voice came in. "I'm at Francis and Maple. I'll try to intercept."

Raphael looked at the map intently. The Triumph was very fast, and Flood was clever—assuming the fight and the shooting had not completely scrambled his brains. To the north of Driscoll there was a rabbit warren of winding streets where he might drop out of sight. But if he stuck with Driscoll after it turned into Nine Mile Road, he would be out of the city with no side streets to dodge into. After that the only alternative would be flight—full-out, pedal-to-the-floorboards flight.

"District Nine, what's your location?" the dispatcher said after several minutes.

"This is Nine. I have a late-model red Triumph with Michigan plates northbound at a high rate of speed on Nine Mile Road. Am in pursuit." The voice that came back was excited, and the siren wailed in the background.

"What is your location, District Nine?"

"Just passing Seven Mile. Subject vehicle is going in excess of one hundred miles an hour."

"All units," the dispatcher said, "be advised that District Nine is in pursuit of a late-model red Triumph with Michigan license plates northbound on Nine Mile Road. Subject vehicle possibly involved in a shooting incident at People's Park within the past few minutes."

"See if Stevens County sheriff can get a unit down there to block him off," Three-Eleven said.

"Yes, sir."

Raphael sat tensely, his map clutched in his hands. "Come on, Flood! Get off that goddamn highway!"

The scanner tracked in silence, the tiny flickering red lights reaching out, looking for voices.

"He lost it!" District Nine said. "He missed the S-curve at Nine Mile!"

"Is he in the river?" Three-Eleven demanded.

"No, sir. He hit the rock face on the right-hand side and then bounced across and hit a tree. You'd better respond an ambulance out here—and a fire-department unit. It looks like we're going to have to cut him out of that car."

The tiny red lights continued to wink, fingering the air, searching the night for misery and violence and despair, and Raphael sat listening alone.

viii

He sat tensely in a chair in the waiting room, a loungelike place just off the emergency admitting area at Sacred Heart Hospital. The night was long and filled with confusion. Much of the human wreckage of the city passed through the wide doors of Sacred Heart emergency, and their cries and moans made the night hellish. The families and beloved of the wounded and the slain hunched in gray-faced shock in the waiting room, wearing mismatched clothes thrown on in moments of crisis.

Raphael did not know Flood's father, and the family telephone number in Grosse Pointe was unlisted. In desperation he finally tried to call Isabel Drake. Her phone rang three times, and then the recording came on. "I'm not at home just now," her voice told him. "Please leave a message at the tone."

He was not really ready when the insistent beep came over the wire. "Uh—'Bel—this is Raphael. Damon Flood—

Junior—has been in an accident. He's at Sacred Heart Medical Center in Spokane. I'm here, too. You'd better call me."

After he had hung up the telephone, he realized that he hadn't given her a phone number or much of anything else. He thought of calling back to add more detail, but could not bring himself to talk to a machine again.

And then he waited, and because he was tired and emotionally wrung, he dozed fitfully in his chair. At four in the morning a crisply starched nurse came into the waiting room and woke him. "Mr. Taylor, you have a phone call—long distance." There was no hesitation in her voice. She knew who he was. He was marked as one of their own—deserving that special kind of courtesy the medical profession gives to those who have survived its most radical ministrations.

"Of course," he said, shaking off the sleep instantly. He rose and followed the nurse through the now-quiet admissions area.

It was Isabel. "Raphael," she said, "I just got in and found your message on my answering machine. What happened?" It was strange to hear her voice again.

"It was an automobile accident," he told her. "He's in critical condition. I tried to get hold of his family, but I can't get through."

"I'll call his father. How bad is it?"

"They're not talking about it. I think you'd better hurry."

"Have you seen him?"

"No. I understand that he isn't conscious. Please hurry, 'Bel. I know quite a bit about hospitals, and the signs aren't too good."

"Oh, dear God! I'll call his father right now."

Raphael held the phone in his hand for a long time after 'Bel hung up, then, on an impulse, he called Denise.

"Hello?" Her voice was warm and sleepy.

"It's me." He felt a bit foolish for having awakened her for no reason.

"Did he . . . ?" She left it hanging.

"No. I just wanted to hear your voice. Hospitals scare me a little. I'm sorry I woke you up."

"Don't worry about it." Her voice was almost contented. "I've never had anybody wake me up in the middle of the night before. It's kind of nice."

"Nice?"

"You know what I mean."

They talked for a while, and then Raphael went back to the waiting room.

At ten in the morning 'Bel arrived. She was dressed in a dark suit and carried a small overnight case. She stopped hesitantly just inside the wide glass doors to emergency, and Raphael went out to meet her.

"How—" she started, and then broke off.

"No change," Raphael replied.

In a single glance she took in the crutches and the vacant space where his left leg should have been. She half reached out to touch him, but let her hand drop. "Is there someplace where we can get some coffee?" she asked to cover the moment.

"The hospital cafeteria."

"Can we leave word here?"

"I'll take care of it." He turned and went smoothly to the desk. He spoke briefly with the nurse and then led 'Bel to the elevators.

"J.D.'s on his way," she told him in the elevator. It was a moment before he realized that she meant Flood's father.

"I'm a little surprised," Raphael said. "From the way Damon talked—talks—I get the impression that he and his father are barely on speaking terms."

"That's nonsense. You should never believe anything Junior says."

"I've noticed."

They had coffee and looked out through the huge windows in the cafeteria at Spokane, spread out in the valley below them in the morning sun.

"Pretty little town," she said.

"Looks can be deceiving."

"Don't be cryptic, Raphael. That can develop into a very annoying habit."

He smiled then. The tone was so familiar that it seemed as if the time that had intervened since their last meeting had simply dropped away. He was surprised to discover that he was not uncomfortable with her. He smiled at her familiarly then, knowing all the lush, creamy opulence that lay beneath her trimly tailored suit.

"You've matured, Raphael," she said, catching the look and arching one eyebrow at him.

Later, back in the waiting room again, because his reserve was worn down by exhaustion, because he needed to talk with someone, and because 'Bel of all people would understand, Raphael began to talk—randomly at first, and then more and more to the point. "I suppose it's my fault, really," he admitted finally. "Damon asked me a dozen times to leave here. If I'd gone—if we'd gone to San Francisco or Denver or Seattle the way he wanted to in the middle of the summer, none of this would have happened."

"Don't beat yourself over the head with it, Raphael," she told him. "You can't go back and change things, and this— or something like it—has been waiting for Junior all his life. You could almost smell it on him."

A sudden thought occurred to him. " 'Bel, who is Gabriel?"

She gave him a startled look. "He actually mentioned Gabriel to you?"

Raphael shook his head. "He lets it slip from time to time. I don't think he was even aware that he said it, but several times he's called me Gabriel. For some reason I get the feeling that if I can find out just exactly who this Gabriel is, I'll be able to understand Damon a lot better."

"Didn't you get my letter?"

"Yes, but I didn't open it. It came at one of those times when—" He let that drop. "I've still got it, though. I've been meaning to read it."

"You should have," she told him quite firmly. "Last spring I had to go back to Grosse Pointe to attend a family funeral. I found out some things about Junior—things I didn't really want to know—but I heard enough to realize that it was something *you* really ought to know about. In some ways I suppose I'm not very admirable, but I do feel a loyalty to my friends.'' She laid her hand affectionately on his. ''I spent a week or so asking questions, and I had the whole story when I came back. I called the college to get your address and found out that Junior had dropped out and left a Seattle forwarding address. I knew that your home was in this state, and I thought he might be following you. That's why I wrote you the letter. I wanted to warn you.'' She looked around. ''Is there someplace where we can talk?''

''The hospital chapel's usually deserted.''

She threw back her head and laughed. ''How perfectly appropriate. All right, Raphael, let's go melt down a few plaster saints.''

Raphael told the duty nurse where they were going and got directions.

The chapel was dimly lighted and quite religious. Sacred Heart *is* a Catholic hospital, after all. They seated themselves, and Isabel began. ''You shouldn't feel any guilt about what's happened to Junior, Raphael,'' she said quite firmly. She gestured at the inside of the chapel. ''You're in the right place. You should fall down on your knees—'' She broke off. ''I'm so sorry, Raphael. I didn't mean—''

''It's only an expression, 'Bel. It doesn't mean anything.''

''All right. You should thank God that it was Junior and not you.''

''Me?''

''That's why he really came here—to destroy you—maybe even to kill you, for all I know.''

''Kill?'' He was startled at that.

''You'll understand more as we go along. I saw a little bit of this myself, but I got most of it when I went back to Grosse Pointe.''

''All right, who's Gabriel?''

''Junior's cousin,'' she answered. ''Did Junior ever tell you very much about his family?''

''Not really. Bits and pieces mostly. I gather that there's

money and that he and his father don't get along too well. You know Damon—he exaggerates a great deal."

"That's a clever way to put it. There *is* money—a great deal of money. Old J.D.—everybody calls him that—hit upon a very simple idea when they were developing one of the newer components in all cars. It's the simplest thing in the world—or so I'm told—but a car won't work without it, and J.D. has the patent."

"No kidding? Damon never said a word about that."

She nodded. "Maybe he considers it beneath him. It's hard to know about Junior. Did he ever tell you about his cousins?"

"I think he mentioned them once—something about a large number of girls."

"There are plenty of girls, all right. The Floods are prolific, but they seem to have trouble producing male children. There's only one other aside from Junior—Gabriel. They grew up together, and Junior hates Gabriel to the point of insanity."

"Hate? Damon?"

"Oh, my dear Raphael, yes. Hate may even be too timid a term. You see, Junior's mother died when he was about four, and J.D. buried himself in the business. It happens sometimes, I guess. Anyway, Junior was raised by servants, and he grew up to be a sullen, spiteful child, delighting in tormenting cats and puppies and his legion of female cousins.

"At any rate, the shining light of the entire family was Gabriel. Because he and Junior were the only two boys, comparisons were inevitable. Gabriel was everything that Junior wasn't—blond, sunny, outgoing, athletic, polite—the kind of little boy people just naturally love. Junior, on the other hand, was the kind of little boy that you send away to military school. I gather that for a great number of years about the only thing old J.D. ever said to Junior was, 'Why can't you be more like Gabriel?' I understand that it all came to a head when the boys were about nine—at Christmastime. Junior had been tormenting one of the girls—as usual—and Gabriel came to her rescue. Old J.D. caught them fighting and made them put on boxing gloves. Then, in front of the entire family, Gabriel gave Junior a very thorough beating, and old J.D. rooted for him all the way.''

''You're not serious.''

''Oh yes. The Floods are a vicious family. After that there was no hope of reconciliation. J.D. told them to shake hands when it was over, and Junior spat in Gabriel's face. From then on he not only hated Gabriel, but his father as well. It was about then that he started being sent away to school.''

Raphael thought about that. ''What kind of person is Gabriel?''

''He's an insufferable prig. He's been trained since babyhood to butter up old J.D.—the rest of the Floods know where the money is. He graduated with honors last year from Dartmouth—J.D.'s old school—and he's now busily backstabbing his way up the ladder in the family company.''

''Good group. I can see now why Damon wanted to get away from there. But what's all this got to do with what happened here in Spokane?''

''I'm coming to that. This is all a little bit complicated, and you have to understand it all before it makes any sense.''

''Okay. Go ahead.''

''Anyhow,'' she continued, ''at school Junior continued his charming ways, spending most of his time trying to bully smaller boys and usually getting soundly beaten up for it by older ones. Since the schools he attended are little WASP sanctuaries, more often than not the boys who thrashed him were blond, Nordic types—replicas of dear Cousin Gabriel. So, by the time Junior was fifteen or so, he'd developed a pretty serious kind of attitude.

''The turning point, I suppose, came at prep school when Junior set out quite deliberately to 'get' the school's star athlete—a blond, curly-headed half-wit who was almost a carbon copy of Gabriel. Junior charmed the young man into accepting him as his best friend—Junior can be *very* charming—and then he planted some cocaine in the boy's room.

An anonymous tip to the school authorities, and the boy was expelled.''

''Flood?'' Raphael said incredulously.

She nodded firmly. ''Junior Flood. After the first time he did it again—and again—not always with drugs, naturally. He turned a promising young halfback into a sodden alcoholic. He introduced another boy to the joys of heroin. A brilliant young mathematician now has the cloud of possible homosexuality hanging over him. One boy went to jail. Another killed himself. Junior's been a very busy young man. He's made a lifelong career of destroying young men who look like his cousin Gabriel. I suppose that in time he might even have worked up the nerve to go after Gabriel himself.''

''And I . . . ?''

''Exactly, Raphael. You look more like Gabriel than Gabriel himself—and of course there's your name. The coincidence was just too much for Junior. He *had* to try to get you. I suppose that's where I came in. I was part of whatever he had in mind, but probably not all of it. Whatever it was going to be, it was undoubtedly fairly exotic. Junior was—is—quite creative, you know.''

''It doesn't hold water, 'Bel. Why did he bother to come to Spokane, then? Wasn't this enough for him?'' He passed his hand through the vacancy where his left leg had been.

She turned her head away. ''Please don't do that, Raphael,'' she said, her tone almost faint. ''It's too grotesque.''

''You haven't answered me.''

''I don't know,'' she said helplessly. ''Who knows what's enough for someone like Junior? Maybe it was because it was an accident and he didn't make it happen; maybe he wanted to gloat; maybe a hundred things. And then I suppose there's always the possibility that he genuinely likes you. Maybe after the accident you no longer threatened him, and he found that you could really be friends. I really don't know, Raphael. I have enough trouble sorting out my own motives—and God knows *they're* elemental enough.''

A nurse came into the chapel, her starched uniform rustling crisply. ''Mr. Taylor?''

"Yes?" Raphael answered tensely.

"Mr. Flood has regained consciousness. He's been asking for you."

Raphael got up quickly and reached for his crutches. " 'Bel?" he said.

"No. You go ahead. I don't think I'm really up to it."

Raphael nodded and followed the nurse out of the chapel and down the long hallway. "How's he doing?" he asked her.

"He'll be fine."

"Lady," he said, stopping, "I've spent too much time in hospitals to buy that."

She turned and looked at him. "Yes. I guess you have."

"It won't go any further, but I need to know."

She nodded. "His condition is critical, and they can't take him to surgery until they can get him stabilized."

"He's not going to make it, is he?"

She looked at him without answering.

"Okay, I guess that answers that question. Lead the way."

ix

Even though Raphael was used to hospitals and was familiar with the stainless-steel and plastic devices used to maintain life, he was unprepared for Flood's appearance. The dark-faced young man was swathed in bandages, and tubes ran into him from various bottles and containers suspended over his bed. Flood's face, what Raphael could see of it, was greenish pale, and his eyes were dull with pain and drugs.

A youngish man wearing a business suit sat in a chair a little way from the bed. He was obviously not a doctor, but seemed to have some official status. He looked at Raphael, but he did not say anything. Raphael crutched to the side of the bed and sat down in the chair that was there. "Damon," he said. "Damon."

"Raphael." Flood's voice was thick and very weak, and his eyes had difficulty finding Raphael's face.

"How are you doing?" Raphael asked, knowing it was a silly thing to say.

"Excellent," Flood said dryly with a spark of his old wit. "How do I look?"

"Awful."

"You ought to see it from in here."

" 'Bel's here," Raphael told him, "and your father's on his way. He should arrive anytime now."

"Terrific," Flood replied sardonically. "That'll be a touching reunion." His eyes closed, and Raphael thought that he had drifted off. Then the eyes opened again, filled with pain.

They were silent for several minutes. The machines that were attached to Flood shirred and whooshed softly.

"Why did you come to Spokane, Damon?"

"It wasn't finished yet," Flood said, his voice almost a whisper. Raphael recognized the tone. Flood had almost been stunned into insensibility by the drugs.

"Couldn't you have just let it go?"

Flood's eyes took on some of their old glitter. "Oh no. You don't get away from me that easily, Gabriel." He seemed a little stronger.

"Damon." Raphael ignored the slip. "I didn't even try."

"Of course not. They never do." Flood caught his breath and twisted slightly on the bed.

"I'll call the nurse." Raphael reached for the buzzer at the head of the bed.

"Get your goddamn hand away from that thing. You always have to be helpful, don't you? Saint Raphael, friend of man."

"Hasn't this gone about far enough?"

"It's *never* enough." Flood's eyes were flashing, and his breath was coming in short, bubbling little gasps. He half raised his head, and then he slumped back on the bed, his eyes closed.

Raphael reached quickly for the buzzer.

"Why does it always have to be Gabriel?" Flood mumbled, his voice barely a whisper. "Why can't it be me—just once?"

"Take it easy, Damon."

Flood's eyes opened then. "You didn't even feel it. What kind of a man are you, anyway? You didn't feel any of it, damn you. Haven't you got any feelings at all?"

"I felt it."

"I *hate* you, Angel."

"I know. Is that why you did this?"

"That's why I do *everything*."

"But why?" Raphael pressed. "I'm not Gabriel. None of them were ever Gabriel. What have you really accomplished?"

A startled look came into Flood's eyes. Then he laughed—a faint, wheezing sound. "Very good, Angel," he said. "You always were the best. It's a damn shame you have to look like that. We could have been friends."

"We are friends, Damon. You might not believe it or understand it, but we're friends."

"Don't be stupid. Don't disappoint me at this stage of the game."

"The game's all played out."

"I got you, though, didn't I? I finally got you."

"All right, Damon. You win."

Flood smiled briefly then and lapsed into unconsciousness again.

It was sometime later when he opened his eyes once more. "I'm afraid, Angel," he whispered weakly.

Without thinking, Raphael reached out and took his hand. He sat for a long time holding Flood's hand, even for quite some time after Flood had died. Then, gently, he laid the hand back on the bed, got up, and slowly crutched his way out of the room.

It happened because he was tired and sick and in a hurry. All Raphael wanted to do was get upstairs, call Denise, and then bathe the hospital stink off and fall into bed. When he came around the front of his car, the tip of one crutch caught the curb, and he fell heavily to the sidewalk.

Because he had not had time to catch himself, the fall knocked the wind out of him, and he lay for several minutes gasping, his cheek resting on the gritty cement. At first there was anger—at himself, at the curb, at the crutch that had so unexpectedly betrayed him—then there was the cold certainty that on this street of all the streets in the city, no one would help him.

He heard a light step behind him.

"Could you give me a hand, please," he asked, hating the necessity for asking, not even turning his head, ashamed of his helplessness and half-afraid that whoever stood there would simply step around him and, indifferent, walk away.

And then a pair of strong hands slid under his arms and lifted, and he was up, leaning against the front fender of his car.

It was Patch.

At close range his face seemed even more darkly somber than at a distance. There was a kind of universal melancholy in that face, a sadness that went beyond any personal bereavement or loss and seemed somehow to reflect the sum of human sorrow.

The Indian bent, picked up the crutches, and handed them to Raphael. "Are you all right now?" he asked, his voice very soft, and his single dark eye searching Raphael's face.

"Yes," Raphael said. "Thanks."

"Are you sure?"

Raphael drew in a deep breath. "Yes. I think everything's fine now. I just got careless, that's all. I should know better."

"Everybody falls now and then," Patch said in his soft

voice. "It's not just you. The important thing is not to let it throw you, make you afraid."

"I know. It took me a long time to figure that out, but I think I've got it now."

"Good. You'll be okay then." The brown hand touched his shoulder briefly, and then Patch turned and silently went on down the street.

Raphael stood leaning against his car watching that solitary passage until the dark-faced man was out of sight and the street was empty again.

O Fortuna, velut Luna statu variabilis

If the subpoena had come a week or two later, they might have been gone. The leaves had turned, and Raphael wanted to be away before the first snow. Denise was unhappy about his being summoned to testify, and they came as close to having a fight about it as they did about anything now.

"It's absurd," she said the morning of the hearing. "I don't see why you want to bother with it."

"I have to go. If I don't show up, they'll send a couple of eight-foot-tall policemen to get me."

"Don't be ridiculous! All you have to do is pick up the telephone. We can get out of things like this anytime we want to. That's one of our fringe benefits. We don't owe anything to their grubby little system. We're exempt."

"No. I won't do that. That's the kind of thing a cripple would do, but I'm not a cripple anymore. Besides, I want to get it all cleared up. Just for once I want to explain who Flood really was."

"Who cares? The judges don't care; the lawyers don't care; the police don't care—nobody cares. They've all got their neat little categories. All they're going to do is stuff him into one of their pigeonholes and then forget about it. That's the way they do things. Nobody cares about the truth, and if you tell them something that doesn't fit their theories, all you'll do is make them mad at you."

"People have been mad at me before."

"You're impossible."

"Will you come along with me?"

"No," she said tartly. "I've got packing to do. If we're ever going to get out of this town, *one* of us has to be practical."

"You'll be here then?" he asked her, looking around at the clutter of boxes in her apartment.

"Where else would I be? What a dumb question."

"It's just that I get jumpy when I don't know where you are."

She smiled suddenly and then kissed him.

The courthouse in Spokane is a very large, sprawling building with a high, imitation-Renaissance tower looming above it. It makes some pretense at reflecting civic pride while ignoring the human misery that normally fills it. As luck had it on the morning of the hearing, Raphael found a parking spot directly across the street from the main entrance on Broadway. He hated parking lots. They were always filled with obstacles that seemed sometimes deliberate. That luck made him feel better right at the start. There was that word again, however—luck. More and more he had come to know that it was a meaningless word. There was a perfectly rational explanation for why the parking place was there. He didn't know what it *was*, but it was certainly rational.

He went up to the intersection, waited for the light, and then crossed. The courthouse lawn was broad and well cared for and was raised above the level of the sidewalk with a stone retaining wall. There was about the whole thing a kind of self-important aloofness that Raphael secretly found amusing. Slowly, step by step, he went up the stairs and into the building.

Frankie was waiting for him just inside the door. Her face was determined, and her dark eyes were flashing. "It's about time you got here," she snapped, looking up at him.

"The hearing isn't for another half hour, Frankie."

"Where the hell have you been? I've been trying to call you all morning."

"I'm shacked up with a girl."

She actually blushed. "That's *really* crude, you know."

"Sorry."

"I have to talk to you, Raphael. It's important." She led him to a room a few doors away.

"Are we allowed to go in there?" he asked dubiously as she opened the door.

"It's one of the places we have here in the building. They have to give us rooms to conduct our business in, because most of the time we're more important in the courtroom than the lawyers. Give us a few more years, and we'll be able to eliminate the lawyers altogether."

They went into the room, and she closed the door. "We're laying for you, Raphael," she warned him. "We've got a couple of crack troops in that courtroom. We've got a lot of time invested in that motorcycle gang. If those hairballs go to prison, three caseworkers and a supervisor are going to be out of work, so watch what you say in there. I know how you feel about us, but watch your mouth when you get on the stand. Those two girls have all the compassion of a pair of meat grinders. They'll hang you out to dry if you screw up things for us. They've been literally sleeping with the defense attorney—who's also a girl, which makes for a *very* interesting situation."

"You've got a dirty mind, Frankie."

"What else is new? Anyway, the defense is going to try to lay all this on your friend. He was the one with the gun, after all. Did you know that he killed two people that night?"

"I'd heard."

"The defense is going to try to picture him as a Detroit hoodlum who led these poor, innocent young local boys astray. If you say anything that damages their case, my colleagues will cream you."

"Why are you telling me this, Frankie?"

"Because I gave notice yesterday morning. I'm quitting. I'm changing sides."

"Hell, babes, don't do that. You're one of the *good* ones."

"Not anymore. You peeled my soul raw when you told me about how Jane Doe got away from us. I didn't realize how much the people we're trying to help really hate us. I can't live with that, Raphael. I cried for three days. I hope you're proud of yourself.''

"Aw, Frankie." He half reached for her.

"None of that. If you start groping me now, you'll get us both arrested."

He stared at her, not comprehending. "You lost me on that one, kid."

"I've got a letch for you, you dumb klutz. If you put your hands on me, I'll peel you like a banana right here on the spot, and I don't have a key, so I can't lock that door."

He had to put a stop to that. "Francesca," he said firmly, "don't even talk about things like that. You know it's out of the question."

"I have enormous self-confidence, Raphael."

He suddenly realized that she was about half-serious.

She sighed. "You've saved three of us, do you know that? You saved yourself, you saved Jane Doe, and you saved me. You got the three of us out of the goddamn system. That may be the only victory for our side in this whole freaking century. That's why you have to be very careful in that courtroom. Don't let them rattle you enough to make you get mad and start running your mouth. Keep it all strictly business, because if you start ranting and raving, and if the wrong judge is sitting on the case, those two girls will have you committed before you ever get out of the courtroom. You watch your ass, Raphael Taylor. Jane Doe and I won't be able to have much of a victory celebration if our glorious leader's in the loony bin."

"They can't do that to me, Frankie," he scoffed.

"Like hell they can't. If you get the least bit excited, they'll have you out at Medical Lake before the sun goes down."

"Maybe I should call in sick." She actually had him a little worried.

"That's what I wanted to *tell* you, but you wouldn't answer your goddamn telephone! It's too late now. If you don't show up at this stage, they'll put out a bench warrant for you. Just go in there, keep a smile on your face, and keep your big mouth shut.'' She glared up at him, her lower lip very active. ''At least I was able to cover your ass a little bit.''

''What?''

''I purged your file. There aren't any reports in it but mine.''

''Why?'' That really baffled him.

''Because you were playing games when you first got here. What the hell were you doing with all those empty bottles? You're listed as an alcoholic, did you know that?''

''I'm *what*?''

''There was a report in your file. It said that there were wine bottles all over that pigeon coop you live in. What were you thinking of?''

He laughed ruefully. ''I was trying to be cute, I guess. They gave me a caseworker I didn't like. I thought I'd give her something to worry about.''

''Dumb! How can you *be* so goddamn dumb? Don't you know that when you talk to one of us, you're talking to *all* of us? That's what those files are *for,* dummy. You owe me at least one roll in the hay, Raphael Taylor, because *I'm* the one who punched the erase button and covered your ass. And I did it with *this* finger.'' The finger she held up was *not* her index finger.

He grinned at her. ''You're a buddy, Frankie.'' He was genuinely grateful.

''They don't have a single goddamn thing on you,'' she continued. ''I even cleaned up some of my own reports. There's nothing in your file that says that you can't walk on water or raise the dead. What are you going to say in there?''

''I'm going to tell them the truth.''

She said a dirty word in Italian. ''They'll eat you alive if you do that, Raphael. Just let it slide. Nobody gives a damn about the truth.''

''I do.''

''That's because you're a weirdo. Just say what they want you to say and get out of there before they get their hooks into you. Your friend is dead. Nothing can hurt him now.''

''I want to set the record straight.''

"The record's *never* straight, you idiot! Haven't you ever read *1984*? They rewrite the record anytime it doesn't suit them. You're spinning your wheels and exposing your bare fanny for nothing." She looked up at him and then threw her hands in the air. "All right. Do it your way—you will any-way—but *please* be careful. Now come here." She grasped the front of his jacket and pulled him slightly off balance. Then she kissed him very savagely.

"*Mar*-rone!" she breathed. "Why do you have to be—" She stepped back and wiped at her eyes with the back of her hand. "I've wanted to do that since the moment I laid eyes on you. You're lucky you're out of action, Raphael Taylor. I'd have destroyed you. I'd have devoured you. If you've never had an Italian girl jump your bones, you don't know what you've missed."

"I love you, too, Frankie." He really meant it.

"I'm not talking about love, Taylor. That might have come later, but there would have been much, much more important things to take care of first. Be careful in there, my Angel. Be very, very careful." She wiped her eyes again. "Now get out of here."

He smiled at her fondly and half turned.

"Raphael?" She said it in an almost little-girl voice.

"Yes?"

"I love you, too, dammit."

The assistant prosecutor was the young man who had been sitting in Flood's hospital room the day he had died, and he was waiting nervously near the elevators when Raphael came up.

"I've been trying to get hold of you all week, Mr. Taylor," he said, coming up to Raphael. "I wanted to go over your testimony with you."

Raphael immediately disliked the man. "Why?"

"No lawyer likes surprises in the courtroom."

"Life is full of surprises. Is this likely to take long? I have a lot of things to do today."

The prosecutor looked at him, a bit startled by his tone. "I'll speak with the judge. I think he'll agree to letting you testify first—because of your disability. To be perfectly honest with you, Mr. Taylor, I didn't really understand what you and Flood were talking about the night he died. Are you going to be getting into that? I mean, is it relevant?''

Raphael drew in a deep breath. There wasn't really any way to avoid it. It all had to come out. "Ask me the kind of questions that'll give me some leeway, okay? It's sort of long and complicated, but I don't think anybody's really going to understand what Flood was doing unless I tell the whole story.''

"I could have the judge delay the proceedings to give us time to go over it if you'd like.''

Raphael shook his head. "I don't have more than one recitation of this in me. It's going to be hard enough to say it once. Shall we get on with it?''

They went into the courtroom.

In due time the judge, a balding man with thick glasses and a slightly wrinkled robe, marched in while everyone stood, and the hearing began.

The preliminaries dragged on for a half hour or so with the nervous young prosecutor and an equally nervous young woman from the public defender's office both behaving with an exaggerated formality that spoke volumes about their amount of experience.

Raphael glanced idly over at Heck's Angels. Big Heintz was there with one side of his face bandaged. Jimmy's nose was broken, and both of his eyes were swollen nearly shut. Marvin's arm was in a cast, and Little Hitler was holding a pair of crutches. There were a dozen or so others—strangers—with various bruises and bandages.

Since some of the defendants were quite young, there was a great deal of polite bickering between the two lawyers about whether or not the juveniles should be separated from the adults. Two hard-eyed young women in professional-looking suits sat protectively near the younger members of the gang, furiously scribbling notes and passing them across the railing to the defense counsel. These were the two Frankie had warned him about.

The judge finally ruled that the problem of jurisdiction could be sorted out later, since this was simply a preliminary hearing. The young woman from the public defender's office hotly took exception, which the judge wearily noted.

"All right then," the judge said finally, "I guess you may proceed, Mr. Wilson."

"Thank you, Your Honor," the prosecutor said. "This is one of three hearings to be held in this matter. At the request of the police department and in the interests of maintaining order, it was deemed wise to keep the members of the three gangs strictly segregated."

"Objection, Your Honor," the defense counsel said, leaping to her feet. "The word 'gangs' is pejorative."

"Sustained," the judge decided. "Select another word, Mr. Wilson."

"Would counsel accept 'groups'?" the prosecutor asked.

" 'Groups' is all right," she replied.

The prosecutor turned back to the judge. "If it please the court, I have one witness who is severely disabled. His testimony may be out of sequence, but he has asked that he be allowed to testify early in the proceedings since he experiences a great deal of discomfort when required to sit for extended periods."

"Of course, Mr. Wilson."

The prosecutor called Raphael's name, and Raphael rose, went to the witness stand, and sat. He drew in a deep breath and pulled an icy, detached calm about himself. Frankie's warnings were very much on his mind, and he knew that he could not allow anything to rattle him. He was sworn in, and then they began.

"Mr. Taylor," the prosecutor said, "are you acquainted with this group of young men?" He indicated the assembled Angels.

"I've met some of them—briefly. They live a few doors up the street from me."

"But you were, I take it, much better acquainted with a Mr. Jacob D. Flood, Junior—now deceased."

"Yes."

"Would you please elaborate on that acquaintance?"

"We were roommates at college," Raphael replied. "He came to Spokane last spring when he found out that I was here."

"You were friends then?"

"I thought so."

"Mr. Flood was educated?"

"Yes."

"He came from a wealthy family?"

"Yes."

"Did he ever explain to you the nature of his association with the group of individuals here in this courtroom? I mean, they do not appear to be the sort of people with whom someone of education and wealth would normally associate."

"They amused him. He had other reasons, but basically it was because they amused him."

"Objection, Your Honor," the defense attorney said, coming to her feet. "Purely speculative."

"I think we can allow a certain latitude, Miss Berensen," the judge told her patiently. "These proceedings are preliminary after all, and whether or not Mr. Flood was amused by the defendants hardly seems to be a major issue."

"Your Honor!" she protested.

"Overruled, Miss Berensen." The judge sighed.

Quite suddenly, perhaps because of the hard chair or his nervousness or the aggravation of the defense attorney's objection, Raphael's left thigh and leg and foot began to ache intolerably. He grimaced and shifted his position.

"Are you in pain, Mr. Taylor?" the judge asked, a note of concern in his voice.

"No more than usual, sir."

The judge frowned slightly and looked down at his notes for a moment. "Mr. Wilson," he said, looking up, "what is the proposed thrust of your examination of Mr. Taylor?"

"Uh"—the prosecutor faltered—"background, primarily, Your Honor. Mr. Taylor appears to be the only person in Spokane who really knew Mr. Flood, and since Mr. Flood and his role in this matter are likely to play a major part in any trials resulting from these proceedings, I felt that Mr. Taylor's testimony would help us all to understand that rather strange young man.''

"Then Mr. Taylor is here not so much as a witness for the prosecution as he is in the capacity of a friend of the court?"

"Uh—I suppose that's true, Your Honor."

"Miss Berensen." The judge turned to the defense. "Would *you* take exception to designating Mr. Taylor a friend of the court?"

"Most strenuously, Your Honor. The man Flood was the instigator of this whole affair. The defense could never accept testimony from his close friend with an *amicus curiae* label attached to it.''

"Your exception will be noted, Miss Berensen. It does not become any of us, however, to inflict needless suffering upon the witness. What I propose is to permit Mr. Taylor to present narrative testimony concerning the man Flood—his background and so forth—in order to allow the testimony to be completed as quickly as possible. Would you accept narrative testimony from the witness based upon *humanitarian* considerations, Miss Berensen?''

The defense attorney seemed about to protest further, but thought better of it. "Very well, Your Honor." She was almost sullen about it.

Behind her the two young women scribbled furiously.

"All right then, Mr. Taylor," the judge said, "why don't you just give us a brief outline of Mr. Flood's background—insofar as you know it?''

"Yes, Your Honor." Raphael thought for a moment, looking at the patch of golden morning sunlight slanting in through the window at the back of the courtroom, and then he started. "Damon Flood's dead now, so nothing I can say will matter to him. It's taken me a long time to piece his story together, so I hope you'll be patient with me. Flood himself isn't on trial, but his motives in this business may be important.'' He looked inquiringly at the judge, silently seeking permission to continue.

"I think we can all accept that, Mr. Taylor. Please go on.''

"Thank you, Your Honor. Jacob Damon Flood, Junior, was born in Grosse Pointe, Michigan. His family is well-to-do. Mr. Flood's mother died when he was four, and his father was totally immersed in the family business. Flood was not particularly lovable as a child, and he was in continual competition with a cousin who appears to have been everyone's favorite—even his own father's. I suppose it finally came to a head during one of those confrontations between Flood and his cousin. Whatever the reason, they fought, and Flood received a very public and humiliating beating while his own father looked on approvingly. As closely as I can reconstruct it, that was the point where something slipped or went off center. He knew who he was. He knew that it was *his* father who was the head of the company that was the source of all the family wealth. I guess that all his relatives kowtowed to his father, and he expected the same kind of respect. When he didn't get it, it unsettled him. He became obsessed with the idea of getting revenge—on the cousin certainly and probably on his own father as well. Of course a child can't attack an adult—or a physically superior child—directly, so Flood transferred his rage and hatred to others—to people who resembled the cousin and whose destruction or disgrace would most severely hurt some older authority figure, who represented his father, I suppose. Does that make any sense at all? I've thought about it for a long time, and it's the only explanation I can come up with."

"It's not inconsistent with things we encounter occasionally, Mr. Taylor," the judge said approvingly. "Please continue."

Raphael took a deep breath and looked down into the courtroom. The two young women Frankie had warned him about had stopped writing and were staring at him with open hostility. "In time Flood was sent to a number of those exclusive and very expensive private boarding schools in the east where the wealthy dump their children. He developed a game—a very personal and vicious kind of game. He made a point of seeking out boys who resembled his cousin. He would befriend them—and then he would destroy them.

Sometimes he planted evidence of crimes or expellable violations of the rules among their belongings—those were his earliest and crudest efforts. Later he grew more sophisticated, and his plots—if that's not too melodramatic a term—grew more complicated. I'm told that this happened several times in various prep schools and during his first two years at college. It was at that point that I met him. We both transferred to Reed College in Portland from other schools, and we roomed together there. I've been told that I closely resemble Flood's cousin, so I suppose his reaction to me was inevitable."

The judge looked startled. "Mr. Taylor," he interrupted, "are you implying that this man was responsible for your injury?"

"No, Your Honor. The accident was simply that—an accident. Flood really had nothing to do with it. I can't be sure exactly *what* it was that he originally had planned for me. By this time he had refined his schemes to the point where they were so exotic and involved that I don't think anyone could have unraveled them. I honestly believe that my accident threw him completely off. It was blind chance—simple stupid bad luck—and he couldn't accept that.

"Anyway, after the accident, when I had recovered enough to be at least marginally ambulatory, I left Portland and came here to Spokane. I didn't tell anyone where I was going, and it took Flood five months to find me. He wasn't going to let me get away from him, but my condition baffled him. How can you possibly hurt someone who's already been sawed in two?"

"Your Honor," the defense counsel protested. "I don't see the pertinence of all this."

"Miss Berensen, please sit down."

The young woman flushed and sank back into her seat.

"Go on, Mr. Taylor."

"When I first came to Spokane, I entered therapy. Learning to walk again is very tedious, and I needed a diversion, so I started collecting losers."

"Losers? I'm not sure I understand, Mr. Taylor."

"In our society—probably in every society—there are people who simply can't make it," Raphael explained. "They're not skilled enough, not smart enough, not competitive enough, and they become the human debris of the system. Because our society is compassionate, we take care of them, but in the process they become human ciphers—numbers in the system, welfare cases or whatever.

"I was in an ideal spot to watch them. I live in an area where they congregate, and my apartment is on a rooftop. I was in a situation where I could virtually see everything that went on in the neighborhood."

"Your Honor," the prosecutor said, "I don't want to interrupt Mr. Taylor, but isn't this getting a bit far afield?"

"Is this really relevant, Mr. Taylor?" the judge asked.

"Yes, Your Honor, I believe so. It's the point of the whole thing. If you don't know about the losers, nothing that Flood did will make any sense at all."

"Very well, Mr. Taylor."

"It's easy to dismiss the losers—to ignore them. After all, they don't sit in front of the churches to beg anymore. We've created an entire industry—social workers—to feed them and keep them out of sight so that we never have to come face-to-face with them. We've trained whole generations of bright young girls who don't want to be waitresses or secretaries to take care of our losers. In the process we've created a new leisure class. We give them enough to get by on—not luxury, regardless of what some people believe—but they know they won't be allowed to starve. Our new leisure class doesn't have enough money for hobbies or enough education for art, so they sit. I suppose it's great for a month or two to know that you'll never have to work again, but what do you do then? What do you do when you finally come face-to-face with the reality of all those empty years stretching out in front of you?

"For most of the losers crisis is the answer. Crisis is a way of being important—of giving their lives meaning. They can't write books or sell cars or cure warts. The state feeds them and pays their rent, but they have a nagging sense of being worthless. They precipitate crisis—catastrophe—as a way of saying, 'Look at me. I'm alive. I'm a human being.' For the loser it's the only way to gain any kind of recognition. If they take a shot at somebody or OD on pills, at least the police will come. They won't be ignored.''

"Mr. Taylor," the judge said with some perplexity, "your observations are very interesting, but—"

"Yes, Your Honor, I'm coming to the connection. It was about the time that I finally began to understand all of this that Flood showed up here in Spokane. One day I happened to mention the losers. He didn't follow what I was talking about, so I explained the whole idea to him. For some reason I didn't understand at the time, the theory of all the sad misfits on the block became very important to him. Of course with Flood you could never be entirely sure how much was genuine interest and how much was put on.

"Anyway, as time went on, Flood started to seek out my collection of losers. He got to know them—well enough to know their weaknesses anyway—and then he began to destroy them one by one. Oh, sure, some of them fell by natural attrition—losers smash up their lives pretty regularly without any outside help—but he did manage to destroy several people in some grand scheme that had *me* as its focus.''

"I'm afraid I don't follow that, Mr. Taylor," the judge said.

"As I said, sir, I collect losers," Raphael explained. "I care about them. For all their deliberate, wrongheaded stupidity I care about them and recognize their need for some kind of dignity. Social workers simply process them. It's just a job to all those bright young girls, but I cared—even if it was only passively.

"Flood saw that, and it solved his problem. He'd been looking for a way to hurt someone who'd already been hurt as badly as he was likely to ever be hurt, and this was it. He began to systematically depopulate my block—nothing illegal, of course, just a nudge here, a word there. It was extraordinarily simple, really. Losers are pathologically self-destructive anyway, and he'd had a lifetime of practice.''

"Your Honor," Miss Berensen protested, "this is sheer nonsense. It has no relation to any recognized social theory. I think Mr. Taylor's affliction has made him . . ." She faltered.

"Go ahead and say it," Raphael said to her before the judge could speak. "That's a common assumption—that a physical impairment necessarily implies a mental one as well. I'm used to it by now. I'm not even offended at being patronized by the intellectually disadvantaged anymore."

"That'll do, Mr. Taylor," the judge said firmly.

"Sorry, Your Honor. Anyway, whether the theory is valid or not is beside the point. The point is that *I* believe it—and more importantly Flood believed it as well. In that context then, it *is* true.

"In time Flood insinuated himself into this group of bikers up the street. The gang posed special problems for him. He'd been able to handle all the others on the street one-on-one, but there's a kind of cumulative effect in a gang—even one as feebleminded as this one."

Big Heintz came half to his feet. "You watch your mouth, Taylor!" he threatened loudly.

The judge pounded his gavel. "That will be all of that!"

Big Heintz glowered and sank back into his chair.

The judge turned to Raphael then. "Mr. Taylor, we've given you a great deal of latitude here, but please confine your remarks to the business at hand."

"Yes, Your Honor. Once he became involved with the gang, I think Flood began to lose control. Crisis is exciting; it's high drama, and Flood was pulled along by it all. He could handle the gang members on a one-to-one basis quite easily, but when he immersed himself in the entire gang, it all simply overpowered him. Being a loser is somehow contagious, and when a man starts to associate with them in groups, he's almost certain to catch it. I tried to warn him about that, but he didn't seem to understand." Raphael paused. "Now that I stop and think about it, though, maybe he did at that. He kept after me—begging me almost—to move away from Spokane. Maybe in some obscure way those pleas that we get out of this town were cries for help. Maybe he realized that he was losing control.'' He sighed. ''Perhaps we should have gone. Then this might not have happened—at least not here in Spokane. Anyway, when I saw the gun, I knew that he'd slipped over the line. It was too late at that point.''

''Then you knew he had a gun?'' the judge asked.

''Yes, Your Honor. There'd been a skirmish between the two gangs, and Flood had been beaten pretty severely. I suppose that's what finally pushed him over the edge. In a sense it was like the beating he'd received from his cousin in his childhood, and Flood could never let something like that just slide. He *had* to get even, and he had to arm himself to make sure that it didn't happen to him again. I think that toward the end he even forgot why he'd gotten mixed up with the gang in the first place. Anyway, when Heintzie's grand and final war came, Flood was caught up in it—hooked on crisis, hyped on his own adrenaline, not even thinking anymore—a loser. I suppose it's sort of ironic. He set out to destroy the gang, but in the end they destroyed him. And what's even more ironic is that all Flood really wanted to do when he started out was to try to find a way to hurt *me*. He knew that I cared about my losers, so he thought he could hurt me by destroying them. In the end, though, he became a loser himself and wound up destroying himself. I suppose that his plan really succeeded, because when he destroyed himself, it hurt me more than anything else he could have done. It's strange, but he finally won after all.'' Raphael looked up at the ceiling. He'd never really thought of it before, and it rather surprised him. ''I guess that's about it, Your Honor,'' he told the judge. ''That's about all I really know about Damon Flood.'' He sat quietly then. It had not really done any good; he realized that now. Denise and Frankie had been right. The categories and pigeonholes were too convenient, and using them as a means of sorting people was too much a part of the official mentality. But he had tried. He had performed that last service that a man can perform for a friend—he had told the truth about him. In spite of everything, he realized that he still thought of Flood as a friend.

"Mr. Wilson?" the judge asked.

The prosecutor rose and walked toward Raphael. "Mr. Taylor, from your observation then, would you say that Mr. Flood was definitely *not* the leader of this—ah—group?"

"No, sir. It was Heintzie's gang, and it was Heintzie's war. The gun was Flood's, though. I think it's what they call escalation. About all Heintzie wanted to do was put a few people in the hospital. Killing people was Flood's idea. In the end, though, he was just another member of the gang—a loser."

"Uh—" The prosecutor looked down at his notes. It was obvious that he had not expected the kind of testimony Raphael had just given them. "I—uh—I guess I have no further questions, Your Honor."

"Miss Berensen?" the judge said.

"Your Honor, I wouldn't dignify any of this by even questioning it. My only suggestion would be that Mr. Taylor might consider seeking professional help."

"That's enough of that, Miss Berensen!" The judge sat for a long time looking at the bandaged and sullenly glowering young men seated behind the defense table. Finally he shook his head. "Losers," he murmured so softly that only Raphael could hear him. Then he turned. "Mr. Taylor, you're an intelligent and articulate young man—too intelligent and articulate to just sit on the sidelines the way you're doing. You seem to have some very special talents—profound insight and extraordinary compassion. I think I'd like to know what you plan to do with the rest of your life."

"I'm leaving Spokane, Your Honor. I came here to get some personal things taken care of. Now that all that's done, there's no reason for me to stay anymore. I'll find another town—maybe I'll find another rooftop and another street full of losers. Somebody has to care for them after all. All my options are open, so I suppose I'll just have to wait and see what happens tomorrow—trust to luck, if you want to put it that way."

The judge sighed. "Thank you, Mr. Taylor. You may step down."

Raphael got his crutches squared away, stood up, and went carefully down the single step from the witness stand. Then he walked smoothly up the center aisle with the stately, flowing pace of a one-legged man who has mastered his crutches and is no longer a cripple. He hesitated a moment at the door. There was still the matter of the two derelicts who had been found shot to death in downtown alleys. He realized, however, that he really had no proof that it had been Flood who had so casually shot them as a means of proving to himself that he did in fact have the nerve to shoot another human being. Raphael also realized that he would prefer to leave it simply at that. A suspicion was not a certainty, and for some reason he did not want that final nail driven in. If it *had* been Flood, it would not happen again; and in any case, if he were to suggest it to the prosecutor or anyone else, it would probably delay the escape from Spokane with Denise that had become absolutely necessary. The bailiff standing at the back opened the door for him, and Raphael went on out.

The two young women who had been in the courtroom were waiting for him in the hall. "Mr. Taylor," the blond one said, "we're from the department of—"

"I know who you are." Raphael looked directly into the face of the enemy.

"We'd like to talk to you for a moment, if you're not too busy," she went on, undeterred by his blunt answer.

"I am, but I don't imagine that'll make much difference, will it?"

"Really, Mr. Taylor," the brunette one protested, "you seem extremely hostile."

"You've noticed."

"Mr. Taylor," the blonde said, "you really should leave social theory to the experts, you know. This notion of yours— it just isn't consistent with what we know about human behavior."

"Really? Maybe you'd better go back and take another look then."

"Why are you so hostile, Mr. Taylor?" the brunette asked. She kept coming back to that.

"I'm bad-tempered. Didn't you study that in school? All of us freaks have days when we're bad-tempered. You're supposed to know how to deal with that."

He could see their anger, the frustration in their eyes under the carefully assumed professional masks. His testimony had rather neatly torpedoed their entire case, and they were furious with him. He'd done the one thing Frankie had warned him not to do.

"I'd really like to discuss this theory of yours," the blond one said with a contrived look of interest on her face.

"Oh really?" Raphael was very alert now. He knew that he was on dangerous ground.

"And you really ought to try to control your hostilities," the brunette added.

"Why? Nobody else does. Could it be that you think I should control my hostility because I'm a defective and defectives aren't permitted to dislike people?"

"We'd really like to talk to you, Mr. Taylor," the blonde said. "Could we make an appointment for you at our office— say next Tuesday?"

"No. Now, if you don't mind, I have things to do."

"We really think we could help you, Mr. Taylor," the brunette said, her eyes hardening.

"I don't need any help," Raphael told her. "There's not one single thing I need you for."

"*Everybody* needs help, Mr. Taylor," the blonde said.

"I don't. Now, you'll have to excuse me." He set the points of his crutches down firmly and began to walk down the hallway toward a waiting elevator.

"We'll always be there," the blonde called after him. "Don't hesitate to call—anytime at all."

She sounded almost like old Tobe. That made Raphael feel better somehow. He was almost safe now—close enough to safety at any rate to take the risk. "If you girls really want to help, you ought to learn how to type," he threw back over his shoulder. Flood would have liked that.

"What's that supposed to mean?" the blonde demanded.

"It's sort of an inside joke," he replied. "It'd take much too long to explain." He stepped into the elevator.

"You'll call," the brunette yelled after him in a shrill voice. "Someday you'll call. Someday you'll need our help. Your kind always does."

He might have answered that, but the elevator door closed just then.

It was good to have it all over. In a very personal way he had put Flood finally to rest, and now it was over.

It was just before noon when he came out of the courthouse, and the autumn sun was bright and warm. He went down the several steps to the sidewalk and started up toward the intersection, moving along beside the low retaining wall.

At the corner the bald, skinny philosopher was delivering one of his speeches to the indifferent street. Although Flood had reported seeing him in various parts of town, Raphael had not really been certain in his own mind that the crazy orator who had greeted him on that first snowy night in Spokane was still roaming the streets, or if he had ever really existed at all.

"Whenever anything is done with one intention," the orator boomed, "but something else, other than what was intended, results from certain causes, that is called chance. We may therefore define chance as an unexpected result from the coincidence of certain causes in matters where there was another purpose."

Raphael stopped and leaned back, half sitting on the low retaining wall to listen. He leaned his crutches against the wall on either side of his single leg and crossed his arms.

"The order of the universe," the bald man went on, "advancing with its inevitable sequences, brings about this coincidence of causes. This order itself emanates from its source, which is Providence, and disposes all things in their proper time and place."

Raphael found himself smiling suddenly. Without knowing exactly why, he uncrossed his arms and began to applaud, the sound of his clapping hands quite loud in the momentarily quiet street.

Startled, the crazy man jerked his head around to regard his audience of one. And then he grinned. There was in that grin all the rueful acknowledgment of human failure, of lives futile and wasted, and at the same time a sly, almost puckish delight in all the joy that even the most useless life contained. It was a cosmic kind of grin, and Raphael found its sly, mischievous twinkle somehow contagious.

Still applauding, he grinned back.

And then, that impish smile still on his face, the crazy man extended one arm to the side with exaggerated formality, placed his other hand on his chest, and took a florid, theatrical bow. His face was a sly mask when he came erect again, and he looked directly at Raphael and gave him a knowing wink before he turned back to continue his oration to the swiftly moving traffic.

ABOUT THE AUTHOR

DAVID EDDINGS was born in Spokane, Washington, in 1931 and was raised in the Puget Sound area north of Seattle. He received a Bachelor of Arts degree from Reed College in Portland, Oregon, in 1954 and a Master of Arts degree from the University of Washington in 1961. He has served in the United States Army, worked as a buyer for the Boeing Company, has been a grocery clerk, and has taught English. He has lived in many parts of the United States.

His first novel, *High Hunt* (published by Putnam in 1973), was a contemporary adventure story. The field of fantasy has always been of interest to him, however, and he turned to *The Belgariad* in an effort to develop certain technical and philosophical ideas concerning that genre.

Eddings currently resides with his wife, Leigh, in the Southwest.

Taking The Quest Across A Strange Continent and Stranger People...

DAVID EDDINGS

THE MALLOREON SERIES